THE
LOST NIGHT

THE
LOST NIGHT

A NOVEL

ANDREA BARTZ

 CROWN
NEW YORK

Copyright © 2019 by Andrea Bartz

All rights reserved.
Published in the United States by Crown Publishers, an imprint of the Crown Publishing Group, a division of Penguin Random House LLC, New York.
crownpublishing.com

CROWN and the Crown colophon are registered trademarks of Penguin Random House LLC.

Library of Congress Cataloging-in-Publication Data has been applied for.

ISBN 978-0-525-57471-2
Ebook ISBN 978-0-525-57473-6
International edition ISBN 978-1-9848-2492-9

Printed in the United States of America

Book design by Lauren Dong
Jacket design by Elena Giavaldi
Jacket photographs: (cityscape) Michael Turek/Gallery Stock; (woman and window) Giacomo Furlanetto/Millennium Images, UK

10 9 8 7 6 5 4 3 2 1

First Edition

For Julia

Prologue

EDIE

I had the dream again: lying on the floor with blood pouring out of me, trying to cry out but I can't make a sound. The scratched floor spreading out around me, round yellow lights overhead. This time, for added fun, I knew someone was coming for me, but I couldn't figure out if it was to help me or finish me off. This morning I finally Googled around to see if there's a universal meaning, like dreaming that your teeth fell out. Apparently all the blood means that I'm emotionally drained, my life force leaking out. One site even noted that it could indicate "bitter confrontations among you and your friends," which is a little on the nose.

I'm still mad about the fight. We've started speaking again, and I can tell she's eager to just pretend it never happened and go back to normal. She thinks she's such a good friend, but she has no idea what's actually going on with me. She never asks. She thinks she loves me, when really she just likes showing the world we're a pair: *This is my cool friend Edie, and never mind whether anything's going on below the surface.*

It's almost funny that she's jealous—you really want all this? I've got a boyfriend who doesn't trust me. A best friend who's using me. Parents who alternately call me up crying or remember I exist only when I'm somehow inconveniencing them. I guess she and I are both pretty fucked up, in different ways.

It's the Fourth of July. Independence Day, as Mom and Dad always insist on calling it, like card-carrying snobs. They're at Uncle John's again this year, Mom probably on her sixth vodka soda, sitting on sweaty lawn chairs and eating overbarbecued burgers and feeling smug about the fact that they're in Connecticut. I scoffed at the idea of going with them, but of course now I'm alone in a musty apartment in Bushwick, writing a stupid diary entry while all my roommates and friends are on the rooftop drinking from red Solo cups and watching some band.

It's sunny, and a holiday, and those are both facts that make things a little worse, because I know I should be enjoying the day like a normal human. It's hard to describe: When I'm out with a crowd and we're having a good time, it *is* fun, I do recognize it as fun, but I don't quite connect with it. It's like I'm eighteen inches away watching all the fun happen. And then as soon as the fun thing is over, a fog settles over everything again.

Okay, I can hear the band on the roof from all the way down here, so I guess I'll head up there. Maybe I'll get up on the ledge, make people nervous. Standing four feet closer to heaven and looking at the sidewalk eight emptied floors below.

Maybe today's the day I'll jump.

PART I

Chapter 1

LINDSAY

Fat chickens packed into factory farms, maggots wriggling like a thick white carpet, buffalo fumbling toward the edge of a cliff: all spacious situations compared to the New York City subway at 6:00 p.m. The doors slid apart, but I was stuck; my fellow commuters barely moved, and I bleated out apologies as I smashed against bodies, squeezing onto the platform right as the doors thudded closed again. I took a few steps and peered through the windows at the people still inside, crammed like stuffed animals at the bottom of a claw vending machine.

I was so tired. A feeling I had a lot these days. A part of me wanted to go straight home, heat up something frozen, and maybe watch old, stupid reruns, but I'd been the one to suggest these plans. In a rare flare of nostalgia, I'd fired off the message, forgetting in the moment that I'd once sworn to myself that I'd never open up Pandora's box. It was almost as if boredom had made me reckless.

I pushed through the throng of commuters at the foot of the subway stairs. Outside, rain made its way through fabric and onto my ass, my knees, my feet. The feeling I'd been wrestling with all day grew, the panicky dread that swells before a first date. What if this reunion mucked up my last good memories from that single, singular year? When I reached the restaurant, an inoffensive bistro in boring Midtown West, a man snapped his umbrella closed in my face and for some reason I apologized to him, knee-jerk.

Inside, I was just pulling out a chair at our table when Sarah entered. She spotted me and waved, and I thought she looked exactly the same. She didn't, of course, and neither did I, a fact I only realized much later that night when I was clicking through old photos, tears rolling down my cheeks. At twenty-three we had that alienoid bone structure, big eyes and sunken cheeks caving into dewy little chins. Now, ten years later, we're old-young and round-faced and just human again.

Then we hugged, and maybe there was some chemical trigger, a smell or invisible pheromone, but the hug felt exactly like it did a decade ago. We relaxed and smiled at each other and thought maybe this would be fun.

"Lindsay, it's so good to see you," she said, dropping into her chair. "You look great."

"So do you!" I chirped. "I can't believe it's been ten years."

"I know, it's crazy." Sarah nodded, eyebrows up. "How have you been?"

"Really good! You know, keeping on. I was so happy to hear you moved back to New York." Once, for an article, I'd read a linguistics study on conversation patterns: In any duo, the lower-power person imitates the speech style of the alpha. I wondered who was following whom here.

"Yeah, I'm glad you reached out. When we found out my husband was getting transferred here, I was like, 'Wow, I don't know that I know anyone in the city anymore.'"

"Your *husband*," I said. "I can't wait to meet him." I'd looked him up on Facebook: He was annoyingly handsome. At least when friends paired up with unattractive people, I could blot at the jealousy with smugness.

"He's great." Sarah smiled and snapped open her menu, looking down. "Are you seeing anyone?"

"No, no one special!" I said brightly. "So how is it being back in New York?"

She scrunched up her features, preparing some middle-of-the-road answer, when the waiter appeared to rattle off the specials. Sarah ordered a vodka martini, and after a moment's hesitation, I asked for my usual seltzer with lime. I didn't often miss drinking, but I knew I'd feel a pulse of envy when her conical glass arrived.

"Oh my gosh, is it okay if I drink?" she asked after the waiter disappeared.

"Of course! I'm totally fine. Otherwise I would have suggested meeting for tea." She giggled and shrugged, and we both went back to reading our menus.

Christ, was this really Sarah? The same literary, witty, hard-partying friend I'd counted among my clique during that first wild year in New York? I'd messaged her the very day she announced on Facebook that she was moving back from St. Louis, forgetting in my sentimentality that things had ended pretty icily. And then I'd felt embarrassed, until a few weeks ago when she'd replied, apologetic, to set a date.

"It's good to be back here, but weird," she said finally. "So much has changed. It almost feels like coming to a new city. But what about you, you still love it?"

"I do," I replied. "I mean, I'm really lucky to still have a job in magazines, and I've been living in the same place in Fort Greene for . . . five years now?" I took a deep sip and bubbles flooded my tongue.

"That's great," Sarah said. "That's definitely a neighborhood I want to check out." She pushed her black hair behind her ears and a few silver streaks twinkled like tinsel.

"Well, if there's any way I can be helpful as you guys look around, just let me know," I said.

"Thanks, Lindsay. It's tough because I want to find a place ASAP, but I also don't want to end up somewhere terrible. Right now we're living with Nate's parents in Trenton." She gave me a knowing look.

"You're in Jersey?! Wow."

"Right? I'm one of those people we totally hated back in the day." We both chuckled.

"Do you keep in touch with anyone from back then?" I asked.

She shrugged. "I mean, just online, like with you. For a while, Alex and I would call or have a little email exchange around the anniversary. You know, raise a glass." She sipped her drink. "Kevin doesn't really update anything, so I'm pretty out-of-date on him. I think he and Alex keep in touch, so I get reports every once in a while. Last I heard, he and his husband owned a little music store in Nashville and he was, like, giving drum lessons."

"Wait, Kevin's *married*?"

She laughed. "You didn't know that? Apparently he met this great guy, like, two seconds after he moved away. A pianist, I think."

Of course—like everyone who moves away from New York. I smoothed a napkin on my lap. A *husband*: Kevin was still twenty-four in my mind, jumpy and juvenile. "When did he move again?"

"As soon as he'd finished his community service. That winter after . . . afterward."

Her face darkened, but then the waiter reappeared and we politely placed our orders, Sarah nodding eagerly when he offered to bring another round. She asked me more about my work, and I learned a bit about the executive recruiting she'd been doing in St. Louis and how now the tables had turned and she had to get *herself* hired and the bar was set high when every headhunter is so good at the game, and my god, the irony. We giggled at the appropriate times. Twice she made a cute hand gesture, her little fists up near her chest like sock puppets, and she was Sarah Kwan again, Sarah Kwan with the cool raspberry lipstick and an impossible crop top and a yard of thick glossy hair.

She didn't mention Edie again until we were finishing dessert, picking at a shared flourless chocolate cake. "It's crazy to think about how much has happened in ten years," she announced. "I was so glad to hear you wanted to get together. I thought about reaching out a few times over the years, but I just wasn't sure after . . . I mean, after how everything went down after Edie."

"That's exactly how I felt, to be honest," I said. "I know I just sort of . . . went MIA afterward. I mean, I guess we were all just grieving in our own way. We were *so* young. None of us were equipped to deal with it." She nodded and looked away, and I realized she wanted me to go on. "I always thought you had it worse than anyone, Sarah. Worse than *everyone*. I mean, you found her. God, I haven't thought about this in so long."

I'd done my crying and then I'd let Edie go, tucking the whole ordeal away so that it couldn't taint what came before. Now I recalled a nugget I'd learned from fact-checking a feature on an innocent man, condemned by poorly recalled witness testimony: When you pull up a memory, you're actually recalling the last time you remembered it—not the event itself. One day, one by one, we'd all stopped refreshing the memory. So I was surprised by how quickly the night came back to me now that I'd called it up. Now that Sarah was sitting across from me and talking about August 21, 2009, in dark, tenebrous terms.

It had been a Friday. A band had been rattling the windows in an apartment two floors up from Edie's place, and a bunch of us were standing around at the concert, drunk or pretending to be. The guitars and bass were so loud, I could feel the vibrations in my collarbone. I remember registering with a flapping concern that I was too drunk, then scurrying out to the street, where a random girl had helped me hail a taxi home. Edie hadn't been at the concert with us; Edie had been home alone, two floors down, crafting a brief suicide note and then pulling out the gun. Her time of death, we later learned, was while we were watching the band, their meandering chords cloaking the single gunshot. The rest I knew from my friends' accounts, repeated so many times that I could see it: midnight, pitch black, Sarah hobbles into the apartment and flicks on the overhead lights, trying not to make too much noise in case Edie's already asleep. Her screams had rattled the whole building, shrill and sharp and with that beelike whine hovering descant just above her cries.

"I know, it was *awful*." She listed forward and I suddenly realized Sarah was drunk.

"You moved back home, right?" I'd always wondered if her parents had checked her into some kind of psych ward. I'd pulled away after a few weeks but continued to watch the amputated friend group from the relative safety of social media; Sarah had gone off the grid completely, deactivating her accounts and only reemerging a few years later with a new, smiling Facebook profile and friend requests all around.

"Yeah, my parents were pretty worried about me. I mean, I was acting like a lunatic, going all conspiracy theorist."

"What do you mean?"

A sheepish laugh. "You remember. I guess I just didn't want to believe my best friend could do that. She trusted me more than anyone, and I didn't like feeling like I'd failed her."

I sat up straighter. *Her* best friend? Who was she kidding?

"I don't know what you're talking about," I said.

"You don't remember?" she continued. "I was running around insisting that Edie hadn't actually killed herself, that it must have been an accident or foul play or something. I know, it's ridiculous."

"Oh, wow, I didn't realize that." Sarah's flair for melodrama resurfaced in my memory like something emerging from the mist.

"It was just strange how different she seemed right before . . . at the end," she went on. "I mean, I lived with her, and we barely said more than two sentences to each other those last few weeks."

"Even less for me—we weren't speaking," I cut in. "And we were always *super* close."

Sarah ignored the one-up. "I was really caught up in that . . . that narrative. It wasn't healthy."

"I'm sorry, that must have been really tough for you, and I . . ." I zipped my thumb out, the universal sign for having gotten out of Dodge.

"Yeah, I understand. I feel like it's all I was talking about back then, but maybe that's just 'cause it was, like, consuming my mind."

"What made you think it wasn't a suicide?" I asked, a little too derisively.

"Oh my god, it was all stupid little things, in retrospect. There was the fact that I found her in her underwear—she was always so perfectly put-together, so that seemed weird."

Right, but it was circumstantial. When we'd talked it out in those first shaken weeks, it had also seemed plausible that she wouldn't have wanted to ruin any of the beautiful pieces in her closet; Edie had treated them like precious artifacts.

"And the gun stuff didn't make sense to me: She was left-handed, but the gun was in her right hand, and the wound was on the right side of her face. Until a forensic expert explained to me that if she used two hands, she could've wound up slightly off-center and just, like, crumpled to either side."

Jesus. She'd talked to a forensic expert? I watched as she slurped the last of her fourth martini.

"But I learned enough about criminology to figure out that there are a few loose ends in any investigation. Because that's how life is."

". . . Unraveling," I supplied.

She smiled. "But yeah, my parents found me an awesome therapist, and she helped me face the facts. I guess we all turned out okay."

"We did. And you shouldn't feel bad about dealing with it however you needed to deal with it. We were all so immature and maybe didn't know how to . . . ask for help."

"You mean like Edie."

I'd been thinking of myself, but sure, Edie, too. What with the debt and the depression and the suicide note on her laptop. The gun pressed against her temple.

"That was some heavy shit," I said.

She poked at her cocktail napkin. "It's still hard for me to believe sometimes. Like, we were at the top of our game. We were having the time of our lives."

"I know what you mean," I said. "Everyone glorifies their twenties, I guess, but for me that period was . . . It meant a lot." I swallowed hard. "And then it ended. It's nuts. Literally, we were dancing around to some stupid band just a few floors up while Edie was . . ."

Sarah narrowed her eyes. "Well, you weren't."

"What?"

"You weren't at the concert."

I cocked my head. "Wait, what? Of course I was."

"You weren't. You went home. I remember because I was mad that none of my girlfriends came with me. Can you believe that? I was mad at Edie while she was, like, committing suicide. Seriously, that took me a few thousand dollars of therapy to work through."

I scoffed. "Christ, Sarah, of course I was there. I pregamed with you guys on the roof, and we took a bunch of shots, and then we went to the show. I went home near the end of the set."

She was shaking her head as I spoke and her expression matched mine: that charged look when you just know, *know,* the other person's remembering it wrong.

"You didn't come to the show." She let out a bleat of laughter. "You didn't! We pregamed together and then you left."

"Sarah, come on," I snapped. "I remember that night perfectly. I was there with you guys." The band with the weird face paint. Music so loud we were part of it, gyrating through every crashing sound wave.

"I mean, I know what I know," she said finally, leaning back and tossing her napkin onto the table. Like she was wrapping up a fight, doing the adult thing.

"That's fine, but I do, too," I told her, sighing and shaking my head. "I know exactly where I was standing. We were off to the left side. The band, something with 'beach' or 'tan' or 'surf' in their name—they were covered in red and black face paint."

"They all lived in Calhoun. We saw them a bunch of times. You're thinking of another time. Anyway." She signaled to the waiter. "Could I get some more water, please?"

We sat there for a while, breathing. Everything was humming: my head, my chest, my hands. Finally she asked if I kept up with any good podcasts and I answered, awkwardly. After a few sentences we fell into a rhythm and Edie slid back into the past.

Outside, in the rain, Sarah and I frantically hugged goodbye and sped off between the raindrops toward different subways. Standing on a clammy C train, my umbrella dripping onto my boots, I let the outrage pour through me again. First there was Sarah's prickly proclamation that she and Edie had been the closest, which was preposterous—everyone knew Edie and I had been inseparable. And here she'd just cut me out of the narrative on the most significant night of our friendship, *snip*. It wouldn't be the first time Sarah had implied that I wasn't in Edie's inner circle but rather a hanger-on, like someone's annoying little sister. All because I hadn't lived with the four of them. Well, no. All because Edie and I had been the closest, and Sarah's jealousy would sometimes waft by like a scent.

Of course I'd been there. I felt a propulsive need to confirm it, to pull up the old photos and messages that would prove her wrong. As soon as I got home, I figured, I'd put this to rest.

I slumped over my laptop at the kitchen table, squinting at the screen to keep it from blurring as my contacts turned gummy. I opened Facebook and blinked at the torrent of my peers' baby photos ("Snuggles!!!"). For the first time in years, I searched for Alex: a profile picture of him and his shiny-haired wife on vacation. From 2016, which meant he didn't use Facebook much. I opened up a message to him, then froze. What the hell could I even say? *Quick question, on the night Edie died, I came with you to the concert, right? Hope all is well, thaaanks!* I closed the message and clicked instead on my photos tab to begin the slow scrolling process of unearthing photos from 2009, sliding backward in time. Eventually I slinked into the right era: me with Sarah, Edie, Kevin, and Alex. I was struck by how good-looking we all were, smooth-skinned and twinkly eyed. Sarah was pretty and serene with that swingy hair and small curvy mouth.

I had the same dirty-blond curls and wide mouth and thick eyebrows I'd since learned to accentuate, but they were easy and unassuming back when I was that age. I'd always felt awkward next to Sarah and Edie, the less pretty friend making an unfortunate laughing face in photos. Now I saw that we were all just lovely, eager and open-faced. Fogging ourselves up with a practiced ennui, sure, but so much younger than we thought we were.

Alex was generically handsome, the stereotypical dark-haired, blue-eyed, five-o'-clock-shadowed Adonis with sleeve tattoos and a self-satisfied smirk. He had That Look; for years I'd stare down a stranger in a store or at a show, trying to decide if it was Alex or one of his ten thousand doppelgängers. Back then, he was a guitarist who made money taking on freelance coding projects and completing them at all hours of the night, and it was sort of sad to look back and realize that the Alex in these pictures had no idea he'd abandon music slowly at first, then with grim finality. Last I heard, he lived in Westchester, in one of those river towns, with a car and a dog and everything he didn't know he wanted.

Aw, and Kevin, such a little goofball. I paused on a photo of him with his band: the guitarist with her pink hair, the fat, greasy lead singer whose confidence trumped his appearance, and little Kevin in the back, his arms and drumsticks a blur. I'd abruptly chopped them all out of my life, but I knew from Facebook that he'd been the second one to actually move away, after Sarah, relocating to Nashville late that year. The gun had been his, a vintage thing he kept in the living room (typically) unloaded, and the guilt surrounding it must have gotten the better of him.

Now he was a grown-up, too. I filed through his most recent photos, annoyed that there weren't any of his husband. *Kevin.* Who'd have thought?

Edie was the quiet star of every photo she appeared in, bony and freckled and so sure of her beauty. I stared at a picture of the two of us until tears gathered in my eyes; I'd both hated and adored her, and for months after she died, I'd felt in my chest a black hole of grief, a sudden gaping absence. She smirked at me from the screen: She had a little gap between her front teeth and long red curls that spilled over her back and shoulders. Edie was the ringleader, the princess whose every wish came true, not because it was also our command, exactly, but because she stated her wants and the very universe seemed to bow to them. When she giggled, when you were in her smile with her, it was magic. And when you weren't . . .

Well.

The problem, I realized, was that the date on the photos showed when they were posted, not when they were taken. I browsed around in the right era, the one after Edie's death, but couldn't find any of that night, anything that could prove my attendance. Which made sense—what a strange, gauche move it would have been, in the midst of our mourning, to toss up a photo of August 21's debauchery. I couldn't remember the band's name or think of how to find other pictures from the show. Frustrated, I kept scrolling, hoping they'd pop up in another image, tagged.

Our little clique was outside in so many photos, drinking out of massive Styrofoam cups in McCarren Park or smoking on fire escapes, stoops, roofs. I remembered that summer, the last one with Edie, how all the bands we saw blurred into a cacophony of synth and Sarah wore that crazy Day-Glo hat everywhere and I was on a vodka gimlet kick. Not pictured: the violent bouts of crying alone, the change in cabin pressure if Edie was unhappy.

I clicked on a photo of the five of us, goofing around in a sculpture park on a weekend trip to Philly. Alex had his arm around Edie, smiling calmly. Edie was looking at something outside of the frame, squinting to see. Sarah and I were posing dramatically, arms up toward the heavens, and Kevin had climbed onto the vaguely humanoid sculpture behind us and wrapped his arms around an appendage.

It won't last, I told them as tears again coated my eyes. Then, because it was late and my anger had simmered into a tired ache, I snapped my laptop closed and went to sleep.

The next morning, I forgot my headphones for the subway ride to work and listened instead to the din of tired people commuting. I heard a sniffle and looked down at a young woman seated in front of me, tears pouring freely down her cheeks. Poor thing. I dug in my bag, then handed her a tissue. She shot me a grateful look and pushed it against both eyes at once.

Wedged against a well-dressed man holding a Kindle milli-meters from a woman's cheek, I debated. *I should throw myself into work.* Then an about-face: *Fuck work, all I want to do is think about Edie.* I was still undecided as I spun through the revolving doors into my building's lobby, a minimalist entry with wavy metal and burbling fountains, all silver and glass and Impressive Business Is Done Here. "I'm really lucky to still have a job in magazines," I'd told Sarah enthusiastically, fifteen hours before hurrying in to fact-check an inane six-page feature on CBD-infused cocktails.

I bumped into Damien, the magazine's video editor and my closest (no, only) work friend, as I headed toward my office. He launched into an elaborate tale of how he'd spent his evening with the police because an idiot UPS worker had left his package out-side his brownstone, where it had promptly been stolen, and now he needed a police report to have his insurance cover it, but the cops were acting like he expected them to *find* the package, and the worst part was that it was a beautiful coffee-table book about circa sixties erotica, but everyone was acting like he'd just ordered porn, and now he had to submit a Freedom of Information Law request just to get his own damn police report from the bureau of criminal records verification or something. He sighed grandly. Damien is the queen of histrionic sighs.

"What'd you do last night?" he finished finally.

"I had dinner with a friend from when I first moved to New York," I said. "It was weird, she mentioned . . . Do you have work, am I distracting you?"

He waved his hand cheerfully and sauntered farther into my office.

"So, ten years ago this good friend of ours killed herself—and the friend from last night, Sarah, she found her."

"Christ, Lindsay, I'm sorry. Did she take a bunch of pills or what?"

"No, she used a gun. And left a suicide note on her computer."

He shook his head. "That's awful. Was she young?"

"We were all twenty-three."

"Damn." We stared at each other. Finally he said: "Ten years ago. You're old."

"Fuck you." I smiled. *Why am I telling you this?* Because he could bring me back to the present, take the gravity out of it. "Yeah, it was really sudden and . . . awful. Been on my mind."

"Why'd she do it?"

"There turned out to be so much weird stuff going on that we didn't really know about until we, like, compared notes in the week or two after," I recited. "Like, her family was struggling and going through some stuff, and she and her boyfriend had just broken up but they were still living together."

"Living with her ex," he said, whistling. "*I'd* kill myself."

"Right?" Why hadn't we seen it as uncomfortable at the time? Well, because bucking conventions had been our status quo. "So anyway, I saw the friend last night, and it turns out right after the suicide, she went totally conspiracy theorist and claimed it wasn't a suicide."

"Jesus," he breathed. "Wait, you're just learning this now?"

"I kinda split from the group after the funeral. They all lived together, and it was . . . We were kinda drifting apart by then, anyway." I sighed. "They were like this beautiful little hipster clique. When Edie died, it all fell apart."

"I need to see these people. Facebook." He gestured at my monitor and I pulled up some group photos.

"She's cute," he said when I pointed to Edie.

"And *there's* the final proof that you are zero-percent heterosexual. She's stunning."

"Did everyone want to fuck her?" He shrugged. "So skinny. You could snap her in half."

"Christ, Damien, she's dead," I said through inappropriate laughter.

He apologized, grinning, then headed for his desk.

I returned to Facebook, to the grid of photos. There were so many pictures of us hanging out in Sarah, Alex, Kevin, and Edie's apartment, which we'd jokingly called SAKE, pronounced like the Japanese wine, unwilling to bear the inconvenience of mentioning all of the tenants' names. Always with drinks around, always with drunk, sparkly eyes. So few of these images stirred up memories; they were like loose leaves or a deck of cards: Young People Having Fun. I seemed to be always there, though I lived two stops away on the subway. Sarah was sort of right: While Edie and I had been best friends for a moment, I'd never quite been a full member of the clique. Once Edie and I had had our falling-out, I'd been just outside, watching them through a sheet of glass.

I scrolled. There were just as many photos of us in other apartments within Calhoun Lofts—beer bottles scattered around, someone flipping off the camera or finding a way to look blasé. It was such an odd building, a full block long and set up like a college dormitory, only instead of small dorm rooms, there were apartments, each tall and rectangular, like a giant shoebox. They came gapingly vacant except for a kitchen and a bathroom crouched in one corner. And into those giant shoeboxes, tenants brought plywood and drywall and constructed their lives: lofted bedrooms resting on stilts with a forest of four-by-four pillars underneath, or cubbylike rooms lining either side of the long walls, so that standing in the central corridor felt like being on dry sand with the Red Sea rising on either side.

Sarah had been the Virgil who'd led me through Calhoun's graffiti-splattered front doors and into its deepest circles. I'd first met Sarah in Manhattan a week or two earlier at a vodka-soaked rooftop party thrown by effervescent PR people for some product or campaign launch. It was August 2008 and I'd just started my first job as a fact-checker at a fitness magazine; Sarah was a junior designer at *The Village Voice,* and somehow both our names showed up in some media directory and garnered us invitations. It felt strange, gulping cocktails at this extravagant party while the stock market teetered and talking heads wrung their hands and both our companies implemented hiring freezes like an early winter frost. We chatted away and exchanged emails and then got lunch at a burrito place, and just like that, we were friends. I miss that about my twenties, that vastness, that sweeping sense that there's room for everyone worthwhile, all the time and space in the world.

Sarah lived with Edie and some other girls at the time, in a different apartment within Calhoun Lofts. I'd heard the building referred to in reverential tones; it was hipster legend. Sarah had invited me to see a show there that Saturday. My outfit and hair carefully planned out and rethought, I'd taken two parting shots of whiskey, boarded the L train, and ridden deep into the bowels of Bushwick.

Sarah met me at the door with a hug and a compliment (I can still taste that tang of relief that I'd dressed acceptably) and brought me first to her apartment to pregame. Stepping into her place, I gasped at the soaring warehouse space with unfinished walls, twenty-foot ceilings, and, on the far end, a wall of dirty windows that looked straight out of a vintage elementary school.

Rap music poured from speakers and my eyes fell on Edie, standing on the couch and dancing with abandon, a red Solo cup held high in one hand. I saw her as if in slow motion: red waves skipping over a cropped gold blazer, a sliver of pale stomach above indigo shorts, all skinny limbs and outsize confidence. Sarah yelled up an introduction and Edie turned her emerald eyes to me and smiled, and suddenly nothing in life was as important as making this girl like me.

Sarah poured us drinks and we sat down with the other roommates. I remember less about them: a quiet girl named Jenna with long brown hair and a bumped nose (she worked in book publishing, maybe?) and an impressively skinny blonde named Kylie, who spoke with a California *raaaaahsp*. Strangers thrown together by Craigslist, but all nice girls, a group that danced and drank and lived well together. I focused my efforts on Edie, who was bright and hilarious and weirdly delighted by everything I said. I did *so well*. I hit that second-drink tingle of wit and found myself thinking that this Edie was everything I wanted my life in New York to be.

She didn't ask me what I did for work; instead we gushed about our close-at-hand *dreams,* her imminent enrollment at Parsons, my plans to write narrative nonfiction so finely crafted it'd make readers' chests ache. We talked about men and Bowie, how we'd both read an article revealing we're about 40 percent stardust and 60 percent hydrogen, or Big Bang dust, and isn't it wild our atoms are as old as life itself. We had such great energy. Even Sarah noticed it and politely faded into herself.

After a final round of shots, the girls led me to an apartment on another floor—another huge rectangular canvas, now decked out with a stage along the far windows, a bar/merch table off to its right, and an especially bizarre construction of living quarters: Over a thicket of four-by-fours, they'd built a cluster of elevated bedrooms, each claustrophobic and squat and opening into an elf-size catwalk, which lipped out into an overhang from which to watch the stage. (A resident I bumped into that night told me that during a brief run of *Romeo and Juliet,* they'd made literal use of it for the balcony scene.)

Our drunkenness swelled, not just from the shots but also from the frenzy: strobe lights, spilled drinks, gyrating masses, a pounding band sporting silver and gold jackets and sequins on their eyebrows. We allowed the surf to sweep us up, dancing along, a pleasant tornado. The night faded to black afterward, like so many after it, when the light of my consciousness would blink back on hours later in my own bed or on SAKE's couch or sometimes atop the small, sweaty mattress of a male Calhoun resident. Periods snipped from my timeline, blacked out, right in the middle of the best days of my life.

That's my lingering impression of our year as a gang: such potent, intoxicating *fun,* a billowing glee I hadn't experienced before and certainly haven't since. A montage of drunken nights spent wandering from floor to floor searching for the source of a pounding bassline, or setting off fireworks from the roof, or drifting around phoneless, unable to find one another in separate sets of staircases. We weren't yet glued to our devices: There was no Instagram to document in flattering light that you'd been included, no location tagging to show you *were there*. For me, it was like a college do-over, reparations for those four years of agonizing over my GPA and pottering around in a medication-induced fog. Calhoun felt self-contained, its own little microcosm, with secrets and a kind of kiddie society and the feel of a grand immersive theater production. We were *so young* but thought we were the wisest bastards on the planet. We didn't run the world, and in fact outside the sky was falling, but we did run that building, eight floors high and a block long on an otherwise undeveloped street in Bushwick.

My pointer hovered over a photo of Edie dancing, and I smiled at the screen. She really did come alive on the dance floor—spinning and popping and shaking and convulsing in a way that somehow looked so fucking cool, so confident and brazenly joyful that others always turned to watch. There was a monthly dance-off, I remembered suddenly, in a sweat-smelling venue by the river, and three times Edie had taken home first prize.

And that smile on her face. I checked the date: June 3, a few months before she died. No one had seen her smile like this in the weeks leading up to her death. Not Alex, whom she would dump just a few weeks later, even as they vowed to be friends. Not Sarah, as the two picked little fights, half antagonizing, half avoiding each other—impossible, of course, in that strange *Alice in Wonderland*-style setting. Certainly not me, in the aftermath of the blowup of the century that left me looking around at the bomb site and wondering how I'd called her my best friend.

I finished fact-checking the cocktail feature and turned my attention to an absurd sex piece about what everyone can learn from polyamorous relationships. An idea unfurled as the day wore on: the state's Freedom of Information Law. A FOIL request, a polite and unignorable demand that the police department pony up whatever I please; I completed them all the time for work, digging up files that writers were too lazy to uncover firsthand. I knew the intricacies of the application form and could certainly make a quiet request under the guise of my research job. If there had been an investigation around Edie's death, as Sarah had mentioned, then there must be a case file. I filled out an online form and got a pop-up indicating the requested files would be sent to me in one to five business days—a bullshit timeframe when the retrieval was almost certainly happening on a scale of nanoseconds, if-then algorithms instantaneously humming in a digital brain.

Near the end of the day, I checked my work email, and midway through responding to an editor, something clicked: I had to get into my old email. I'd blathered tons of juicy stuff in messages to and from Edie back in the day; we'd written constantly about weekend plans, her relationship dramas, the previous night's party recaps. Maybe inspecting them now, with my fact-checker's eye, would reveal something I'd missed, a cry for help or a pall of depression I'd been too young to grasp. Or perhaps I'd written something about the concert that night—maybe there was proof, documentation of my whereabouts. I'd abandoned the account years ago, and the service no longer existed, so there was no simple reset password button. But there must be some way to crack it back open, wriggle inside.

And I knew who could help. I texted my friend Tessa late in the afternoon; she was always surprising me with the digital lock-picking skills she'd picked up in her library sciences program. She invited me over later that week—Damien, too, if he was free.

I couldn't resist checking Facebook one last time before shutting down my computer. I scrolled a bit further and my heart jumped: Deep in one of Sarah's photo albums was a little thumbnail that looked familiar. Full-size, it was four men scuzzing around onstage, keyboards and guitars and synth. They all had black and red stripes painted across their faces. It was a perfect match with the concert I'd been picturing for August 21—a wild show that rattled a random Calhoun apartment. I looked at the date and my stomach sank. This night, the one pictured at least, had been a full month before Edie died.

Chapter 2

The wine shop on Tessa's block was closed, but the bodega wasn't, so I picked up a six-pack and carried it awkwardly, the bottles clinking inside their cardboard carrier within the bodega's plastic bag—a pointless beer turducken—past Tessa's doorman and up the ancient elevator and to her door. Marlon, her cute terrier mutt, bounded up to my ankles and crouched, wagging his tail hysterically.

"Lindsay!" Tessa gave me a cursory hug and grabbed the beer. "My favorite kind, thank you!"

"Didn't want to show up empty-handed. It smells amazing in here." Something garlicky and rich.

"I made risotto. Here, come help me make a salad."

I followed her into the kitchen and tapped a magnet on the fridge in the shape of a mug of Guinness.

"Your trip! I forgot to say thanks for the postcard." I don't know if she sends them to everyone or just to me because she knows how much I love her handwriting: the hip, squared-off lettering of an architect or artist, angular and typographic.

She smiled and swung the fridge door open, pulling the vegetable drawer out noisily. She always has fresh vegetables, not limp and forgotten and sometimes rotting white and green like mine. "Of course! You know, there's exactly one post office left in all of Dublin, and the nineteen-year-old behind the counter acted like she'd never seen a postcard before." She dropped a clatter of veggies in front of me and produced a cutting board.

"Well, you *are* the last person on earth still sending them."

"It's true. I should know, I catalog this shit all day."

I turned on the tap and began scrubbing the vegetables. "So tell me about Dublin!"

"It was fun! Rainy. I mostly just drank Guinness with Will."

"Sounds amazing. Is he coming tonight?"

"Eventually. He's at work." She banged around, cleaning up. Her kitchen's all gleaming white and chrome. "Do you know what time Damien's coming?"

"Oh, he said to eat without him—it'll be eightish. Apparently Trent teaches spin on Thursdays, and he obviously can't miss that."

She laughed. "How's everything for you? Work?"

"Ohh, the same." I sliced a head of cauliflower right through the center and peered down at it. How like a brain it looked, the woody white just like a brain stem. For just a second, I saw the ruffled pink organ in front of me, blood spurting from the bottom.

"Are you still working crazy hours?"

I blinked the image away. "Only during shipping weeks. When we're sending everything to the printer. And I care less with every passing month, which makes me sort of untouchable. So it's fine. Should I cut up both tomatoes?"

Tessa looked back at me and nodded. "Still not interested in looking around for another job?"

I rolled my eyes. "There aren't that many print magazines around anymore, Tessa. And they know I'm good at what I do. We can't all love every second of our amazingly perfect jobs like you."

She let out an awkward laugh. "Sorry. So tell me again what you need me to break into your old email for?" She'd turned back to the stove and the hood swallowed her words.

"It's sort of dumb," I began. "I randomly had dinner the other night with this friend from when I first lived in New York. And remember how when I was twenty-three, my best friend committed suicide?"

Tessa nodded, still bent over the pot.

"We started talking about the night it happened, and Sarah—

the friend I just saw—we, like, remembered it really differently. It just got me thinking, that's all. Set some nostalgia in motion."

"You remembered it differently?"

"It made me realize how little I actually dealt with it at the time." I didn't mention Sarah's odd claim about my whereabouts; I still felt sheepish about the discrepancy. "Instead of grieving and leaning on my other friends to get through it, I just cut them all off. I was so self-absorbed at twenty-three. Everyone is, I think."

Tessa nodded and tested a bite of risotto.

"It's almost weird that . . . that I haven't *thought* about how odd my reaction was, if that makes sense. I never really tried to figure out why I reacted that way. And now I'm curious to go back through it with a little perspective."

"And you really think your old emails will help?" Her tone was friendly, just curious, but I heard my voice growing defensive.

"I've just been thinking about it, is all. The ten-year anniversary is coming up next month—maybe that's subconsciously why I contacted Sarah in the first place. Not to psychoanalyze myself or anything. But I'm the head of research at *Sir;* I fact-check things all day long. Maybe I'm finally equipped to go over this one more time and then be done with it."

"What are you hoping to figure out?"

"Why she killed herself, I guess."

"Was she depressed?"

"She was. She must've been. But she never told anyone, so it was pretty shocking. And it all happened around when she was fighting with everyone. I'd even been planning a dramatic friend breakup with her."

The kitchen vent whirred. "Just be careful that you're not circling back to find reasons to blame yourself or anything," Tessa said. "Healthy people don't kill themselves. That's not something anyone else can drive you to do." She turned around and I smiled at her. Sometimes Tessa can sense the anxiety I'm creeping toward before I even realize it. She wiped her hands on a towel. "Let's eat."

She asked about my folks in Wisconsin (fine; hadn't talked to them since Easter) and Michael, the sort of dodgy guy I'd been seeing. I asked about her archivist job at Columbia (excellent) and her and Will's upcoming anniversary trip to New Zealand (stressful but exciting). We were almost finished when I noticed she hadn't grabbed a beer; she was sipping water, occasionally crossing to the fridge to refill her glass.

"I brought Two Hearted Ale for you!" I called, suspicious. She froze, wide-eyed, and I gasped. "You are not . . . are you? Is that— *Tessa!*" My voice rose to a screech as we both broke into laughter.

"We haven't even told our parents yet," she said as I released her from a hug. "Mine will be in town next weekend, so we figured we'd tell them in person."

"*Tessa,*" I said again. Just above my grin, my eyes filled with tears. "I'm so happy for you! Holy shit." I'd known that she and Will were vaguely trying to get pregnant—she'd begun seeing an acupuncturist to regulate her cycles and improve her chi or whatever—but she hadn't mentioned it in months.

"I'm only eight weeks along, so don't tell anybody," she said. "I kind of feel like crap all the time, so I want to complain to everyone, but apparently I'm not supposed to talk about it yet."

"I won't say anything. Morning sickness?"

"Mostly just feeling exhausted and . . . off. It's like being hungover all the time. And all I want to do is drink wine."

I squeezed her hand. "I'll make you amazing virgin ginger cocktails. And run errands and do whatever you need, obviously." I clicked my tongue. "Tessa, you're going to be a *mom!*"

I gave her another hug, my tears soaking into her shoulder. The idea of taking care of Tessa cheered me; typically *she* was the one with her shit together, mothering me.

"When are you due?"

"End of February." She shrugged again, like she was sick of talking about it. "It helps to see you excited because I keep forgetting it's exciting. I'm just focused on pretending everything's normal."

"You totally fooled me! Jeez. Thank you for making us dinner and, you know, being willing to help me with these emails."

"Of course! Should we go into the office? I've been thinking about this challenge all day."

I stopped in the bathroom first and froze as tears again filled my eyes, suddenly, like a bell clanging. I blinked into the mirror and steadied my breath. I was happy for Tessa, of course, excited to meet Baby Hoppert. But there was also—what? Jealousy, a wistfulness? I peered hard at the feeling until it crystallized: that awful tug of feeling left behind, overlooked by some unseen orchestrator. All of my Facebook stalking came into sharp focus: Sarah giggling about her in-laws in New Jersey. Alex and his apartment in the burbs. Even Kevin had a goddamn husband now. Where was I the day adulthoods were distributed?

I stretched my mouth into a smile and breathed hard until the tears cleared. Biological trickery; I'd researched it once—fooling the body into some semblance of ease. I cleared my throat and headed into the office, dropping into Will's fancy desk chair. Before Tessa could begin typing, the doorbell chimed, sending Marlon into barking conniptions.

"Hello, darlings!" Damien called as soon as Tessa opened the door. He gave us both French-style cheek kisses.

"A huge thank-you for keeping your spinning shorts on," I joked. He looked like a Greek god.

"I aim to please."

"Do you need food?" Tessa broke in, already heading down the hall to make him a plate. Standing around her kitchen island, Tessa shared her big news again and Damien responded like the bro I sometimes forget he is: He smiled and said, "Hey, that's fun!" and then, after a question or two, changed the subject. Once, at the office, I'd witnessed a copy editor proudly showing him her engagement ring, which he'd barely glanced at before chirping, "It's cute!" Yet he'll *lose his mind* over a puppy on the street.

When Damien had finished eating, Tessa herded us back into the office.

"So we're playing detectives?" Damien asked as he dragged in an extra chair. "Because I'm a regular Sherlock Homo. Just call me Fancy Drew. I'm like a . . . Hardy Boy?"

"Too far," I said, smiling.

"The real mystery is why Lindsay wants to look through her old inbox," Tessa said.

I couldn't quite articulate it myself. To figure out why Edie killed herself? To check how I'd overlooked Sarah's hysterical breakdown afterward? To confirm, beyond the shadow of a doubt, that I'd been up at that concert when the unthinkable happened?

"To remind myself how far I've come since I was twenty-three and a hot mess," I said lightly.

Damien raised his beer. "Never change."

Tessa began to type. "You're sure you don't remember your old password?"

"Absolutely not. I can barely remember my current one." I pulled out my phone and sent my music to the speakers set high in the walls. Classical guitar filled the room—intricate flamenco music to score whatever calisthenics Tessa was doing online. I watched over her shoulder: codes being entered, archives unlocking.

Tessa and I had become friends six years ago when I approached her, tipsy on bad wine, at a bookstore following a reading that sounded interesting but wasn't. Whoever was supposed to come with me hadn't shown up, and I'd felt embarrassed about the seat I'd reserved with a scarf and then guarded jealously, turning people away until the event began and I became a rude person next to an empty chair. Afterward I'd swigged a big plastic cup of free wine and headed for the door, pausing just as the alcohol hit me to ask Tessa if I knew her from somewhere—her face, it was tickling my sense of déjà vu. She hadn't seemed to remember me, but we played the maybe-from game for a while, spitting out our biographies in quick, successive questions, then gave up and started chatting and totally hit it off. Eventually I introduced her to Damien, and to my delight, they got along famously, too. I'd felt so pleased, the creator of a happy elective family after a long period of loneliness. Tessa's a good yin to my yang. If only she'd been a man.

The front door slammed, and for a second time, Marlon yelped and sped off. Will drifted in, tall and waifish and drowning in a suit. He smiled and dropped his palms onto Tessa's shoulders.

"Hey, hon," she murmured without looking up.

"Hi, Will!" I called out, half standing to give him a hug. "Congratulations on fathering my new niece or nephew!"

"Mazel!" Damien added.

Will beamed. "Thanks, guys. We can hardly believe it."

"How was your day?" Tessa asked, still typing.

"Not bad. They accepted the plea bargain on that case I was telling you about. What are you guys up to?"

"Tessa's hacking me!" I announced.

"Is that so?" He grinned and leaned on the credenza. I like Will, who had been Tessa's husband of only a few months when she and I became friends. The two of them had met on Match .com at a time when people still believed both that one could find a soul mate online and that that belief was worth paying for. (Tinder has since disabused me of both notions.) At first I wasn't sure what to make of his soft-spoken manner, the way he'd just smile at Tessa's jokes and grow calmer and muter the funnier she got, but now I know it's their introvert-extrovert pas de deux. He's a card-carrying good guy, the kind I myself haven't encountered on dating apps in years.

"She's helping me bust into my old email account. Because I'm an idiot and I can't remember my old password."

"You know, Tessa, the unauthorized access of an email account is a felony," he said, nudging a wheel of her chair with his toe. "Additional civil liabilities, too."

"I'm authorized!" she replied. "Besides, with the dirt I find in here, she'll know better than to come after me."

"To mutually assured destruction," I laughed, and we clinked our water glasses.

Will wandered off to change out of his suit, and Marlon trotted after him, tail wagging. Just as the guitar music hit a dramatic crescendo, Tessa murmured, "There, that should . . ." and struck the space bar. Words swarmed the screen.

"It's not pretty," she warned, "but it's all here, everything in your inbox and sent folder from 2009."

"There's no way they taught you that at library nerd school," Damien said.

Tessa stretched, smiled. "I used to hack into corporate servers in high school. I had issues with authority."

"Damn, girl," Damien said. "Quit making me question my orientation."

She turned back to the screen. "It's not directly from the server, but the archive was backed up in the cloud, probably because at some point you pulled it into a program."

I frowned and then said, "Outlook?"

"That must be it. It's kinda unwieldy, but I can index it for you." More typing, more clicking. "Want me to drop all the emails into our shared folder?"

Something fluttered, apprehension at the idea of Tessa and Damien having access to my potentially embarrassing emails—the dumb stuff I cared about at twenty-three, the sexual quirks of whomever I was seeing, the cringe-y tales of how wasted we all had been. Really, it was a miracle that I'd made it through my twenties in one piece, protected only by the hubris of youth. I remembered making out with someone in the back of a camper as it barreled down the FDR Drive; his long-haired bandmate had volunteered to drive us back to Brooklyn, gesturing with his beer: "I shouldn't be okay to drive, but I am." How, *how* had we made it there safely?

Drunken disasters. There'd been the Warsaw Incident, but I hadn't emailed about it, had I? Either way, I hadn't met Tessa or Damien until years after that nonsense, so the names would be meaningless. But. Still.

I said sure. When she lifted her fingers from the keyboard and leaned back, I wanted to jump right in, push her out of the way, and start reading, but instead she crossed her legs and smiled.

"I used to write long emails back then, too," she announced. "We spent so much time composing these novel-length messages, you know?"

"I know. Texting really killed the long-form personal confession." I shrugged.

Damien finished his beer with a little *ahh*. "Didn't you used to write essays? Like Modern Love–type stuff?" he asked.

"Oh, *god*." I let out a laugh. "Yeah, that's the exact kind of thing I was writing when I wasn't treating emails to my friends like diary entries. I was always frustrated because I never had any good material. I didn't really like that many guys and the ones I *did* like didn't seem to like me, so I never had much to write about."

The real answer was a longer one: I'd wanted to be a writer since I was little and had stumbled only by accident into the realm of fact-checking—a decent specialty in a shaky field, but just literal steps from the job I'd actually wanted. I'd had a few minor successes in my early twenties—a feature in the pretentious literary magazine *n+1,* a few clips in the fitness magazine that employed me—but I'd stopped pitching in my midtwenties, when all the staff writer jobs disappeared and journalists with résumés as long as the *Iliad* competed for the same editors' attention. And I'd made peace with it long ago. I was a damn good research chief, and *Sir* was one of the nation's oldest and most solid men's magazines in the industry.

"You should think about submitting again," Tessa nudged. She scratched at her button nose.

"Oh, maybe someday." I cleared my throat and added, "*Anyway.*"

At home I dashed into the bathroom as soon as I got inside, and I stared at the inside of the door as I peed: a cheap door painted white, snowy when I moved in but now covered in black scuff marks. The area around the doorknob was a dirty beige; a crack bisected the door partway up. The kind of things a landlord deals with between tenants, a quick slap of paint to blot out the last renter's marks. Five years on, the mess was all mine. Five years. It had seemed like such a nice, adult apartment when I'd first moved in.

I sat down at the table and bathed myself in the computer's bluish glow. I opened up the text files Tessa had made and realized that it was going to be more of a nightmare than I'd anticipated; each email was in its own file, some of them with the earlier exchange clinging to the bottom of the message but never organized into conversations. I could sort them by date, which split conversations up over weeks, or by subject, which glommed convos together but strung them into a senseless timeline. Shit.

Instead I searched for "Modern Love" and found three sad little emails, each ending with a polite rejection, two form letters and one that seemed at least a tiny bit more personal ("Sorry to say I don't think this is quite a fit, but thanks for trying me with it"). Even all these years later, rereading these replies sparked a mix of disappointment and self-consciousness. I opened up the piece that got the longest answer.

I Don't Want to Be Sedated

A very determined cricket has chosen the tree outside my window as his podium. I love him and pity him and feel for him as he chirps his question mark over and over into a dark street. There don't seem to be many other crickets in Bushwick, and with the odds against him, I worry that his trills will slow, that his optimism will flag.

My own odds ought to be much more favorable: The city holds millions of single men, and the company I keep— beautiful, creative young Brooklynites—pretty much comprises the graduates of gifted and talented programs from high schools all over the world. The options are excellent. The problem is me.

I don't mean to be difficult to impress. I didn't pick this particular pickiness. It's the butterflies in my stomach, I tell you. It's like they're sedated or possibly bound up in cocoons.

It's so very easy to get dates in New York City. Anyone with an internet connection and mild self-portraiture skills can line them up in a few quippy sentences. It's so hard to get good ones. When I came to the city six months ago, I felt nervous before each first date, sipping a cocktail and listening to Beyoncé and swirling on bronzer as I fought down the urge to vomit. All those nerves, not the good kind of eddying in my torso, but motion nonetheless.

Now I don't get nervous at all, a change that strikes me as a little sad. *He'll be fine,* I predict, *and I won't really want to see him again.* I'm almost always right. At night, I lie awake and wonder why the butterflies refuse to stir. I fear they know something I don't, something dark and jagged about me. The skeletons in my skeleton. The reason I don't quite deserve it.

The last time they showed any movement was when I met Jonah, a cute bearded fellow, at a concert in the fall. I liked his wide grin, his unbounded enthusiasm. He'd moved from the Midwest to Manhattan only three weeks before, and I was into the idea of an unspoiled specimen, too fresh and transparent to be over everything already. He and I sat knees to knees at a bar, and the little moths showed movement, an unfamiliar, almost-forgotten rustle.

He ghosted after the third date.

It's nice to know the butterflies haven't calcified, but I'm not entirely sure I'm glad I met Jonah. It's made hollow first dates even hollower since then, two strangers in a mahogany booth deciding to become estranged. But I keep

going to shows and parties, keep setting up dates, keep
entering bars with a smile and a question mark on my face.
Like the cricket, like the bird in the children's book who
keeps on asking and asking and asking. Are you my lover?

I must have written it before I fell for Lloyd. Aw, little awkward Lindsay. A girl I'd like to reach back and hug. Except that I wouldn't have too many soothing words for her, I suppose. If only she knew the trend wasn't temporary, that in a decade she'd be as old as Jesus with a list of sex partners exceeding her age but no identifiable capital-B boyfriend in the ensuing years.

And Jonah—him I just barely remembered, a dull "Ohhhh, right." That idiot.

Time to start reading emails then. I attempted to sort them by date but accidentally brought them up by size, so the one at the top had huge files hanging off of it as attachments. Edie's subject line: "HOT BUSHWICK JAMZ." I opened it and found twelve .mp3s tacked onto a quick hello—oh god, it was a playlist, from back before songs streamed through the air, when we bought music piecemeal (or ripped it off LimeWire) and uploaded it into devices that didn't yet intuit what we'd want to hear based on our constantly fine-tuned preferences. I popped in earbuds and dragged the files into my toolbar's long-dormant iTunes player: first, a lush synth-heavy number with braided, building chords. I hit next: a dramatic eighties-style hit, something appropriate for the climax of a John Hughes movie.

I skipped ahead to a stripped-down head-bobber with reverb-y guitars and droning male voices. I could picture them, onstage just inches from Edie and me in a semilegal venue: a troupe of skinny guys in plaid shirts or big trench coats, nodding their heads with their hair shaken over their faces. I read over the band names and smiled—lots of woodland creatures, a few colors. None of them had gone on to greatness, which probably would've made Edie and me turn on them anyway.

We'd loved going to shows together. One night I had turned to

Edie from the packed audience of a concert, what felt like the millionth, and the whole crowd was so excited and the band onstage was killing it and Edie and I had just locked eyes, happiness rushing up through me like froth. She'd reached out and squeezed my arm with both hands, and for one second, life was perfect.

Edie had that air of never seeming to care what anyone thought of her, which of course made everyone desperate for her approval. She spoke lazily, softly, and people leaned in to listen. She smiled and raised an eyebrow when you said something dumb, a look that hurt like a hot iron. And when she laughed, when you got it right and she tipped her head back to guffaw . . .

I hit forward again and got an intense drum intro, then a hyperpulsing bassline: same venue, different punk kids onstage sweating and flailing while the crowd slammed into itself. I pictured us playing the song on Edie's computer speakers, shaking our hips as we applied eyeliner and got ready for a night out in Williamsburg. The music felt ageless now; it was angry but somehow defiantly joyful, a middle finger to the sky.

As the song pummeled into my headphones, I searched by date and found the last email Edie ever sent me. It was a group email from our mutual friend about her coworker's show at Spike Hill that Friday (*the* Friday); Edie had replied-all to say that she was probably going to stay in. No other emails from her that week, which made sense given our big blowup the weekend before.

I decided to work the other way, beginning with the oldest emails, from January. We volleyed back and forth almost daily, mundane emails peppered with our own affected shorthand: "see you on fridaze" and "let's get some burr" and "sofa king" as our go-to adverbial clause ("sound it out," she'd prompted on first usage). She complained about her fashion-school classmates; I told her about a hot but "possibly aspy" boy who'd left his socks on during sex. A sense of privacy infused every email, our own little world. People have described romantic relationships to me that way; perhaps this was the closest I'd gotten.

I saw a long chain that had tracked in one email, indented

further and further so that my first email to Edie was a skinny column along the right; the subject line was "UM." I started at the bottom:

From: Lindsay Bach <lindsay.bach@gmail.com>
To: Edith Iredale <eiredale1@gmail.com>
Fri, Jan 23, 2009 at 2:06 PM

LADY. WTF happened with BC after I left last night? There was so much heat between you guys that everyone else was, like, shielding their eyes. Did anything happen??

From: Edith Iredale <eiredale1@gmail.com>
To: Lindsay Bach <lindsay.bach@gmail.com>
Fri, Jan 23, 2009 at 6:16 PM

Ugggghhh I am so hungover I want to DIE. Isn't he insanely hot? I know you've seen him around here too but there's something about his voice, and those eyes when he's listening to you . . . I want to have sex with his voice, Lindsay. Someone should come up with a way for me to do that.

But to answer your question, NO, don't be stupid, of course nothing happened! I wouldn't do that to Greg. It was totally innocent, just . . . intense. I don't know. He got my number and said something about hanging out in Calhoun this weekend but right now I can't even wrap my head around it. I'm going to have to make him use a voice changer thing like they do on TV so that I can be around him without spontaneously orgasming . . .

From: Lindsay Bach <lindsay.bach@gmail.com>
To: Edith Iredale <eiredale1@gmail.com>
Sat, Jan 24, 2009 at 12:10 PM

Okay, I am glad to hear you two didn't jump each other's bones because it TOTALLY FELT LIKE THAT WAS ABOUT TO HAPPEN. Just saying. Did you figure out where BC lives?

From: Edith Iredale <eiredale1@gmail.com>
To: Lindsay Bach <lindsay.bach@gmail.com>
Sat, Jan 24, 2009 at 1:45 PM

He's on the 4th floor, way east, which makes sense why I
hardly ever see him. So wild, I can't believe we bumped
into him in Manhat. Ugggh. Do you want to watch a movie
tonight? Greg's friends are going to some bar that has
bocce ball, but I really don't think I can rally ...

I skimmed further; the conversation veered off into plan making. But god, I remembered that night, Thursday, January 22,
apparently—clear as if it were playing out documentary style before me.

The holidays were over and we were cold and bored. Weekend after weekend, we drank cheap whiskey and did lackluster,
shuffling dances in the back room of Royal Oak, one of our go-to
shitty bars. We racked up Friday after Friday at Calhoun, picking our way up and down littered staircases in search of another
sweaty party or arbitrary open band practice or glimpse of the hot
guy Edie had a Building Crush on. We sat in booths and sipped
drinks instead of talking and finished too many nights with sad
free pizza at The Charleston.

Until that night when, in a burst of motivation, Edie and I rode
the train all the way to the Lower East Side to see some British
band she knew about; the rest of our friends had been too SAD-
addled to make the trip. After the show, we downed whiskey-
gingers and held shouted, jerky conversation over loud music and
were just about to call it a night when in walked Building Crush
with a crew of cool-looking friends: model-y, thick-banged girls
and a cute blond dude in an acid-washed denim jacket. Building
Crush, of course, turned out to be Alex, but it was his friend I
homed in on—ashen hair curved in a triumphant windblown wave,
like he'd just stepped off a crotch rocket. High cheekbones and a
square jaw around an impish grin. The goofy sidekick in a Molly

Ringwald movie. Energy that bounded out spastically, bouncing off of things.

What followed was one of those New York City nights that we were too young to see as special: Alex wandered over with a confident "Hey, are we neighbors?," setting in motion the whole movie montage. The blond dude, Lloyd, not of the building, said his friend had given him the code for her fancy condo in the East Village, and we walked there together, Lloyd running ahead to entertain us with stupid antics like climbing into and then reclining in the basket of an abandoned crane. Edie and Alex followed a half-block behind, talking and smiling shyly. It was an unexpectedly warm January night, and we all felt young and drunk and free, pretty hipsters in an ad for jeans.

Lloyd was a photographer with an insane ability to take a good shot of anybody; he snapped away on his iPhone 3G, and every time he flicked it around to let us see, we squealed in delight, our faces just the way we liked to think they looked. Humoring me, he took my shitty Razr flip phone and lifted a lighter above me as I held a cigarette and looked pensive. It was perfect. Longest-running Facebook profile photo to date, until I grew old enough to realize the fake-smoker thing was gross.

I think he was in a band, too. God, all the men of that era were both photographers and in shitty bands.

We clambered onto the roof of a gorgeous condo on Fourteenth, one I wasn't ever able to locate again, and one of the girls magically procured a stereo and we danced to stupid nineties tunes. Lloyd kept us moving, pulling me in and then whipping me out to spin. Alex and Edie found some lawn chairs and settled in a little ways away, talking sleepily, while Lloyd finished a bottle of whiskey and, with a holler, ripped off the cover of a drained pool I hadn't even noticed and vaulted himself into the deep end, demanding that we grab the stereo and climb in with him.

I still remember those smooth white tiles, how we threw off our coats and danced in and out of the deep end, laughing hysterically as one by one we lost our footing on the center's slanted floor. Lloyd did pull-ups under the diving board. We discovered the stars over-head and clutched each other in delight of them. We were dizzy and drunk. The night screeched to a halt when I threw up into a drain, and Lloyd helped me clomp down to the street and obtain a cab home. But that happy little aquarium made the rest of winter survivable: a ceramic vault where the music boomed and swelled.

I'd gone on to develop an enormous crush on Lloyd, the jelly-kneed, stomach-flipping kind that only strikes every five years if you're lucky. (I squinted at the emails again: of *course* Edie's hadn't asked if anything had happened between him and me.) I felt a little heart flip, remembering my intense infatuation. Then my mind jolted ahead to how it ended, and a sinking feeling rushed in to replace it.

But *Greg*—there's someone I hadn't thought of in a while. Edie's boyfriend at the time, the reason nothing could happen between her and Alex on that magical January night. Greg and Edie had begun dating shortly after I met her; I couldn't remember how they met, but there was something cute about it, something seren-dipitous that she got a kick out of sharing with people. Greg was older and intimidating, with a real job and expensive clothes and a condo by the water in Greenpoint. He rarely made appearances in Calhoun; Edie often headed to his apartment after a late-night show or dance party with the rest of us. Now I wonder what emo-tionally stunted thirty-two-year-old man wants to date an impul-sive twenty-three-year-old with a bit of a drinking problem, but at the time, he was a catch.

What had happened to Greg? I searched for his name in my inbox and confirmed they'd broken up in February 2009, shortly before Edie had begun dating Alex and moved into his apartment (*the* apartment, SAKE, the one with Sarah and Kevin—plus me as an honorary roommate). That had been such a fun spring and summer, right before everything went wrong. The first summer of Real Life, a hot season pulsed into the year instead of twelve demarcated weeks before the next semester. We were adults, we thought, but still soused on the sense memories of summers past.

And my friendship with Edie had been everything. I remembered a rainy afternoon when we'd holed up in my bedroom, drunk on boxed wine and high on our mutual friend-crushes. We were playing Truth or Truth, killing time with probing queries: detailed sex questions, humiliating childhood stories. It was thrilling and personal, like staring into each other's eyes.

"What's the worst thing you've ever done?" she asked, setting her glass on my windowsill. I adjusted the pillow behind my back, squeezing it flat and pushing it around.

She realized I was stalling. "I'll go first," she said, turning to pour herself more wine. "My mom planned this big dinner for my eighteenth birthday. She was cooking all day—and she hates cooking—and she'd invited some family and close friends. It was all really unlike her; normally she'd just pick up a cupcake that day or whatever and I'd celebrate with my friends." She took a long sip, then wiped her wine-stained lips. "So that morning she and I got into a huge fight—like, an all-out-screaming, plate-smashing fight. And I yelled 'Fuck you!' and stormed out of there. Then I proceeded to email everyone except my mom and tell them the dinner was canceled because I wasn't feeling well. I stayed over at my friend's that night, ignoring her calls, and when I came back, my mom didn't say anything. Then my dad told me that she'd still cooked everything and set it all out and sat there while nobody showed up. She had no idea I'd canceled it." She closed her eyes. "I mean, she *is* a bitch, but I still feel bad about that."

I scooted over on the bed and rested my cheek on her shoulder. She tipped her head onto mine and we sat there for a minute, pop music playing in the background.

"I can beat that," I offered finally. "It's about my parents, too. Only I was younger." And I told her the story they told me not to share, the one that scorches my cheeks and forehead still. When I finished talking, she raised her chin up to look at me, then nuzzled it back against my hair. She's still the only other person who knows. Knew. Now there's no one again.

It was hard to put a finger on exactly when my friendship with

Edie began to come apart at the seams; by July, we were having icy half-fights via email, infuriating ones where I'd write something long and detailed and she'd respond, with neither punctuation nor capitalization, "sure" or "what time" or "k." Edie said no to more and more group activities and closed herself into her little white room, especially sad because its square windows looked out not on the world but on the apartment's gloomy interior. Alex and Edie broke up in July, too—just a few months after they'd finally gotten together—for reasons neither of them really bothered to explain, adding that they were going to stay friends and not move out or anything. Now I saw that it was probably FOMO that kept either from being the one to leave, fear of missing out, fear of being ostracized, seeming maturity masking massive insecurity. It had to have been uncomfortable.

That summer, Edie and Sarah spent more time than ever hanging out in my apartment, a tiny but comfortable share with cracked walls and scuffed linoleum floors and a normal layout, a quiet roommate from Washington State, bedrooms with windows onto the street below. I felt a humming anxiety that the Calhounies must be instantly bored in my apartment, unstimulated by its lack of weird wall hangings, life-size portraits, or swings suspended from the ceiling. And I was jealous, too, jealous and in awe of the offbeat creatures in Calhoun and other Escherlike buildings who could coolly live in those strange setups. They did it so casually: "Oh, this?"

I found Greg's full name in an email and Googled him; strange how he'd felt so firmly in the past by the time Edie died, when in reality she'd been his ex of only six months. Time felt different then, stretchy and wide. I found him listed as a partner at some tech-y, startup-y architectural firm, beaming at me from a poorly framed headshot. The website was a confusing mass of buzzwords: "breakthroughs" and "collective reach" and "strategic partnerships." Gross. No contact information for him, just a physical address somewhere in DUMBO. I saved the listing and returned to my archives.

A name hit a nostalgic note in the February emails, and I clicked through to something I'd sent a friend from college who was teaching English in Italy, someone I lost contact with in the ensuing years. It started out with boring catch-up talk, but the middle of it made my stomach squeeze:

> Sometimes I just feel like such an idiot next to Edie. Like, so incompetent. The other day I was complaining to her about my boss and she was like, "Lindsay, you know everyone and their dog is unemployed right now, so you can see why she expects you to be working late and not complaining, right?" And she's RIGHT, but it's also like, Why can't you ever just be on my side? Or sometimes when I'm asking for her advice on guys, she'll ask what I said or look at what I've texted and she gives me this wide-eyed look like, Oh my GOD, how do you not know how to talk to boys? Which maybe I sort of don't. She's just so GOOD at everything. I know I just sound jealous, but it's not that. It's something, though . . .

Wow—I hadn't realized that I'd noticed so early how uneven the power dynamics of our friendship were. Later, I'd worked out that we were the kind of friends you make fresh out of college, when the only thing you have in common is doing fun things together. And so, after months of passive-aggressive torment from Edie (and quiet complicity from the rest of our friends, who were just happy her scorn wasn't directed at them), I'd made a grand decision: I'd extricate myself from this group and start over with kinder, happier, less self-obsessed people. I was planning to tell her that very weekend. I'd been prepped for that discussion, equipped and braced, and then she'd died. It was awful.

For her, of course. Well, for everyone. But especially for *me*. It was ridiculous, but in addition to the squall of confusion and grief and shock, there'd been a ribbon of annoyance—like Edie had skipped out on the confrontation by killing herself. I'd been so over her, how she was always making me feel like a charity case, like the one who had to be fixed. And then she'd disappeared.

She'd died dramatically, too, still a magnet for attention, with coverage of her death all over the blogosphere. Canonized, deified, the exact fucking week I'd planned to finally put an end to the toxic relationship. And so I'd left. I'd stopped talking to them all. And everyone thought it was because I was racked with grief—which I was—but it was also a convenient excuse to get the hell away.

I leaned back and felt my pulse thumping in my neck. I'd never put it together like this before—never allowed myself to see Edie's death in this light.

These were sick, stupid, childish thoughts. I poured myself a glass of water and swallowed them all.

I checked the time: 10:12; not late. So, before I could think too hard about it, I texted Michael and asked what he was up to.

My phone chimed a few minutes later. "Working late. What about you?"

Stupid noncommittal text. Obviously, Michael, I'm alone and bored and wanting you to want to see me.

"Just got home from dinner. Feel like watching a movie when you're done?"

He waited six minutes to answer, just long enough for me to pee again and wander around and burn holes into the screen with my eyes.

"Sure. I'll text you when I'm heading out."

Forty minutes later, I hadn't heard back from him. I checked in, hating myself for it. He said he could leave in fifteen and was that too late? I waited four entire minutes, the longest I could hold out, and then answered: "No, it's fine, come over when you can."

Chapter 3

Michael showed up a little before midnight, handsome and smooth. Four months we'd been sleeping together, occasionally with dinner or another sufficiently datelike activity beforehand; I knew I was too old to put up with this, but the thought of seeking out something more fulfilling made me so, so tired. We settled onto the couch and he was as witty and charming as ever, quick to steer the conversation to himself when it was clear I was feeling sullen. Sometimes this annoyed me; right now, it felt like warm relief, chatter I could wrap myself in like a blanket. Eventually I stood to make us tea and he suggested we turn in instead.

I was in the woods behind Uncle Bob's farm, steadying a pistol in my hands, clicking through my pre-fire checklist: fighter's stance, hand throttled high on the grip, thumb curled down for strength, trigger hooked inside the joint. I knew Edie was behind me, watching, and I was furious with her, anger streaming into my forehead and hands, a primal, frenzied, out-of-control urge to hurt. It occurred to me that Edie didn't know not to step out in front, and then it happened: She was picking through the trees, treading over roots, headed straight into my crosshairs. I closed my left eye and took aim, and the recoil shook me awake.

I lay still, heart racing, something eager and carnal still pulsing through my veins. I slowed my breathing, beating down a flare of bewilderment and shame, then willed my brain to delete the dream from my memory. Michael, next to me, was snoring.

Hours later, he woke me up by kissing my neck, a gentle, urgent move that always roused me. I swam up to the surface, blinking the wool from my eyes. Then Michael was there, solid and warm and sour-breathed, and I pulled myself awake enough to kiss him, hard.

Almost as soon as he came, he slid back on the bed and gently pushed my hips flat, working his tongue against me. He was good about this in an unsexy, pragmatic way—tit for tat, keeping us in a tie. At first I didn't think it would work, my mind suddenly cluttered with flashes of the dream, but I forced them aside, listening hard to my own deepening breath. Afterward he kissed my belly and wandered off, naked, to toss the condom and drink water and stretch his long arms; then he climbed back into bed.

"What are you thinking about?" He exhaled it as I nudged my head onto his chest, and I felt rather than heard the words. The lover's laziest question.

"Do you ever get blackout drunk?" I asked.

He let out a surprised chuckle. "I mean, not lately. But in college and my twenties, of course. Why?"

I looked around the room, thinking. Postorgasmic oxytocin was probably needling through my brain like truth serum, inky and insidious.

"I've just been thinking back to those days. Remembering. Well, remembering what it's like to wake up and not remember anything, which is sort of a Möbius strip of remembering."

He stroked my arm absentmindedly. "I mean, it's a normal part of being young. Figuring out your limits, and hopefully you have friends there to take you home and keep you safe and give you Gatorade."

"That's true." I scratched my forehead. "It's weird that it's normal, though, isn't it? It's weird that we aren't more terrified of it. Like, what did ancient civilizations make of it? Shouldn't we be more freaked out by people walking and talking and, like, interacting with others when a critical part of their brain is offline?"

He considered. "What actually happens? Are the brain cells too fried to pull up memories the next day?"

"No, I looked into this once." I laughed. "Not even for an article, I was just curious. It's actually that your brain isn't laying down memories. It stops recording. So not even extensive hypnosis or something could bring those hours back up."

I heard the smile in his voice. "I knew you'd have researched it."

"It's what I do." His hand stopped moving near mine and I wove my fingers into his. "What's the worst thing you've ever done while blacked out?" I tossed it out like a statement, a challenge.

"I got into a fistfight once," he offered. "Stupidest thing. Apparently this guy bumped into me in a bar and I was wasted and in a bad mood about something—a lady, probably—and I was like, 'Hey, fuck you, man.' And he turned around and said something threatening like, 'You wanna go?' And even though he had about eighty pounds on me, apparently I was like, 'Let's go! Right here!' And all my stupid friends were just watching like assholes as I took a swing at this guy. Who came back and punched me, busted up my nose, and threw me onto a table. So idiotic." We both giggled. "What was yours?"

There were options. The Warsaw Incident, which of course I'd never tell him. The time I'd spent my entire savings on round-trip tickets to Balikpapan, Indonesia (I'd drunkenly agreed to go to Bali and was five hundred miles off the mark); the time I'd come home late and inexplicably screamed at my messy roommate, shoving her tub of dirty dishes off the counter and then cutting my foot on broken glass during my defiant, wobbly exit. Lloyd flickered into my mind, too, the terribleness of that one morning after, but I swallowed and rattled off my default blackout story.

"I was out one night and started talking to this guy," I began, "and we had a bunch of drinks together, and then I think I invited him over, but he was like, 'Ehh, I just want to stay here with my friends.' Which, god knows what was actually going on, but I was *pissed*. So I went outside to hail a cab—this was when you had to actually look for them on the street—and some girls who, in retrospect, must have also been wasted saw me looking all furious and were like, 'Fuck him, come hang out with us!' and we went into the bar next door. I don't remember anything after that, but the next morning, when I finally woke up and went to check my purse for my wallet and phone, I reached in and pulled out"—I mimed it, the slow vertical reveal—"someone else's purse. Like a clutch? The entire thing was in there. And full of this poor girl's stuff—wallet, phone, lipstick, keys. I remember shuffling out to the living room where my roommate was watching TV and going, 'Hannah, I did something really, really bad . . . '"

"So you turned into a pickpocket?!" Michael was laughing now. I giggled, too, but I could still feel it, that balloon of shame, the feeling of fumbling into the past and finding nothing but air.

"That's the thing, I don't even know! Did I take it by accident? Did she ask me to hold it and I got lazy keeping it in my hands, so I dumped it into my purse? I have no idea! I didn't recognize her at all."

"God. What'd you do?"

"The phone was dead, but I had her name from her driver's license. I tried to find her on Facebook but didn't have any luck—for all I know, the ID might have been a fake. So I put on clothes and walked in a hungover stupor to the bar the random girl had brought me into and left it there—I said it looked like mine so I'd taken it by mistake. And then I just avoided that bar for the rest of time. I still have no idea how that bag ended up in my purse. I hope I didn't mug anyone."

He squirmed a bit, gently shook me off his shoulder, and rolled onto his side. "Are you a mean drunk? Is that why you stopped drinking?"

He said it teasingly, but I felt myself blush. "I guess. Back then I was, at least. My friends used to joke about having to keep me 'on-leash.'"

He snorted. "What's funny is that normally when you've had too much to drink, you wake up feeling like you've done something bad even though you haven't. But I woke up with a busted-up face. And you woke up with someone else's bag. So the guilt response was *correct*."

"I know, right?" I giggled again. "I looked into that, too. Your serotonin receptors are all messed up; basically gives you depression for the day." I fitted my elbow over his waist and sighed. "I don't miss that."

"Why did you stop drinking?"

Impressive that he'd made it this many months without asking, really. "I had this disastrous thirtieth birthday when I had way too much to drink," I said into his neck. "I finally put two and two together that . . . I mean, you've probably seen my pill bottles around, I've been on a few different things for depression and other stuff and yeah, I finally decided that alcohol wasn't really a helpful chemical to combine with my fucked-up brain." I normally avoided this entire topic—the stimulants as a kid, the benzos in college, the antidepressants now. That I don't remember life without mood-stabilizing drugs, that I'm not entirely sure who I'd be without them monkeying around with my neurotransmitters. But I was feeling so open, vulnerable.

"What happened on your birthday?" he asked.

"Well, I'd invited people over, and there was a huge snowstorm that day, so nobody came. The only ones who made it were my friend Tessa and her husband. He left early because he had to be in court the next day, and when it was just Tessa and me . . ." My face burned. "I blacked out and got kinda mean. About how all my friends sucked and she'd turned into a Smug Married and stuff. I said some terrible things; she didn't speak to me for days. They weren't even true, I don't know what I was talking about. After that I was like, 'Maybe this isn't such a good idea.' It hasn't actually been that hard. My life doesn't revolve around drinking like it did when I was younger."

He was quiet for a second. "Well, I don't think your brain's fucked up." He lifted my knuckles to his mouth and kissed them.

I laughed. "I mean, thanks. Obviously I'm . . . fine. But I miss it every now and then."

"If it's not an actual addiction, maybe you could just have one? I always figured you were in AA or something."

And in all these months, he'd never asked. Which probably said something about the seriousness of our relationship. "No, it's nothing like that. So maybe. I don't know. I don't really wanna keep talking about my . . . *shriveled and blackened brain*." I added a little bravado to show I was joking, but it fell flat. After a moment, I slid my limbs back and got up to make us coffee.

At my desk, blinking at a story about radicalized Algerian immigrants, I fantasized about whether anyone would notice if I just stopped doing my job. I'd still show up, of course, moseying into meetings and making small talk in the break room; I just wouldn't *produce* anything. The thought experiment left me feeling pretty unmotivated, so I convinced Damien to venture out for lunch with me. He gossiped about the junior editors as we walked; I think it bothers him that there's a younger, hipper clique of gay men on staff now. I figured we'd bring our food back to the air-conditioning, but he insisted we eat outside even though it was 100 degrees, so we plodded to the Elevated Acre, a bizarre rectangle of Astroturf tucked between office buildings. Businessmen in suits were splayed on the fake grass like well-dressed starfish. We chose a spot along the edge and I fanned myself, wishing I had a sun hat.

"This is what . . . the sixth summer in a row that's the hottest on record?" I eased the lid off my salad.

"I know. You feel especially bad when you're here, surrounded by, like, hundreds of floors of energy consumption."

"Oh, the buildings around here are probably mostly LEED-certified by now." We looked around, chewing thoughtfully. "My dad's a civil engineer and he says the reason he retired is that everyone was making him build, quote, buildings for fearmongering, tree-hugging hippies, unquote."

"Yikes. I always forget you're the product of gun-toting right-wingers."

"That's me." Why had I brought them up? Picturing them, I felt an arrow of unease.

He leaned back against a step. "I love the idea of you as a teeny six-year-old pointing a loaded shotgun."

"Rifle," I corrected. "A twenty-two-caliber rimfire rifle. Single shot."

"And you were actually six? I was being cute."

"Sixth birthday present. Every little girl's dream." I'd wanted the Totally Hair Barbie, but eventually I came to like shooting with my dad. He was calm at the shooting range, predictable. Unlike at home.

"Remember when I met them and they kept asking me where my accent's from?" Damien said. "Took me forever to realize they just couldn't detect gayness."

"Oh god, that was awful. And hopefully that was the only time they'll ever come to New York." Damien was likely one of the first black men they'd encountered socially, and they'd said plenty of unintentionally racist things—"That's really great that you're educated, that you got your degree!" I couldn't imagine how awkward things would've gotten if they'd picked up on his sexual orientation as well.

He kept laughing. "They were sweet. You're still not talking?"

"I mean, we get further and further apart on our political stances with each passing year. To the point where it's hard to have a conversation. We're basically down to obligatory phone calls on birthdays and major holidays."

He shrugged and sucked on his straw. "It's *family*. You only get the one."

"Yeah, and my family voted directly against my well-being and safety. And yours." It was a convenient excuse, though not the real reason. It'd been a little easier avoiding them the last few years—so many fellow New Yorkers were outraged with their own red-leaning folks and I could just follow suit.

"But they raised you!"

"And I didn't . . . I didn't have the greatest childhood with them. I don't want to talk about it."

Damien shrugged easily and I envied his mellowness, how he could always make me feel like the hysterical woman by contrast. We gazed out at the grass. A pigeon was plodding closer and closer to the head of one of the supine businessmen. He had his eyes closed, unaware.

I tried a joke. "My dad's an amazing shooter," I said. "When he'd go to retrieve his target, with all the holes in the bull's-eye, he'd always say he was gonna put it on the front door for any guy taking me on a date to see."

"Did you go on a lot of dates?"

"Ha! No."

"No high school boyfriend?"

A ping of shame: Even after years of friendship, Damien didn't know that the answer was no, not then, not ever. "Nah, definitely not cool enough for that. I was a weird kid. And I was chubby."

He laughed delightedly. "Oh my god, you must have been adorable!"

"No, it was just bad-chubby." Once or twice I'd awkwardly asked the nerd clique if I could be in their all-female dinner-and-photo-taking group for homecoming, but that was the extent of my social life. In college, too, I'd made mostly drinking buddies, other girls in my dorm who partook of the cheap whiskey I procured from a junior and stored under my bed. I'd availed myself of the university gym and Madison's legendary party scene, discovering in alcohol and the occasional Klonopin all the mood-lifting effects I hadn't in SSRIs. But close friends hadn't come until I moved to New York, far away from my parents, the ones who only occasionally wanted to claim me. Far away from my whole sad youth, really.

"Hey, did you ever find anything in those emails?" he asked, as if hearing my thoughts.

"Not really. Just a reminder that I was twenty-three to the max."

He laughed. "Weren't we all?"

That night, I kneeled on the floor and pushed dusty boxes around under my bed until I'd found what I was looking for: old photo albums, anachronistic even then, cute ones with bikes and planets on their covers and endless permutations of the Calhoun gang inside. There were stacks of loose photos, too, and I carried everything into the living room, piling it on my lap.

Damn, had Edie *ever* taken a bad photo? She'd awed me even then, and sometimes, alone in my insecurity, I'd play out the impossible scenarios: Did Edie ever fart? Trip? Say the wrong thing and then blush bright red? For twenty-three years, she floated through life a few inches above us messy, gaffe-prone mortals. And then . . .

A photo of me pointing at my new cartilage piercing, coral pink and swollen. My fingers floated up and found it; ten years later, I still walk around with the piercing ring in. I remembered that day, early in the spring: I'd vaguely mentioned wanting a new piercing and Edie had jumped on it, declaring Saturday "bruncture day" because we were to get drunk at brunch and then make our way to a piercing place. I'd been distracted and nervous as we picked at our eggs, but I tried to hide it, to mirror Edie's effortless cool. I lay on the piercing table, my head flopped to the side, while she flirted with the tattoo-covered piercer; he smirked at her as he snapped on his gloves. Later, she told me she could see my pulse pounding in my neck. With the steel hoop in place, Edie had hugged me and bought me iced coffee at the café across the street. As we'd browsed the racks of nearby vintage stores, I kept touching the earring, the flash of pain a permanent reminder of our "bruncture" bond.

I opened another photo album: Here were Sarah and Edie, monkeying around on the boys' guitar and drum kit. Here were Kevin, Edie, and me, playing a drinking game while snow piled against the windows. I'd been so delighted to be part of a group, and a hip one at that, the kind of club that kids all over the nation would kill to be in. I turned the page: Here were Kevin and Edie, giving cheesy smiles and middle fingers to a flyer posted on Calhoun's front door.

I squinted at it and remembered: People were trying to make TV shows and movies about our kind, and someone had hung flyers around the building to cast for a reality show; from what the gossip blogs reported, the concept was "hipsters in incongruous situations," kids dressed like us working on farms and struggling through military boot camp. Sarah and Alex had been so irritated by the whole thing, so scolding whenever anyone used the h-word around them, but Edie had remained amused, simultaneously above and inside of the whole amorphous mass.

The grin on Kevin's face. Nothing seemed to get under his skin. Kevin, who'd snicker good-naturedly or crack an off-the-wall joke or make a farting sound with his mouth if the moment got too prickly, if you were feeling self-conscious or judged or small.

My feet moved before I knew exactly what I was doing. In the kitchen, I had his profile pulled up in seconds. He had his phone number listed. It's a habit I picked up from being a fact-checker: Don't think, just dial.

"Hullo?" It was him. Everything in me buzzed.

"Is this Kevin?"

"Yes, it i-is." The suspicious singsong of anyone who suspects a telemarketer.

"Wow, hi! It's Lindsay Bach. How are you?"

"Whoa, hey! I—I'm good, and yourself?"

"I'm good, thank you, I'm really good. So, I know this is so out of the blue—"

"Hey, I'd really love to catch up, but I'm actually waiting on another call? From one of Evelyn's doctors."

Evelyn? Was he straight now?

"I'm so sorry, I didn't mean to—"

"No, not at all, it's just my daughter—you don't even know who Evelyn is, do you?" He chuckled and for the second time that week, ten years dissolved; it was his same whispery titter, *tssh-sh-sh-sh*. "But listen, can I call you right back? Just at this number? It shouldn't be long at all."

I took that to mean I wouldn't ever hear from him and so was elbow deep in soapy dishes when my phone rang a few minutes later.

"Hello!" I cried, after too many rings. "Everything work out okay with your daughter's doctor?" I'd meant it politely, but it came off as invasive.

"She's . . . Yeah, I heard back from him, so no worries. Thanks for waiting. What's up?"

"Um, thanks for calling me back. I'm actually calling 'cause . . . well, I just had dinner with Sarah, if you can believe that."

"Sarah! How is she?"

"She's good, she just moved back to the city, so . . . it was nice to catch up. Her husband's job transferred him here."

"That's good, that's good. You tell her I said hi."

"Yeah, definitely." What would happen if I just blurted it out: *So Sarah claimed that I wasn't at the concert the night Edie died. Isn't that insane?*

I went with the smaller, sillier revelation instead. "We spent a lot of time reminiscing about the old days. I didn't remember that she'd had that weird freak-out where she was insisting Edie hadn't committed suicide."

"Ah, that's right." He sang: "Paranoia, paranoia, everybody's coming for Edie."

"It was the least suspicious suicide of all time, right? Gun near her hand, suicide note on her computer." I drummed my nails against the counter. "But I have to say, hearing it now, all these years later . . . I mean, maybe I'm just glorifying our youth, but it did kinda feel like, 'Yeah, why *would* Edie kill herself?'"

"I mean, I always thought that was bullshit." He said it quickly, casually, like he'd been waiting for the chance to tell someone.

I froze. "What do you mean?"

"The suicide thing. I told the cops that, too, that just a few days before her death she looked me in the eye and told me she wanted to live to be an old lady."

I had to grab the edge of the counter to steady myself. "Wait, what?"

"I can't—it's a long story. But, dude, people don't just up and kill themselves out of the blue. They think suicidal thoughts and they get their affairs in order and they tell people about their plan and then maybe, *maybe*, after one or two false starts, they do it. That wasn't Edie."

I was silent, my mouth hanging open, so he went on. "I don't want to go into it, but she had, like, a health scare that I helped her through, and she came out of it basically determined to live forever. She talked about how there was still so much she wanted to do, it was like she was begging the universe to let her make it." A thump, like he was doing something else as he soliloquized. "Not that Edie believed in that shit, at least as far as I know."

"And you told the cops this?" I finally said.

"Hell, yeah, I did. But they didn't listen. I think at first they thought if anything, I was somehow involved and trying to pass off the blame. It was scary enough getting arrested in the middle of all that. Possession of an unlicensed firearm, a Class A felony, punishable by up to a year in jail: I must've heard it a hundred times."

"I forgot about that. You took a plea deal, right?"

"Yeah, pretty lucky to be a white kid with no priors. Fifty hours of community service and a thousand-dollar fine. I was such a dummy, keeping that thing there. But yeah, I think the detectives thought something was going on between Edie and me after I was the one she dragged to the ER with her."

The ER? I started to interrupt, but he barreled over me.

"Which is a whole 'nother story. They tried to spin it into

another reason she committed suicide, but believe me, they're wrong, nothing about that whole shebang would make her kill herself."

Another few clunks. What was he doing?

"What was the health scare?" I asked.

"Nah, it was embarrassing for her, I don't wanna go into it."

"Did anyone else know about it?"

"No, I don't think so."

"What makes you so sure it wouldn't have made her suicidal?"

"I don't wanna play twenty questions, Lindsay. Suffice it to say that out of respect for the dead, I don't want to talk about it, but if you'd like to trust me, I can say with one-hundred-percent certainty that she was not a suicidal girl."

We both sat with that for a second.

"So you think someone killed her?"

"I mean, seems like the only other option."

"Who, then?"

"Fuck if I know. She'd pissed off a lot of people in that building."

"What do you mean?"

"I mean, I have no idea who did it. But she was always shucking people off. I said *shucking*." He chuckled to himself, *tsh-sh-sh*. "Didn't y'all ever notice that about her? She spent her whole life in Manhattan, but it was like she didn't exist—no friends from her past, no stories of crazy high school nights or friends from way back—and then, uh, she was the center of everything, and then she'd be gone again, leaving a bombed-out group in her wake. I don't think she could help it."

A chronic friend-defector. I'd noticed it as well but had thought—hoped—she was like me, floundering through her early social life until the right people, the right friendships, appeared.

"Well, if someone did it, I want to figure out who," I said.

He tittered again. "Hey, be my guest. You know absolutely everything I know at this point, but maybe you'll have more luck." *Clunk* clunk *click*. "Or maybe we're both wackos."

"Why didn't you back up Sarah? When she was saying she didn't think it was suicide?"

"Yeah, that worked out really well for her. Total pariah, shipped off to the loony bin. But unlike me, she wasn't under suspicion by the poh-lice." He drew it out for effect. "I'm glad you saw her, healed some old wounds. She still nursing her suspicions?"

"No, not at all. 'I was young and stupid, I was grasping at straws,' that kind of thing." I chewed on my lip. "I never even knew she had this conspiracy theory. I kinda stopped talking to everyone right away."

"Right, I think I knew that. The whole period is a blur for me, it's kinda hard to remember who was around when."

Did he know anything about my disputed whereabouts that night? It was as if he were addressing my unasked question.

"But I'll tell ya, if you can somehow figure out what really went on that night—" He cut himself off suddenly. "Lindsay, I gotta run, my husband's on the other line."

"No worries, thanks for talking to me."

"Y'all take care of yourself."

You all? Me and whom?

"Thanks, Kevin. You, too." I hung up and looked around the living room. *Figure out what really went on that night.* Clearly I didn't remember as much as I thought I did. I'd been drunk, but it had just been a brown-out: I had strong snippets of each portion of the night, scene after scene after scene, like an intricately set-designed play. Up on the roof, sitting on the cement and chasing shots with beer. Then we'd all decided to head to the concert—no, Kevin had had a show in Greenpoint, it was just me and Alex and Sarah—and there was the flurry and racket and energy gust of a drunken location change. Then the show: Even Sarah's photo hadn't convinced me I was thinking of another night. I could *see* it, the guys in red zebra face paint rushing around the stage. Strobe lights and a ball spitting green dots over the crowd and what looked like hundreds of sweaty revelers dancing to the noise. The alcohol hitting me all at once and the sudden, billowing conviction that I needed to be in bed. Had I shouted goodbye to them or just left? Had Sarah somehow missed me?

Figure out what really went on. My damn brain was no use, a recorder with damaged tapes: 2009 was on the early end of the accidental police state we all live in today, where whipping out your camera to document everything is the norm. I remembered a story I'd fact-checked about Big Brother–type surveillance in which a filmmaker had mused that there's so much more amazing material for documentaries today, because there are cameras absolutely everywhere.

Something clicked: my camcorder. My silly-looking Flip cam, a strange little thing with only a single function, a box with a big red record button that made videos we'd watched almost exclusively on its tiny screen—I'd carried it around in my massive vintage purse at almost all times. We used it rarely and randomly, and I'd been so bad about connecting the gadget to my computer that all the videos lived on the camcorder. There likely wouldn't be many; I had a habit of deleting videos after a single viewing, especially when the clip showed me embarrassingly drunk. But maybe something had survived, some clue we'd overlooked that would bristle with meaning now.

I could picture my Flip cam, could almost feel its shiny plastic coating in my fingers, its shape readying my palm for the iPhone that would soon doom it. Had I tossed it during one of my moves? I began pulling things out of the hall closet, snapping open bags and boxes and piling them on the floor. Nothing. I moved on to the cabinets around the TV, yanking out board games and old magazines and outdated electronics and other things I knew an adult shouldn't still own. Then I pulled every dusty storage bin out from under my bed, flinging through old scarves and purses I couldn't bear to give away, travel-size toiletries, expired pills, a sad cornucopia of detritus tucked into the pockets of my life. Then I flicked off the light and fell asleep, fully dressed and with my home in shambles, Facebook open on my laptop, fogging up the apartment with old, invisible air.

I dreamed about the camcorder, a creepy dream where Edie was still alive but somehow trapped inside its plastic walls, speaking to me through the little screen. Half awake, I grabbed my phone and murmured the storyline into its voice memo app, sure it was urgent, that my sleeping mind was onto something. When I played it back in the morning, my own voice sounded spooky and halting, the narrative meaningless. "She was inside but also behind," it intoned, between long pauses and thick swallowing noises. "She said 'four corners' and . . . and I was outside in the fields and I knew them from other dreams." I deleted the file midway through listening.

As I clattered around, making coffee, something echoed in my mind: *inside but also behind*. It repeated itself, a loop in a DJ's mix, until I froze and felt the idea blossoming.

I dropped the spoon, black grounds scattering, and hurried into the living room. My bookshelf hulked along the wall, as long as an elephant and unusually deep. I yanked away books on shelf after shelf, revealing the random stuff I'd stashed behind them, in the dusty space along the cabinet's back. And there it was, inside and behind the third row, sandwiched between a laptop charger and an obsolete Kindle. My Flip cam.

I carried it into the kitchen, then discovered it had an outdated jack, something I couldn't connect to my laptop. I set it on my counter and texted Tessa to ask if she could borrow an adapter from work. When she hadn't answered an hour later, I pulled on clothes and tromped to the dollar store at the end of my block. Nothing inside costs a dollar, but that place is like the goddamn Room of Requirement: ant trap, sunscreen, dish tub, lawn ornament, whatever you need, it's there in a section you've never noticed before.

Tessa texted as I was cracking open my laptop to try the new cord.

"I should be able to borrow that. What for?"

"Thanks, but no need, I already got the connector. I found my old Flip cam."

"From back then?"

"Right. Update: I'm not so sure it was a suicide now."

It showed she was typing for a while, so I waited for something long, realizing with a spritz of embarrassment that she was probably going to chide me for writing something that legally loaded in a text.

Instead: "How come?"

I called her, but she rejected it.

"Still in the office," she texted. "Trying really hard to finish something."

On a Saturday? "No worries—let's talk later."

I wanted to pull the videos onto my laptop, but my machine wouldn't recognize the old files, the systems a decade apart; still, the cord managed to siphon over some power and after a few seconds an outdated graphic appeared on the camcorder's screen: FLIP VIDEO.

Navigation was a mess; I couldn't view all the videos at once and discovered that I had to browse to the right or left to view them. The first was from March 2009, us waving and cracking up in the car, Alex behind the wheel, Edie navigating, Kevin inexplicably speaking in a bad French accent while Sarah and I howled with laughter. Another from later that month: a mess at first, loud EDM and green shapes fizzing in crazy circles, until I picked out our silhouettes and realized it was Edie on the dance floor in the back of a bar.

I skipped forward, forward, forward, hitting the last video just eleven skips later; so there were only twelve on here, a small batch. One, from May, began with Edie smiling into the camera like an anchorwoman, fuzzy in a streetlamp's sallow glow.

"Edie, tell us what just happened," my voice prompted from behind the camera.

"Well, we just had a bit of a run-in with the law," she replied.

A male voice murmured something off-screen and I prompted him to repeat it: "She just saved our asses, that's what happened." It was Alex, sounding stressed.

I panned to him and he sucked on a cigarette. "What happened was we were pregaming in McCarren and Kevin had a whole six-pack sitting next to him like a fucking idiot," he said, turning to his left to shoot a glare. "Then a cop car pulls up with its lights flashing and they take all our licenses and tell us that drinking in the street would be a—what was it?"

"An eighty-dollar fine for drinking in the street, but it's three hundred twenty if you're in a public park," Edie supplied, to general agreement.

"Then what?" I said. My voice sounded nasal.

Alex blew a plume of smoke. "Then Edie gets up and walks over to the cop car—"

"—even though they told us not to move." Sarah's voice, off-camera. Something sat up in me like a cat. So spooky, hearing the same voice I'd just heard over dinner, but younger, frothier.

"Right, even though they told us not to move," Alex continued, "and she's over there talking to them for like five minutes, and then they come back and say we're really lucky we're over twenty-one and they've already hit their ticket quota for the night, and they watched us dump our beer and then off they went."

"Edie, what'd you say to them?" I panned back to her.

She shrugged, still smiling. "I just said we were all dumb, unemployed kids who should've known better, but that we'd never do it again," she said. "And then I told them my roommate had called 911 last week after a man followed her into the building and forced himself on her in the foyer, and he matched the description of the serial rapist who's been running around Williamsburg, and the cops who came to take her statement were so nice, and the work the policemen do is so important."

"It isn't true, for the record," Sarah called, still off-screen. "About the rapist being in our building."

"But there is a serial rapist in Williamsburg, that's true," I said.

"Yeah, maybe the cops should worry about *that*," Alex muttered.

". . . and then I cried," Edie finished sweetly, with a shrug. Someone said something, then repeated, "Do it." So the camera zoomed in to Edie's head, her face, then just her eyes, shakily, and Edie looked hard into it until fat, pretty tears broke free.

The video ended and I Xed out of it, alarmed by Edie's intense stare. I hit next: There was a Fourth of July barbecue with a shitty band performing on a rooftop; a mass of skinny humans in lamé bathing suits and bright eighties patterns and so much exposed, tender skin. Edie had climbed onto the brick ledge along the edge of the roof, standing up so she could see the stage. Fearless. Watching it now made my ribs contract. In the video, I screamed, "Get down from there, you moron!" and Edie just turned and waved.

Then there was a little video from mid-August, just a few days before Edie died, thirty seconds of the four of us—no Edie—playing Jenga in a bar's leafy backyard. The game's pieces had dares Sharpied onto them by previous players, and Sarah pulled one that instructed her to post a photo of herself wearing the Jenga box as a hat. She was reluctant and Kevin spazzed around, hyping her up, squishing his big grin into her photo.

That was it. Nothing new about August 21.

Perhaps there was a recently deleted folder. I held down the center button to try to call up a new menu and . . .

Black. I pressed the forward and back buttons and still just black. I hit play and the screen said "No new videos." I'd deleted them all. Fuck.

Fighting down panic, I texted Tessa and Damien for help, then Googled "how to recover deleted Flip cam videos." Incredibly, there were how-tos, dozens of them. I had to convince my computer to play nice with the camera, and then I had to download a sketchy-seeming program called Recuva ("pronounced re-cuh-va!" according to the cheerful Southern dad in the YouTube tutorial), but a half-hour later I had an ugly-looking folder just bursting with old videos.

The new file names were meaningless, but I counted forty-three of them. An uncensored batch of video files, up from a dozen—now we were getting somewhere. I checked the file creation dates and saw, with a pulse down my arms, that one was from August 21, 2009.

I dragged it into my iMovie player and turned up the volume. The video jerked around in the dark for a while; there was music, tinny guitars. Tones of black and gray, the indistinct din of people hanging out. The time stamp read 10:48. When had Sarah found Edie? Shortly after that, wasn't it, around 11:15, 11:30? The video was long, twenty-three minutes. What was I recording? Finally, 2009 me found something to focus on: I'd turned the lens to the New York City skyline and stopped wobbling long enough for it to focus. We were up on Calhoun's roof; it had a great view of Manhattan.

Sarah's voice rang out from my computer's speakers. "Alex, can you hand me another beer?"

"This is our second-to-last Tecate, people." It was Alex, off-screen as I'd struggled to zoom in on the Empire State Building. I realized why the cityscape looked odd: no One World Trade Center yet.

"What are you doing, Linds?" he called out. "Come back here."

I'd responded with a single giggle, whipping the lens around to face them. I could feel it now, the bubble of pleasure that he wanted me there. A place in the circle.

Figures formed in the dark: Sarah and Alex lounging on the cement roof, facing the same way like sunbathers at the beach; dutifully, they waved. I hit pause and mapped my friends out like pieces on a chessboard: Kevin had already left for the big show with his band. I remembered him being on the roof earlier in the night; a headliner might not go on until midnight, but he'd want to watch the openers. And Edie. As far as I knew, at that moment

Edie had been alone in SAKE. Pawing with interest at Kevin's vintage gun, sadness swelling around her like purply smoke. If the story I'd heard was wrong—if Sarah and Kevin were right, and Edie hadn't been alone in the final moments of her life—then this recording could be everything. An unchanging record of who was where, when.

I hit play: I'd wobbled over to the group and caught a span of the sky as I sat. Someone must have grabbed the camera from me—Alex, I could tell when he hooted, "Say something for posterity, Linds." He was aiming at me, and suddenly I was staring into my own eyes. Old me looked surprised, squinted hard, and for a moment I had the eerie feeling that we were looking at each other, that she could see me. Then she—I—laughed and shrieked, "Give me my camera, you fucktard!" Christ, no wonder I'd deleted this mess.

The lens made another pass around the roof, a drunken version of the slow pans you take at tourist destinations. There were fuzzy orange orbs here and there, unfocused—probably other groups hanging around on the rooftop, kicking off a balmy Friday night by drinking in the dark. Someone else wandered up and I jerked the camera in surprise. Male voices said hey and asked if we had a light; everyone chattered, the staccato of cross talk.

"You guys seen . . . ?" one said right near the Flip cam, loud enough that the microphone picked it up but not clear enough to make out the name. Jim? Jen? Jan? Then the guys wandered away and I caught their backs, cigarettes glowing between their fingers. One of them was wearing ironic light-up sneakers that glittered in the night.

"Where's Edie?" I asked as Alex fiddled with the iPod attached to a speaker. I panned to Sarah, who was smoking serenely.

"She's a fucking bitch," I heard myself add matter-of-factly. It was loud but not angry—the know-it-all tone of a little kid sharing a dirty fact.

"I know, I'm glad she's not here," Alex said back.

Sarah murmured something inscrutable, then repeated it to

Alex's "Huh?": "You're on tape!" she said again, pointing at the lens.

"I don't fucking care." His voice rose to a bellow. "I want that bitch out of my apartment!"

I whooped in agreement, so loud next to the Flip cam's mic, then shouted, "I want to push her off this building!"

"I want to slit her throat!" Alex hollered back. He grabbed the camera and leaned in close, steadying it on his face. He giggled. "I'm just fucking with you. It's cool."

He let go and suddenly the view swooped down to my feet and stayed there for a second, then went black as the tinny sound blared on. As the seconds ticked by, understanding dawned: I'd *thought* I'd turned the camera off and had instead left it recording, in a purse or pocket or something. We were only three and a half minutes in.

As nausea curled inside me, I jumped ahead in few-minute chunks, confirming by the blackness and slivers of butt-dial din that this was it—nothing but accidental recording. A little gurgle of female voices around the eight-minute mark, too muffled to decode. But in the last twenty-eight seconds, the sound died down and then—color again. I rewound the video and leaned forward. In the darkness, I heard the metallic clank of me clomping down stairs. Then I saw the bright yellow of Calhoun Lofts' hallways, and I must have been walking, bobbing a bit as I lifted the camera waist-high and burbled, "Oh, whoops."

Then the lens swept up one more time, long enough for two symbols on a door to come into focus: 4G. SAKE. Edie's apartment.

A little lean forward and my hand on the knob, the click of the door opening.

My voice, surprised, an inaudible warble. Projected like it was meant for someone—a greeting, not to myself.

A quick flash of the hardwood floor inside. And then, with a jumble of fingers, I'd turned the camera off.

PART II

Chapter 4

GREG

I had just bought a little tub of Greek yogurt and was thinking inane thoughts about how it always comes in a wider container than regular yogurt and why is a man eating yogurt sort of fey and effeminate, anyway? I sat down at the counter along the window and peeled back the top and noticed four peaks in the white, vaguely creepy remnants of the electric udder employed in the factory, when She walked in.

She had freckled skin and a halo of soft red curls. A sunbeam struck her, movie perfect, as if she traveled with her own light source, a perpetual spotlight. She slid her eyes around the little deli, pausing on me, holding my stare for just a moment before sauntering up to the register.

I put my eyes on my book and read nothing as she ordered a strawberry chicken salad. Then she scraped back a stool at the other end of the counter. Only a few seats away. Jesus, that *air*. She felt me looking at her and glanced over just enough, just as I feared I'd never get a glimpse of the eyes again, as she ate and read a book of her own, a near-smile on her lips.

I knew I should say something, something polite and unimposing and easy to back away from should she not, you know, want strangers bothering her during lunch. Which, of course, she probably did not. The man with the yogurt leering and blathering and treating the place like a despicable Murray Hill hookup bar.

So, frozen by the stupid stalemate I'd created for myself, I continued to study a page of the Murakami novel in front of me. And right as I was working up the nerve to get up and say hello, she checked the time on her phone, snapped her book into her purse, and headed for the exit.

As she yanked the glass door open, she glanced back—at me, definitely right at me—and I grinned, a full-toothed hapless grin that was the closest thing to communication I could toss toward her exiting body. She smiled—just long enough to make sure I saw it—and was gone.

When I got home from work that night, I opened my laptop, embarrassed for myself, and went to Craigslist's Missed Connections section, that graveyard of hypothetical relationships for introverts and pussies everywhere. The words *This is fucking dumb* cobbled themselves into a mantra, complete with a monomaniac theme song, as I scanned the day's sad pleas.

> Location: Café Green on 57th St.
>
> Subject: To the guy at the other end of the counter . . .
>
> Body: . . . Thanks for the smile. It made my day.

My chest and dick distended in unison. This was her, this was fucking *her*. This was insane. I clicked respond. I stared at the cursor and realized I had no idea what to say. I couldn't even remember what she looked like, just an impression of glinting eyes and a ludicrous certainty that this woman was interesting, full of captivating ideas, opinions, and stories.

I stood up and got a beer out of the fridge. I sat down and messed around on Facebook, on blogs. Finally, I returned to the Craigslist email and wrote something that would, I hoped, be complimentary without freaking her out.

> Subject: that guy at the other end of the counter . . .
>
> Body: . . . had nearly finished his yogurt so that he could nonchalantly peek at you while you ate your salad. (okay, maybe it was a stare. sorry.) before you left, i wanted to

tell you with neither presumption nor agenda that you're
beautiful. maybe you'll give me another shot, or maybe
we'll bump into each other again. anyway, thank you for
giving me the unlikely opening to do a deed left undone . . .
you definitely made my day.

greg

I read it through a couple of times and deleted the second-to-
last sentence—there, now I'd done everything I could to distance
myself from the drooling ogre bro vibes I didn't want to emit.
The response came two days later, days mercifully packed at the
firm—I was developing a set of construction drawings for what
eventually became a facade in Park Slope. So the mystery woman
wasn't even humming in my subconscious when a reply showed up
in my inbox.

Greg—

I've never posted on Craigslist before, not even to sell a
couch or anything. And I did it on a whim the other day,
not expecting a response, let alone one so kind. So thank
you. I keep rereading it and smiling. Hmm, so many things I
could say next, but I'll start with a question: What were you
reading?

Edie

I wrote back that night, answering and returning the question.
She wrote the evening after that. We asked the typical questions.
Senior at NYU. (So much younger than I'd thought.) Living in
Bushwick in one of those insufferable dormlike self-contained
hipster havens. Born and raised in New York, which explained
that phlegmatic expression earned from a lifetime of discovering
things before everyone else. I learned her verbal tics, the lilt of her
sentences and the subtlety of her wit. I found her on Facebook

and stared and stared and stared at the tiny blurry profile photo I could access, too stubborn to send her a friend request. I couldn't mentally call up an image of her, just a sharp sense of attraction. Which almost never happens to me. What good is a photographic memory if the cap's on right when you need it most?

I told my friend Lexy the story, leaving out the bit about the woman being an undergrad. I knew she'd react with the appropriate amount of awe and delight and excited clapping. I've known Lexy since college, one of those truly platonic friendships that way too many women insist can't exist. Sitting at a picnic table on the back porch of a barbecue joint, wearing a coat and pretending it was a warmer spring day than the thermometer indicated, she actually flung a rib down at one point to throw her hands over her mouth. I knew she'd just love it.

"You guys are gonna get maaaried," she sang when I'd finished.

"Dude, she hasn't made any mention of actually meeting up in person, and it's been over a month. I'm beginning to think she's in a full body cast or something."

"Or that you're writing back and forth with someone who just happened to be in the deli and observed the whole thing and is doing this to fill a certain emptiness in his or her life."

Jesus, that hadn't even occurred to me. That's the thing about Lexy. She's getting her Ph.D. in American history and will just extrapolate the shit out of something you thought you had figured out.

"You think I should ask her out?"

"Uh, yeah. She's probably wondering why you haven't tried to see her yet. Actually, if she was smart, she'd think *you* were the fat, lonely impersonator."

One end of Lexy's chartreuse scarf kept sliding off her neck and down across her boobs. I was waiting for it to land in her pile of sauce.

Lexy was right—it *was* weird. The intimacy was fading from the email exchange, and now I had no choice but to ask her out, which of course would sound creepy or awkward no matter how I phrased it because I'd already waited so damn long. I asked Edie to call me. She wrote back with her number instead. I dialed it right after work one day, settling into a bench in Central Park among a row of peacoat-swaddled locals.

It rang once. Twice. Someone with a clipboard was making his way down the line, asking for money for some kind of project.

She picked up on the third ring.

"Hello?"

It was nice to hear a real hello, the way we used to answer the phone before we always knew who was calling. Her voice was huskier than I'd imagined.

"Hi! It's Greg."

She said "Oh, hi!" just as I continued to speak, and then I stopped, and then we both listened to silence for a second.

"How are you?" I lumbered on.

"I'm good! Just got off the subway. Sorry if I sound out of breath. How are you?"

"I'm fine! Thanks. I'm . . . sitting in the park, actually."

"Oh, nice. Central Park?"

"That's the one!"

"Ahh, jealous! Do the trees have buds on them yet? I love buds and those little puff things at the end of pine trees. I always promise myself I'm going to make it into the park before they open up and then I forget and remember in, like, June."

"The trees are still looking pretty dead from here. But actually . . ." My god. A freebie. "Actually, I was calling to see if you'd like to get together this weekend. Like for a walk. In the park."

"Oh! Umm . . ." It was either deliberation or thinking hard, trying to work out her schedule.

"The buds are gonna be here and gone before you know it. Honest to god, I can see, like, six big leaves just from here."

She laughed. I loved it—a kind of throaty *ha ha.*

"I have brunch plans on Saturday, but . . . after that? Like at three?"

I couldn't remember the last time I'd been excited for a date.

I got Lexy's good-luck text as I climbed out of the subway at Eighty-sixth and headed west, motoring around tourists. Edie was standing outside the entrance, pecking at her phone. Prettier than I remembered, another little punch of *damn*. She smiled and waved and waited awkwardly for me to cross the street as the light lingered on DON'T WALK, and then she pulled me into a hug, all wool to wool and warmth to warmth.

We tromped around the reservoir for an hour, hands in our pockets, smiling at each other as we talked. That aura was there again, that weird magnetic pull. Finally she veered off the circular path and sat on a bench. I sat down next to her and allowed myself an unabashed stare—this time, I vowed, I'd remember those high cheekbones and that heart-shaped mouth.

"I have to tell you something," she said finally, staring out at the water. A row of ducks was lined up on what must've been a beam just under the water. It looked like two dozen birds had arbitrarily formed a straight line.

"Go for it." I slung my arm over the bench's back.

"It's . . . Okay, it's weird now because I haven't told you before. I'm actually—when you and I first met, or ran into each other or whatever, I was just kind of casually starting to see someone, but now we're . . . exclusive." She mumbled the last word, but it still came out sounding heavy. Ex-*clooo*-sive. No matter how you mean it, it forms pretension in the mouth.

It hit me like a force, like a big wave of energy shot off of her and struck me in the side, but I just nodded and stared out at the reservoir. "Got it," I said.

"But I really do care about you," she said urgently, turning to me. "I really hope we can still hang out and talk and everything."

I nodded slowly and shot her a smile. "Of course." I withdrew my arm from the back of the bench and fished my phone out of my pocket to check the time. "I should think about heading back, though."

I really didn't mean to sound sullen, I didn't, but neither of us was any good for conversation as we trudged back to the subway.

We should have ridden the same line, but I made up some dinner plans so that I could drop her at the stop.

"At least she was honest with you," Lexy texted back.

"I guess," I responded.

The emails with Edie petered out; I can't remember who finally didn't write back, which probably means it was me. Spring slipped straight into a hot and muggy summer, and my work started to take on that nihilistic pall. I kept on thinking about Edie, the playful smirk, the warm hug through the coat. I still couldn't conjure up her image and I kept her in the back of my mind whenever I turned a corner in the city, hoping she'd appear.

Then right at the most merciless blast of summer, when a third of my coworkers had been quietly let go, when my 401(k) had shriveled to a few curls of bills, when it was so hot I just sat and sweated and thought hazy hateful thoughts about nothing and no one in particular, she texted. She wanted to get drinks. And could I meet her at nine.

The week after that is foggy, no clear chronology, just a set of moments, a real-life movie montage. Her lowering her chin and looking up at me through those eyelashes, saying exactly the words I'd been longing for like autumn: "broke up," "single," "another round." Kissing in the street while a parade of drunks and late-night revelers ambled by. Her sinewy back as I unclasped her bra. Eggs Benedict. Watching someone make enormous bubbles in McCarren Park. The pillows with the zigzag stripes on her little lofted bed.

We were a We. And we had to last, we just had to, because how many fucking stars had aligned to bring us together in the first place? She delighted in telling people the story of how we met, pausing for effect in the same places, raising both hands to recount how she'd never, *never* posted anything on Craigslist before, not even for furniture or anything. I took so many photos of her with my Mark II—at the beach, over dinner, at the park, on my love seat—and put a few of the best onto my phone, an iPhone back before everyone had them. Sometimes I'd pull up an image I'd shot of her and just stare, taking in the details like I was sizing up an especially impressive building.

I discovered I wasn't the only one enchanted by her; her little roommates, thin and sparkly eyed, worshipped her as well, including the creepy brunette Edie counted as her closest confidante. Men of all ages went googly-eyed when she let out her laugh. She had her own gravitational pull, the calm black hole at the center of a swirling galaxy. I'm not sure if she knew it. She floated through life, the air bending toward her in her wake.

Four months became five, then six. I kept snapping photos of her, trying to capture what I'd lose when I couldn't see her. I had dinner with her odd, unbalanced mother and her spooked, distant father in their Upper West Side apartment. We took our first big trip together, a week in Berlin coinciding with an architecture conference I was invited to attend, right in that last aching stretch of winter when you stare at the skeletons of trees and just long for them to be leafy already. The city delighted her, with its white asparagus and crisp museums and citizens who were just like us Brooklynites only they stayed out later and spoke multiple languages. On the flight home, she slept in my lap while I stared at the TV screen in front of me, a head cold gathering in my skull like storm clouds. By the time we landed, the congestion had commandeered my lungs. We collapsed into bed that afternoon, and I woke up the next morning with a ridiculous combination cold/flu.

I didn't want her getting sick, too, so we spent the week in our own beds, her stopping by late at night to bring me Sudafed or soup. But something changed that week. It was the same dimming of intimacy that'd begun in our email exchange so many months before. She had less to say at dinner and interesting new reasons to crash alone in her own apartment. I observed it helplessly, like a passenger watching his boat recede into the distance.

She came over one night with the sole intention of breaking things off; I knew it the second she walked through the door. I was washing out a bowl lined with vinaigrette and thinking that the little flecks of spices looked like undigested food. We'd made vague plans to rent a documentary, but when she walked in and closed the door and draped herself over a chair at the kitchen table, I thought, *Well, fuck*. I don't remember anything she said, just the tunnel-like feeling of multiple gunshot wounds as she fired off lines about stagnancy and not growing and something being different and just not right. I actually teared up and she hugged me close, letting the drops gather on her sleeve. When it was all over, she picked up her purse and walked miserably out the door.

About three weeks later I figured out that she was dating Alex, a friend from her building whom I'd never liked. The fact was painfully easy to gather from a little Facebook stalking. I was shocked and then totally alarmed that I was so shocked. And then I just felt really stupid.

"God, so she's one of those girls who's always seeing someone," Lexy said. "That makes so much sense. You didn't pick that up from talking about exes at all?" We'd both ordered whiskey neat in a dim new bar in Lexy's neighborhood. Sometimes I appreciated her refreshing lack of sympathy—from everyone else it was bordering on pity.

"I mean, I have a lot of ex-girlfriends, too."

"But you're a *guy*. There are about fourteen eligible men in this city, and it's totally normal for any of them with their girlfriend light on to get snatched up like that." She actually snapped her fingers, and I admired the theatrics. "For a woman, it's a mind-set. Do or die. That's why some women always have a boyfriend when others haven't had one in, like, six years. You just think to yourself, 'Okay, you'll do' and keep lining 'em up."

She saw my eyes drop and knew she'd gone too far.

"Greg, you're a *catch*. The point I'm trying to make here is that you could go on Nerve and have five hot girls clamoring to date you in all of thirty seconds."

"It's just—it's weird that I was so wrong about her. Apparently I'm really fucking terrible at reading people."

She put down her glass and asked the bartender for more water. I could see her assembling her thoughts. "There's just no such thing as absolute reality. There's no such thing as ever reading anything quote-unquote right." She pressed a napkin on the small puddle around her glass. "You and I could be standing together and both see, I don't know, a guy bump into an old lady on the subway, but our *experience* of it would be totally different. And that's just a douchebag and an old lady, action, reaction. Dating's probably the most subjective experience there is. You're experiencing another person. A fucked-up, complicated, enigmatic human being."

We sipped our drinks.

"So you're saying . . . what? That I'm wrong and she's *not* kind of a bitch?" I let out a half-laugh.

"I just mean that it's not weird to look back on someone or something and realize that your read on it at the time was completely different from how you'd interpret it now." Lexy nodded to herself. "I met a guy at this party, that one Mandy had while you were out of town? He'd just published a memoir, and I asked him how his friends felt about him exposing all their shit. He told me, 'You'd be amazed at how bad people are at recognizing themselves in print.'"

"So basically I'm not delusional, we just had different versions of each other in our heads."

"I'm saying we're all delusional. And we're all just trying to find someone whose delusions line up with our own."

I couldn't decide if that was encouraging or depressing.

"And people do?"

"People do what?"

"Find someone whose delusions line up with their own?"

"Apparently people do, Greg. Apparently they do."

———

For a few months, I bumped into Edie here and there, the way denizens of this city always do. At first we made polite conversation, smiles forced, auras tense. Then one day that summer, we saw each other in a grocery store. I was heading up the escalator and one of us would have had to make an effort and I was tired and in a bad mood and so we didn't. I didn't have histrionically bad feelings toward her, just tiredness, just a sense that we were no longer worth each other's time. A few weeks later, while I was at a conference in DC, someone texted me something confusing, so I Googled her and up popped an obituary. I couldn't believe it. It didn't mention a cause of death and there wasn't really anyone I could ask; I was out of town during the funeral, too, so I sent her parents a bereavement card and that was that. It's horrible, of course, sad that she died so young, but it also felt strange and thick and faraway. Someone I loved doesn't exist anymore. You pretend after a breakup that that person disappears, but in this case she did.

I know that's what should haunt me the most, but what actually snags my mind from time to time, even all these years later, is how we met, the improbable connection, the perfect How We Met. I don't understand why the universe wasted the whole scheme on that ephemeral redheaded fairy and a relationship that wasn't going to work. *Maybe we weren't supposed to speak to each other at all and Craigslist messed with the natural order of things,* I think to myself, staring at a wall of gleaming white Greek yogurts. I pull out five because my wife likes to take them to work. Maybe we were a miss from the start.

Chapter 5

LINDSAY

T he Flip cam video ended with a freeze-frame of blurriness. I sat stock-still for a few seconds, then felt a curious rise through my torso, neck, and face like a glass being filled with water. A sudden muted hum like dipping your ears underwater. Then another punch of thick nausea.

Because the realization had hit me full force: I was there. After screaming that I wanted her dead, I had visited Edie in her living room the very night of her death. Drunk, murmuring, over-Edie's-bullshit me, in a rendezvous I had no recollection of whatsoever.

Thoughts like popcorn:

Did I never make it to the concert, then?

What did I say to her?

What did I see?

What did I do?

Maybe she was already dead?

The time stamp. On my screen, I clicked back to the moment I'd opened the door: 11:11 (make a wish!). When had Sarah called the cops? I Googled around a bit before I realized that duh, this was an absurd thing to expect to find. Case files. I needed those case files.

I returned to the video, my stomach whirling. I cued it up to my entrance: navy-blue nail polish on my fingers, the smooth *clack* of the door opening. I listened over and over to the exclamation I'd made when I looked inside. It was gibberish, "[inaudible]" on a transcript. I listened to it enough times that the distortion eventually organized itself into a nonsensical phrase, namely me chirping "Heavy skies senile?," and then that was all I could hear.

"Heavy skies senile?" Rewind. "Heavy skies senile?"

Fuck. Fucking brain hearing it wrong, latching onto the wrong words, the wrong interpretation.

Well, and. Fucking brain going totally offline at 11:11 on August 21, 2009.

A surge so sudden that I barely made it to the bathroom in time to vomit, hot tears and snot streaming down my face. When I finally sat back, I leaned my head against the wall and wept, weirdly enjoying the sound of the wet sobs bursting out of my throat. I listened and cried until I heard my phone vibrate in the kitchen. It was Tessa, finally seeing my text about un-deleting videos.

I called her, tears welling again as the phone rang, and I panicked about what I'd say when she picked up. Her "Hey!" was so inappropriately cheerful.

"Tessa, I was *there*," I said, my voice wobbling. "I found a video from that night that I'd deleted right after, but in it I go to her apartment and—"

"Slow down, Lindsay, breathe," she broke in. "I can't hear anything you're saying. Are you okay?"

"No, that's what I'm trying to tell you!" The sound of my own croaking voice spooked me.

"What's going on?"

I took a long, quavering breath. "Can you come over?"

A beat. Then: "I'm on my way."

I texted Damien, too, but again he didn't respond. As Tessa sped across the East River, I watched the other videos; they were spastic, twenty-second snippets of drunk postgrads messing around. What was I looking for? In one from July, we passed a joint and discussed what our entrance music would be if we walked out to a song like a pro athlete taking the field. I suggested "Queen Bitch" for Edie and laughed cruelly, and she responded by playing it on her phone and remarking, "Oh, Lindsay, it's cute when you try to be mean!" A ripple of annoyance. Was that a clue? Was that evidence?

Tessa set her watch to ping mine when she got close, and at the sound I walked to the window and watched her lock up her Citi bike on the street below. Cars whizzed behind her and I pictured it for a moment, a drunk driver careening off the road and onto the sidewalk, Tessa pinned to the bike-share structure from the waist down. My heart sped up at the thought and adrenaline shot through my limbs. I blinked again; she crossed the street and made her way up my stoop, then leaned on the bell. I buzzed the front door and heard it unlatch a few floors below.

I'd sprawled on the sofa. "Don't you have those keys I gave you?" I asked, dangling a leg off the cushion.

"Somewhere. I didn't realize getting up to let me in would be the death of you." She set about making me tea, banged a cupboard.

"Thanks for coming over," I called. "I hope you weren't in the middle of anything."

"It's fine. Will and I were just watching TV."

"Oh." I scooched deeper into the couch and slung my knees over the armrest. "Well, I'm glad you're here. I'm actually having this internal battle where I don't want to tell anybody, but I think I'll go crazy if I do that."

Tessa carried over a steaming mug. "Just tell me what happened. We're gonna figure it out."

I leaned my head back and groaned. "I don't even know where to start."

"You said on the phone you were there? Start there."

But I didn't start there. I recounted Sarah's casual admission that she'd questioned Edie's cause of death, then launched into my call with Kevin, his reveal about a mysterious ER visit and a prescient conversation with Edie earlier that month, right before she died—his conviction that she wasn't suicidal.

"Okay, that would definitely freak me out," she said when I paused to rub my face. "But Sarah also course-corrected once she got a little perspective, right? She can't have been *that* convinced if she dropped it afterward."

"That's true. Everything she mentioned on Monday was really flimsy. I can see why she kinda grew out of it."

"What *was* she basing it on?"

I tugged at the teabag's string. "Like, she mentioned how the gun was in Edie's right hand, but she was a lefty like you. How she was found in her bra and underwear, that kind of thing."

Tessa scrunched her nose. "I see why it all feels . . . alarming when you look at it through a new lens. But, Lindsay, you know that's not much. And the two people behind this theory were Sarah, who's rescinded it, and Kevin, who maybe felt motivated to not believe it was suicide since the gun was his."

Jarring, the way the names popped out of her mouth. Like hearing your cousin call your father "Uncle Mike."

"You mean so that he'd feel less responsible?"

"Right, exactly. How would you feel if your friend used your gun to kill herself? Maybe it was easier to pin it on some big, bad, anonymous monster, you know?" She picked at a hangnail. "All the adults in the situation, the detectives and her parents and everyone, concluded it was suicide, right?"

"I know, I know." I pulled in a deep breath. "But there's another thing. The reason I actually started poking around again is that . . . well, I think I told you Sarah remembered something differently from the night that Edie died. I have a memory of being up at this concert with her and Alex while Edie . . . while it happened, and Sarah was like, 'No, you weren't there, you'd already gone home.'"

"Whoa."

"I know, it was really weird, she was adamant about it. But of course I was there, I remember it. I was drunk, but not wasted or anything. So I just kinda thought I'd . . . you know, prove her wrong. Obviously this was an important night to me."

"But you said on the phone you think you . . . I couldn't really understand you."

I pulled my laptop off the coffee table and cued up the last few seconds of the video. "Watch this."

When it ended, she continued to frown in confusion.

"This is *the* night," I told her, pointing. "And based on the time stamp, this is right around when Edie died. And look, I walk into her apartment. My fucking frenemy is about to die and I just waltz into the room."

It was so absurd, said aloud, that I almost cackled. Tessa frowned and watched the end of the video again.

"You're sure that's you?" she said.

"The person walking into the apartment? Yes, I'm sure."

"But you're not sure she's in there."

"Tessa, the timing works out perfectly. And I'd just seen all my other friends."

"Where?"

She hadn't viewed the first few minutes of the video yet. I blushed, knowing she was about to hear Alex and myself slandering the dead, but I hastily rewound it anyway. She watched, her eyes narrowed.

"Whoa, I didn't realize you and Alex had such strong feelings about Edie."

"I don't remember either of us saying that. I don't even remember being that pissed. In normal, sober life. But they'd broken up and were still living in the same apartment, and Edie and I weren't on great terms, and . . . I'm kind of a mean drunk," I finished lamely.

"I've seen it." She said it without thinking and the moment froze up, all awkward.

I cleared my throat. "So it pretty much had to be Edie in there."

"What about Kevin?"

"He had a show that night. In Greenpoint."

"And there's no one else who could've been in the apartment?

Seems like enough time passed that any one of those friends could've walked in . . ."

"I know, but the timing, it's right before Edie . . ." We exchanged exasperated looks.

"So let me get this straight," she said. "You're saying that now that you know you went into the room, you think you actually . . . what, found her body and didn't tell anyone?"

"Or saw something I shouldn't have. Like who was in there with her." The thought blinked on like a lightbulb: This would explain so much. Lindsay Bach's Pathetic Decade. I'd fact-checked a story once about the health consequences of harboring secrets, how the chronic gush of stress hormones eats away at the brain. What if you don't even know about the skeletons in the closet?

"Or you walked into an empty room. Or your friends were in there refreshing their drinks or smoking pot or something and the time stamp is an hour off. I mean, right?"

"Maybe. But, Tessa, what if I saw, like, the smoking gun and was too drunk to realize it? Up until this morning I was convinced that I'd just gone to the show with my friends and then gone straight home. Or what if I said something awful to her right as she was feeling depressed and had a gun at her disposal? I was raring to tell her off, you know."

"I thought you were convinced it *wasn't* a suicide now."

"I don't knooow. Ugh, I just wish I could *remember* this moment. I had no idea I blacked out, and that's really scary." A headache throbbed against my nose and forehead. Beneath it, behind my eyes and temples, was a shadowy thought, one I desperately didn't want to dredge up.

"Okay, okay." She refolded her legs under her. "This is . . . you're not thinking straight. Let's talk this out. What do you remember from that night?"

I'd gone over it so many times in the weeks and months after, and then again this week, my brain finding and then easing into those deep, ancient grooves. "I went over to their apartment around maybe nine thirty, normal time," I said, "and Edie wasn't there. I was on edge because I'd pumped myself up to have this friend breakup talk with her. I kinda casually asked where she was and somebody just said she was around and would maybe meet us later." I could see exactly where each of us was sitting and even knew what I was wearing: a way-too-short denim romper and white Keds. "The rest of us were pregaming in the apartment. I think Alex was playing bartender. And I was drinking extremely fast because I was nervous about seeing Edie. I was already feeling pretty tipsy by the time we went up to the roof. And then Kevin left for his gig."

I finished my tea, now cold. "We were up there for a while, and then we came back inside and walked over to the party. I mean, I don't really remember walking there, like actually being in the staircase, but why would I?"

"Then what?"

I sighed. "The band was like synth-pop—god, what'd we call it? Synth-wave? Chillwave! We were dancing like idiots and bouncing off each other and stuff. And then I had that moment of clarity when you realize you're too drunk, so I left and a random girl smoking outside helped me hail a taxi. I couldn't stop thanking her." I swallowed. "That's what I remember clearly. But Sarah swears I never came to the show. I figured she was just remembering it wrong."

"It sounds like you remember it pretty well."

"I thought so, too. But the video . . ."

The thought again, beating at the inside of my skull. I resisted as it threatened to take shape, to crystallize. My eyes welled with tears, and Tessa pushed me on: "What happened the next day?"

"Well, I woke up at home on my bed, fully dressed. I had the worst hangover of my life, which made the entire next day especially fucking surreal."

"God. I'm so sorry, Linds."

"It was bad. My phone was dead, so by the time I saw all the texts, the cops and everyone had already left. I was so sick, I remember throwing up in a sewer grate on my walk to the subway and then buying Gatorade at a bodega and rinsing out my mouth. So gross. When I got there, Sarah was sitting on these steps just outside the front door, and her face—oh my god. I sat down next to her—I was, like, fighting the urge to vomit, and my head hurt so bad I could barely look at her straight—and she just looked at me and she goes, 'I found her.' God, it broke my heart."

It'd been a beautiful morning, breezy and cooler than normal, and a bird had chosen the nearest tree to sit and sing its little heart out. I'd gazed at it, wishing I could tear its lungs out and make the sound stop.

"How did she find her?"

"She came home to start getting ready for bed and found the body."

She closed her eyes. "Jeez, poor Sarah. How'd she seem?"

"The next morning, you mean? She just seemed exhausted. Obviously they hadn't slept all night. Sarah's and . . . I think Alex's parents were coming in that day. That's right, Kevin had spent the night in jail 'cause of the unlicensed firearm and was waiting to talk to the DA, and then he was gonna go stay with Alex's family. So everyone was just waiting to be brought back to hotels." I'd felt jealous, to be honest: accosted by this news and then too many steps behind and away to get any support. None of my so-called "friends" had asked if I'd wanted to go with them; I'd just waited until they'd all left, then gone home, climbed back into bed, and bawled.

Tessa stood up and crossed into the kitchen, bending to root around in her backpack. "You said you and Edie were on bad terms?"

"Yeah. We were basically inseparable for a year. And then I started to feel like our friendship was sort of based on me being fucked up and her being more together than me."

Tessa returned with a bar of dark chocolate; she broke off a chunk and handed the rest to me.

"That's why I'd made up my mind to separate myself from her, which would mean also separating myself from the whole crew, which was scary. But necessary, you know? Deciding felt very adult. And then a week before she died, we had this stupid fight over nothing." I held out the bar and she took it, foil crinkling.

"What happened?"

I let the chocolate melt on my tongue for a moment. "It was so inane. The weather was shitty and someone had invited me over, maybe Sarah, and I'd brought a bunch of DVDs in case everyone felt like being lazy and staying in. Edie still wanted to go into Williamsburg and I was jokingly being whiny, you know, 'It's raaaaining, let's staaaaay,' and she just *snapped*." I could still see the look on her face, could still feel the blow of her shrieked words. "She just started screaming that I was the most selfish and controlling person she'd ever met and that I was always acting like I owned the place when it wasn't even my apartment." God, it'd hurt. The bruise resurfaced, still fresh. "Then she stormed out of the apartment and all of us were like, *whoa*."

"Whoa is right," Tessa said. "Did you ever talk about it?"

I shrugged. "She texted the next day and just said she was sorry for, quote-unquote, flipping a bitch, and that she'd been stressed about other stuff. I'd been thinking about cutting ties anyway, so I just told her it was fine. But after that, things were . . . tense. It was like she'd cut me off before I could do the same."

Tessa set the chocolate on the coffee table. "'Stressed about other stuff.' You didn't ask what?"

"Not really. I mean, everyone was stressed out. It was two thousand fucking nine. Edie's parents were about to lose her childhood home, Kevin and Alex couldn't find real jobs, Sarah had been laid off . . ."

"I remember," Tessa said. "That era, I mean. All these weird aftershocks and this feeling like . . ." She hesitated.

"Like right after an earthquake, when you're not actually sure if it's about to get worse," I offered.

Tessa nodded.

"You were still in Chicago then, right?" I asked.

She nodded again. We sucked on our chocolate. "I might have asked you this before, but I forget: Why was Kevin keeping a gun in the apartment?"

"Oh, it was awful. The good little Southern boy had this antique pistol from his grandfather that he kept in this chest in the living room—like a steamer trunk? He loved that gun. It didn't occur to any of us that you can't just randomly have an unlicensed firearm in New York. It was hardly ever loaded, and he never let us touch it. Apparently he'd gone target shooting in Bucks County the weekend before and just hadn't dealt with it yet. God, he'll never forgive himself."

"Would Edie even be comfortable using it?"

"I dunno. I can't think why she'd have touched it before."

Tessa nodded and looked down. I pictured the gun in Edie's slender hands. Maybe she'd pointed it at herself—or at me—just to fuck with me. It felt like something she'd do.

"I bet she'd never even held a gun before," I added. "New York City's not exactly a place where you grow up hunting." Unlike Bumfuck, Wisconsin. Unlike me. And then the thought blared on, so loud I couldn't stop it: I would've known exactly how to use Kevin's gun. It would have been the most natural thing in the world. And I knew what an uncontrollable surge of anger could cause me to do. Had I . . . could I . . . ?

With a crack, Tessa snapped another piece of chocolate from the bar. "So whoever had the gun had to know it was there and get it out of the chest to use it?" she asked.

I took a breath. "I'm, like, ninety-five percent sure it was put away. I mean, the living room wasn't that big and we were all hanging out there earlier that night, and I certainly don't remember seeing it. But it could have been out, sure."

Tessa nodded. Her line of questioning, her certainty that it was someone else and had nothing to do with my friend-breakup fantasies, was giving me some relief, so I followed it, haltingly: "If we limit it to people who knew about the gun and where he kept it, it's still a ton of people. He wasn't secretive about it. We were more worried about it getting stolen than anything else. God, we were stupid."

Tessa smiled sadly. "The age of invincibility," she said.

"Exactly."

She considered. "I take it you didn't find anything helpful in your emails?"

"I don't even know what I was looking for. Obviously I didn't find one that was like 'Hey, Lindsay, good thing I spotted you at the concert and not anywhere near Edie's apartment on Friday.'" I shook my head. "I just don't know, Tessa. I don't know what I don't know. And this goddamn video . . . it means that whatever I don't know is a lot bigger than I realized."

Softly: "Lindsay, I'm sure that whatever you're worried about . . . that you said something, or saw something . . . I'm sure that's not the case. The odds that everybody had it wrong and you're just discovering this ten years later, based on this one totally inconclusive thing . . ." She opened both palms.

"Not everyone," I countered. "Look at Sarah. Look at Kevin."

"I hear you," she said. "But at the same time, this seems like something where there's no obvious way to get to the bottom of what happened. So if you just want me to listen, I'm here. But if you want my advice, I think you should just walk away. Nobody else is even *thinking* about this stuff all these years later."

"If you thought someone had hurt your friend, wouldn't you want to know?" I couldn't tell her how much I needed to know, how I wouldn't be able to live with myself until the truth had come to light. A tear slipped out and I brushed it away. "I'm a fact-checker, Tessa. If I'm grossly incorrect about this formative life event, I'd like to know. Besides, I've already requested the case files."

"I understand." Tessa leaned down and hugged me awkwardly. "Then I'll help."

Chapter 6

The next morning I woke up convinced I was overlooking something, something I'd looked at but not seen, a prickly cocklebur riding along unnoticed. Was it a photo on Facebook? A detail from the videos? I'd sent the August 21 clip to both Tessa and Damien, hoping one of them would notice something I hadn't. Ugh, both of them listening to my voice, drunk and garbled: "I want to push her off this building!" I squeezed my eyes shut another moment and rolled out of bed.

Lloyd buoyed up in my mind, so I searched for him in my old email database. It didn't take long to find my email to Edie from April, the day after Lloyd and I had finally hooked up, drunken sex three months in the making on my end and perhaps two hours on his:

> E—my head is pounding and my insides all hurt and oh my god let's never ever drink whiskey again, but I don't even care because I am seriously walking on air. OH MY GOD. I like him so much it's embarrassing. I am sitting in my cubicle beaming like an idiot even though I'm super hungover and my hair smells like smoke and I clearly didn't shower before booking it into work. He is sofa king hot. I'll tell you more about it tomorrow, but the short story is: REALLY GOOD. Remind me to tell you his story about the dishwasher. He got my number in the morning and said he'd text and I'm a liiiiittle bit panicking because I haven't heard from him but I'm sure it's fine. Gah, did that really all

happen last night? I'm not sure I'd believe it if there weren't witnesses. OMG. SO HOT.

I grinned retroactively at my airheaded tone. I'd seen Lloyd only a couple of times after that magical January night on the rooftop; Alex and Lloyd had had a falling-out shortly after, Edie had told me, one that precluded Alex from directly setting us up. I can't remember now why I didn't just take matters into my own hands, since I knew Lloyd personally, since it shouldn't have been that hard to ask him out for drinks. He didn't live in Calhoun, so I didn't bump into him much; maybe he'd been coolly distant ("Oh, we've met before?"), and yet I continued crushing, undeterred.

The story of the dishwasher was gone, too, lost to the ages, but I remembered other pieces of that Monday night. Edie and I were hanging out in some strangers' Calhoun apartment, a weird space with a hammock suspended from the ceiling, so loose that when you sat in it, your body sunk into an *L*. We were standing around, drinking bad whiskey out of mugs, when Lloyd and another dude walked in. It all felt a little miraculous: that he was there at all, that Alex (Edie's new official boyfriend and Lloyd's ex-friend) wasn't; that Edie, knowing I had a huge crush on the guy, had given him a big wave and then backed away once he jangled over to say hello. I was blushing fire-red, but Lloyd had been friendly, had picked up the conversation. God, I could still remember it now: the mounting excitement as Lloyd didn't turn away, the delightful realization that every time he took a few steps to refresh his glass or speak to someone else, he came back and rejoined me. That mutual unspoken thrill: *This is happening.*

I couldn't recall much about the sex now except for a belated certainty that it was *not* good; at the time I was so thrilled to be making out, so grateful when someone chose to unwrap my body instead of the body of any of the other women in the room and building and Brooklyn and world. I had a vague memory of him crashing down next to me and falling asleep within seconds of coming, and I lay there smiling into the night, my heart beating fast: *He likes me, he likes me, he likes me.* Which, of course, made everything that came after all the more upsetting.

On Sunday, the unlikeliest day for bureaucratic progress, the case files appeared in my inbox, compressed into an attachment like a present ripe for the opening. In a few seconds, I had everything open: the coroner's report, police notes, incident report, autopsy report—a novel-length pile of information all about my onetime best friend's death. I checked the total page count: 124 pages, too long to print. So I clicked on whatever came first alphabetically and began reading. It was an autopsy report, dense and clinical:

> *Autopsy authorized by: Dr. Allan Dennis for New York City*
> *Identified by: Fingerprints and dental comparison*
> *Rigor: Absent*
> *Livor: Purple*
> *Age: 23*
> *Race: White*
> *Sex: Female*
> *Length: 65 inches*
> *Weight: 117 pounds*
> *Eyes: Green*
> *Hair: Red*
> *Body heat: Refrigerated*

God, I could practically hear Dr. Dennis bleating off the stats to a lab tech with cool detachment, Edie's body on a table just like on TV shows. The report described her clothing next: just the polka-dot bra, stained with blood, and the red lacy thong. Such an undignified way to die.

> *EXTERNAL EXAMINATION: This is the unembalmed*
> *body of a white female which weighs approximately 117 pounds.*
> *and measures 65 inches in height. The physique is ectomorphic.*

*The head hair is red, wavy, and long, measuring approximately
21 inches in greatest length. The irides are green.*

Ew, *which?* Try *who,* asshole. I did some searching: "ectomor-
phic" means thin and delicate; irides are irises. Jargon fogging up
such simple truths.

*The teeth are natural. The fingernails are painted purple. There
is a small transverse pale linear scar in the lower quadrant of
the abdomen. Other distinctive markings are absent on external
examination.*

I leaned back and breathed heavily. My gut was threatening to
take over, an expanding ball of nausea and alarm, but I fought it
back with research mode. *This is what I do,* I told myself. *I research.*

*RADIOGRAPHS: Postmortem radiographs of the head
and neck reveal several radiopaque fragments in the front-
right skull/brain. Cranial X-rays demonstrate sizable missile
fragments in the central head region with additional fragments
in the right forehead region and smaller fragments dispersed
throughout the midcranial region.*

I searched for "radiopaque" and then felt stupid for not just
sounding it out: opaque to an X-ray or similar radiology. Duh.

*INTERNAL EXAMINATION: A 2.5-inch circular area
of scalp hemorrhage is present around a gunshot entry wound
in the forehead region. Additionally, an individual 3-inch
circular scalp hematoma is present over the vertex as well as
a hemorrhage surrounding the laceration over the external
occipital protuberance. The calvarium is intact. Upon its
removal diffuse subarachnoid hemorrhage is evident. The
brain weighs 1,280 grams. There is a perforating track through*

the brain, described below. Other than this, no underlying
abnormalities are evident in the brain.

I was shaken enough to pause my reading and search for it: The average weight of an adult female's brain is 1,198 grams. Smarty Edie.

PATHOLOGIC DIAGNOSES: Gunshot wound of the head
Entrance: Side of the head; close range of fire
Path: Skin and subcutaneous tissue of midline parietal scalp,
frontoparietal skull, dura, frontoparietal brain lobes, corpus
callosum, base of the skull, hard palate, tongue, and floor of
mouth
Associated injuries: Laceration of the right medial cathus of
the eye, extensive skull fractures, and contusions of the left
and right periorbital tissue
Missile: Multiple fragments of copper-colored metal in the
brain and sinuses weighing, in aggregate, 162.8 grains

Okay—a handgun bullet would be at least 120, maybe 180 grains. I hated that I knew this, that so much gun information was tucked away in my own brain.

OPINION: This 23-year-old white female, Edith Iredale,
died of a gunshot wound to the head. According to reports, the
decedent was found in her apartment with an antique pistol
near her body. Autopsy revealed a close-range entrance gunshot
wound to the side of the head that fractured the skull and
damaged the brain. Fractures at the base of the skull caused the
appearance of bruising around both eyes. This gunshot wound
also damaged the roof of the mouth (hard palate) and the tongue.

Postmortem toxicological testing revealed a blood
alcohol concentration of 0.054. There was a high level of
3,4-methylenedioxymethamphetamine (202 ng/mL) in the blood.

Whoa. Alcohol I expected, but drugs? I searched for it and it rang a distant bell: Molly, a potent form of MDMA that had a resurgence in the spring of 2009. A fifth of Calhoun's residents were probably on it on any given Friday. But Edie?

> *The presence of gunpowder stippling, gunpowder particles, and soot on the skin surrounding the entrance defects is consistent with a close range of fire (less than 2–3 inches). Gunshot particles deep in the brain tissue suggest a close-range shot consistent with suicide, although accidental death should still be considered a possibility.*

I could only skim the rest: section by section descriptions of opening her up with a Y-shape incision, peeling out her organs, weighing them, making pithy observations. Then there was a matrix repeating the levels of drugs and booze in her splayed-open body. The report ended on a note of finality, some of the only improperly used periods capping five pages of sentence fragments:

> *CAUSE OF DEATH: Gunshot wound to the head.*
> *MANNER: Suicide.*

I leaned back and breathed deeply through my nose, waiting for my stomach to unclench. Then I opened another file folder: dozens of free-floating emails between the police department and city officials. They swirled like snowflakes, unindexed, and I thought dully of my own emails from that era banging around on my server. I opened one at random: It was a New York City Police Department spokesman telling city employees that Edie probably killed herself. "Police are on the scene of a possible suicide in Bushwick that occurred by 11:30 p.m. I will provide you with updates," it read. A two-liner, letting everyone know no foul play was suspected.

I clicked on a folder named after the detectives assigned to the case and realized it contained notes from their interviews with us, handwritten in comically terrible handwriting and scanned. There was one from their discussion with me, labeled LBACH, which touched off a strange thrill in my ribs. I opened it and struggled to read the jottings:

> Bach, Lindsay
> #594
> 23 yo
> Friend for abt 1 year, met through Sarah
> Call next morning, returned to scene
> Night of incident: Roof w Kotsonis, Kwan, Reed approx
>   9:30 pm. Drinking beer, gin prep by Reed. Reed left for
>   Matchless 10 (CHK). Grp to concert in 6E approx 11.
>   Took cab home (CHK)
> Fight with Iredale on Saturday 8/15 re: "controlling,"
>   unexpected
> Conf. breakup bw Iredale + Kotsonis around 7/4; cause
>   unknown
> Decedent moody, withdrawn
> Iredale "never used drugs"

I remembered that interview, a few days after Edie's death: the freezing-cold interrogation room done up to look a little cozy with a coffee machine and ugly cushions on the chairs. I'd felt so young and scared, tempted to ask if I should really be speaking to them without my parents being present.

And the notes were so vague. Had I told the cops that I'd headed to 6E with the crew or that the rest of them went out while I hailed a cab? I scanned the jottings again: interesting that I'd said Kevin had made our first drinks; I thought it was Alex. I looked around for notes from my friends' questionings and brought up Alex's, squinting again to read the scrawls:

> Kotsonis, Alex
> #488

24 yo
Met Iredale in winter, approx. January 2009, can't confirm.
  Building, other apt.
Dated 3/09-7/09. Lived w Reed, Kwan & Iredale moved in
  4/09 (apt 4G, scene of unattended death)
"Growing apart" no details
Night of incident: Last saw decedent approx. 5:30 pm.
  Night of: apt w Bach, Reed, Kwan 9:30, then roof;
  Reed to Matchless Greenpoint. Drinking gin; no drugs.
  Left for 6E (CHK) w Kwan and Bach.

I leaned back and pursed my lips around a long, slow exhale. There—Alex knew I went to the show. Although the notes made it sound like we'd gone directly, while the Flip cam video showed I'd made my way from the roof to SAKE. How drunk had we all been? I heard Alex's voice again, low and trundling: *I want that bitch out of my apartment!*

I scanned the notes from the interview with Sarah, whose last name they erroneously spelled "Quan" (or, once, "Kwon") instead of "Kwan." It started the same as Alex's and mine—the origin story of their friendship, mention of a meaningless fight not long before, similar memory of the beginning of The Night. Then:

"Tiny fight" w Bach when Bach left; Quan & Kotsonis to
  concert apt 6E check.

I read it twice more, my eyes circling back at the end as if it were music and I'd bumped against a repeat symbol. A tiny fight? I thought hard but couldn't remember anything, either the dustup itself or a later mention of it. There was the burbling sound on the Flip cam video a few minutes in, but nothing I could decipher. Had it happened in my memory's seams, while we were worm-holing between the roof and the concert? Although she said here in the report, too, that I hadn't gone along to 6E. A direct contradiction, one the detectives hadn't caught.

I'd read once that in emotionally distressing moments, your brain can rewrite an ending, stitch together a memory that feels real. After Columbine, for example, the school principal swore he'd made it through a job interview with a potential new teacher and had offered him a gig, while everyone else—the candidate, his secretary—insisted he hadn't gotten nearly that far. Distressed, we construct realities that feel just as real as the world around us. Whose brain had concocted a new version of that night—mine or Sarah's?

I kneaded the back of my neck. All these factoids, all these nuggets I took such pleasure in uncovering as a fact-checker—not pleasure, exactly, more like scratching an itch, stamping out a red-hot drive to know, discover, confirm. Making the world orderly and predictable and objectively real. I'd always assumed I'd wound up as a fact-checker by accident, when there were more open roles in research than in the features department. But maybe some part of me had always been scratching away, clawing at the coating over things I'd forgotten.

I pulled my messages up in front of the detectives' notes and texted Sarah: "Can you call me?" I stared at the screen, willing the bubble to appear that would mean she was responding, but . . . nothing. I thought briefly of looking at her social feeds, trying to gauge where she was right now, why she was taking so long to reply. In 2009, it was harder to keep tabs on people. You had to wait for them to come to you. I suddenly remembered long nights of drawing out text conversations with boys—seeing their responses, setting my phone down, sipping a beer, and taking three hours to respond. Just 'cause.

Alex, then. Everything tightened at the idea of confronting him, of speaking to the dude who'd spoken so poorly of Edie moments before she died. I had no idea he'd had that revulsion pulsing just under the surface. But it was like jumping into a cold lake: I found his number in his email signature and texted before I could think about it. He wrote back right away: "Whoa hi!"

"Can you hop on the phone?" I typed back. I wanted to just

call, since I knew he was literally holding his cell. Ten years ago I would've just dialed. Fuck this era.

He took longer to write back this time. "I could call in like an hour? Hope everything's okay???"

"Please do, and thank you!!" I stood up and walked to the bathroom, staring into the sink and watching the water swirl into the drain. I began to feel that urgent drive, faraway at first and then with growing intensity, somewhere deep in my low back and groin: Keep going.

I opened the notes from the interview with Kevin gingerly, as if winding a jack-in-the-box. It occurred to me that he could be my tiebreaker, the third vote on whether or not I'd made it to the show; then I remembered he'd left for his own concert while we were still pregaming on the roof.

The notes began the same as the others, how they'd met in spring 2009 when Edie and Alex started dating, how she'd moved in with them along with Sarah in April. It was hard to picture the conversation—little Kevin shifting between bad postures while two detectives gave him the third degree, arrested for the first time in his cheery life. It sounded like Kevin started to get emotional next, noting that he and Edie had become better friends and that she'd cried to him about fights she'd had with Sarah and me.

Which would have been surprising enough in its own right, since I could barely imagine them exchanging more than pleasantries, but then this sentence boomed out of the document like a cannon:

Accomp decedent to ER early August, likely 8/4, when she complained heavy cramping; visible blood. Assume miscarriage. Left + not discussed/told friends. CHK.

Jesus. The ER visit he'd mentioned. I pulled up my email index from that era and searched for August 4, apparently a Tuesday: mundane emails to coworkers and one from Sarah mentioning an upcoming party, reminding Kevin he still owed rent and finishing with "BTW, anyone seen Edie in like a week? Is she officially avoiding everyone or just me?" Kevin had responded about the rent the next day, diplomatically ignoring the stuff about Edie, and the thread had petered out.

Back in the cops' scribbles, I saw that Kevin went on to say that he'd had a show the night of Edie's death and had taken his bandmate's van to Greenpoint. They'd been the headliners, taking the stage around 11 p.m., and he'd only heard the news when he turned his phone back on around 1:00. I verified it on fact-checking autopilot: a tweet from the venue from early August 22, 2009, thanking Static Pony for a BRUTAL NIGHT.

I set aside the detectives' notes and searched for Edie's medical records. I saw dental records, an annual OB-GYN visit, and then bingo: admission forms from Mt. Sinai Medical Center, dated "8/4/09, 9:06 p.m." Retrieved on official police business about a week after the interviews took place. I scanned Edie's frantic handwriting on the intake forms, noting that symptoms had begun around 5:00 p.m. but she'd never had cramps this intense before and she was experiencing bleeding heavier than any period. Poor thing, on a scale of 1 through 10 she rated her pain a 9. I hit page-down; she was seen by 10:48, where, according to her discharge forms, a doctor determined she'd had a completed miscarriage—confirmed with a surgical dilation and curettage, which sounded scary, and then an ultrasound, which sounded expensive—and had been approximately six weeks along. She was given relaxants, monitored overnight, and released in the morning. And off Edie went, back to Calhoun Lofts. No longer pregnant and with no one to confide in but, oddly, Kevin.

Oh, that poor girl—holing up in her sunless room to mourn and heal in solitude. I returned to the autopsy report, poring more carefully over the organ-by-organ rundown at the end of the document. And there it was, ripe for the noticing:

Thickened uterine tissue suggested early pregnancy; progressing normally before spontaneous abortion.

Six weeks before early August. Mid-June, shortly before she and Alex split. Had Alex known? Had she been planning to keep it? And why the hell had Kevin been the one to accompany her?

I returned to the main index. There was a folder named D_ ASUSEEEPC that I'd been avoiding because I found its name so inscrutable, but finally I opened it and gasped, all the blast-from-the-past sensations pinging around my skull. There was a screen-grab of an old computer desktop, files and icons everywhere like stickers on a little girl's notebook. Asus was a kind of computer. I Googled the folder name and there it was, Edie's clunky old laptop: the Asus Eee PC 100HE. There was just one other file in the folder, a Word document. I clicked on it and felt my breath catch in my throat.

The suicide note. The Word document had been opened at 8:12 p.m. and then auto-saved at 11:44, around the time when the first responders appeared. I cross-referenced time stamps: My Flip cam video ended at 11:11; the 911 call came in at 11:32. Damn—a part of me had hoped I'd absolve myself here, that somehow I'd wandered into the room with a camcorder minutes *after* Sarah had called the cops. A video I'd coincidentally deleted shortly after, assuming it was a gross drunk record of us embarrassing ourselves. Only to rediscover it almost exactly ten years later. It rushed up through me again like a geyser, a sharp *What the fuck?*

But an autosave told us nothing. I opened the Word file; it was so old I could only view it, not access it. It blinked back at me, three mini sentences I hadn't actually seen with my own eyes (as far as I knew), but that we'd heard about and discussed among ourselves:

I love you. I'm sorry. Goodbye.

All at the top left of the page, uncentered, unstyled, ugly. That didn't seem like Edie, either—she was a visual creature, she liked symmetry and pretty, arty things. She would have centered the note, a few inches on the top and bottom, that middle *I'm* marking the center like a spire.

How easy it'd be for someone else to fake the note. Three sentences, no detail. Really, it couldn't have been more than a two-step cover-up, one easily gleaned from decades of TV watching: Press her fingerprints onto the gun and leave it near her; grab her laptop, open a file, and hastily type something out. (Had she used a password? If so, her closest friends would have known it; we were constantly passing around computers, pulling up YouTube videos or photos or music for all to enjoy. Which meant our fingerprints would be on everything as well.)

I checked for tags on the file, any additional information. I rubbed the edges of my fingernails across the flat pads of my thumbs and stared hard. What was I missing?

I got up and poured a glass of water, an old trick a former boss had taught me to do whenever I was stumped. Walk away, come back to it with fresh eyes. I slid the suicide note aside and checked online what metadata a circa 2009 .doc file typically shows. Something slid into place: Date Created. Why had the embedded info on this file shown me Last Opened and Saved At, but not the creation date? I checked again—the Created On listing was blank, two little hyphens where a date should have been. What a bizarre thing to be missing.

There was nothing else in this folder, nothing else from her Asus. I selected another one and felt something rip through me.

Five death-scene photographs—all time-stamped JPEGs. They were still just a string of letters and numbers, their file names, but if I double-clicked I could see Edie the last way that any of us saw her.

My heart banged. I guzzled my glass of water, spilling a little onto my chest. My hand shook as I set the cup back on its coaster.

I filled my lungs up with air and pushed it out. One look, all at once, careful and thorough just to see if there was anything odd in the periphery, anything investigators had missed. I would keep my eyes moving, not on Edie's, not on her bruise-ringed gaze.

I moved the pointer, ready to click, then sat back again. Could I do it? Face the nightmare that'd haunted Sarah for months?

Would this fuck with me, too, weave its way into a dream or vision or made-up memory of the moment after the gun went off, me standing there with the recoil still pulsing through my arm?

I balled both hands into fists, mashed them into my chin, a bad silent-film actress pantomiming indecision. Then my right hand jolted out and double-clicked.

A notification. Password-protected. Pursuant to New York State law, inaccessible without a key.

Annoyance took over, and I played around with different apps and programs and ways of seeing previews, all to no avail. I gave up and Xed out of the folder, awash in relief. *Tomorrow I'll ask Tessa to find a way to access them for me,* I thought showily, knowing full well I never would.

I chose a folder labeled SWMODEL399MM, then realized it contained technical specifications about the bullet and gun. I moved on to the next folder and gasped: the 911 call, a recording and a transcript. My mouse hovered over the audio file, but I couldn't do it; instead, I opened up the text.

> NEW YORK POLICE DEPARTMENT
> Brooklyn, NY
> 9-1-1 CALL TRANSCRIPT
> 9-1-1 CALL FROM: Sarah Kwan
> CALL TO: NYPD 9-1-1
> DATE: 8-21-09
> RE: 11-441957
>
> **Q: Christopher Fuchs**
> NYPD Dispatcher
> A: Sarah Kwan
> A: Oh my god!
> Q: (Inaudible) 9-1-1 (inaudible) this call is being recorded.
> A: Is this 9-1-1? Oh my god. Hello?!
> Q: It's 9-1-1.
> A: Hello?! (Unintelligible.)

Q: Ma'am, I need you to stop screaming so that I can hear you.

A: My friend, she (unintelligible)! Oh my god!

Q: What's happening?

A: Oh god! No! Oh my god! My friend is all bloody! She needs an ambulance!

Q: What's wrong with her?

A: Oh my god. You need to send someone! Quickly!

Q: Ma'am, listen to me. I need you to calm down so I can understand what's going on. What's wrong with your friend?

A: I think she's been shot!

Q: You think she's been shot?

A: There's blood on the ground, oh my god, oh my god.

Q: Listen to me. I need you to stop screaming so I can . . .

A: (Unintelligible.)

Q: Ma'am, are you listening? Take a deep breath and calm down so I can understand you.

A: (Unintelligible) . . . touch her, don't touch her! Is it OK if he checks her?

Q: Before anyone touches her I need you to give me the address so I can send the ambulance right away. OK?

A: [redacted] Hurry, oh my god, please hurry.

Q: OK, the ambulance is on its way, now listen, I'm going to transfer you to the paramedics so they can give you CPR instructions, OK? Don't hang up.

A: Wait! So he shouldn't touch her?

Q: Listen to me, I'm going to transfer you to—

A: There's no pulse! Oh my god, he said there's no pulse, please hurry, please hurry.

Q: I'm transferring you, don't hang up! (Call is transferred to NYFD.)

Mr. Gonzalez, NYFD Dispatcher
Q: New York Fire Department.

Mr. Fuchs, NYPD Dispatcher

Q: NYPD with a transfer (inaudible).

A: . . . please, oh my god!

Mr. Gonzalez, NYFD Dispatcher

Q: Fire Department, what's the address of your emergency?

A: [redacted] She's not breathing, she doesn't have a pulse.

Q: [redacted]

A: Oh please hurry!

Q: What's the phone number you're calling me from?

A: [redacted] Quickly! Please?

Q: [redacted]

A: That's right, yes.

Q: What's your name?

A: Sarah Kwan. Oh my god, I don't know what to do, she doesn't have a pulse, oh my god.

Q: OK, exactly what happened?

A: Please hurry!

Q: (Inaudible.)

A: It looks like she got shot! In the head!

Q: With a gun?

A: Yes! Oh my god, I see the gun, oh my god, oh my god! It's by her hand!

Q: OK, ma'am, I'm sending the paramedics right now. They're on their way. Please do not touch the gun.

A: Oh my god, oh my god! (Sobs.)

Q: How old is she?

A: How old is she?

Q: Yes, her age.

A: Twenty-three. (Inaudible.)

Mr. Fuchs, NYPD Dispatcher

Q: Hey, FD, hold on a second. Did she shoot herself?

A: I don't know! It looks like it! There's a gun! Oh, please!

Q: You see the gun?

A: Yeah, it's right by her! It's on the ground next to her.

Q: OK. We'll get the police and the paramedics . . .

A: Where are they? Where are they?

Q: I need you to not touch the gun, OK? Can you do that?

A: I don't know what to do, oh my god, I don't know what to do. (Sobs.)

Q: Ma'am, I need you to calm down and listen to me. Do not touch the gun, OK?

A: OK. OK. Please hurry. Oh my god.

Mr. Gonzalez, NYFD Dispatcher

Q: Ma'am, the paramedics are on their way, I need a yes or no answer, is she breathing?

A: No!

Q: Can you feel again for a pulse?

A: He just did, there's nothing.

Q: Who did?

A: Anthony, he's the landlord. He came in when he heard me.

Mr. Fuchs, NYPD Dispatcher

Q: Are you the only people in the room?

A: No, more people are by the door now. Wait, I hear sirens, are they here? Is that the ambulance?

Mr. Gonzalez, NYFD Dispatcher

Q: Sarah, the police are there. I need you to go to the front door and let them in and lead them upstairs. Can you do that? Stay on the line.

A: OK. OK.

Q: Make sure someone clears a path so they can get through. OK?

A: (Inaudible.)

Q: Sarah, they're going to need to be able to get inside in a hurry, make sure people get out of the way.

A: OK. OK. Over here! Please hurry, she's up here! Get out of the way!

Unknown Officer
Q: OK. (Inaudible.)
A: Where's the ambulance?
Q: The ambulance is on its way.
A: (Unintelligible.)
END OF CALL.

I sat back, my heart pounding. Then I reached out and closed the file; I felt dirty, like I'd just done something unseemly.

Anthony. At the peak of the night's party, drawn by the sound of screams, Anthony had appeared. Calhoun's sketchy landlord, the creepy and cryptic Anthony Stiles. The memory of him mushroomed in front of me, so vivid I felt it like a force: Anthony Stiles, who half behaved like a slumlord and fucked a number of tenants and always had a thing for Edie. Jesus Christ. Anthony Stiles.

What had he been doing, skulking around Calhoun within earshot of SAKE? Why hadn't Sarah mentioned him? I picked back through the detectives' notes until I found him: He'd told them he'd been alone at home, in his fancy apartment just steps from Calhoun, when a tenant had called to alert him of the commotion. The notes didn't specify *which* tenant, because the NYPD wasn't big on competency that night, apparently.

I Googled his name and a headline came up, an old news article on a snarky city website: BUSHWICK LANDLORD FOUND DEAD IN HOUSE FIRE. I clicked through to the article and the photo on top made me squirm—eight years later, he was fatter but still smirking, still far too confident for his lot in life.

> *Anthony Stiles, the 51-year-old owner of Bushwick's Calhoun Lofts, was found dead after firefighters brought a massive blaze in a Bushwick apartment under control Tuesday morning, officials said. The victim was pulled from 250 Boerum Street, near Bushwick Avenue, after flames erupted around 2:35 a.m., NYPD and FDNY officials said. Stiles, who lived in the*

building, was found on the first floor and pronounced dead on the scene. Three firefighters were treated for minor injuries at the scene, an FDNY spokesman said. Investigators believe there were no other tenants in the two-story building. About 140 firefighters helped bring the blaze under control at 5:47 a.m., according to an FDNY spokesman. The unit's fire alarm failed to deploy and firefighters only responded after neighbors called in to report the blaze, officials said. Investigators are still trying to determine what caused the fire.

What the fuck? I returned to my search results for further updates but found none. In my job, this was the kind of detail I hated, the one that pushed the other, neater facts out of place, forking off into too many possible explanations. It could have simply been a fire, that kind of thing happens. It could've been arson but unrelated to Edie, of course. There were so many tenants in that building, all those possible enemies, and so many sleazeball slumlords winding up dead around the city for reasons that never became clear. Hasidic landlords with buildings in Williamsburg and tens of thousands of dollars of debt turning up broken and bloodied in car compactors, that kind of thing.

Or it could have something to do with Edie. He knew something, maybe, or someone knew something about his guilt and made sure he paid for it. God, dying in a fire. If you're already asleep, do you die of smoke inhalation, or are you awake and screaming, burned at the stake?

The fire had been eighteen months ago; we'd all moved on and missed the headline. But we'd sort of tacitly worshipped Anthony back in the day, this strong-jawed Peter Pan with a thick beard and the confidence a forty-three-year-old man should have but should never exercise around throngs of postgrads. He'd inherited the lofts in his thirties and would only periodically maintain them, showing up primarily for unscheduled appearances at parties and shows. He'd called Edie "Red," and she'd feigned disgust while complaining that he'd burst into the apartment right as she was getting out of the shower to let her know about a new building code, refusing to leave as she stood there dripping. Even the guys had begrudgingly thought Anthony was cool, with his sleeve tats and long hair and wild stories about touring with his band in the nineties.

He was around a lot, but I'd interacted with him directly only a handful of times. Once I'd been stumbling out the front door, hungover from the night before and rumpled from sleeping on SAKE's couch. I'd been wearing something ridiculous, my top and bottom both inches too short—a sexless walk of shame. Anthony had been standing out front, surveying from a few yards away an overflowing and likely vomit-splattered Dumpster.

"Hey, you got any cigarettes?" he asked.

I did, a pack I carried around like gum, although I rarely smoked, and only when drunk.

"I'll pay you for it," he offered, but I waved his dollar away.

He smiled at me, then leaned in for a light. I always felt self-conscious about this part, concerned I'd mess it up, but I didn't.

"Smoke with me?" he said, but my stomach was already convulsing with nausea from all the booze I'd consumed the night before.

"I promise I'll find a way to make it up to you," he said, smirking again, and for a moment I felt special, even though he promptly forgot me.

God, how could we not have seen that he was the biggest, creepiest loser in the world?

Not that he deserved to die. Probably.

My phone rang and my heart skidded up my arms and out my fingers. I stared at Alex's name for a moment before answering, briefly blanking on why I'd decided to call him.

"Lindsay! What's going on, are you okay?" He still had a rich voice, low and resonant.

Suddenly I clammed up, and the enormity of what I needed to ask rushed in: Why did you hate Edie? What really went down between you two—when you were together, as you split, and then afterward, while you continued breathing the same beer-smelling Calhoun air? But it was my turn to speak, so I began forming words, the way you make up lyrics to sing along to a song you only sort of know.

"Sorry if I worried you," I heard myself say. "I know this is out of the blue. I've been reading through my journals from back in, you know, our party era." A lie: I hadn't kept a diary during those years, instead abandoning journaling sometime in early college. It was something I always vaguely regretted but felt too old to change, like being unable to play the guitar or sail or understand football. "We had *so* much fun. Like, so much fun I don't understand how we functioned on a daily basis. Do you remember that?"

He chuckled but still sounded bewildered. "Of course! That whole era was crazy."

I opened a silence and he filled it. "Yeah, I've been thinking about that, too. We were poor as shit and living in that shithole and had no idea whatsoever."

"Right? We were basically living in squalor. Which got me thinking about that horrible landlord you guys had, remember Anthony Stiles?"

Another beat, too long. "Yeah, that guy sucked."

"I did a search for him the other day," I went on. "After he came up in my journal, like, whatever happened to him, right? Turns out he died in a fire over a year ago. Isn't that insane?"

"Whoa. Just like a random house fire?"

"Yeah, they never figured out the cause, but it was in the middle of the night. And I looked back even further and it turns out he was convicted of statutory rape a few years before that, which is especially terrifying. Because wasn't he, like, sniffing around at parties and stuff all the time?" The rape charge was a lie, but Alex wouldn't think to investigate it.

He kept his voice even. "I think so. Although I feel like he was dating someone in the building those last few months we were there. Right?"

"I have no idea." Had that person called Anthony the night of Edie's death? It was like a mosquito bite, south of painful: a reminder that *they'd* remained the kings of Calhoun just as I was written out of the narrative. With finality, right as I prepared to tell them all off in a glorious, Oscar-worthy monologue. God, the hubris. "Do you remember who?"

"Someone I thought you girls knew. I dunno. You'd know better than me if you were just rereading your diary." He considered. "What, you think the rape charges are related to the fire?"

"Oh!" I said it like my teeny lady-brain couldn't possibly have drawn such a connection. "I didn't even think of that, do you think it could be?"

He grunted. "I don't know. Maybe somebody didn't like him for being a rapist. You shouldn't rape people."

"I agree. One should not."

He let out a humorless *ha*.

"I was reading an entry about this warehouse party we all went to," I tried, "like out on Knickerbocker or something. Remember those huge ragers that Kevin's friends used to throw? Apparently one was carnival-themed and there were naked trapeze artists and shit. I was so scandalized."

He laughed again. "That actually rings a bell," he said. "Wasn't that the party when Kevin spent the entire night trying to pull this dude from another band and then at the last minute the guy left with the douchebag in the marching-band cap who planned the whole party?"

"Ha, oh my god! It was like a drum-major cap! With the feather plume?" Thank god I'd reviewed those emails.

"And Kevin was sooo wasted and he kept going, 'But I'm the drum major! I'm the major . . . of the drums!'" Alex said, laughing hard.

"And drumming on things! As we dragged him out of there!"

"That's it! That's it!" Alex said. He came down again, sighed. "God, that kid was funny."

"Do you ever hear from him anymore?" For some reason, I

didn't feel like mentioning that I'd called Kevin a few nights earlier.

He made a noncommittal noise. "Jaclyn still sends him a Christmas card. I always figured he'd pass through New York at some point and look me up, but it's been a long time now."

"That makes sense," I uttered when the silence between us ballooned. "Oh, so guess who I had dinner with last week."

"Sarah?"

"How'd you know?"

"We don't have *that* many more people in common."

"Oh, I thought maybe you saw she posted about it or something."

"No, but I think I saw she moved back to the city, right?"

"That's right, for her husband's job."

"How is she?"

"Really good! It was nice to see her."

He didn't ask more and I could feel it, how he wanted to wrap things up, the same way the girlfriend widens her eyes and pats at her partner's shoulder when she's ready for him to stop talking to you. Why hadn't Sarah been terrified of Alex? How could she run around claiming—to everyone, *to Alex*—that Edie had been murdered, when the deceased's own arrogant, hot, seemingly-adult-but-actually-twenty-four ex-boyfriend had just declared that he wanted to slit her throat?

I want that bitch out of my apartment! His voice had sounded younger then, warbly and immature. Did he remember saying that? Did he know that others had heard it?

I cleared my throat and found my fact-checker voice. "Oh, there's something I wanted to ask you. Have you—actually, is it okay if I ask you something about Edie? I've just been thinking about her a lot, with seeing Sarah and the anniversary coming up, but we totally don't have to talk about it if you don't want to." Another trick I'd picked up from my editor friends: Make the interviewee feel like not answering your question makes him the biggest dick in the world. It worked; Alex murmured me on. "Did you guys ever talk about either one of you moving out when you broke up? I was reading some stuff about . . . that period and how she and Sarah were over at my place a lot, kind of awkward in that Calhoun apartment . . ."

"Not really. We were broke and moving's so expensive. And we had our own rooms, at least."

"And she didn't think to go stay with her parents or anything."

"Well, no. But that doesn't surprise me."

"What do you mean?"

"I just . . . I didn't like them."

"How come?"

"It's a long story," he said.

"I have time."

"See, I kinda don't." It was so unexpectedly rude, I clutched a hand to my chest.

A new idea. "So I take it you don't talk to them at all? I was just thinking, I came across some really great photos that I thought maybe they would—"

"I don't talk to her mom anymore."

"What about her dad?"

"Lindsay, you know her dad is—did you not hear this? Her dad died."

"Oh my god. From what?"

"Suicide. A few years after . . . afterward."

"Oh my god," I repeated.

"Yeah, I mean, they'd lost their daughter and their home and apparently he still hadn't been able to find a new job . . . and presumably he had a predisposition to mental illness or whatever. So sad."

"That's terrible."

"I know. Pretty shocking when it always seemed like her mom was the unstable one."

This rang a distant bell. "Remind me, she used to show up at Calhoun sometimes, right?"

"Yeah, she was . . . odd. Clinging to her youth, a little obsessed with her daughter. I remember she used to come crying to Edie whenever she was having, like, marital problems, which I thought was really weird."

"Yikes. Do you know what happened to her?"

"She's still kicking around Manhattan, as far as I know. She's a psychiatrist, so maybe she finally figured her own shit out." He swallowed. "We obviously didn't keep in touch, but I used to look her up every once in a while. She got remarried at one point."

"Well, that's good. Jeez." So I should probably stop thinking of her as Mrs. Iredale, like a little kid.

"Yeah. Whoa. Way to bring the mood down."

"Right, sorry." An opening, a bleak one, but I took it. "Well, since we're already on the subject of depressing things, Sarah mentioned something I . . . I hadn't known about Edie back then. That maybe didn't make her look great, but I wanted to ask you about it." A lie, but Sarah *could* have been the one to tell me about the miscarriage, right?

"Look, I really don't want to sit here and talk shit about Edie. Okay? She apologized way back before all—"

"No, of course not, neither do I. I'm sorry, I . . ." My ears caught up with me. She apologized? "Wait, you knew?"

"That she was cheating on me? That's why we broke up." A beat. "Wait, what were you talking about?"

Everything was alert, my eyes, ears, hands. The fact slid into a waiting slot: one motive, humming away. And if she'd been cheating on him that summer . . . whose baby had she lost?

Now I definitely couldn't mention the miscarriage. I rifled around for a red herring. "I was just going to ask about the drugs," I said. "Sarah told me that the autopsy showed that Edie had Molly in her system, and I don't remember her ever using anything. So I wanted to ask about that."

"Oh. Well, shit. Now I feel like an asshole."

"No, it's okay," I said. "That's totally not shocking or outside the realm of possibility for me. I knew Edie was sort of . . . boy crazy."

"Look, we don't need to get into this."

I spotted a new tactic. "You know how Edie and I were fighting a lot that summer? Understanding what went down could help me make sense of that. Make peace with it, even."

"What, with her cheating? Why would that matter at all? You don't even know the guy."

Was it Greg, maybe, Edie's cool architect ex-boyfriend? How could it be someone I didn't know, someone none of us knew about?

I let a few seconds drip past, then added a tremor to my voice. "I just want to understand what happened," I half whispered, "for closure." It sounded like something from a movie. When had my life knotted into a telenovela? Could I please go back to last Wednesday, when I went to Pilates and then binge-watched canceled television, cranking up the sound so that I could hear it over the air conditioner?

He heaved a big, manly sigh. "She put a stop to it after a few times," he said, "after I found out. But it was . . . terrible."

"How did you find out?" I prodded.

"Does it matter?"

"I don't know."

"It doesn't." He let out a bitter little laugh, and I heard a *plunk,* like he was doing something else now. I sat with that, flipping through everyone I could think of. That building was so big, floor after floor of people tucked into plywood rooms like tchotchkes in a shadow box.

"Also, I didn't know," he said, when the quiet grew too large. "About the drugs. I didn't think she ever used anything, either."

"Huh."

Again, the silence fizzed.

"Maybe that helps explain it," he said. "Why she would kill herself. Because she was on something."

"Fucked up," I managed. Chemically, metaphorically, her, this. I didn't even know how I meant it. Me.

Alex said he'd better "let me go" and mechanically we exchanged pleasantries. Then he hung up and I pictured us both seated in our apartments, peering miserably into the past.

Chapter 7

I looked up at the kitchen window, which faced a brick wall, while the world shifted to make room for this revelation. How had Edie had a secret affair without any of us noticing? I saw her at least a few times a week; the other three *lived* with her, for Christ's sake. Then again, she'd been distant as soon as that June, hanging out with the crew less, wandering off on her own more. God, how little I'd known her. I flashed back suddenly to myself in my apartment the night after my big fight with Edie, crying to my kind but distant roommate who'd had no idea what to say, bleating between hiccups that it wasn't just the things Edie had screamed at me, it was *me,* my own judgment, shaken to its core. I couldn't believe I'd trusted her; I'd befriended her with these scales fitted firmly over my eyes.

I poured some seltzer into a juice glass and drank it down. The movements made me feel purposeful: Adult Woman Recaps Bottle and Places It Back in the Fridge. Then I called Tessa and she invited me over, sending a car to pick me up. I called Damien on the way and begged him to walk the few blocks from his place to hers, and he reached her front door just as I was getting out of the car.

In Tessa's chic, white living room, I stroked Marlon's soft back and told them everything I'd learned. Damien sipped the rosé he'd brought over. From a leather chair, Tessa listened, making notes on a notepad and nodding, a neat row of her cool geometric letters. Something about her manual note-taking soothed me. So anachronistic, a librarian still in love with physical things, card catalogs and musty books and those checkout slips glued inside the cover, stamped with date after date after date.

"Alex is looking insanely sketchy, right?" I concluded. "Between this and that crazy shit he said out of nowhere on the tape."

"I still haven't watched it," Damien announced, and Tessa rolled her eyes and brought him up to speed.

"He's the hot one, right?" he added, after taking it all in.

I sighed. "Yes, Damien. And I thought Edie was obsessed with him. So I'm pretty shocked."

"Seems suspect that he never told anyone, the police or anything," Tessa said. "Not to mention the fact that he told the cops you came to the concert with him. He and Sarah can't *both* be right."

I nodded. "It's weird, right? I need to figure out exactly how that went down. It wasn't gonna happen on the phone." I rubbed at the spot between my brows. The third eye. "I wonder if I can get him to meet up in person."

"Good idea. In a public place, obviously." Tessa tapped the pen cap against her lips. "I mean, whoever did this is probably not going to be very helpful."

"I know." *If* somebody else did this, if this wasn't me running on a hamster wheel until I concluded it was indeed a regular old suicide, just like I'd always believed.

"Whomever she was sleeping with sounds pretty suspect, too," she added. "Alex said it ended when he found out? Maybe someone didn't like that."

"Maybe. I wish he would've told me who it was."

"Yeah." She doodled on her page, a slow spiral.

"You know, I'm impressed with how much ass Edie was getting," Damien said. It was a playful blow dart, and we all laughed. Marlon stirred, disturbed by my shaking torso.

"Right?" I said. "She conquers her building crush and then almost immediately starts sleeping with someone else on the side."

"Didn't you say you used to have a building crush, too?" Tessa asked.

I sighed. "No, the guy I was kind of obsessed with didn't live in Calhoun. And it only culminated in hooking up once but still took over my brain for, like, a year." The hurt had felt so senseless and embarrassing. *This wasn't a thing,* I'd reminded myself over and over. It was like turning around after bowling a gutter ball, hoping to share an exaggerated shrug, only to discover that none of your friends were watching anyway.

"Ooh, what happened?" Damien said. He narrowed his eyes. "Was the sex bad?"

"I mean, yeah, but it wasn't that. Oh, god. His name was *Lloyd,* of all things." Confessing felt like a comfort, an abrupt hook from the horrifying thought of Alex hurting Edie. "I met him on a totally random night in the winter and then built him up in my mind as this Adonis for a few months. Then one night we were at the same party and ended up hooking up. Cue months of me pining over him as he didn't return my texts, and then cue me waking up on Edie's couch one morning and her saying, 'Umm . . . you gave Lloyd a black eye.'" I was blushing, I could feel it, even all these years later. "Apparently I wandered into a party where Lloyd was, presumably made a fool of myself hanging all over him as he, like, casually tried to get rid of me, and then—just as Edie found me, lucky-slash-unlucky me—I guess I tried to playfully hit him with a pillow and somehow my elbow clocked him in the eye."

A new thought, opening like an umbrella: *Had* it gone down that way? I'd seen his black eye later, as I refreshed his Facebook profile obsessively. He and I hadn't spoken again, and I'd avoided the topic with Edie. Maybe she'd lied for my benefit. Maybe I'd confronted him, screamed in his face, thrown an object or an elbow or a punch.

"Serves him right," Damien announced.

The front door jangled and Will walked in, clearly surprised to see Damien and me. He looked exhausted, and I promised, without prompting, that we'd be leaving soon.

"No, no, you're always welcome here. I'm going straight to the gym, anyway." He headed into the hallway.

"Lindsay, you're welcome to stay in the guest room if you don't feel like schlepping," Tessa said once he'd left. "Use it now, before we turn it into a nursery."

"I'm not invited?" Damien teased.

"Oh, please, you live five minutes away," she replied.

I laughed. "Nah, I'll leave you guys alone. Oh, but one other thing: I looked up Calhoun's landlord," I said. "Major creeper who had a weird crush on Edie."

Damien lifted his pointer finger. "Pedophilic slumlord? I know the type."

"Exactly. Apparently he died in a fire the winter before last."

"Whoa. Like, arson?" Tessa asked.

"Unclear."

Damien leaned forward. "Maybe he killed Edie and then God struck him down for it! That would explain everything."

Tessa played along. "You're right! Case closed. Let's go celebrate."

We raised our water glasses, and Damien downed his rosé.

"Oh, I almost forgot, I have something for you," Damien said to Tessa. He rushed off to the foyer and I fought down a flicker of hurt, that Damien was already done with this topic. A moment later, he returned with a little bag from the neighborhood's most bourgeois baby shop.

Tessa reached inside and pulled out a gray onesie with the words FUCKING ADORABLE splashed across the front.

"I love it!" She rose to kiss his cheek. "Although I'm not sure how Will is gonna feel about our kid having *fucking* on his or her chest."

"Well, the store also had adorable pink and blue things, but until you do a highly Instagrammed gender reveal, I—"

"Sex!" I corrected.

Damien turned to me. "What?"

"It's a biological sex reveal—we won't know the gender until they're old enough to have a gender identity."

He lifted his palms. "Linds, you can't be yelling 'Sex!' while

I'm speaking and expect me to keep my train of thought. On that note, I gotta go—I have a date tonight. Lindsay, keep us posted on the murderous hottie, 'kay?"

He and Will left at the same time, an odd couple with Will's skinny legs popping out of his gym shorts and Damien's muscled body encased in well-tailored resort wear. Tessa set her feet on the coffee table and leaned back.

"You doing okay, Linds?"

"I don't know. I think so. I just . . . that video. Christ. I'd give anything to just go back in time and be a fly on the wall, see what happened next. Fuck, I'd give anything to make the *camera* keep recording. Literally."

"We'll figure it out. It'll be okay."

I nodded. "I hate that she was cheating on Alex," I blurted out.

Tessa raised her eyebrows, waiting.

"I mean, I guess it makes me mad. That she was doing that. And then I'm mad at myself for judging her because, c'mon, she's dead." Something that's always bothered me about cheating: It seems so greedy. I would gladly take just one partner. You need *two*?

Tessa nodded. "I mean, cheating sucks, but it happens. Either way, you're not wrong for feeling your feelings."

"Have you ever been cheated on?" I asked.

She kind of laugh-sighed. "Okay, I'm going to tell you something," she said. "Years ago, I became totally convinced that Will was cheating on me. We had kind of a rough first year of being married, and then he was traveling all the time for work and coming home late, and I just thought, 'Dammit, I'm one of those women. I'm the idiot wife.'"

I could barely hide my shock. Sweet, boring, definitely-not-as-hot-as-her Will? "Why didn't you tell me?"

"I didn't tell anyone."

"So what'd you do?"

"Oh god, this is embarrassing. I installed a keystroke logger on his computer."

"A what?"

"A keystroke logger. You can get it at, like, Office Depot. It records everything someone types so you can see it remotely."

I frowned. "Why not just hack into his computer? Or, like, look at it when he wasn't around?"

She shook her head. "You can clear your search history. You can delete emails and texts. This shows you everything they've ever *typed*." She bowed her head. "I can't even look at you. I know, it's so bad."

"No, I get it. You just wanted to know. So what'd you find?"

"That he'd been seeing a therapist. Because he loved me and was afraid he was gonna fuck things up. I felt like such a crazy person."

"Oh my god. Well, I'm relieved about that ending. And you're not a crazy person. Love makes people crazy."

"*Fear* makes people crazy," she added, or maybe countered.

I nodded slowly, unsure of what else to say. I'd always thought their relationship was close to perfect, the Platonic ideal. Knowing about this rocky patch, even all those years ago, made me feel sad for Tessa, but also . . . what was that soft fizz? Relief?

"Sorry, I'm not helping," she burst in. "I'm just saying shit. But listen, it's gonna be okay."

I thought for a moment. "Can you do me a favor and look into the landlord for me?" I asked. "Anthony Stiles. I did a cursory search and found the fire, but maybe—"

"I'm on it." She nodded emphatically, then finished a scribble in her notepad with a dramatic dot. *Stiles*, cross the *t*, dot the *i*. Stick a needle in my eye.

"But, Tessa, I know you've got a lot going on with the baby and work and everything else. So please don't feel like you need to—"

"You'd do the same for me," she interrupted.

"Can I at least take you out to dinner this weekend to say thank you?" I pressed my palms together. "Or we can order in some Thai and watch movies that'll make you really excited about motherhood. Like *Rosemary's Baby*!"

She giggled. "I wish, but Will and I are going up to the house on Friday. The city smells are getting to me."

"Rain check, then," I told her, careful not to let my face fall. The house in Saugerties. Coincidentally, they'd closed on it the same weekend when, a few years back, a pipe had burst under my kitchen sink. For weeks, I had to sleep in hotels as contractors ripped at the cabinets and floor. Tessa had called to check in from their new pinewood cabin, and the heavy envy I'd felt had been almost too much to bear: Here I was stuck with no partner, no dream job, and no apartment, and Tessa was rounding the bases with home number two. I'd cried often that month, ugly sobs that took me by surprise as I blow-dried my hair or got ready for bed.

In the morning, I rode the subway clutching a greasy pole and thinking about Alex. A suspect so obvious, it was laughable: the cuckolded ex-boyfriend, spurned and *right there* that evening. I was standing in the break room, making a cup of coffee, when a circuit connected—a cuckolded ex-boyfriend, recently spurned: We had another one of those in the cast. Why didn't anyone suspect him?

I'd found Greg's architecture firm back when I'd first broke into my old email—no contact info, just a physical location and a generic info@ email address. The address was in DUMBO, a cobblestoned neighborhood in Brooklyn, just one subway stop from my office. I blocked out a fake lunch on my work calendar. *Greg, I'm coming for you.*

At noon, I emerged at High Street and wandered the wrong way for a while, confused by the area's angled streets and sudden dead ends from the two bridges plunked there. Eventually I found Greg's building, a block-long behemoth with bookstores on both ends. No doorman, so I rode the elevator to the fourth floor. No receptionist there, either, so I wandered the hallways, watching the numbers until I came upon suite 418.

It was one of those open offices, sunlit and dissected by four absurdly long tables, hip men clacking away at computers along them. Many were standing and the rest were rolling around on Aeron chairs. Ringing the whole space were beds of snake plants and zanzibars, thick and green and leaning gently toward the windows.

"Can I help you?"

The only person free from the long tables was a tall guy at a standing desk near the door. I realized with a little jolt that he was almost intimidatingly hot: thick black hair, big brown eyes, a sharp suit in contrast to everyone else's hoodies. I smiled and clacked over. "You look like you run the place."

He grinned. "I'm just an assistant," he said.

"So not yet. Got it." I leaned on the desk. Thank god I'd thought to apply lipstick on the subway. "And yet you're the only one with your own desk. Seems like there's nowhere to go but down."

He shrugged, looking pleased. "No one cares what I think about open offices. But yeah, I don't mind being on my own over here."

I giggled like he'd said something wickedly clever. "So I'm looking for someone I think works here," I said. "Greg Bentley?"

"He does!" he said. "But he's not in right now."

I felt the same complicated release I get whenever someone doesn't pick up the phone: relief and annoyance. "Oh, is he traveling?"

"He's on paternity leave. Another . . . four or five weeks at least."

"Well, that's exciting! Boy or girl?"

"A boy." Lucky kid. Life like a game set to one level easier.

"That's great. Wow."

"He's picking up his messages once a week," he said, doing something on his computer. "I can pass something along?"

"Oh, that's okay." There was a sudden joyous shout from a corner. I turned and saw that one of the frosted glass doors along the back wall was marked PLAY.

"Game room," the man explained. "They're probably playing cornhole."

I nodded. "Anyway, thanks for your help. I was just in the neighborhood and thought I'd stop by and say hi."

"Old friend?"

I smiled mysteriously. "Sort of."

"Ex-girlfriend?"

"Interesting guess!" I laughed. "But wrong again. He used to date my best friend."

"Oh. That had to be a while ago; he and his wife have been together for . . . I don't know, this is their fourth kid."

"It *was* a long time ago. Anyway, thanks for your help."

"Do you have kids?" He leaned to his side. The ease of an attractive white man who, obviously, gets to decide when the conversation's over.

"I don't. Do you?"

He chuckled. "Nope, no kids. Are you married?"

"You're sure full of questions."

He laughed, gave that winning smile. "I'm trying to figure out if I can ask you out."

My cheeks burned. "Oh, I thought you—oh. Well, sure. Let me give you my number." I looked around for a pen, then realized his fingers were aloft over his keyboard because he was not, like me, old and analog. I recited it, then added, ". . . and I'm Lindsay."

"Josh," he replied, reaching out to shake my hand.

A classic Hot Man Born in the Nineties name. I forced myself to maintain eye contact. "Well, I better get back to work," I said finally. "And no need to mention me to Greg, I'll catch him some other time when he's . . . back in action." Then I spit out a goodbye and shot back into the building's labyrinthine hallways.

No one at work had noticed my absence, of course. I returned to the architecture firm's website, telling myself it was to learn more about Greg but knowing it was to research Josh. The babe wasn't anywhere on the site, so I forced myself to at least reread Greg's bio. He was an accomplished man, one who'd worked on several impressive-sounding buildings around Manhattan before co-founding this technology-driven firm, one of the first to employ 3-D printing.

Next I combed through my old emails, looking for signs of Greg. I found remarkably little, although I did figure out how they'd met: a motherfucking missed connection on Craigslist, which, Jesus Christ. It was the kind of ridiculous thing that would happen only to Edie, whose life played out like a single-shot mumblecore: hip parties. Fashion school. New boyfriend, probably dovetailing with the ones before and after, obtained in a cool, unique way that also underscored how desirable she was. Then I felt a rush of nausea, aware that I was once again envying a dead girl.

Why had we called each other best friends? We were young, after the period when you could declare someone your bestie but still young enough to crave it, the way a twelve-year-old lusts after a place at the lunch table. She was my girl crush, and my adoration fed her.

But that's not it. She could be such a good friend, when she wasn't obsessed with her own problems or mad at you about something. I thought back to my twenty-third birthday, when we'd gone to see an Australian band at Glasslands, a wood-paneled venue with terrible bathrooms and reliably cute bartenders. I'd deemed the keyboardist hot, and as soon as the show ended, Edie had dragged me to the lip of the stage and introduced me as the birthday girl as he helped break down gear. He'd invited us into the greenroom and we'd spent the evening drinking with the Aussies; twice, she'd pulled me into the bathroom to make sure I liked this guy, that I was still having a good time.

I'd missed her *so badly* in the weeks and months after her death, even though I'd been planning to split from her anyway, even though the departure was almost mine. Over and over, I'd think of something funny or ridiculous or sarcastic to share with Edie, and sometimes I'd have my phone out by the time I realized I couldn't text her. Nor could I contact any of the other Calhounies, off grieving in their building's rambling halls. Instead I'd worked hard to find new friends, ones to whom Edie meant nothing, and I'd watched with slight surprise as time rolled past.

That night I dreamed I was in Calhoun again, stumbling through the halls with something behind me, my legs clumsy and useless, bruises blooming on my shins and knees. The apartment numbers on the doors that lined the corridor kept changing, so that no matter which way I went, SAKE slipped farther and farther away, 3G, 4H, wrong wrong wrong. I turned around and suddenly knew, with certainty, it was Alex behind me, Alex coming for me. I started awake gasping for air, terrified, like I'd been a hairsbreadth away from dying.

I stared at the ceiling for a while, picking back through my phone call with Alex two nights earlier. Why hadn't Edie moved into her parents' apartment after the breakup, if only for a week or two? She had her own room there, and things with Alex must not have ended well if, two months later, he was standing on a rooftop, screaming "I want to slit her throat!" into the night.

Edie and I had bonded a bit by complaining about our insufferable parents, but I'd never met Mrs. Iredale. Everyone else had, which made me feel a little excluded; she'd helped Edie move in and the other roommates complained about her occasionally showing up at Calhoun, smelling of whiskey and banging on the door of 4G. She was like the kooky old woman in the crumbling house that the neighborhood kids call a witch, one-upping one another with mad tales. Who was this woman?

On the subway ride to work, I hatched a plan, a madcap scheme that shoved Alex further, further, further out of the frame. I'd talk to Edie's mother—figure out if she had any suspicions or details she'd kept hidden. From my desk, I used an app to hide my number and called her landline, a rare 212 area code on an island of untethered communications. She picked up and I asked if José was home (*Why José?* I thought, even as I said it), then apologized, hung up, and began gathering my things. I wasn't sure what I'd tell her at her front door, but I had a twenty-five-minute bus ride to figure it out.

As I rode north toward Morningside Heights—an odd neighborhood near Manhattan's knobby tip, one where old row houses unfold down both sides of the street—my brain kept sifting; mentally I stepped over the people I'd talked to like bodies scattered across the ground: Sarah, Tessa, Kevin, Damien, Alex. I peered out the window, where rain coated the street, and my mind wandered over to last year's horrific accident in the Bronx, the one where a bus collided with a big rig, veered into a pole, and had its top sliced off by a sign. Fourteen people dead after rolling around like popcorn inside. I imagined it for a moment, this bus suddenly airborne, screaming and limbs and the stiff punches of seats, windows, other bodies.

The bus was frigid and I wrapped my arms around me, feeling the staticky fluff of goose bumps—one of those silly leftovers from evolution, like the tailbone and appendix. But most of our adaptations are good ones. I remembered a story I'd fact-checked about a Japanese doctor who'd been arrested for surgically disconnecting young men's fear circuits, plucking apart their brain fibers like a threadbare tapestry. It was a for-service hire, a dimming of the amygdala in a half-dozen humans, suddenly preternaturally brave. But also stupid, self-endangering. Fear is a survival mechanism, as any half-witted high school biology student can tell you. Darwin knew that dead men don't reproduce.

But the impulse to rewire a brain, that I knew all too well. My own parents had worked hard at it, mucking around in my skull— chemically rather than surgically—from the time I was old enough to have a personality.

Middle school: me at my ugliest; Dad's eyes as he turned to me, a mixture of fury and fear. The oval of blood growing syrupy on the floor. I read once that seventh grade is exactly when your brain undergoes its biggest changes since infancy, overproducing brain cells and then killing off most of them. Letting them duke it out for survival. Which is ironic, really, since seventh grade is a bunch of confused preteens doing the same thing.

I dashed outside at my stop and stepped through the rain toward Mrs. Iredale's home. Her town house was orange brick and cute, with bay windows and navy trim and a small front yard in need of mowing. Next door some kids were playing in their own wet patch of lawn, stomping into puddles with their brows knitted in concentration. On the porch, my hand jumped out and rang the doorbell before I could stop to think about it.

No answer. Again, the relief/disappointment cocktail.

"What's your name?" It was one of the girls next door, her wet hair matted to her face.

"I'm Lindsay." I flashed them a smile. "What's your name?"

"Sophie." She picked a bathing suit wedgie unflinchingly. Kids can be so unflappable. "What are you doing here?"

"I wanted to talk to Mrs. Iredale. I was friends with her daughter."

She cocked her head. "Mrs. Iredale?"

Shit, was this the wrong house?

"Can I help you?" It was an adult voice, a knowing voice, coming up the path behind me.

"Mrs. Iredale, I'm Lindsay. Edie's friend. I'm—I'm sorry to bother you." I was struck, frozen. She was beautiful, with silver-streaked hair and Edie's freckles and a serious expression on an otherwise impish face.

"It's Ms.," she said. "Ms. Iredale."

"I'm sorry. That's right. I'm . . . I've been thinking about putting together a little commemorative video of Edie to share with her friends," I continued, cursing myself for wasting all that time on the bus *not* coming up with a better lie, "and I thought you might be interested in sharing some photos. And I have to tell you,

I tried to find your number or email address and just wasn't having any luck, but I saw your address online and was heading up to Riverdale this morning anyway, so . . ."

She peered at me. "You found my address but not my email?"

I shook my head, felt the rush of blood to my cheeks. "I'm sorry, that came out like a save-face kind of thing—to be honest, I had the idea when I was already on the bus here."

"The commemorative video? Or coming to see me?"

"Oh, coming to see you, I mean. I'm doing the video either way. I found a few videos of all of us on my old Flip cam and thought it would be nice to edit together something I could share on Vimeo, so . . ."

I thought she'd interrupt me, but she just stared. I hung my closed umbrella off of the porch and shook raindrops from it gravely. They floated in a cloud before falling.

"Do you want to come inside and dry off?" Mrs. Iredale finally said.

"That would be great, if you don't mind. My friend told me she's running late, too, but I can get out of your hair in just a minute."

She unlocked the door and held it open for me. She was almost a foot shorter than me and this felt wrong, oafish me wandering inside with a trail of wet footprints in my wake. I suddenly wondered why I hadn't brought her a gift, some chocolates, flowers bound and wrapped in cellophane.

"Tell me your name again. Lizzie?" She pulled out a towel and handed it to me. She moved suddenly, jerkily.

"Lindsay," I told her.

"Were you one of Edie's roommates?"

"No, but I was really close with all of them—Sarah and Kevin and Alex." I said their names deliberately as a drumbeat, watching for a reaction between each. I thought I saw one after Alex, a tiny pulse around her eyes, but I couldn't be sure.

"So you were a later friend. I thought for a second you were one of her earlier roommates. In Calhoun Lofts, right?"

"Right. Calhoun." I wasn't keeping up, wasn't saying the right things.

"I see." She watched me scuff my shoes across the welcome mat, and, feeling childish, I bent and started to unlace them.

"Lindsay," she repeated. "I do remember you. Edie liked you."

Liked to control me, maybe. "Well, you know how wonderful she was. Thanks for letting me step inside for a second." I lined my shoes up by the door. "I've been thinking about her a ton, and honestly, just seeing your face—seeing the resemblance, it helps. I know that sounds crazy." I looked down at my hands. Suddenly I was twenty-three and obsequious to grown-ups again.

When I looked up, Mrs. Iredale was giving a tired but real smile. "Thanks for saying that."

"She was just magnetic. From the very first time I met her, I remember being captivated by her. So much wit and sparkle and life."

Mrs. Iredale was one of those people who stares blankly as you speak, waiting until the end to react. It creeped me out and tripped up my speech—like when you're on the phone and hear your voice echoing back.

"How did you know her again?" she asked.

"I met her back in . . . let's see, 2008. Through Sarah, actually, whom I knew from working in magazines."

She looked around. "Would you like to sit down? I think I left the coffee on."

"Sure." I followed her into the kitchen. "So as I was saying, Sarah and I met randomly and, you know, quickly became friends." She held up a carton of half-and-half and I nodded. Then she frowned like I'd made the wrong choice. "So Sarah had me over to their apartment one night. That was back when they lived with those other girls."

"I liked them," she interrupted, leading me into the living room. "We had them over for dinner a few times."

So she'd clearly liked the old roommates better than the SAKE ones. Had she not approved of Edie moving in with Alex so quickly?

"Well, Edie and I just really hit it off. And we became friends and hung out all the time at my apartment near Calhoun or, you know, at their place. It was . . . it was such a good era, having that really close-knit little group of friends."

Mrs. Iredale perched on a love seat and blinked at me, both hands wrapped around her mug. Her tempo unnerved me, the random things she would and wouldn't respond to.

"Robert and I didn't really get a chance to know that group," she said finally.

"Well, we all became friends right after we graduated from college," I said. "The rest of us had just moved to New York. Maybe Edie just wanted that . . . that sort of faux independence you think you've got when you're in your twenties. I remember feeling so grown up."

Mrs. Iredale cocked her head. "Looking back on it, I feel bad for you guys," she said unexpectedly. "I mean, not you in particular. Your generation. Promised everything and then, you know. Toppling off a cliff."

"You mean . . . ?"

"The recession. Obviously it hit those of us with mortgages and retirement accounts harder. But . . . Edie graduated in May 2008, poor thing." She made a gesture, her fingers winging upward, and I felt the hairs rise on my arms: exactly the same motion Edie made. I hadn't seen it in ten years.

"You know, I think that's the reason a lot of people back then—my age—would take on this really affected air, just this blanket disapproval of everything," I said. "Like 'Oh, this band sucks, and that book sucks, and mainstream society is lame, and capitalism is a joke.' If you refuse to align yourself with anything, you don't give anything any power."

"Interesting." From her terrible posture, she lowered her head and took a sip of coffee. "Edie was like you. Always quick to cobble together a narrative and fit everything into the bigger picture. When she was small, she'd make little books that told the story of her day before." She laughed, a rich, musical sound. "Eventually they just kept showing her making her book about the day before. They got pretty boring. But she loved it, her little record-keeping. And then the second she could write, she was filling up diaries as fast as we could buy them."

"That's so cute!" I smiled at the thought: hundreds of scarlet-haired Edies coloring in yesterday's coloring session, an endless hall of mirrors. "What was she like as a kid?"

"She was the shyest thing when she was little." She slid her palm across the armrest, back and forth. "Then she turned ten or so and really came out of her shell."

"Center of attention," I said before I could stop myself.

She looked at me. "Yes, that's true."

"Did she develop . . . was she depressed when she was younger?" She blinked at me, and I hastily added: "I know you're a psychiatrist, so I thought maybe—"

"We didn't know," she interrupted. "We should've been watching for it since it was in her family history, but we didn't know until after."

"Us neither." I shifted in my seat. "You were pretty close with her, right? I know you came by Calhoun sometimes to see her."

She stared hard at me, expressionless. "She was my daughter. I liked seeing her."

I swallowed. "Well, did you talk to her about what was going on at Calhoun? Like, with Alex and everything?"

She picked up her mug and drank deeply, then set it down with a clink. "Lindsay, I know what you're doing here."

A cold spring of shock. I stared at her, my cup frozen in front of my throat.

"I'm not stupid," she continued. "You're not the first conspiracy theorist. But Edie killed herself. It wasn't a freak accident. There wasn't any foul play. Suicide."

I brought the mug back down to my lap but couldn't speak.

"She was depressed," Mrs. Iredale continued, "and she hid it very well. But she was under a tremendous amount of pressure, and then she'd experimented for the first time with ecstasy, which is extremely problematic for someone with her delicate brain chemistry. I wish there hadn't been a gun at her disposal, but if it hadn't been that, it would have been another way. I saw her just hours before it happened. She didn't seem well."

It hung in the air for a moment. "Wait, what? You saw her?"

She shrugged. Then I caught it, a weird tic near her eye. "I came by to see her that night. Are you here to find out what we talked about, like that's the missing piece?"

I didn't answer. Everything was moving too fast. A coffee drip slid down the side of the mug and coated my fingers.

"I was there to deliver more bad news: that we were losing our home and could no longer help her out with her tuition. Not exactly the best revelations when you're, as it turns out, fighting with your friends and going through a breakup and recovering from a medical emergency."

My insides lurched. She knew—of course she knew about the baby, of course the autopsy report hit her eyeballs first—but it jarred me, how she tossed these things off like a grocery list.

So Mrs. Iredale had been in Calhoun the very night of Edie's death. Now busily trying to convince me it was nothing but a suicide.

Something clicked. "Wait, other conspiracy theorists?"

She sighed and the same eye flicked again. "It's been ten years, Lindsay. I think you should go." There was a calm confidence in her syntax, as if it made perfect sense. As if I'd spent a decade on the armchair in Edie's mother's living room.

Sarah, right? She had to mean Sarah. I should talk to Sarah.

"I'm sorry, Ms. Iredale. To have taken up your time. I know there's nothing I can say to make you believe me, but for what it's worth, I didn't come with a . . . conspiracy theory." I wiped the drip on the side of the mug. "Guess I just miss her."

She shook her head. "You can't know," she said. "You don't

know what it's like. I think about her every single day. And how I should've tried harder to persuade her to come back home with me, to talk some more." She sighed and rubbed her temple. "I'll never forgive that kid for convincing her to go back inside."

My stomach did something gymnastic. This was too much all at once. The rain throbbed against the window and she glanced at it; *when it rains, it pours,* my neurons spit out.

"Who convinced her to go back into Calhoun?"

"Some boy she was seeing. He was texting her the whole time we were talking, and she must have told him where we were because eventually he showed up to escort her back inside." She looked out the window again. "He introduced himself, seemed pretty polite. But maybe if we'd had more time to talk . . ."

Not Alex, whom she'd met before. "Do you remember his name?"

"Oh, what was it . . . Roy, I think. He told the cops the same thing as me—that she seemed really upset and shaken by our conversation." She whipped her head over to look at me. "And no, he's not a suspect. He was photographing a concert that night, and he headed straight into Manhattan for it. There were witnesses."

Who the fuck was Roy?

"Wait, not Roy," she announced suddenly, almost proudly. "His name was Lloyd."

Chapter 8

For a moment my mouth gaped open like a fish's. Edie was seeing Lloyd? *My* Lloyd, the object of my obsession? Did people know?

"Are you sure they were dating?" This was just a month or two after Edie and Alex had split. The next revelation blared: Maybe Edie had been cheating on Alex with Lloyd earlier that year, too. Perhaps he was the other man Alex wouldn't name.

She narrowed her eyes at me. "Well, it sure seemed like it."

And then the question boomeranged back into me. *Did I know?* Had I seen something that summer? Had my intuition finished a puzzle and sat proudly back until I was drunk and uninhibited and suddenly able to catch up? Was there a split, forgotten second when I *knew* on the night of August 21?

"She was sick," Mrs. Iredale announced, "and she was upset. Edie was someone who turned to relationships for—for comfort, so it doesn't surprise me she was seeing someone new. He said it was casual. Afterward, I mean."

Alex told me Edie had ended the affair "after a few times"; if my hunch was correct, she'd picked it up again after they'd broken up. Or maybe she'd never quit.

"Of course. I'm sorry."

Mrs. Iredale stood, crossed as far as the fireplace, and stopped. "Lindsay, there aren't . . . things don't always fit together the way you want them to." I thought of her late husband, of the moment she learned her daughter was dead; I stared at the dark circle of coffee in the bottom of my cup and nodded. "Whatever you're trying to go back over and see how it looks if you piece it together a different way—it won't change anything. It just is what it is." She turned and walked into the kitchen.

I stood to follow her and noticed a few framed pictures propped up on the mantel—one of Mrs. Iredale and a nerdy older guy, presumably her second husband, on vacation somewhere warm. Another of Mrs. Iredale and her late husband—god, he looked just like Edie, gangly and good-looking—waving under bright layers on a ski vacation. And one of Edie, teenage and lovely, sitting under a tree and reading obliviously while the wind tangled her halo of hair. I gazed at it, half expecting her to look up at me and wave. *Edie*, I whispered silently. *Did you know you'd grow up to be kind of a bitch?*

In the kitchen, I handed my mug to Mrs. Iredale and watched her load it into the dishwasher. "I get the feeling you didn't know about Lloyd, so I'm sorry if that was . . . by design on Edie's part or something," she said. An observant woman, like Edie. She closed the dishwasher and looked out the window, toward a bird feeder. "No sign of the sun coming out. I'll get your umbrella."

The umbrella promptly snapped inside out, and I arrived at the bus stop soaked and bedraggled, damp hair spooling across my forehead and neck. I climbed into the bus's brightness and caught my reflection in the window. The bags under my eyes had ballooned, the lines from my nose to my mouth deeply etched. Had that been a help or a disaster? I felt the questions growing and multiplying, two for every one answered, spreading like cancer cells.

On the one hand, Mrs. Iredale had a point, one mark in the suicide column: The stew of mental illness, drugs, and a pounding stream of bad news did point to the conclusion that she and the cops had come to. On the other hand, why the fuck had Edie been seeing Lloyd? If he came out and collected her, and he didn't live in Calhoun, then certainly they must've clambered up to her room together . . .

We wheezed to a stop at a red light, and I turned over another odd detail: What had Mrs. Iredale been doing there just hours before the potential crime? "You can't know," she'd said. A slip, a tell that she was holding something back?

Her reason for rushing to Calhoun felt flimsy, too. Late on a Friday night, why bolt all the way to Bushwick to tell Edie something that could wait until morning? The condo would be foreclosed; they'd no longer be covering her grad-school tuition. Upsetting, but not earth-shaking—more Edie's parents' problems than her own.

I played it out, the outlandish scenario: Could Mrs. Iredale have waited in SAKE with a gun, a fake suicide note already typed out on Edie's computer? I couldn't picture the woman getting into the building without anyone noticing, although she did know the way; she'd slipped inside to knock on SAKE's door a few times before. I pictured her biding her time in the dirty hallway. Parties blaring in from every side, the boozy flotsam and jetsam of our hard-partying lifestyle littering the floor. Ridiculous.

It certainly didn't sound like Mrs. Iredale thought I had anything to do with it. *Edie liked you.* Well, she liked everything I wanted, too. And unlike me, she got it.

My phone buzzed against my hip, and it was Alex fucking Kotsonis, well of course. I made up my mind to let it go to voice mail and then answered it at the very last second.

"Hey, Alex!"

"Hi! It's . . . I was gonna say 'It's Alex.'"

"Yeah, your name came up." I glanced outside again: lightning julienning the western sky.

"Old habit, I guess." He laughed. "So look, I was thinking more about what you said the other night about Edie having drugs in her system, and I realized I kinda hung up before I even asked anything about that. Because that's super weird. We both know she didn't use anything. Right?"

"That's what I thought. But it's in the autopsy report. Hang on, let me look at it." I put him on speaker and pulled it up. " 'There was a high level of,' here goes, 'methylenedioxymethamphetamine in the blood.' That's Molly."

"Huh. I mean, everyone in the building was kinda into it, so it wouldn't have been hard to get. I just don't know where or when she would've taken it."

"Yeah, it's strange, right?" I said. "And that drug makes you happy. You don't kill yourself on it."

"If anything, people die because they jump off balconies and stuff. Makes you feel like Superman. Invincible."

Maybe it'd turned Edie into even more of a braggart, a mean girl. Perhaps it made her say just the wrong thing to the exact wrong person who happened to be with her at that moment. Take me, for example: a little sniping on Edie's part, maybe a snotty proclamation about Lloyd or about our clique's true allegiance or about any one of my three thousand weak spots, could've set me off. Every clue, it seemed, offered dozens of possible interpretations.

"What are you doing tonight?" I blurted out. "Let's get dinner," I went on, when he didn't say anything, "or just, like, grab a drink after work. It'll be fun! We're not too old to be spontaneous, right?"

He half laughed. "Maybe—I had a project I was going to finish up." I knew this was my shot, the universe plopping Alex in front of me like a cat dropping a very dazed mouse.

"Alex, I think the fact that neither of us has firm plans tonight is a sign from above." I kept my voice light. "It's shitty outside and God wants us to get together and eat, you know, caloric things."

" 'Caloric things.' You really paint a picture with words." I could hear it, the crack as he relented. "Can we meet near Grand Central so I can catch the train straight from there?"

I beat him to the restaurant and sat flicking through his photos on Facebook. He was still dreamy; I'd always had a vague crush on him, but he was Edie's and way out of my league. I'd felt lucky just to be friends with him, to sometimes be spotted in public in such handsome company. Most of the pictures were of him and his wife: on vacation, at a play, at a wedding.

He pushed open the door and moved like I remembered, solid and with an easy swagger. He perked up when he spotted me, and I stood from the dinky table to give him a hug. He smelled warm and autumnal, and for a moment, my only thought was that it was good to see him. Then I remembered everything I needed to ask him, the simmering spite toward Edie that had only come out when we were drunk and my Flip cam was rolling. For a moment I saw it like a scene from a horror movie: Edie in her undies turning around just in time to see Alex raise the gun. I gave my head a little shake and began exchanging pleasantries. *This must be what it's like to be a sociopath.*

"I'm so glad you could be convinced to come out tonight," I said. "It's been way too long. How's everything?"

"Yeah, this was definitely unexpected. I'm good."

We caught up politely: Alex was still working for the same company, still happily married, now looking to buy a home in Tarrytown. The waiter appeared and Alex began ordering a glass of wine, but I convinced him to make it a bottle. I've found it's not hard to hide the fact that I don't drink a single sip of my "half."

I flashed back to us as buddies, hanging out on a cold winter night, drinking cocoa with schnapps and playing Before and After, a stupid word game we made up that involved easing band names into unrelated portmanteaus. Radioheadphones. Ace of Base-jumping. Once he and I had almost died of laughter over increasingly elaborate plans to open Destiny's Child's Pose, a yoga studio that played early-naughts R&B.

"Well, I'm at *Sir* magazine," I volunteered.

"It's been a while now, right?"

"Five years!" I nodded, eyebrows high. "They just switched us to a new platform that makes more interviews and photos and original documents and stuff available to the reader, so it's like figuring out the whole fact-checking ethos anew."

"That's great. That's really great." Now he did the deliberate head bob. "Always good when it's dynamic."

The wine appeared and Alex had to do the dog and pony show, swirling, sniffing, tasting, approving.

"You're in Cobble Hill?" he asked.

"Fort Greene, and yep, also going on five years now! It's a New York City miracle. I've got the nicest landlord, so I just haven't seen a reason to leave. He owns this woo-woo place called Healing Hands Reiki on the ground floor and lives right above it, so I'm his only tenant." Aggressive hairpin turn: "We've come a long way from Bushwick."

"Yeah, the lofts were pretty shitty, huh? Weird to think about us living there."

"*I* didn't. I knew better."

He chewed his bread, smiling. "That's right. But we were only there, what? A little less than two years. We had some good times in that loft."

"Hell, yeah, we did."

"On track to be the best years of my life, weirdly. I still can't believe—" His eyes popped up and the waiter leaned in to set down our food. Goddamn waiters and their impeccably bad timing. Alex picked up his fork and got quiet again.

How had Kevin put it, back when this all began? "Figure out what really went on that night." Alex had answers, but getting them was going to take more work than I thought.

"Do you still play guitar at all?" I asked between bites.

He shrugged. "Not really. I used to play when I got home from work sometimes, but lately I've just been too tired."

"You used to be really good," I said lamely.

"A couple guys at work and I keep talking about starting a band together. Jam out like a bunch of old losers. Hard to actually make it happen, though."

I poured him more wine and then looked back down at my noodles.

"Fleetwood Mac and Cheese," I said.

"Oh my god." He nodded his approval. "Well played, Bach. Okay. Um . . . Aimee Mann-agement funds."

"Oh my god, we're so *old*. You never would have come up with that back in the day." We both cracked up, and just like that, ten years between us splintered apart.

"I have to tell you, seeing you and Sarah in the flesh in the span of a week is pretty surreal," I said.

"Do we look old to you?"

"Well, now I realize how old I've gotten."

Alex laughed. "You look the same! Do I really look old now?"

"Oh, sir, I think you dropped your fishing pole!" I mimed handing something back to him; he played along. "But no, none of us looks old. I guess it's more that twenty-three seems absurdly young now. I've been looking at old photos and . . . god, we were babies. You know what I realized?"

"What's that?"

"Remember Edie's boyfriend, Greg? That older architect she dated right before you?"

"Sure." He kept chewing, listening attentively. No particular ire toward the man she'd left for Alex.

"He was our age, like now, when he started dating Edie, who was twenty-three. Can you imagine?"

He considered. "I guess I have buddies who date girls that age. But yeah, seems a little . . . stunted. Like, what do they even have in common?"

"Apart from the unshakable belief that he's a demigod?" I cracked, and he guffawed. "Edie had mentioned in an email that her mom liked that dude. Which, you'd think a mother would be suspicious of a grown man interested in her postgrad daughter."

"That so?"

No, it was a blatant lie. I had no idea how Mrs. Iredale felt about Greg. But I nodded.

"Well, I can't imagine her mom had anything nice to say about me."

This again. "Why do you say that?"

He shook his head. "Never mind."

"No, I'm curious! You said you didn't like them." *It's a long story,* he'd said on the phone. And when I told him I had time: *See, I kinda don't.*

"It's just—we had a weird . . . incident."

The waiter leaned in to refresh our water. Fuck.

"Why are we talking about this again?" Alex said in the ensuing silence.

"Alex, I want to tell you something."

He raised his eyebrows.

"I know about Lloyd."

His eyes widened and I held my breath. If my gamble was wrong and Lloyd *wasn't* the paramour Alex had been referring to . . .

"What?"

"I actually knew him."

"You *did*?"

"Yeah, I met him the same night Edie did. Well, the same night you and Edie met for the first time officially."

"In the city?"

"Yeah, we ended up hanging out on a rooftop on Fourteenth."

He squinted at me. "You were there?"

Ouch. "I was indeed!"

"Huh." He leaned back and looked around suspiciously. "In my head it was her old roommate."

"Which one?"

"I forget her name. She had the nose." He outlined a bump over his own face. What a nice descriptor for him to use.

"Well, it was me," I continued, "and I remember you bros seeming pretty tight, so I was really surprised he'd do that to you."

"Oh, we stopped hanging out long before he and Edie started hooking up."

Lucky break that he hadn't asked how I'd found out about the affair. Men's brains really do work differently—without the real-time social mapping, perhaps, the 3-D blueprints of relational information. "Right, you guys had a falling-out. Did he start hooking up with Edie as, like, a revenge thing?"

He snorted. "Revenge? We weren't on a soap opera." He shrugged. "It was just some dumb elementary-school shit. He borrowed my nicest guitar and fucked it up and refused to fix it. He was also this brilliant deadbeat who was too high and coked up to actually accomplish anything. We got into a stupid fight and I told him so. I used to have some anger issues."

More wine appeared and we both waited through its uncorking. Another lucky break: He was still a fast drinker.

"Anger issues?" I asked finally, spinning the ruby liquid around in my glass.

"Dude, let's stop talking about this. As we already established, we were stupid twenty-three-year-olds." He scrunched up his mouth. "Actually, I think I was twenty-four."

"You're right, it doesn't matter." I picked up my fork again. "How did you find out? About Edie and Lloyd?"

"Come on, Lindsay."

"I wanna know! You don't think we *always* wondered why you guys broke up? You were so weirdly secretive about it!"

"Cool, so you guys were just talking about us all the time."

We'd regressed; we were bitchy twentysomethings again.

"Well, I think it matters! We were worried about you two. And nobody would tell us what the fuck was going on."

"Well, maybe it was nobody's fucking business!"

"But it was! We were all in that apartment together—"

"You didn't even live there!"

He'd struck a tuning fork and I let it ring out. The sting crept into my eyes and I willed them to fill with tears; one hard blink and a drop slipped down my cheek.

"Look, Lindsay, I—"

"No, it's fine." I smeared it with my palm.

"I didn't mean to hurt your feelings. It's just . . . not fun to talk about."

Why, because you killed her? "I get it. It's hard for me, too. Especially because we . . . she and I were fighting. So even up until the end, I didn't have the warmest feelings."

An endless second as I waited to see if he'd take the bait: *Me too, it was so hard to go on living together* . . . "Yeah, that sucks," he said finally.

Ugh. "Sarah brought up how Edie was kind of . . . disengaging from everyone that summer," I offered. *Like you, you idiot. I caught you on film saying you wanted to slit her throat.*

"I mean, we'd just broken up."

"I know. That must have been so hard deciding to stay friends and roommates and everything."

He shrugged. "I guess."

I refilled his glass and put a palm on his forearm, summoning my most earnest, empathetic face. "I'm really, really sorry about Edie and Lloyd," I said.

"Yeah, it was bad." I waited for him to go on. "And I found out in the worst way possible."

He froze long enough that I murmured, "You can tell me."

He stared at my fingers, then slowly turned over his wrist. He slid his elbow back a few inches until our palms touched; my whole arm lit up and I willed myself to focus.

"We were sorta having some trouble anyway," he said, "fighting all the time and trying to fix it in the stupidest way possible. And she decided to stay at her parents' place because they were out of town. I was going to go over and surprise her, bring flowers, right? I mean . . . I was really into her." I nodded him on. "I called her as I was walking over from the subway, pretending I was still in Bushwick, and she picked up and sounded normal, said she was watching a movie or whatever. Then the doorman let me upstairs and I got to their door, and for some crazy reason it wasn't locked and I followed the noise to the bedroom, and . . . yeah, you can't fucking unsee that."

I remembered research discussed in my human sexuality class in college, how for a woman learning a partner's deeply in love with someone else is the most painful thing imaginable, but for a man, sexual infidelity—another person's body where his once was—is impossibly hurtful. Infuriating. Crazy-making.

"Wow, I'm so sorry," I said. Then: "How on earth did you keep living together after that?"

"It was pretty idiotic in retrospect," he said. "They saw me storm out, and she stayed at her parents' for a few days, calling me nonstop to cry and apologize and say how important I was to her." He shrugged. "I felt bad. And I still loved her. And she had so much shitty stuff going on with her parents and school and everything. So I guess it felt like breaking up but not kicking her out was, like, the adultest thing to do."

Slowly, slowly, our fingers were moving until they interlocked. He had such nice hands, strong fingers with neat fingernails.

"Why didn't *you* move out?" I asked.

He stared. "It was my apartment," he said simply, like it was obvious that a king couldn't be cast from his castle. What's the word? Abdicate.

"What was it like living together after that?"

"Oh, fine. Obviously sort of uncomfortable, but fine."

Except for the repressed rage, the kind that came out in front of a camcorder the night of Edie's murder.

"So you forgave her? That's amazing. I don't know if I could have done that."

He shrugged.

"I guess I'm, like, extra-obsessed because I don't remember her last night very well." I stared at the purple ring beneath my wineglass, a stenciled splotch.

"You were pretty wasted, right?"

I nodded. "For a long time I really hated myself for it," I said softly, adding a tremor. I willed my eyes to fill up with tears again, and slowly, they obliged. "Here was this pivotal night and I wasn't there for her, I wasn't . . . It was like I wasn't there."

I peeked up at him: He had that wild male look in his eyes, the expression men get when a woman is crying and they'll lop off their own hand with a scythe if it'll make the female freak-out stop.

"It was . . . Lindsay, you know you didn't miss anything. It was just a normal night, until it was . . . I mean, the most horrible night imaginable."

I pulled my fingers out from his and ran my knuckles against my tears. "I don't even remember being at the concert with you guys," I went on. False: I could see and hear and feel it now, a memory richer than real life. "I don't even know what we talked about or how everything went down. And I couldn't ask anyone because I'd seem like a crazy person, trying to make it about me."

"Lindsay. You know it's . . . you shouldn't feel that way."

"I'm sorry, I wasn't planning to bring any of this up," I lied. "I guess I've just had this . . . this preoccupation lately of wanting to piece together what happened. Where everybody was, what we were all doing, when we—when *I*—last saw her. That way I could . . . well, I'd *know,* and I could stop wondering."

He rubbed his eyes with his fists. "Shit, Lindsay. You really want to know?"

I nodded.

"It's exactly what you already know. Edie was avoiding us. Kevin left to go play a show and the rest of us took a bunch of shots—gin or something, something bad—and headed to the show. You got surprisingly drunk, so you said you were gonna go home."

"So I did go to the concert?"

"Yeah." He frowned. "As far as I can remember. You were there, right? Or did you leave right before?"

"I'm not sure, which is creepy. I know I was out front and a random girl called a car for me." I shook my head. "If only there were some way I could just go back and look, you know? Something that could tell me what happened." Would he bring up the camera? Did he even remember it?

He put on his man-laying-out-the-truth voice. "Lindsay, there was nothing any of us did or didn't do that led to Edie's suicide. It doesn't work like that. It sucks, and I know we all wish things had gone down differently, but it just is what it is. She was clearly a very troubled girl."

So faraway, another cheesy line from a movie. Again, I tried it on: About two months after the breakup, could Alex have walked over to Kevin's open chest, picked up the weapon, and pulled the trigger? Dropped it in his panic and tapped out some semblance of a suicide note? Absurd. But there had been no signs of a struggle, just Edie in her underwear, high on ecstasy and still frozen—in Alex's mind—midcoitus with Lloyd.

How well does anyone really know their friends? Edie was proof that the answer is: not well at all.

I let the conversation veer back into normalcy, tapering off the sniffles and throwing in a few snappy jokes to prove everything was all right. He kissed my cheek as we hugged good night, and then we headed in opposite ways in the dank post-rain night.

As soon as I got home, I poured La Croix over a pile of ice cubes and called Tessa, omitting the detail that stuck out like a blinking light: our fingers, interwoven.

"God. As if he weren't looking sketchy enough already," she said, after I brought her up to speed. "Means, motive, and opportunity, right?"

"I know." I sank into my couch. "God, I really don't want it to be him. I've always liked him, you know? And I always thought it was so noble that he and Edie kept living together after the breakup. Which is ironic, I guess, if that's what put him over the edge."

"I'm worried about you," she said. "If he really did this and he thinks you're getting close to figuring it out . . ."

Alex wouldn't hurt me, right? I stood up and slid the curtains closed. "It's not like I could go to the police right now. I have no proof."

"I know. But . . . maybe it's time to cool it on pressing him. He knows you met with Sarah, who was the first person to suspect that Edie was murdered, right? And now you get in touch all full of questions . . ."

She was right, but I told my thousandth lie of the day. "I'm fine. You don't need to worry about me."

We'd said good night and were about to hang up when I blurted it out: "Is everything okay?"

There was a long silence, which told me everything.

"Tessa, what's up?"

"It's nothing, we don't need to talk about it."

"Are you kidding? I'm here. You can talk to me."

A swallow, then a sniff. "It's just . . . we're okay. Will just found out he's not getting his bonus this year, and we were already barely keeping up with the mortgage on the Saugerties place, and now with this baby coming . . ." Her voice cracked.

"Oh, Tessa, I'm sorry. That's so stressful."

"Thanks." She kind of laughed. "And everything I've read about pregnancy is like, whatever you do, do not flood your body with stress hormones because it'll mess up the fetus, so I'm doubly freaking out about—"

"—about the fact that you're freaking out," I finished. "Aw, Tessa. I want to give you a hug through the phone. Should I come over?"

"No, it's okay. We're seeing his parents next week and they'll probably want to help and it'll all be fine." She sighed. "I'm sorry. I try to be sensitive of whom I'm complaining to. I know it's kind of shitty to be like, 'Ooh, my house, and my husband, and my baby.'"

Hearing it so bluntly, I teared up, too. I had no idea she'd been shielding me. "Honestly, you really don't need to think like that," I said. "This sounds weird, but it actually . . . it kind of helps? I mean, it sounds awful to say it makes me feel better, but, like, it reminds me that life is still life, and ticking those boxes doesn't magically make everything better."

"We all have our shit," she agreed. I *did* feel better, and I struggled to home in on whether or not that was a betrayal. "I mean, especially with all this crazy Edie stuff."

"I'm fine," I told her again, pierced by the change of subject. "I'm okay."

It wasn't until I was changing into my pajamas that something hit me, a breaker of fear and fury, horror at Alex, jagged resentment and disgust and those barbs of jealousy toward Edie, dead and gone and still messing with me anyway.

"Fuck this," I whispered aloud, because I was *done,* done scuba diving in the past, unearthing horrible things about my friends that I couldn't share and would never unknow. Suddenly I was crying so hard that it was like I'd never existed outside of this cry. I smeared the tears so they stung, then flopped down and slept with the yellow lights on overhead.

Chapter 9

Around noon the next day, my phone chimed. "Hey, it's Josh!" it read, exclamation point standing tall. "How's it going?"

I was supposed to wait—Edie would have demanded it, she'd been my flirt-texting Cyrano back in the day—but I figured this kid might as well know now that dating a thirty-three-year-old does not leave room for bullshit games.

"Hey!" I texted back. "Just at work. How are you?"

I stared at the screen until I saw he was typing back.

He stopped typing. Fuck me.

"Just walking in Brooklyn Bridge Park."

Now what? Tease him for making it sound like he's jobless? Say something about the park? Why hadn't he asked a follow-up question? What Would Edie Do?

"I can see DUMBO from my building," I typed. "Wave." I'd have to actually enter a conference room to look east, but, technicality.

No response. Two minutes passed, then three.

Then: "Ha, nice, you in FiDi?"

"Yep. How are things on your side of the river?" God, I was bad at this.

"View's better from here. You're only one ferry stop away."

What did that mean? An invitation? A statement of fact?

Then he wrote again: "I'm by Ignazio's. Come have pizza with me." Three pizza-slice emojis to underscore his point.

Something pitched in my chest. Damien walked by just then, so I pulled him in.

"Wait, who is this?" he screeched, delighted.

I blushed as I scrambled for something to say—I hadn't mentioned that I'd been stalking Edie's ex and couldn't think of a suitable meet-cute for a guy ten years my junior. Damien had moved on from the Edie mystery and I didn't want him to know how fixated I'd remained.

"He's waiting!" I spat, handing him the phone. "He's a dude I met. Answer now, info later."

Damien scrolled. "Well, do you want to have pizza with him?"

"I mean, sure! Yeah."

"Hmm." He stroked his chin stubble.

"Can I just say that? Pizza, sure?"

Damien looked up, eyes sparkling, and I dropped my face into my hands. "I am horrible at this."

Damien started typing. "What kind of pizza do you like?" he asked.

"What?"

"Damn it, Lindsay, this is not a drill! What kind of pizza!"

"Uhhh, I don't know! Pepperoni!"

He hit send and handed the phone back to me just as my cheeks started to hurt from laughing. He'd written: "Meet me at the dock. I'll take pepperoni."

"What the hell, Damien! He's supposed to bring me pizza to go?"

"I'm really glad you said pepperoni. Because it's phallic." He leaned on my desk and sighed happily. "Mystery man, bring me your big, hard pepperoni."

"Jesus Christ. He's writing back." We both leaned in to watch.

"You got it. Be there in twenty or I'm eating both slices myself."

Damien whooped. I gathered my things, ignoring his screeching request for more explanation.

"If you're not back in an hour, I'm calling the Coast Guard," he called as I hustled to make the 12:30 ferry.

———

I stepped onto the dock in DUMBO and spotted Josh, back behind the gate and clutching a greasy white bag. We waved hello when I was still twenty feet out and then he lifted the food up near his head; I gave a dorky thumbs-up. Finally we were together and he gave me a one-armed hug hello, with one of those little air pecks somewhere near my ear. He was handsomer than I remembered, tall and broad-shouldered. Why did he want anything to do with me?

"Hi!" I said. "Is that for me?"

"Half of it. I got the same thing."

"Can't go wrong with a classic." Everything I said dated me. *My dating skills are dated,* I thought crazily. *I date datedly.*

"Should we sit down?" We settled on a bench, looking out at the skyline, a mosaicked cliff of brick and glass.

"Which building is yours?" he asked. I pointed it out: a gleaming silver one next to a big black spire.

"That's the Tress building, right?"

"Yeah, I work at *Sir* magazine."

"Seriously? I used to read that!"

"Not anymore?"

"I think my subscription ran out. Wow, what do you do?"

"I'm the research chief."

"So you research the articles?" He'd succeeded in sliding out the slices, each on its own paper plate.

"Not exactly. I fact-check the articles after they've been written. Well, I lead the team that does." He handed me the top plate, which was probably a nice gesture, but it meant its bottom was soaked with oil, so I couldn't set it on my lap. I pleated the slice and took a bite.

"Wow, so you're a boss lady."

"I guess. Tell me more about what you do."

"You know, it's just boring operations stuff."

"Do you want to be an architect eventually?"

"Not really. I studied civil engineering and got really into the technology piece: 3-D printing and advanced CAD, that kind of stuff. Kinda figured I'd end up at a startup, but they hired me first."

"Well, they do have a cornhole room," I cracked. He smiled, chewing. "What's it like working for Greg?"

"Oh, he's the best. Really good guy, really smart. Everybody loves him."

"Are you just saying that because he dated my friend? You can be honest. She dumped him."

"No, I'm serious, he's awesome. Your friend really missed out." He shot me that beautiful goddamn grin, and something between my chest and stomach cartwheeled.

"All right, I believe you." I worked up something new. "So how long have you been there?"

"Two years last month."

"Since right after college?" *Please let him be older than twenty-four.* "Yep!"

Twenty-four, then. A barge glided by, majestic in the sun's glare. "And do you like it?"

He shrugged. "It's good, they treat us well. Eventually I'll probably start my own company."

Right, easy as pizza pie. "Doing what?"

"Probably with 3-D modeling. Making it more accessible to the masses."

"So that the masses can do . . . what?"

"Whatever they want. Print their own custom orthotics. Or jewelry. Or, like, a bust of their great-grandfather. There are instructions online now for printing and constructing a functional handgun."

Handgun. This was the arrhythmic pattern of the last couple of weeks: periods of distraction, of time passing normally, and then *screeeh*, jolt, and crash.

"Do you think that has, you know, ethical implications?" I dabbed my lips with a napkin.

"I don't know. It's just a tool. You know the phrase: Guns don't kill people—people with guns kill people. So it's kind of a stretch to say that people who design 3-D models for guns kill people. Right?"

I sighed. "I guess. I mean, I grew up in a gun family; I'm not anti-gun. It's just . . . wild to think about."

"What would *you* wanna print out?" he said.

"Ohhh, gosh. Well, definitely not a gun." Two assholes careened by on blue and white Jet Skis. "When will we be able to 3-D print a time machine?"

He laughed. "Once we master quantum physics. We're getting there."

"You think?"

"Sure."

I thought for a moment. "That would make it 4-D modeling!"

He chuckled. "When would you go back to?"

August 2009, obviously, so I could stay home that night. Maybe order sushi, walk over to Videology, and rent a DVD.

"It's funny we always talk about time machines transporting us back in time, right?" I said after a moment. "You could jump ahead, too."

"That's true. And it'd be a lot easier to go that way, if we could just figure out how to move at the speed of light."

"I guess that's less appealing, since we eventually reach the future, anyway," I said.

A ferry tooted its horn.

"A physicist would argue that we're always in the now," he replied.

"So would a philosopher."

He laughed. "This is pretty heavy for a pizza lunch."

He caught my eye and held his perfect smile, his thick hair rumpling in the wind, and for a moment, a small, embarrassing part of me wondered if he was my time machine, my wormhole back to when I was twenty-three and happy and free.

———

"So did you guys have sex on the dock?" Damien called as soon as I got back to my office, loud enough for others to hear.

"Damien!" I beckoned him in and closed the door. "I found out he's twenty-four years old. And he brought me my own slice of pizza. I feel like the prettiest girl in all of high school."

He laughed, his eyes glittering. "You said you were chubby in high school, right? Chubby High School Lindsay would be cheering this hot bitch on." He leaned against the door. "Chubby Lindsay would have eaten a whole pie."

"All right, all right." I spun slowly in my chair. "I can't even believe I went out with someone so young."

"It was just pizza. Does he know your age?"

"No, and now that I haven't mentioned it yet, I feel like it's this dirty secret." I laughed. "Do I have my graduation year on LinkedIn? He must *never know*."

"He's probably into the fact that you're older and wiser." Damien considered. "But he clearly isn't just in it for the sex, because you hung out midday. This is fascinating. Maybe the youngs have, like, circled back to playing the long game."

"I'll take what I can get."

"How did you meet this kid?"

"I just stopped into . . . my doctor switched floors and I accidentally wound up at the wrong suite number," I said evenly. Was I getting good at this? "I asked for directions and we ended up chatting for a minute. So wild."

He nodded approvingly. "Okay, so what *would* Fat High School Lindsay say?"

"Hey, wasn't I Chubby Lindsay a minute ago?"

"Adorable either way. Oh, speaking of being fat kids together, are we getting dinner before the show tonight?"

"The show?"

"Alvin Ailey. Don't tell me it's not on your calendar."

Oh, Christ. "I didn't forget! Just . . . I mean I did right now, but I'm in. It's at Lincoln Center, right?" Damien loves modern dance and always gets us pairs of plush seats at the major companies' shows, Cedar Lake, Martha Graham, Paul Taylor. (Except for that brief period in 2016 after Damien dated a Paul Taylor dancer, then broke up with him on the basis of bad conversation and disappointingly uncalisthenic sex; Paul Taylor had been unmentionable for two whole seasons.) We get dressed up—nothing annoys Damien like attendees in jeans and sneakers—and sit together, enthralled, watching athletes spin their art.

"Yep, Lincoln Center." Damien headed for the door. "I'll get us dinner reservations in the neighborhood. I can tell you forgot, Linds. Put on some lipstick."

As we walked to the 1 train, weaving around the after-work mobs, Damien chattered away about his Labor Day plans, the final Fire Island trip. A part of me was grateful that he was over the Edie drama—he was an unchanged figure in the murk of swirling unknowns. I didn't want to tell another soul about Alex, about what he'd probably done, because saying it might make it true. The secret was like a storm cloud, growing larger under my skin.

At dinner, too, I tried to be upbeat, tried to keep up my end of the conversation and remark at appropriate times. Greg had been another dead end, but out of it had come a few feel-good minutes with Josh, time that reminded me that there's a here and now. And if I was really going to close the book on Edie, I had to come back online, to an era when we weren't guzzling shots and bumming cigarettes and dancing with strangers and always moving just a little faster than real life, jerky and frenetic like early motion pictures. Maybe Edie didn't need me revisiting her final hours. Maybe I didn't need to know whether I had made it to the concert or what'd happened after I'd opened her door and turned off my camera. Maybe the past really had passed.

But at the theater, the first act was lyrical and slow, not enough to keep my mind from wandering. The troupe spun and rolled in perfect, languid unison, and I found myself combing through the case files again, impressions rising like balloons: Kevin waiting at the ER, Sarah fumbling with her cell phone, Anthony reaching through the blood to feel for Edie's pulse. Me, drunk and blank-faced, opening a window to let in the heat as my taxi wove its way through the night.

The second dance was more my speed, with a pulsing drum-beat and spastic motion. My eyes settled on a corps member shorter than the others, with red hair and pale creamy skin; from back here, she reminded me of Edie, graceful and quick. I let my eyes relax and watched the dancers braid themselves together, now sideways, then a small explosion and limbs sticking out at awkward angles. Suddenly all of the dancers but the doppelgänger bolted offstage, and the music switched to something mournful, deep, and soulful. The redhead slunk in and out of the spotlight, moving slowly and then crashing into odd contortions, hitting the stage so hard that we could hear the thud from our balcony seats. I glanced over at Damien and saw that he was riveted, too, then realized I was crying, unassuming tears leaking down my cheeks.

I cheered when it was over, hollering when the woman took her solo bow, letting the roar of applause cover up my sniffles as I pulled myself back together. At intermission, Damien and I stood among the throngs, sipping drinks.

"So that last one got to you, huh?"

I wasn't sure he'd noticed. "Yeah, it was beautiful."

"You seem quiet tonight."

"Do I?"

"You can talk to me. You thinking about your friend?"

Goddammit, he'd invoked the secret code, the way to split me into a million sobbing pieces: He was nice to me.

"I—I'm sorry," I said with a high-pitched laugh. The faucet of tears was on full blast.

"Whoa. Here, come here." Damien led me away from the crowd, which had begun streaming back into the theater, and set-tled us on a sofa in a random recess.

"Babe, I didn't realize this was bringing you down so much! You haven't mentioned it in a while."

I shook my head. "I can tell you and Tessa think I'm being compulsive or whatever. But . . . you know that feeling when a situation is just totally out of your control? It's like that. Only it's about this really horrible thing that already happened, and the reason I wasn't in control was because I drank too much." I groaned. "You saw the video—you heard how Alex and I were saying awful stuff about Edie that night, how we wanted her dead. And it's just . . . it's really upsetting to think that he or I could've . . . I don't know. Said something awful. Or that he could have done something awful." Or that I could have seen something awful, witnessed the two of them fighting, him posturing with Kevin's gun. Or, or, or.

"Ohhh, girl." He pulled me into a hug. "You know what they say about suicide: Nothing anyone says or does—"

"I know, I know." I slid away from his arms. "But it's still really disturbing that I went and talked to her. I'd always thought she was alone in her apartment the whole time. Nobody really saw her that night at all, after she parted with her dude of the moment." Fucking Lloyd.

"So I have a confession," he said. I raised my eyebrows. "I haven't looked at your video. But I will! I'll do it tonight. I'm a *video editor*, Linds. I can definitely find something you didn't notice."

I want to push her off this building, I'd screamed. Suddenly I wanted Damien to delete it, eliminate the record of Alex and me fantasizing about her death. Muffled music swelled from inside the auditorium, and I rested my head on the back of the sofa. "Focus on the last few minutes," I told him, and he nodded.

At home, my eyes fell on a stack of glossy photos, piled like a brick on a side table, the old photo albums on the floor underneath. I picked up the snapshots and recognized the image on top: Kevin and Sarah on the subway, next to me and too close, so Kevin's head was huge. On his other side, Sarah peered over, her mouth distorted a bit: midword.

I realized with a happy spritz that I remembered this day: It was a springtime outing when the five of us—no, four, Alex couldn't make it for some reason—had made our way upstate from Grand Central, hungover and slow-moving and pausing too long to gaze at the station's teal ceiling. The plan was to hike the hills around Cold Spring, though none of us had proper footwear. I'd bought two disposable cameras at a bodega that morning, and we'd had no choice but to develop the images.

I smiled as I flicked through them; Edie had had the brilliant idea of turning hiking into a drinking game, and every time someone spotted a trail marker, everyone else had to drink. She never beamed in photos like me, instead turning away or smirking sleepily, always so effortlessly cool. There was a selfie she'd taken of both of us where she was pretending to bite my hair (perhaps the wind had been flopping it onto her face?), and I could still feel the weight of her arm around my shoulders, the thrilling calm of owning half an imaginary BEST FRIENDS necklace.

I paused on one: It was the inevitable shot of our shoes, four pairs on the dirty train's floor. The others were beat-up, but mine were still shiny new, Keds as white as fresh snow. I could sort of recall the point of these pictures: We were proud of how shabby our shoes got, evidence of all the dirty hipster spelunking we'd done. For a moment I peered at it, feeling the realization coming, a gushing sensation like ice on a frozen river fissuring and running free. Then I lunged at my laptop, pulled up Facebook, and began to search.

There it was, posted September 26, 2009, by a work friend I'd clung to after severing the SAKE crew: another foot shot, my shoes on a picnic blanket with strawberries and baby carrots and chips nearby. My white canvas sneakers were the worse for wear, scuffed and gray. But there were two unmistakable spots on my right toe, each the size of a pencil eraser. Rusty red and permanent.

Panicked, I clicked through more photos of myself, further

and further back in time. When had the dots appeared? My stupid shoes were so often cut off, photos from the knee or waist or shoulders up, or most of my body obscured by buzzing throngs of other twentysomethings. Finally, one of me playing on Kevin's skateboard in McCarren Park, arms out, wobbly terror in my eyes. August 8.

Heartburn rang out in my ribs. Two weeks before Edie's untimely death, at least, the shoes. They were spotless.

I woke up to a text from Damien: "Who's the baddest bitch? I'm the baddest bitch."

I sent question marks back, but he didn't answer, so I hightailed it into work and left my office door open for him. He burst in ten minutes past our normal call time, the bastard. He was grinning like the goddamn Cheshire cat.

"So it was surprisingly easy to clean up the audio," he announced. "I ran it through this filtering app that factors out the effect of a mic being covered by fabric or wrapped up in your hand or whatever. Listen."

He held his phone out as the familiar footage rolled: a moment's focus on 4G, my hand opening the door. Then instead of "Heavy skies senile?" I heard my own voice in a surprised little chirrup: a gasp, then "Have you guys seen Alex?"

It took a moment for it to sink in. Damien was still grinning.

"See?" he said. "You didn't come upon her all alone and goad her into killing herself. Alex, neither. She was already in there with someone else."

Relief like a shower: Someone else was in the room, not Alex, someone else who must have done this. Someone else who could've picked up the gun. Alex was innocent. And my Keds—what a stupid notion—that was chocolate syrup or ketchup or barbecue sauce on them, just as I'd figured at the time.

Then fear buzzed in me: *Someone else was in the room.* Someone who may have killed Edie and gotten away with it. And he could very well know that I'd been poking around in the past.

I stared at the final frame, a blur of brown and black as I'd hit the button to stop recording.

Someone else was in the room when Edie died.

PART III

Chapter 10

KEVIN

When I was in my early twenties, things were pretty fucking good, and I knew it. Not great—I was aware of the big list of wants hovering on the other side of the greener-grass hedge, how cool it'd be to have more sex, more money, another six inches or so in height and wingspan, that kind of thing. But shit was pretty good. I had a cheap roof over my head, space for the entire drum kit, and not a soul in the building who'd complain if I got the urge to play at one in the morning, two o'clock, three o'clock (rock); a buddy, Alex, who was good at guitar and willing to jam with me pretty much whenever I wanted; girl roommates who were always finding fun shit for us to do on weekends, apple picking and weird-ass art exhibits and outdoor shows and whatnot; a stupid but manageable job making mochas and cleaning espresso machines with other equally bleary-eyed friends at a coffee shop within walking distance of my place.

And this was back when basically nobody had a job, hiring freezes and mass layoffs all over the place like avalanches, like those videos of huge chunks of what looks like a mountain breaking off and speeding toward hell. That's what it felt like, everything around us dropping with insane speed while I stood in the middle of my happy snow globe with shit whiskey and cool people and a few dollars and my drumsticks. Maybe not everyone appreciated it, but I knew we had it good.

So I guess I was pretty cheerful because I was on to that, and maybe in some subconscious way I was trying to convey that to everyone else, too: Dude, stop shitting on everything and come listen to this new album with me, it's pretty good. Everyone was so negative all the time and I thought it was so funny, so affected. Rolling their eyes and hoisting up their noses at Murray Hill bros and Ugg-clad girls and popular songs and clueless parents and med-school-attending high school friends and themselves, hate hate hate hate. That was how it felt, like Duck, Duck, Goose only when they got to themselves they looked surprised and whispered "Duck!" too.

I remember once my roommate Sarah came home all upset because a guy on a packed subway had called her a "hipster bitch" after they got snappish about fitting through a door or something. She was all morose and finally our friend Lindsay asked what was up and when Sarah told us, Lindsay was so outraged and sympathetic, but I couldn't stop laughing. Remember that word, "hipster"? It was the oddest thing, slippery as an eel, meant as a compliment when some out-members used it (like the *New York Times* speaking breathlessly about a new "hipster art installation"), but as an insult when certain out-members (see: the subway asshole) and even in-members (see: anyone dumb enough to utter the word inside Calhoun) used it. There were silly Tumblrs about it, stupid books picking the so-called "subculture" apart. We all wanted to naturally, effortlessly be hipsters without anyone calling us hipsters, we wanted to be the definition set forth by the supremely uncool editors of the Style section, but we would sooner die than let anyone know that, and also who the fuck cares what those losers at the *Times* think is cool? The fuck do they know about coolness? God, it was so funny then and it's hilarious now.

So basically I just liked reminding everyone that yeah, ludicrous shit was going down and our parents' net worth was plummeting, but we were doing just fine, the kids are all right, and so much is so funny if you know where to look. And I think Edie liked that, saw a bit of a kindred spirit, because she was amused, too, she was confident and gave zero fucks. I really didn't know her that well when she first moved in with Alex and me that spring, had seen her around the building a bit, had the occasional beer with her in a Calhoun hallway or open-door living room. Alex seemed to like her a lot and when two rooms in our apartment opened up, the weird hippie chick from Portland and the mustachioed bro from Minnesota suddenly deciding to split, Alex seemed pretty thrilled about Edie moving in. Smiling to himself as he wandered toward the bathroom, that kinda thing. And it seemed like they were being smart about it, her still having her own separate room so they'd still have solo space. See? Shit's not all bad.

It blows me away to think that Edie moved in in April and was dead by Labor Day. It felt like *so much time.* What was it about that era that slowed down the clocks and made every month feel brimming and eclectic like my steamer trunk in the living room? It reminds me of camp: Mom sent me one summer when I was nine or ten, and when I learned from her years later that the whole thing had been only three weeks long, I was blown away. Because so fucking much had happened, I was sure it had been the whole summer: best friends, alliances, enemies, crushes, breakups, entire operatic narratives compressed into twenty-one days. That's how Calhoun felt, each week its own ginormous plotline.

And it became a story line with a big twist when I came home and Edie's shorts were covered in blood. Years later, the first time Evelyn had a seizure, as I sat bored and antsy in the hospital waiting room, I thought about that night, how preternaturally calm I'd been in that insane moment of crisis. I don't believe in God as a big, bearded dude surrounded by winged angels, but I sort of wonder if that night with Edie was the universe testing me, like, Can he handle it? Is he gonna keep his head and take care of her, or is he gonna lose his shit?

And I kept it together, made her tie my black hoodie around her waist to cover the blood, shhh'ed her as she fretted through the boogers and tears about getting her blood all over it, got the name of the hospital out of the all-business paramedic to whom I for some reason wasn't really a person, showed up in a cab myself a half-hour later and sat politely in the waiting room, headphones blaring, snoozing on and off, occasionally wandering to the front desk to make sure I hadn't missed her.

When she finally stumbled back into the waiting room, she looked dead; her eyes were glazed and unfocused, fucking freaky, and she stared at me for a moment like I was a stranger, like whatever was happening inside her head was reality and I was part of this TV screen inconveniently stretching across her eyeballs. I waited for her to snap out of it, but after a few seconds I realized it wasn't gonna happen, so I grabbed her arm and led her through the door, and we stood in the blazing sun as I called the only cab company in my phone.

If it was a test, I'm glad I passed it because now I have Evelyn and she's the most beautiful thing I've ever done. But Edie. Fucking pity. For two weeks I felt like a hero, all the more noble for being a secret one, and then bang, a bullet took her down, blood pouring out of her like spilled wine a second time in as many weeks.

Not *a* gun—*my* gun.

What kind of idiot keeps a sometimes-loaded gun in a huge catacomb of open doors and drugs and booze with drunks wandering in and out like sleepwalkers? How was I such a fucking idiot? There was a feeling of trust, though, one I can remember but can't bring up, everyone sort of hating but mostly adoring everyone else in this secluded little scene, good people who were trying to make art and putting up with all the grossness of our building and New York City and themselves and one another in order to get there.

I remember a huge snowstorm sidelined the city late in the winter, and through some collective osmosis we all agreed to lock the doors to the outside and open the doors to our apartments and thus began a forty-eight-hour rager, bands jamming and joints passing hands and at one point throwing my body with four other near-strangers against the door to the roof, then running out shrieking and throwing snowballs and making angels in the snow. Someone put together a snowman and stuck a cigarette butt on it as a dick. We were all idiots, hopped up on camaraderie in a mostly scared and scorning outside world. But I was the idiot who owned a gun.

I would lock the trunk, that was my big smart move. That was, I figured, close enough to a gun safe. Only when the gun was loaded, when it was armed and dangerous on August the 17th, 18th, 19th, 20th, and 21st, in the year of our lord 2009, fucker was out just waiting for me to put it away. I spent a lot of time thinking about that the first year, walking through it in my mind frame by frame: how I came home on the 17th and dropped my messenger bag onto my bed where it sat for a few hours; how that evening I got out the pistol and the box of bullets and carried them into the living room, prepared to lock them away; how Edie had been in there on her laptop, had said something when I entered and we'd started to talk; how I'd registered that the trunk was still locked and my keys were back in the room and I'd take care of it later; and that's when the scene sorta fades.

So many idiotic microdecisions, so many times I could have prevented the whole thing. I like to think there's an alternate dimension where I locked the gun away, another, happier Kevin out there, hopefully not too different, hopefully still with Glenn and beautiful Evelyn and a nice house and all the stuff I'm grateful for, but also where Edie is alive somewhere, a stylist like she always dreamed of being, putting together beautiful outfits like art.

I replay the day of the ER visit, too, moments of it that clung to my memory like dryer lint, maybe because they held some clues or maybe just 'cause memory's funny like that. I remember her staring out the window on the cab ride home, like I wasn't even there, and then saying something so softly the silence hissed and I wasn't sure she'd said anything at all, and then I whispered, "Huh?" and she turned suddenly and said, "Alex," again, like it was a statement. I was like, "What about him?" and she said, "Don't tell him," and then turned back to the window as the cab scuttled along the street.

How she waited until we were almost at Calhoun's front door to whisper, "Let's walk in separately, and please don't tell anyone," then turned on her heels and headed down the block. How I thought about following her, watching her thin body recede and knowing I'd do nothing so that distance would make the decision for me. I went inside and took a shower and got ready for work. Alex looked around all curious, no doubt wondering where his new ex-girlfriend had spent the night. No one ever assumed I knew anything.

Two days later I found my hoodie spread out on my bed, newly washed and blood-free. For some reason, imagining Edie in the laundromat, rubbing extra detergent into the stains, was just the saddest fucking thing.

For about a week she acted impressively normal, a bit withdrawn, but everyone still chalked it up to the breakup. So I did my best to be normal, too, goofing off with the group and keeping everybody laughing. It seemed like a fluke that I was the one among us who helped a friend through a miscarriage, such a random, adult problem that just happened to thwack into me like a fly ball.

Then a few days later, I found her smoking on the front steps of the building, watching a little brown bird hop around the tangle of the block's only tree. I sat down next to her and accepted a cigarette.

"You know what I've been thinking about?" She always had a musical voice, animated like a singer's.

"What's that?"

She exhaled a long stream of smoke. "It sucks to die when you're old, but not that much because you've already spent so long on the planet, being human. And it sucks to die as a baby—or even before you're born—but really not that much because you haven't had time to, you know, grow attached to shit here. To really get into the whole human-being-on-planet-earth thing." She tapped a bit of ash off the end. "So the worst thing is a young adult dying, like our age. Because you've just woken up to the fact that you're a person, that you get to be an actual being and you're not just, like, a little human robot on the conveyor belt your parents pushed you onto when you were little. But you're not old yet, it's not like 'Whew, really lived that up.' It'd be like—I don't know—leaving right before the movie gets good."

We smoked together for a minute. Two girls stepped around us to get into the building, both wearing cutoffs.

I said, "I think the media and whoever else get way dramatic when a young person dies—so much ahead of her, that kind of thing. Like the 27 Club." I didn't want to call her out as a cliché, but I also couldn't ignore that she wasn't exactly making a new observation.

She shrugged. "I guess."

"Were you thinking about . . . Did you think something bad was gonna happen at the hospital?"

She rolled her eyes. "Something bad *did* happen, Kevin."

"I know, but I mean—like, did you really think you might die?"

She shrugged. "Maybe. I've been thinking about it more since then, though. And how weird it is that there was another life inside me." She put her hand on her stomach. "Something that would have grown hair and teeth and worn clothes and gone through the conveyor belt and come out the other side, you know?"

I'd figured we'd never discuss the whole ordeal. I realized that up until that point, I'd only been about 80 percent sure it was even a miscarriage. Some other mysterious lady issue seemed plausible, too.

"But you're saying maybe it wasn't as bad for . . . ?"

"This little sac of cells." She took another drag. "It sucks it died before it could get out there and do anything, but at least it didn't know what it was missing. Me, I would be so fucking mad if I didn't get to stay here and *do* everything. I mean, not that I thought it was a him-or-me situation or anything, it wasn't like the doctors were standing around going 'We can operate to save the child, but it'll endanger your life.' The thing just up and died. But I guess I could have died. It could have implanted funny and stayed there building up an infection that'd blow me up from the insides. How much would that have sucked?"

I gave a slow, emphatic nod as I sucked on the end of the cigarette. I still wasn't sure what she was getting at.

"I want to fucking *do* shit. I don't want to live forever, but I want to go balls-to-the-wall until I'm old and can leave contentedly, you know?"

"I hear you. That's awesome. You should fucking do stuff, Edie. You're smart as hell."

"Thanks." She crushed the cigarette butt and wrapped her arms around her knees, all freckles and bones. And that was that.

It was the only time we ever talked about her miscarriage, ever acknowledged it head-on. She was dead a few days after that, sprawled on our floor amid a beehive of accusations that she'd been depressed, erratic, contemplating taking her own life for days or weeks or months. It was bullshit, such bullshit. Homegirl wasn't suicidal. Homegirl wasn't going anywhere. Edie sucked a funnel of smoke into her lungs and felt fucking alive, dizzy with everything she had to get done before she got old enough to exhale, a long, contented sigh, tired but happy with all that she'd pulled off.

Chapter 11

LINDSAY

Damien's smile melted as he watched me react. "Not the relief I was expecting," he said.

An urgent command from somewhere deep: *Lie*. "I *am* relieved. Oh my god, it's like a four-hundred-pound sandbag was just lifted off my shoulders. I was just so surprised I . . . I froze up. I really didn't think you'd find anything." I pictured SAKE and swapped in suspects next to Edie like paper dolls: Was Sarah in the room? Anthony? Kevin, somehow? My stomach clenched: Had I seen Edie with Lloyd?

Damien shrugged. "It wasn't hard," he said. "I was just excited to find something that would burst your bubble on the whole theory that you or Alex went in alone and picked a fight or whatever. Right?"

"Absolutely." I pressed my hand on his arm. "Wow, this really changes things. Was there anything else in the video?"

"Not really, no. The footage of you guys at the beginning—you were on a roof, right?—it was about as clear as it was gonna get. There's a little conversation with your friend, just her deciding to go to a party. But that's it. You were movin' around like a ninja." He swept both hands into a fighting stance, and I giggled for his benefit.

"Thanks so much for doing that, Damien. This is . . . that's a game-changer."

"*De rien, de rien*." He grabbed his phone and tapped at it. "There, I just sent you instructions on viewing it. Now please tell me you're gonna let this go. Tessa is worried you're getting all OCD about it." He kept tapping at his phone, so he missed my hurt expression. Then he frowned and leaned in closer to the screen. My chest froze over.

"What is it?"

"You aren't gonna believe this," he said, still staring.

"What? Tell me!"

"Son of a bitch," he said. "The cops found my pornography book."

I plopped into my chair. "I thought it was erotica?"

"Turns out somebody dropped it in a library return box, of all things. With the plastic wrap still on. Look!"

He turned the screen to show me a washed-out cell-phone photo of a book on a white desk. The cover displayed nothing but four letters—*PEEK*—and a picture of an erect penis. In grayscale.

He flipped his phone back around and smiled at it lovingly. "Talk about a hardcover, am I right?"

"I'm very happy for you and your penis." I turned back to my computer.

"I am having a hell of a day," he said. "I better buy a lotto ticket."

"When you win, don't forget us little people!" I called as he headed for his office. Wow, the cops accomplishing something. Unlike the useless detectives who'd investigated Edie's death.

I logged into the video-filtering app Damien had sent me and listened until I found the conversation with Sarah. "Tiny fight," she'd called it. Four minutes after I'd tossed the Flip cam into my purse and we'd all presumably headed inside.

"I'm gonna go," my voice announced. The words tumbled together: "Hominago."

"You're not coming to the show?" Sarah, sounding cross.

A beat. "I gotta go home."

"Ugh, nobody ever wants to do anything fun anymore."

My voice rose in confused indignation: "Fuck you, I'm fun."

"Just go."

I had to listen to it twice to make out what I'd said next: "What about Edie?"

"Forget it. Just go then. Are you taking a cab?"

"Yeah, I'll get one. I'm fine."

Another pause, some fumbling, then my voice again: "What about Kevin?"

"Just go home, Linds."

"Whatever."

The sound of stomping; no additional dialogue. The conversation made me uncomfortable: Sarah's sudden animosity, my own disgruntled curse. Sarah *had* tended to grow annoyed when others got drunk and fumbly, that much I recalled.

I listened to it again. What about Edie and Kevin? Was I simply suggesting other people she could hang out with, forgetting in my fog that Kevin had left for Greenpoint? Where had Alex gone? And was there something more to Sarah's *Forget it. Just go* at the mention of Edie?

An editor dropped in to discuss a story, and I quickly closed out of the app. I wouldn't share it with Tessa. I wouldn't share it with anybody.

Over the next few days, Damien didn't mention the video again, and I did my best not to think about it, occasionally waylaid by the hard-brake feeling of it wafting into my consciousness. Then everything would speed up, a sense of not knowing, of wanting to know *so fucking hard* I could scream, stomp, pound my fists against God's chest.

One evening, as I was leaving the office, I paused at a window on my way to the elevator; the world was darkening sooner, summer tipping into fall. Twentysome floors below, people were just visible picking their way across streets and sidewalks.

Thoughts swarmed every which way, directionless. Whose baby was Edie pregnant with? Was she planning to keep it? Why didn't she tell anyone but Kevin? Why didn't Kevin tell anyone? Why was fucking *everyone* near 4G that fateful evening—Lloyd to comfort Edie by Calhoun's front doors, Edie's mom to deliver bad news, Sarah and presumably Alex to see a band just a few floors up?

I leaned my forehead on the glass and closed my eyes. *And me, cruising straight to SAKE to force a friend breakup.*

And now there was a new thought, humming underneath like a pipe organ's deepest note. Now that I knew Alex hadn't been there, now that all I was left with was my own drunken self calling "She's a fucking bitch!" into the night sky. What the hell had gone on in there?

When I got out of the building, I turned left instead of right. I wasn't entirely sure where I was walking until I saw the pier in the distance, jutting out over the water near the massive heliport, where copters thrummed and floated like gigantic dragonflies. Of course. I'd take the East River ferry to Williamsburg, a route that hadn't even existed when we'd lived in the area. I climbed to the upper deck and looked east, feeling small and dazzled by the glittering skyscrapers along Brooklyn's shore. So much silver and glass now, propped up like dominoes in the evening light. The ferry pulled into the South Williamsburg landing, and I clambered off between two condos and disappeared into the neighborhood I once knew.

At first glance, it wasn't so different: town houses and old churches and drinking establishments on so many first floors, but with names I didn't recognize. I turned onto Kent and rooted around for an overlay of what this street had looked like in my time—crummy semilegal concert venues, cheap apartments, grassed-over lots with graffiti on the particleboard fences enclosing them. Now, good-looking, well-dressed young professionals swarmed out of the office buildings and into the waterfront condos.

Around the corner, I froze at the sight of Mugger's, one of our old haunts, my heart suddenly clanging, afraid that—what?—I'd open the door and find Alex and Kevin and Sarah and Edie in the corner, big-eyed and brazen under a garland of tacked-up Christmas lights? I went in, and the familiar smell, beer and sweat and old beat-up walls, hit me like a sound wave. One night we'd co-opted the casual karaoke in the back room here, signing one another up for increasingly ridiculous songs: Alex covering TLC, Sarah on Alice Cooper. Someone put me down for a Talking Heads song that apparently everyone knew but me, and when I'd started to look miserable, Edie had jumped onstage with me, sharing the mic and pulling me into crazy dance moves and turning the whole thing into a not-mortifying experience. I could still remember the high-pitched thrill of that night, playing what Kevin had dubbed karaoke roulette, freezing at the end of every song to see if my name was up next.

I sat at the bar and ordered a ginger ale. A couple walked in and picked a booth near the door, her thin and long-haired with epic eyeliner, him bearded and broad and confident. They looked so nonchalant about each other, so unimpressed that they'd found a partner, and I watched them for a little too long.

"You just getting off work?" The bartender was drying glasses with a towel, a cute, short guy in a sweater despite the heat.

"That's right. Taking a walk down memory lane, actually."

"Oh, did you used to come here a lot?"

"A very long time ago. It looks pretty much the same, though."

He nodded easily and leaned against the counter. The door screeched open behind me and my heart froze up: For one moment I knew, absolutely knew, that Edie was walking into the bar. Why was I so afraid of her, still?

Instead, two bros sauntered in, making too much noise, monkeys hooting.

"You all right?" the bartender asked, smiling. He'd seen me jump. I laughed and assented, but the thought hit me: *What the fuck am I doing here?*

Suddenly I was old, exposed, the sad, single woman drinking alone among the children. Abruptly, I pictured my parents, and in piped the diatribe I sometimes find myself spitting into the silence: *You were afraid of me, but I should have been afraid of you. If you'd been braver, maybe I'd have grown out of it. Maybe my brain could have matured, the unbridled blossoming everyone else's neurons seem to enjoy. Maybe I wouldn't have these black, gaping bullet holes in my own memory. Maybe I could have grown up like everyone else managed to do.*

I glanced up and realized the bartender was looking at me; I'd been almost talking to myself, my expression curled into a mask of anger. I flashed him a smile and swept myself outside, gulping in the twilight air. I turned in the direction of the subway; a cab rounded the corner and I nearly stuck my arm out.

But I was so close to Calhoun now, just a few more bends, and I realized I'd hazily imagined myself getting inside—seeing if traversing those old, dark passageways would stir up anything useful. Maybe I'd try the walk from the rooftop to 4G to see just how far I'd drunkenly stumbled to SAKE. I crossed the overpass and glanced down at the Brooklyn-Queens Expressway, clogged with cars. The heat was thick, sticky, changing form and coalescing into the cicadas' hum.

I turned a corner and stood stunned for a moment: What the fuck was this? In place of Calhoun Lofts were two ugly buildings, all green glass and white molding. I took a few steps forward and craned my neck, as if these buildings were just a front and my home-away-from-home was hiding back there, obscured from view.

So it was gone. How had I missed this in my research? I pictured the demolition, a wrecking ball tumbling the cinder blocks in slow motion, a crane pawing at the foundation like a curious dog. I imagined the door to 4G buckling and then collapsing like cardboard; I saw the cubbylike bedrooms crumbling one by one. It was gone. The last clinging particles of Edie's blood wiped totally clean. I felt something complicated in my chest, grief and dismay and relief and horror twisting around like fingers in a fist.

The front door to one of the buildings swung open and out popped a middle-aged woman carrying a small fluffy dog, which she set on the sidewalk. She bent to fix its collar and then jumped back—the thing was already peeing, splashing onto the cement directly in front of the glass doors. I turned away and called myself a cab; even as I waited, I felt a drowsy relief in entering my address.

In the taxi, I leaned my head against the backseat and cracked open the window. Outside, an endless scroll of bodegas and nail salons and cheap clothing stores unfurled. After a moment, my phone buzzed in my purse and I pulled it out to see, with a little jolt, a text from Josh: "Did you work on this?"

I clicked on the link he'd included: a *Sir* feature on a secretive Silicon Valley lab that claimed its user-friendly CAD program would revolutionize—nay, democratize—design.

"Someone on my team did," I wrote. "Why?"

A thumbs-up. Then: "People were talking about it at the office today."

"Nice. I think it's kinda bullshit, tho. All hype like when the Segway debuted."

A split second after hitting send, I realized he was too young to remember the Segway hoopla: mounting excitement over an invention that promised to transform transportation and then *splat.*

After a few more blocks, I tried again: "How's work otherwise?"

He didn't reply. Didn't even cue up the little bubble that meant he was typing. With a rinse of embarrassment, I turned off the screen and slipped the phone back into my bag.

At home, I stared at my laptop for a moment before giving in and searching through old news for Calhoun's death sentence. It'd been sold to a developer and torn down in early 2017. The Google News search had brought up other stories, too, and I remembered why the space we'd adored had always had a sinister vibe to outsiders: the confusing junctions, exposed pipes, scuffed-up walls and wood, and eternal carpet of beer bottles and cigarette butts. I clicked on a story from 2012: EXPLOSION ROCKS BUSHWICK

APARTMENT BUILDING. Anthony Stiles had been refurbishing the lofts one by one to justify a massive rent hike, and some idiot contractors had coated the floor in sealant and left it unattended to saturate. When the vapor reached the pilot light of the unit's stove, *kaboom*. No one had died, but someone on the street had been hurt when the windows blew out.

Anthony had died before Calhoun was sold, and apartment and condo listings from the shiny new development sprinkled the internet. Most included a photo of the entryway as I'd seen it, white walls and green glass.

I thought again of Mrs. Iredale, bloodless and storm-eyed, standing with Edie right on that same patch of sidewalk. Ten years ago, on a Friday evening, she'd traveled all the way to Bushwick to tell Edie that her childhood home had been foreclosed and that they'd no longer be paying her grad-school tuition. Edie's classes were surely about to start, far too late to apply for financial aid. That must have been disconcerting, destabilizing for Edie. And instead of reaching out to any of us, she'd contacted Lloyd for comfort.

Lloyd. My fact-checker light blinked on: Mrs. Iredale had dropped something verifiable, the kind of fact that—were it in a magazine story—I'd need to confirm before the issue could go to press. "He was photographing a concert that night," she'd said, back when I was still trying to figure out who the fuck Roy was, "and he headed straight into Manhattan for it. There were witnesses."

It didn't take long to find the album archived on an event photography site: the band Man Man at Webster Hall, dozens of shots of the hairy musicians adorned in colorful hats and thick cloaks of sweat. There were photos of the after-party, too, cigarettes and whiskey drinks and cool, overexposed moments of candor. Lloyd had a photo credit on each one and the time stamps put him at the show at Edie's time of death.

Of course, for obvious reasons, he wasn't *in* a single one.

I made a valiant but doomed attempt to find audience members' photos of that very show, in case Lloyd was visible onstage, but it was just too long ago, a time when files were organized and tagged so haphazardly. Instagram didn't exist; Twitter didn't let you post images. *Fuck.* I pressed my knuckles into my temples, fighting down a headache, then returned to the keyboard and searched hard for Lloyd himself.

Lloyd Kohler—not an especially common name, but after 2010, the man became a goddamn digital ghost. No website, no number, no email, not even a city. Just a smattering of forgotten photos, saturated and archaic, credited to him and hosted on other companies' sites. Maybe he'd wiped his digital identity clean, like Tessa was always telling me to do—technological and informed and afraid of everything the government had on us. Or maybe he was just an off-the-grid hippie these days. Both seemed equally plausible.

I padded into the kitchen and poured a glass of water. Stories are like mazes, an early boss had told me. When you hit a dead end, you just turn around and try another way.

Alex picked up his cell on the second ring.

"Hello?" He sounded as eager as I felt.

"It's Lindsay again," I said. Then when he didn't answer: "Lindsay Bach."

"Oh, hi! I'm sorry, I don't have you in my phone and I thought it was . . . We made an offer on a place in Sleepy Hollow, and the home inspector was supposed to—"

"I just needed to ask you something," I blurted out, afraid he'd rush me off the phone. "It's about Lloyd. I'm sorry, I know you don't want to talk about him, but it's important."

"Lloyd? Lindsay—"

"I know you guys fought. I know you had a big blowout. But do you know if he and Edie ever fought?"

"What are you talking about?"

"You're the only one who knows," I said, my voice taut, "we're the only ones who know about them, so you're the only one I can ask."

"Lindsay, what's going on? You don't sound right."

"He was with her, Alex," I said. "The night she died. She talked to her mom and then out walked Lloyd to take her away. They were still seeing each other." The long silence crackled. "I'm sorry."

"You know this how?"

"Um . . . anonymous tip," I said lightly.

"No, if you and I are the only ones who know, who told you? Did you talk to him?"

"Should I not have? Is he dangerous?"

"Lindsay, you need to tell me what the hell is going on."

"Is he? Is Lloyd dangerous?"

"What? No. Lloyd's a dick, but he's not dangerous. Or at least he wasn't the last time I talked to him."

"When was that?"

"Lindsay, what is this?"

"When did you talk to him?"

"Ten years ago. Okay? We met up a few months later—after Edie—and he manned up and told me the truth and apologized. Now can you tell me what's going on?"

"He wasn't violent?"

"No, I told you."

Well, maybe he hides it, I thought. *Like I have for the past twenty years.* "Did you know they were hooking up again?"

"Not while it was happening. But, like, it wasn't cheating. We weren't together anymore."

"But he still felt the need to come to you and tell you and apologize?"

"I mean, yeah. Bro code."

I scrunched my eyes closed. "Do you know what they talked about? Him and Edie, on her last night?"

"She was just upset. Because of her mom."

"And her mom told her . . . ?"

"Lindsay, you know this. That they were losing their condo. That they couldn't pay Lindsay's tuition."

But why rush to Calhoun to tell her? I froze, another question solidifying: Why did *any* of us know what they'd talked about? Edie hadn't had time to tell us. Lloyd couldn't. How had this intel leaked? Had Mrs. Iredale mentioned it to someone—Sarah, maybe?

"I met with Mrs. Iredale," I said. "Not Lloyd. That's how I knew."

"Now that is legit not a good idea."

"What?"

"Talking to her."

"How come?"

"You just don't want to fuck with that lady. Trust me." *We had a weird . . . incident,* he'd said in the restaurant, before polishing off his water glass.

"Tell me what happened. I know something happened with you and her parents."

"Lindsay, have you lost your damn mind? This is nuts." Why did he keep using my name?

"Please, I won't try to talk to her again. I promise. Just tell me and you'll never hear from me again."

"That's not what I . . ."

"Alex, please."

He let out a sigh. "Are you okay? Do you need me to call someone for you?"

"I'm fine. I just bumped into Mrs. Iredale and learned about Lloyd, and the whole thing really shook me. I'll feel better knowing I'm not crazy for finding her . . . unsettling."

The phone line sizzled: three seconds, four.

"Okay," he said. "Just please don't tell anyone. So, when Edie and I first started dating, she was in her second semester of fashion school, right? And I started to notice that more and more, she just wasn't going to class. And at first I thought, whatever, fashion school's probably not that hard for a smart girl like Edie, maybe she just doesn't need to be there, y'know?" A beat. "But after a few weeks, I started to question it. Like, are you getting notes from someone? Aren't your finals coming up? Don't you have, like, papers or assignments or something due? And it didn't take long to figure out that she was just willingly flunking out of school. Well, I dunno if 'willingly' is right, but letting it happen. Like, failing all of her classes and not seeming that concerned about it."

"Whoa! And she didn't say why?"

"No, it was really weird. She was just, like, don't worry about it. I didn't want to be an overbearing boyfriend or whatever, but I couldn't not worry about her."

"You were worried that . . . that what, that this was a sign she'd given up on life or something?"

"That she was not right," he said quickly. "It was just . . . I don't know if it was some kind of, like, episode or something, but it was bizarre. Edie was super smart. She went to NYU. And working in fashion was her dream, so what the hell was she doing flunking out? And not just getting Ds and Fs, I mean actually not turning shit in and getting incompletes. That can really fuck you over."

"Well, to play devil's advocate, everyone was pretty pessimistic about their professional lives back then," I pointed out. "I could see how pursuing fashion in 2009 could feel kind of pointless."

"But then you formally withdraw from your classes and go work in a clothing store. You know? This was super weird. And I knew her mom was a psychiatrist and would probably know what to do if Edie was having a breakdown or whatever, so one day at work I thought, Fuck it, and I called her."

"Her mom?"

"Yeah. When I told her, the first thing out of her mouth was 'You didn't tell anyone, did you?'"

The sweep of goose bumps up my arms.

"That was her response?"

"Well, then she backpedaled and said this was the kind of thing they wanted to handle within the family and she'd appreciate my discretion, for Edie's sake. She said, 'Do you think it's drugs?,'

'No,' 'Do you think it's alcohol?,' 'No,' and that was basically it. Edie and I never talked about it, so I don't even know if she knew, y'know, that I'd told her mom. But she started going to class again. I'm lucky we were so goddamn in love, otherwise she'd probably have been furious with me."

I wandered over to the couch. "But that left you with a bad taste in your mouth toward her mom."

"I mean, obviously. What a psychopath."

A tense silence, like we were both shocked by what he'd said.

"Anyway, I gotta go," he said. "You're okay, right?"

"Yeah, you don't need to call my mom on me."

Another long silence.

"G'night, Lindsay." Then he hung up.

I stared at the ceiling for a few seconds. I shouldn't have made that final, knee-jerk jab. It was my instincts working faster than my judgment (see easy callback, crack joke). I wrote out a text to Tessa and Damien, then deleted it. I'd have to pick through this tangle myself.

So Alex wasn't suspicious of Lloyd, who'd formally apologized to him. But he didn't like Mrs. Iredale, either. What kind of mother responds that way to her struggling daughter? Who cares more about how her child reflects on her than the kid's actual well-being? The whole flunking incident added another dimension to the suicide theory, too; if Edie had been checked out as soon as that spring, it wasn't a huge leap to think she'd be suicidal come August.

Spring semester, 2009. I plunked around in my old emails, searching for mentions of school from Edie: *classes, study, midterms, grades*. Nothing telling. And again I got wrapped up in reading our old threads, scenes that felt only tangentially related to my own history, story lines like something on TV: In one from March, I described how I'd found myself in the bedroom—the makeshift coatroom—at a lackluster house party the night before, digging through layers of fur and fringe and suede for my own vintage jacket. A man had entered and rifled around for his coat, too.

"One of those nights, hmm?" I'd said, smirking.

"I just feel like," he'd hesitated, his shoulders slumping. "To-night was so forgettable, you know? Years from now, I'm never going to remember it."

Then he'd glanced up under heavy brows and our eyes met, and he took a step closer to me, and I let out a giggle as suddenly we were making out, hard, rolling around on the crumpled pyramid of outerwear. After a minute or two, someone in the doorframe cleared their throat and we'd pulled away, laughing. Before he could say anything else, I'd snatched my coat and darted out into the street below.

I did remember that, vaguely. I forget if he was cute. That wasn't the point.

A knock at the door, and my heart seized up. I closed my laptop and crept over, then peered through the peephole. Gasping, I flicked the deadbolt and pulled the door open.

"Alex."

He had his chin tucked and his brow knitted, all broody. "Can I come in?"

I held the door wider and watched him step inside. This couldn't be real; this was an odd dream, the details all wrong.

"Nice place you got," he said, even though it's really not. He stuffed his hands into his pockets and walked over to the couch.

"What are you doing here?"

"I wanted to see you."

"Oh." I was befuddled but remembered my lines. "Can I get you something to drink?"

"That'd be amazing, yeah. Do you have some whiskey or something?"

I nodded and walked into the kitchen, then opened the cabinet over my fridge. In the back was a dusty bottle of scotch, something a clueless research assistant had gifted me for Christmas. I'd almost given it to Damien on the spot, but instead I stuck it back here next to a small fire extinguisher.

"Ice?" I called.

"Nah, neat."

Robotically, I handed it over.

"Thanks," he said. "You don't want any?"

I took a long breath in and out. "Alex, I don't drink."

"But at the restaurant—"

"I didn't drink anything. I just didn't want to make a big deal out of it."

He sat on the couch and looked up at me. My whole torso tingled, my chest and belly.

"That's not it," I heard myself say. "I wanted you to drink, because I wanted you to open up. About Edie."

He patted the cushion next to him and I sat obediently.

"There's only one Healing Hands Reiki in Brooklyn," he said finally, with a grin.

"I'm impressed you remembered." I looked down at my knees. I'd changed into sweatpants after I got back from Bushwick and now I wished I looked cuter.

"It's a memorable name." He sighed and looked straight ahead. "I was in an Uber to Grand Central and found myself putting it in. As the destination. You really worried me on the phone."

I shrugged. "I was just disturbed by everything Edie's mom told me. She's a disturbing woman."

"That's for damn sure." He put a hand on my shoulder. "I just don't understand why you're going back into all this stuff. So many years later. If I can help, I wanna help."

His hand slid to the back of my neck, and like gravity was pulling me, I leaned into him. His chest smelled like autumn; his hand rubbed my far shoulder.

"Alex, I found this horrible video," I told him, and my eyes filled with tears.

He craned his neck to look at me. "A video?"

"From the night Edie died." A tear broke free. "Here, I'll show you." I stood up and got my laptop from the table, careful to leave a few feet between us when I sat back down. His knees sloped toward me as I found Damien's email with the cleaned-up clip; I hit play, then hooked my heels on the sofa and wrapped my arms around my shins.

"I want that bitch out of my apartment!"

"I want to push her off this building!"

"I want to slit her throat!"

I could feel Alex cringing next to me. When the screen darkened, I hit stop.

"That's all there is," I lied. "The rest is just it recording inside my bag."

"All these years you've had this, and you never told anyone?"

"I just found it," I said. "I must have deleted it that same night. I just found my old camcorder and figured out how to recover deleted videos."

"Wow. Did you show Sarah?"

I shook my head. "It scared the shit out of me. And the fact that neither you nor Sarah ever mentioned it makes me think . . ." I trailed off.

"I one hundred percent do not remember that," he said, pointing at the computer. "I seriously don't. My mother didn't raise me to talk like that, dude. I don't even know." His voice was getting higher, his head shaking back and forth—a basketball player insisting he didn't just foul.

"I know. Obviously, I feel the same way. I mean, yeah, we'd been fighting, and I wasn't totally happy with her, but I would never . . . wish her harm." I picked at my fingernails. "So you don't remember this conversation at all? Or me having a camera?"

"Not at all. Swear to god."

I nodded. "I believe you." I didn't want to show him my squabble with Sarah, when I declared I wouldn't come to the concert—my alibi, the spot we both assumed I'd been. And I definitely didn't want to show him the end of the video, the part where I stumbled into SAKE. Because I didn't want him to suspect me. Ten years later, an unsolved death hanging in the balance, and I cared most about his esteem.

"So you don't remember deleting it?"

I shook my head, then looked at him slowly. Who's to say *I* deleted it, really? Couldn't it have been someone else, perhaps the other person in the room, alarmed to discover a recording device jangling around in my bag?

"So this is why you had so many questions. About Lloyd. And Edie's mom."

I nodded. "I can't shake this hunch that it wasn't a suicide. That something happened to Edie."

He didn't reply and I pressed my forehead against my knees. "My friends think I'm obsessed," I murmured, "like this is taking over my life. But you get it, right? Why we need to figure it out?"

"Of course. That doesn't make you obsessed. It just makes you a good friend. Hey, don't cry."

I turned away. Why had I shown him the video? Tessa, Damien, and now Alex: Everyone promised to help. And then they dug a little deeper and told me to back away.

"Just let me know if you think of anything else, okay?" I said. "I tried to track Greg down, but he's out on paternity leave. Oh, I want to talk to Lloyd—do you have his contact information?"

"Not anymore, no. Maybe you can find it online?"

I shook my head and stood up. "Don't worry about it. You should probably be getting home, right?"

He stayed planted. "So you haven't said anything to Sarah?"

I shook my head again. "I've been trying to sort of pursue this on my own. Back when we had dinner, she had a lot of conviction that her whole Edie-was-killed theory was stupid."

He propped his elbows on his knees, his chin on his knuckles. "But it might not be. Let's talk to her. She might not know what she knows."

I raised my eyebrows. "Good point. She did follow the same thread, albeit ten years ago." Never mind that I was a little afraid of shining a spotlight on her memories: Alex and me screaming our hexes on Edie from the rooftop, the little tiff before she headed to the concert.

"Ask her to lunch, something casual," he said. "I'll be a surprise.

We won't say it's to grill her, obviously—just a little reunion. Maybe it'll knock some memories loose."

"I'm on it," I told him. It was nice, having someone else plan the next move—someone decisive and confident, too. In fact, it was hot.

He glanced back at the laptop. "We don't need to mention the video. Do you want to send it to me? I can check if I recognize anyone else in it or anything."

The nausea boomeranged back. "I just don't really want it, you know, in the cloud." Never mind that Damien and Tessa had copies already. God, if anyone else found it . . .

"Isn't it already in an app?"

"Just a filtering app."

He frowned. "Tomorrow I'll send you an invite for a file-sharing method. Encrypted. You probably shouldn't be keeping that on your hard drive, just in case . . ."

"In case what?" Suddenly I was crying again.

"Aw, Bach. It'll be okay." He rose and leaned forward, and I let him wrap his arms around me, my tears streaming into the warmth of his collar. I leaned back and he kissed my forehead; then I turned up my chin and suddenly we were kissing, urgently, his warm soft mouth on mine.

I yanked away first and froze, his face an exact mirror of my shock. Finally I shook my head and wiped the tears off my cheeks dramatically, with the backs of my hands, the way little girls do.

"I'm sorry," he half whispered, and then he was gone.

I returned to my computer, trancelike, clicked on the folder of Flip cam videos, and opened one from early June. I'd thought it was one of the gang at Rockaway Beach, one where Alex and Edie couldn't keep their hands off each other, where they embraced in the chest-high water, laughing and kissing and bobbing like a single buoy. Self-flagellation, something to make me feel extra terrible after what I'd done.

But I mistook the date and what popped up instead was a dark scene in a bar. With a little effort, the lens focused on Sarah and Kevin, playing Jenga and sipping beer. Why did we play so much Jenga? Everyone waved languidly at the camera and went back to what they were doing. The Levee, that's where we were, a beer-y dive near the subway stop. Sarah was gossiping—her old room-mate Jenna had been caught selling drugs in Calhoun, and rumor had it that Anthony the landlord had really been the one dealing, but he'd thrown her under the bus, the exact kind of microcosm-y drama we thrived on—and begging Kevin, who probably knew the drug scene better than most, for more details. Kevin was doing his usual reserved shtick, neither confirming nor denying.

"Is it true Jenna and Anthony are sleeping together?" Sarah asked, a little too eagerly.

"Why don't you just ask her yourself?" Kevin said, poking a middle block loose.

"That'll be the day," she replied.

"Hey, let the man focus," my voice broke in. "We're going for a new world record." Slowly I scanned the tower of blocks, from the bottom to the top. Then I zoomed in on his maneuver. Kevin had chosen one of the last three-block levels left, and the move threat-ened the whole stack's structural integrity.

Kevin took a break, flexed his fingers. "I feel kinda bad. I mean, a bunch of people in Calhoun deal."

"A *bunch*," Sarah offered, smacking her glass on the table. "Shit." The stack tumbled over, slow mo at first and then in a big crash. A few pieces skittered across the floor and I canted the camera down, focusing on the downed blocks for a few seconds before turning the Flip cam off.

Sarah *had* been so on top of the gossip, so quietly in the know. Onward, forward with the plan. I texted her and she agreed to come see me in the city that weekend. But to minimize her com-mute from New Jersey, she asked that we meet near Penn Sta-tion, which meant hanging around New York's tourist-clogged hellmouth. I sent the info to Alex, all business, and he responded with a thumbs-up. He never did send me the video encryption link he'd promised. Perhaps he, too, had a hard time remembering anything we'd talked about before the kiss.

At work, I had a simple goal: to think of anything but Alex's mouth on mine. I failed miserably and nearly doubled over in shame when Tessa texted, cheerfully asking how I was doing. I didn't answer. My mind kept showing me snippets: a married man, on an errand his wife didn't know about, sitting on my couch and sipping secret scotch. His hand gently guiding my head to the crook of his neck. The kiss like a stamp on my brow and then his eyes meeting mine . . .

I grabbed my phone and opened my messages. My text to Josh the night before was still unanswered: "How's work otherwise?"

I drummed my fingers on the desk, then tapped out another message: "I confirmed everyone at Sir thinks the design startup is all smoke and mirrors, too. So your job should be safe. ☺"

A few minutes passed, then thirty. Then an entire afternoon.

Chapter 12

The Saturday subways were all delays and reroutes, but I still arrived early to the diner off Thirty-fourth Street. I sipped my bad coffee and felt my quickened pulse thumping in my fingers and neck.

Sarah burst in sweaty and frazzled and ten minutes behind schedule. "I walked the wrong way at first," she gasped by way of apology. I waved it away and sped through the obligatory chitchat, my eyes on the entryway.

The front door jingled and Alex appeared, slick with sweat. He looked handsome and eager, like a golden retriever, and I watched him until Sarah cut herself off midsentence and twisted in her seat. Then she whirled back to me, confused.

"Alex, over here!" I waved, and he grinned and sauntered over, pausing to give us both hugs. I let go before he did. Sarah was smiling now, too, but still looking flummoxed.

"Well, surprise!" I said as Alex slid in next to Sarah.

"That's for sure! I had no idea you guys were even back in touch!" Sarah leaned her elbows on the table.

"Yeah, we bumped into each other, and I thought it would be fun to get together," I said. "Impromptu reunion."

Sarah and Alex fumbled through some polite catchup. As I watched them, an eerie feeling spread through my stomach and ribs. Here was the crew from the rooftop, sitting in the same triangle ten years later, drinking sweaty cups of ice water instead of beer and shots.

"So, Lindsay, you said you had something to discuss," Sarah prompted. "Was that just a ruse?"

"Actually, I did want to talk to you guys. Together. I've been reading more about Edie's death, and I sort of suddenly realized I have the skills to really examine it. And, like, the distance, maybe?"

Sarah's face was politely blank, a passenger waiting for the flight attendant to take her drink order.

"I basically—I'm realizing I don't remember it as clearly as I thought I did, like maybe I did actually black out, and it's this missing piece of my memory that . . . that you guys were all present for, and that was really bothering me."

She'd stiffened. Alex kept his eyes on his place mat.

"I went through the case files, and like you said, it just—it doesn't add up," I said. "I can't believe I'm saying this ten years after you . . . after all of it. But it's been keeping me up at night. We owe it to her to get it right."

Sarah looked at Alex, then at me. "So what's your question?"

"I just—I don't have all my memories of that night. And so I guess I came to . . . to ask for yours." My voice cracked on the last sentence, but I kept the rush of tears from breaking free.

Sarah's chin trembled and she turned to gaze out the window. "I'm sorry, Lindsay. I'm sorry you were spared the life-altering experience of finding your roommate with a bullet in her head because you'd had too much to drink. But I don't feel like it's a good idea for us to talk you through it so you can implant some false memory of being there."

"Harsh," Alex said, knee-jerk. We were still. This time I blinked hard and let the tears fall, one from an outer corner, one from inside, along my nose. I felt the pink steam of shame, of disgust with myself.

"Am I wrong?" she said to Alex, eyebrows high.

"I'm sorry," I said before he could answer. "I really didn't think through what I was asking. I know it's not fair. I . . . I'm sorry." I swallowed with effort and began to rise from the booth. My thigh stuck on the vinyl and made a ripping noise.

"You know, I was basically ostracized for saying it wasn't a suicide," Sarah offered.

"I'm sorry I wasn't there for you," I said, sitting back down. "I didn't even know you were going through that. But I'm sure everyone was . . . It was hard enough to process as is."

"Look, we were all having a hard time," Alex added, as if that were an apology. "We were worried about you. Like . . . now we were losing *two* friends instead of one."

She nodded. I felt a childish spray of annoyance: three friends, right? Weren't they sad to see me go?

"Listen, I'm really, really sorry nobody listened to you." I leaned my head against the booth and closed my eyes. "For what it's worth, Kevin told me he didn't think it was a suicide, either."

"Really?" They said it almost in unison.

I nodded.

"I didn't know that," Alex said accusingly, and I shot him a look: As far as Sarah knew, *all* of this was new material.

She sighed. "So Kevin had his suspicions, too. I can't figure out if that makes me feel better or worse."

The waitress came by; Alex got a beer, and Sarah ordered chicken noodle soup, an odd choice. It was strange to watch our old dynamic creeping in: analytical Sarah; confident, patronizing Alex. His fingers brushed mine when he grabbed his glass, and I pulled my arm away; I had to focus.

"Did Kevin say anything else?" Sarah asked.

"No, just that I should figure out what really happened that night."

"And you looked into it? What'd you find?"

"No real bombshells." Well, apart from the incriminating Flip cam video. "It's weird that the cops didn't talk to Greg, isn't it? The guy she dated before you, Alex."

"I did; I looked into him," Sarah replied.

"Really?" Alex and I both turned to look at her.

"Yeah, I was in total Nancy Drew mode for a while. He was out of town for a conference the week Edie died. He gave a presentation, so it was pretty well documented." We must have looked astonished. "I went deep on this."

"Did you know her mom was there that night?" I said.

She nodded.

"You *did*?" Alex perked up.

"Yeah, the night she died. Shortly before you came over. I told the cops, and it always bothered me how little they wanted to hear it. Like, I was staring at the guy with the pen thinking, 'Aren't you going to write this down?' "

"What'd you tell them?" Alex asked.

She let out an old, tired sigh. "Well, Edie and I were alone in the main room—I was in the kitchen doing dishes, she was on the couch drinking whiskey and typing away into that diary she kept on her computer—and her phone rings. She talks into it for a little bit, sounding angry and I'm trying not to listen, especially since I'm still annoyed with her. Then she hangs up and says, 'What the f-word?' Like, loud enough and then with a waiting air, so I turned around and said, 'What?' She made a face and said, 'My mom is here.' " Sarah played with a lock of hair. "I remember looking around and noticing the bong and cigarette butts and empty beer bottles and stuff everywhere, so I was like, 'She's coming in here?!' And she said, 'Don't worry about it, I'll just go meet her,' all annoyed like I'd told her her mom wasn't allowed in. So she grabbed her purse and walked out. That was the last time I saw her. I mean, alive."

The diary—Mrs. Iredale had mentioned it, too. I made a mental note to double-check that I hadn't missed it in the case files.

"Alex, where were you during this?" I asked.

"Earlier that night? I was hanging out with Kevin and his bandmates. We went to the taco truck." He was tearing the cardboard coaster into shreds. "Her mom was pretty intense, right?"

"Super intense. Always made me uncomfortable," Sarah concurred.

"You think her mom did it?" I said, looking back and forth at them. I knew even as I said it that it was a crazy leap.

But Sarah took it seriously. "Probably not. I dunno. Edie didn't really seem to like her parents, but . . . I mean, her mom was obsessed with her. I dunno why she'd kill her." Her soup appeared and she sprinkled it with oyster crackers.

"But it's chilling she was there that night, right?" I pressed. "What if she hung around after they talked and then snuck up to the apartment?"

Alex crossed his arms. "That's a lot of luck, to get all the way in and out without anybody seeing you. It was a Friday night—there were people everywhere."

"Well, no one saw Edie going back to her own apartment," I said. "Or—if there was someone else, if we're correct that she didn't kill herself—nobody saw *the other person* coming in or out. Calhoun was a labyrinth." It was its own dimension. Maybe portals lurked below the staircases and between the floors, wormholes for sudden inexplicable entrances and vanishings.

Sarah shrugged. "I told the cops about her stopping by, but they never even made a note about it. Actually, how'd you figure it out?"

"I went and saw her last week. Her mom."

"Whoa. What'd she say?" Sarah asked.

I flicked a glance at Alex, then leaned forward. "She told me she left Edie with the guy she was secretly seeing. Lloyd."

She frowned. "He had the bouffy blond hair, right?"

"Wait, you knew about him?" Alex said.

Her eyes bulged, then dove to the bowl in front of her.

I started laughing. "This is so ridiculous." I was surprised that this revelation still stung—that I now cared more about Edie sharing the secret with Sarah than having the secret at all. The sudden singe of feeling Left Out. "This is like a fucking soap opera. I forgot what a drama magnet Edie was."

A tense silence.

"That's why we broke up," Alex offered finally. "I found out about Lloyd when we were still dating. So if you were . . . Lindsay said you guys always wondered what happened."

Sarah's cheeks were scarlet.

"I had a huge crush on Lloyd, which Edie knew about and encouraged, so *that's* not humiliating or anything," I said. The teensiest part of me wanted Alex to feel jealous. When had I slept with Lloyd? It was before he and Edie had begun hooking up, right?

Sarah tilted her bowl to collect the last of the broth. "I talked to him, back in the day. Just 'cause I knew they'd been seeing each other, but then I figured out he was the last one to see her. But his alibi held up, and he didn't really have anything to add. He'd been in the neighborhood and Edie had texted him begging him to come, like, rescue her from her mom. They talked by the front door a minute, he had to leave to shoot a concert, and then—I mean, we know he was onstage when it happened."

I frowned, working through the timeline. "He told you they were at the front door?"

"Uh-huh."

I shook my head. "You said this was around when I came over. And I didn't see them. Alex, you didn't either, coming back from the taco truck."

"I probably took the side entrance," he said, cocking his head. "You reach it first if you're heading east. You would, too, if you were coming from your apartment."

"That's true." How different would my life be if I'd walked one hundred and fifty feet farther? I turned to Sarah. "When did you talk to Lloyd?"

"That fall, right in the middle of everything."

Ten years ago. "Had you met him before?"

She shook her head. "Edie had pointed him out once, but they never really hung out at Calhoun. I guess where you could see them." She nodded at Alex. "I only talked to him that one time."

"Alex, you could have seen them at Calhoun that night, talking to her mom."

He shrugged. "Guess you're right. They were lucky I took the other door."

"Sarah, do you still have his contact info?"

"Seriously?"

I nodded. The waitress tipped more coffee into my mug, brown liquid sloshing everywhere.

"Of course not."

"Okay."

Now Sarah leaned back. "I just wish I could figure out what she was *doing*," she said, "for that last ninety minutes or so. She said goodbye to Lloyd—didn't tell him anything about where she was going—and then she obviously didn't come back to the apartment, because we were all still in there. There's just this . . . gap."

The lost hours.

"Maybe her mom called her down again," I said. "After Lloyd left. They talked some more, they're getting eaten alive by mosquitoes, so Edie brings her back inside to your apartment, which is newly empty."

"The gun—the weapon was Kevin's gun, though, something in the room," Alex said. "Her mom wouldn't have known it was there."

"I'm not saying it was *premeditated*," I pointed out. "Who the fuck knows what went on? Maybe her mom insisted on coming in to look for something, or to, I don't know, tell Edie to pack up and go, and they were fighting and things got out of hand. Maybe it was an accident."

Sarah shook her head. "We have the phone records. Lloyd was the last person she texted. Her mom couldn't have called again."

I bit my lip. "Okay, but maybe—"

"This is crazy," Sarah announced, a little too loudly. "We're talking like I did when I was twenty-three and grieving and trying to make everything a lot more complicated than it actually was. Right?" She slurped her ice water. "Like, no, life isn't actually a soap opera and the simplest answer is probably the right one. There's a reason nothing you've uncovered during your . . . your *investigation* proves anything different."

The three of us watched one another across the booth, across the ten years.

"But if Lloyd left the concert early," I said, "maybe he quickly got all the photos he needed and headed back to—"

"Lindsay, stop. Do you hear yourself? Do you have any idea how you sound?" Sarah pressed her palms flat on the table. "Look, with Edie . . . I loved the girl, but she had a lot of enemies. We could probably fill a stadium with people she had a beef with, right?" She let out a mirthless chortle. "She was smart, and funny, and incredibly charismatic and all that, but she could also be really horrible to people. I lived with her—I saw that firsthand. I mean, weren't you guys fighting at the end? If I didn't know you better . . . hey, you grew up shooting guns, right? You knew Kevin's gun was there, you wandered away from the rest of us before the concert, you don't remember a . . . a *fucking* thing from the night—"

Alex piped up: "Hey, you know—"

"And I know what you did."

We locked eyes. Did Sarah know about the Warsaw Incident, the drunken disaster Edie had promised not to share? Had she betrayed me?

"To your mom. When you were a kid? Edie told me."

Not the Warsaw Incident—something worse. We stared at one another and the entire room vibrated with my heartbeat, *bum bum, bum bum, bum bum*.

She pulled the napkin off her lap, folded it carefully. "I said if I *didn't* know you better. Look, at the end of the day, I think she was really depressed, and she took some drugs that messed her up even further, and she was alone and everything sucked and she made a really bad decision."

Sarah knew. The dark childhood secret I'd let slip just once, soused on my friendship with Edie, deep into a game of Truth or

Truth. I looked down at my hands, limp and folded in my lap like sleeping kittens. *What are you two capable of?*

"But we're still here. And, Lindsay, it's been ten years. Ten *years*. If Edie were sitting here right now, she would look all of us in the eye and tell us we should move the heck on."

I felt rage rising within me, a steamy red spiral, but I fought it, moved my gaze back to the window and the people crisscrossing on the sidewalk outside. All consumed by their own little dramas.

"You're right," I said softly. "You're so right. I'm sorry, Sarah. I'm sorry to bring this up."

"It's okay. I understand it's—it's not something you can talk about with a lot of people," she said. She slapped a ten-dollar bill on the table, an odd, cinematic move, and said she'd better go. Alex and I slid out of the booth and gave her clumsy hugs. She was heading for the door when I remembered a final question.

"Sarah, wait." She turned and peered at me, and I cleared my throat. "We had a little tiff that night, you and I, right? Right after we came down from the roof. About my wanting to go home and not come with you to the show?"

She nodded slowly. "That sounds right. I hate having to walk into stuff like that by myself."

"Then where was Alex?" We both turned his way.

He raised his eyebrows. "Guys, I did a lot of coke back then. And I know you girls weren't into it. Pretty sure I stopped on another floor to do a line and then met you at the show. I mean, right?"

We all looked at one another. Frustration swelled and my instinct, suddenly, was to cry.

"That sounds right," Sarah said finally. "I remember finding you at the show. Well, see you later." She headed for the exit.

Alex was looking at me oddly. " 'What you did to your mom'?" he said.

I shook my head, tears breaking free again, and walked past him toward the door. He called my name a couple of times, but I turned just long enough to say, "Alex, please don't." It was one of those silver days, overcast and still too bright, and when the door swung closed behind me, the air swallowed me right up.

On the subway ride home, I let this new horror unfold: *Sarah knew.* I couldn't believe that Edie had told her, that all this time, another person knew what I'd done back in middle school. At the diner, I'd been too stunned to ask Sarah when Edie had shared it and why. Maybe Edie had gleefully gossiped about me, the same way she complained to me about Sarah; maybe she'd worked hard to keep both of us privately convinced we were in the number-one-friend spot. I felt a blast of nausea and tipped my sweaty forehead toward my knees.

Middle-school Lindsay. I'd spent two decades scraping away any signs that, deep down, I was a violent, dangerous creature. In fact, for years I'd felt secretly relieved that Edie, the only other person who might think that, was long dead.

I checked the case files as soon as I got home, but Edie's diary wasn't among them—another timeline lost, her brief life instead flattened into phone records, ER discharge papers, a bloodless autopsy report. I dug around under my bed until I found the bag I was looking for, a small stack of old sketchbooks and diaries slipped into a canvas tote, and pulled out the spiral-bound note-book I'd been picturing.

I'd journaled sporadically in middle and high school, bored and lonely and newly determined to hone my writing skills. The act soothed me, the way my clacking fingers turned my brain's chatter into narrative, something finite, controllable. I would type up entries on the hulking computer in my room because I didn't like my own handwriting. I still don't: rushed and leaning this way and that, too often unreadable. Crazy-person handwriting. I'd fiddled with the page settings to get the margins right, so that I could slice the sides off with an X-ACTO knife and glue them into this notebook.

It's funny, come to think of it, that my parents let me keep an X-ACTO knife in my room. Perhaps they didn't know about it.

I opened the journal at random, to sometime early sophomore year. Printers were shittier then, strips of black missing in the middle of lines of texts. *Read between the lines,* my neurons fired at random.

> *I'm ravenous all the time now. Mom says it's nerves, but I know it's whatever they switched me to. They thought it was the Zoloft giving me headaches, though they haven't gone away and now I'm convinced it's this quiet hell of Onalaska, Wisconsin. M&D have eased up on the surveillance compared with last year, I guess because I'm almost 16 now and "making very promising progress," as Dr. Mahoney wrote recently in an email Mom printed out and stupidly left on her desk: That's how you discuss your dog in obedience school, not your daughter. I can't wait for college. I don't understand why people are so content to be here, imagining their whole lives spooling out without trying anything new or experiencing anywhere better.*

What followed was a boring tale of being stuck at piano lessons, waiting for my parents to pick me up while a popular girl drove up for her own lesson and made polite, banal conversation. I could tell even from my written account that I'd been the bitch in the situation—so shy and self-conscious that I'd come across as hostile. How had I gone from hating popular girls to becoming one's best friend?

I flipped forward a bit, the pages shuffling awkwardly under their glue. Josh was popular in high school, I decided. Maybe not prom king, but definitely prom court.

It was toward the end of that year that I started admiring my artsy classmates. I wrote something gushing about Michaela Leonard, a painter in eleventh grade who'd made a blog tribute to men in black-framed glasses. She let me burn copies of some of her CDs: The Get Up Kids, Weezer, The Dismemberment Plan. I could almost picture them, nacreous in my leather CD wallet.

I couldn't play a CD now if I tried, I realized. I'd fact-checked a story once on futurists' predictions, and one had commented that we're in the digital dark ages: A few short centuries from now, historians won't have any way to access the pixels and bytes into which we funnel our lives. The predigital stuff, this glue-y journal in my hands—that was what survived.

Sarah must have heard me, some weird tin-can-telephone telepathy stringing from my cerebrum to hers, because the next day she texted me a photo of a number written in curly, girlish handwriting. "Found my Moleskine from back then," her message read. "This = Lloyd."

I called him immediately, doubting he'd have the same number ten years on anyway. There was some clicking, then the sound of fumbling. "Whoa! Hello?"

"Hi, is this Lloyd Kohler?"

"Yep. Whoa, I was just trying to use my phone and you were there. Who is this?"

"My name's Lindsay Bach. I know this is random, but we have a good friend in common from a long time ago. In New York."

I felt my shoulders rise, ready for him to hang up.

"And who's that?" he said finally.

"Please hear me out if you can. I'm calling about Edie Iredale."

Another massive silence. I went on: "I'm sure you don't remember this, but you and I actually hung out a few times around then, too. Edie and I bumped into you and Alex Kotsonis and some girls one night in Manhattan and ended up on a rooftop. Hanging out in an empty pool." And, later, having terrible drunken sex. And, later still, being engaged in battery, when I blackened your eye. My fridge clunked on, humming through the silence.

"Familiar. Fourteenth Street, right?"

He remembered. I felt a small, pathetic spurt of pleasure.

"Yes, that's the one. And I know you and Edie kept seeing each other later. I don't mean to bring up anything painful, but I'm just trying to"—I hesitated—"get some answers."

"Ha. Is this like *High Fidelity,* where you talk to all her exes, only the twist is that she's dead?"

I tried mirroring. "Pretty much, except that in the movie version, Catherine Zeta-Jones had nothing helpful to say. I'm hoping you can do better."

"Doubt it. Why the fact-finding mission?"

"I think someone killed her," I said. "I don't think it was suicide."

Another long wait and I began to regret my frankness. Why couldn't I stick with the old party line, that I was looking back and trying to understand why Edie did what she did? What about this kooky kid, on whom I'd had a breathless crush *ten years ago,* made me blurt out the truth?

"What makes you say that?" He had one of those preternaturally calm voices, like an actor who manages to make all his lines sound improvised.

"Mostly little stuff." Like that she was with someone in her living room shortly before the gun was fired. And that I'd walked into that living room moments before it happened, raring for a fight. It hit me in another wave: *What the hell happened?*

He groaned. "You know, I was stupid-lucky I had to work that night. Otherwise who knows what kinda story the cops woulda spun. Jealous lover or whatever."

My heart pounded in the pads of my fingers.

"So you did talk to the cops."

"'Course. They were pretty fucking incompetent, though. Didn't even bother with me until I called 'em a few days later to ask what they'd found."

"They didn't track you down?"

"No, stupid NYPD just figured it was a suicide, case closed."

So much candor. I slowed my breathing.

"Didn't Edie's mom see you, like, take Edie inside? Didn't she tell the cops?"

"Fuck if I know what she told 'em. They just didn't seem that interested."

I flopped onto my bed. "And did you have something to tell them?"

"Huh?"

"About Edie. About how she seemed, or . . . how her mom seemed, or something."

"Nah. I mean, they were both crying, her mom had just told her they were basically broke, right? She started texting me like whoa, begging me to come get her. So finally I did. I was only a couple blocks away."

"Did you talk to her mom at all?"

"I mean, I introduced myself. Tried to be polite. It was awkward as hell because they were both crying. She was, like, wild-eyed."

"Edie?"

"No, her mom. Like, she really didn't want Edie to go. Edie said her mom was freaking her out."

Freaking her out? Edie's mother was an odd duck, but she seemed composed. "What exactly did Mrs. Iredale say?"

"Look, I dunno. She bounced as soon as I got there. And Edie didn't really wanna talk about it. We only had a couple minutes before I had to leave for the show anyway. I was dragging around all my gear."

"Where was Edie headed when you left?"

"Just back inside. I figured she was going to her place." He started laughing. "Lady, you're better at this than the cops, you know."

"The cops. They never spun together a . . . jealous-lover story, like you said?"

"Buncha clowns."

"What'd they miss? *Were* you jealous? I know you were keeping your relationship a secret."

"Ah, fuck. We were just stupid fucking kids. Hanging on to each other while the world, you know, crumbled around us."

This was the Lloyd I remembered, ADD-addled and talking like a beat poet. I felt a pulse of envy that he'd chosen to cling to Edie, not me.

"What are you talking about?"

"Fuck if I know. I'm pretty bombed."

I waited him out.

"Let me tell you something, Lindsay."

"I'm listening."

A little exhale, like he'd just finished a deep sip. "When the ground splits open," he said, "the only smart reaction is to run."

The fuck?

"What do you mean, when the ground splits open?"

"I mean that's what we were living, babe, you, me, Edie, everyone back then. When we were coming out of this fucked-up phase of politeness and fake prosperity and everyone believing they just had to act proper to get everything they'd ever dreamed of on a silver platter."

I gave a noncommittal "Mmm."

Again, the sound of swallowing. "Edie was bored out of her mind," he said. "Oh, I remember. She was getting a useless degree in like theoretical clothing design, and she was stuck with Alex because they lived together, right?"

I assented.

"And she had those rich, miserable parents in the city and she just, I don't know, she totally got it. We were just, you know, living our way through it."

I felt him wait for me to say something, so I tried mirroring again, some faux-hippie shit. "Proving that, like, you weren't gonna let the monster shaking the tree take you down."

"Exactly. You got it." He tittered. "And now we're back to being hubristic motherfuckers and everyone who's doing semi-okay feels even more entitled to act like they earned it, survival of the fittest, dog-eat-dog meritocratic bullshit."

I pictured him now, hair long and scraggly, brain cells desiccated like overbaked cookies.

"When did you start seeing her?"

He giggled. "You really do sound like a cop."

"I'm not." Suddenly, recklessly: "I think I might have been involved. In her death."

Surprised silence, then laughter, full-on guffaws. "The fuck are you talking about?"

"We were fighting, I know how to use a gun, I was blackout drunk, and I was hanging around her apartment that night. I'm—that's why I'm investigating."

"Well, shit." He collected himself. "Here I thought *I* was an alcoholic."

"Fuck you." Panic was fanning out inside me: Why had I told him, what had I done?

"Go ahead, Sherlock. I'm an open fucking book."

Everything tightened. "Do you think she killed herself?"

"I dunno. I guess not if you killed her."

"I'm serious."

"I mean, she had some fucked-up stuff going on, but so did everyone else."

"Like what?" Had he known about the miscarriage?

"Aw, you know. Secret love affair."

I rolled my eyes. "Can you think of anyone who'd want to hurt her?"

"Nah. Edie was cool. I mean, unless *you* secretly hated her."

I was growing dizzy; the room tilted like I'd just gotten off a roller coaster. "When were you guys actually hooking up?"

"Fuck if I remember."

"Can you try? When did it start, what season was it?"

"Ohhh, fuck. Let's see. I ran into her at a bar in my neighborhood, she was with . . . I think she lived with the girl. And we were sitting outside so it had to be summer. Actually . . . I think it was one of the first truly nice days, so maybe May?"

A roommate? Sarah?

"Was she Asian?"

"Edie?"

"The friend she was with."

"No . . . I mean, I don't think so. I don't really remember what she looked like. I didn't, like, hang out with her friends. Obviously."

"And what happened?"

"Uhhhh, she recognized me, and we talked, and finally her roommate left and it was just us and we made out in the bar and then I took her back to my place. Which was sort of just a mattress on the floor in this shitty-ass railroad apartment in Bed-Stuy, so after that we just went to her parents' apartment whenever they weren't around."

Right, as Alex had said. "And you knew she was seeing Alex?"

"I mean, yeah, but it sounded like it wasn't going great. And it's not like he and I were talking."

"You'd fought?"

"Stupid thing over a guitar."

Okay, so their stories matched. "When was that?"

"Hey, I know, let me just check my blog!" Sarcastically, with mock cheer.

"I know, I get it, it was a long time ago." I sighed, felt a shudder in it, and decided to go with it. "I'm just trying to piece this together. Ten years too late." I made sure he heard the wobble in my voice, added a loud sniffle for good measure. The silence bloomed between us and I tacked on another sniff and murmured, "Sorry."

"Listen, babe," he said. "It was a long time ago, so don't hold me to anything. But I think Alex and I stopped hanging out, I don't know, maybe February or March of that year? Winter sometime. And Edie and I started hooking up around May, and it lasted maybe a month or two before Alex . . . found out, so we stopped for a while. And then picked up again after they'd broken up, but didn't, you know, tell him at the time, obviously."

"Did you and Alex, like, have a stupid manly fistfight at some point or anything?"

"Nah. I just avoided him."

For a moment, a scene stitched itself together in front of me, one that made sense: Edie and Lloyd canoodling in her apartment for some reason, Alex walking in on them, altercation, grabbing of a gun, Edie tries to intercept, shots fired. Then I remembered Lloyd had been up onstage snapping photos of a band.

"I don't actually think I was involved. I was just trying to get you to open up."

"Ha. Okay."

A long silence.

"Are you gonna tell anyone?" I asked.

"Who would I tell?" Another swallowing sound. "I'm just a drunk piece of shit."

I heaved a sigh, my stomach aching.

"Well, I gotta boogie," he announced. "Good luck to you, kid."

He hung up and I lay staring up at the ceiling, where a long crack snaked out of the doorframe, forked into two, and petered out just above my head.

I passed a few lonely nights eating dinner in front of the TV, willing Josh to text, Josh or Alex or Michael or someone, someone who'd want me to come out of my apartment and in doing so, to materialize again. At night I lay around my apartment and scared myself, imagining shapes hulking in the corners, wondering what was behind the shower curtain as I peed. Looking up into the mirror sharply, like I could catch the phantom lurking over my shoulder. Instead I just saw my own face, eyes pooled in blackness, cheeks sunken like a skull's.

Early one morning, I awoke with a start, sweaty and twisted in my sheets and unclear if the heat had triggered a bad dream or vice versa. It took me a moment to register the fake blue light casting shadows on my bed—my laptop, which I'd left open and blank, was lit up now. An automatic update or something, I figured; I crept over, prepared to snap it shut.

My email was open—probably the last thing I'd looked at before bed. I almost closed the screen without reading it, fighting off that ache of curiosity.

Mostly stupid stuff, newsletters and promotions.

And one at the top, from fourteen minutes before.

> From: Edith Iredale <eiredale1@gmail.com>
> To: Lindsay Bach <lbach@tress.com>
> Wednesday, August 14, 2019 at 4:06 AM
>
> *Don't.*

Chapter 13

I thought about calling Tessa on the spot, even though it was four thirty in the morning and there was nothing in particular she could do. But I'd stopped updating her on the investigation, her and Damien. I battered around the apartment turning on lights and checking locks. Finally I forwarded the email to Tessa with a plea to call me. I felt anger building like a panic that no one was up to help me, that I was alone in this lunacy, getting emails from the dead.

Tessa called a little after seven, her voice scratchy, and I put her on speakerphone.

"So somebody hacked into Edie's account and sent you that?" she said.

"Apparently! Unless we're now of the belief that the dead can fucking send emails." I looked around again, grateful for the buttery light that pressed in from the windows, washing away the shadows.

"So . . . we think this means what?"

"This means someone knows I've been poking around and wants me to stop. Right? Probably whoever else was in the room, whom I just missed with my camera. I mean, what else could it mean?"

"Is it a threat?" She sounded a little more awake now. "Should we call the police?"

I took a long sip of coffee. "Is that a stupid idea?"

"It just might be hard to explain. Or to get them to do anything for you. I mean, since there wasn't an actual verbal threat. Hang on, let me ask Will."

I picked at my cuticle as they discussed it in muffled voices. "Okay, I'm right," she announced, suddenly loud. "Since there wasn't an actual threat, let alone a quote-unquote credible one, there's not much they'd do. Do you want me to look into the header info?"

"Header? Is that like metadata?"

"Sort of. It's the data involved in getting an email from Point A to Point B. Maybe it'll show who actually sent it."

A sprig of hope. "Yes! That's a great idea. Thank you." We were quiet for a moment.

"Lindsay, this is fucking weird. This is scary."

"I know."

"Are you still talking to people about this? I worry about you. I was already worried about your emotional well-being—"

"You mean my mental health."

"—but now I'm actually worried for your safety," she finished. She didn't correct me.

"I'll stop," I told her, wishing it were true, wishing I could. "Let me know about the header, though, okay? But I'll delete all my files and everything. 'Cause you're right. This is getting weird."

"Do you want to stay here tonight?"

"No," I said, because my next move was to keep searching.

Lying in bed that evening, I finally found a photo on the website of Nicky Digital, a then-ubiquitous party photographer: Lloyd on-stage, adjusting his lens, a few feet behind Man Man's bespectacled drummer. So his alibi did check out. Lloyd really was handsome, with his striking bone structure and tousled blond hair. We'd had sex in April, a month before he and Edie had begun hooking up. Of course he didn't want to keep fucking me. Nobody ever does.

I set the computer on my nightstand and flicked off the light, exhausted but unable to sleep. For hours I lay in a fugue state, my body mostly asleep but my mind still meandering, curling like a mist over a landscape of thoughts of Michael or Alex or Josh, somewhere else, probably real but possibly my own invention. *I feel lonely,* my brain quietly announced, and hearing it so baldly, my eyes welled up. I fell asleep in a fuzzy sleeping bag of self-pity.

Rain pinged against my air conditioner. Morning. I padded across the room and pulled the curtain aside: a downpour, splattering against the window and turning Fulton Street into a smear of green and gray. A perfect day to feel sorry for myself, to believe and not-believe that Edie was murdered, that the world was stiff and cruel and somebody out there wanted me dead, too. A taxi almost hit a jaywalker, the driver leaning on the horn instead of the brakes, and beneath an umbrella I could just make out a lifted hand, the middle finger held high. I blinked away the tableau of what would've happened if the jaywalker hadn't gotten out of the way in time. Supine on the ground, a limb crushed flat. Bystanders circling up stupidly. A scarlet pool rippling outward from his body, mingling with the rain and—

My watch and phone and laptop all vibrated at once from different parts of the apartment. I squinted at my computer, and it took me a minute to make sense of the incoming message. Three letters, all from Josh: *Hey.*

At seven forty-five on a Thursday morning. Was he still out partying or something? It'd been more than two weeks since I'd seen him, since we'd sat on a bench and said stoner-y things about moving around in time, in the fourth dimension. I knew I should make him wait a bit, punish him for the unanswered texts and the fortnight of silence, so I puttered around, cleaning up the living room and brewing coffee and putting away clean dishes and it'd still only been eight minutes and I'd run out of things to do, so fuck it: *Hey!*

"What's up?" he typed back.

"Not too much," I wrote. "You?"

"Same."

"Big plans for tonight?" I said, because I was suddenly bored, because this was boring and some bizarre cocktail of boredom and fear was making me reckless.

"Still figuring it out. You?"

"Same." Then: "Let me know if you want to meet up later."

"Yeah, def!" he said, right away, and I glared at the phone for its succinctness, for being the conduit for an answer that could either mean yes, we'll meet up, or yes, I'll let you know if I feel like it.

Alex updated his Facebook photo that day, a beaming picture with his perfect wife, and I glared at them both. After work I show-ered and shaved my legs, just in case, and as the sun sank behind neighboring buildings and nobody contacted me to do anything, I slipped into a robe and reopened the old email archives. I poked around without a clear plan, knowing I should be more system-atic about this, I should at least be recording my search terms. I cringed my way through a few email exchanges with Edie where I clearly wanted to ask about Lloyd; I hadn't known they were sleeping together and still saw her as my connection to my crush. I brought him up with faux casualness, begging between the lines for an update. I'd finally broken down and sent him a text, labori-ously composed to strike the proper breezy tone, and he hadn't responded, which filled me with a wash of shame.

Dating sucks. Fuck Josh; I didn't want to see him anyway.

But he did text, a little after ten, and I was immediately ner-vous, looking around like a trapped animal.

"Hey! You out?"

"Just finishing up dinner," I lied, then instantly regretted it: He could ask where, he could fact-check me.

"Come hang out!" he replied. "I'm at Jimmy Rhoda's."

I looked it up: a dive bar in Bed-Stuy, a gritty, gentrifying neighborhood that reminded me of the Bushwick I'd known.

"Will you be there for a bit?"

"I'll wait for you," he said, and, unsure what else to do, I sent him a smiley face and ducked into the bathroom, heart pounding like the circa 2009 playlist I put on the speakers.

I was about to leave when I turned around, stepping back to the cabinet over my fridge. The scotch was still there, next to the fire extinguisher. *In case of emergency.* I thought of Josh's gleaming smile, then of Alex's soft lips, fringed by a five o'clock shadow. I froze like someone at the top of the high dive and then took a swig straight from the bottle, chasing it with water and then swishing some mouthwash so I wouldn't smell like a damn alcoholic. I coughed at its golden burn, and as my cab coasted along Myrtle Avenue, I felt the forgotten, familiar sensation—booze prickling outward from my belly. I was going to meet Josh's friends, which was strange but somehow casual, a hurdle I'd never crossed with Michael but that I'd sail past with Josh before we had any reason to think it mattered. I wondered how many of them would be sitting around with him. I wondered, too, if they'd think I looked nice, clad for more or less anything in tight jeans and a racerback top. Surely Josh would think I looked pretty. Surely that's why he invited me.

I pushed open the bar's door without noticing the bouncer murmuring at me from the side, and I had to back out to hand him my ID. Then back inside and the music crescendoed, something hip and bass-y, and I took a few steps in and scanned the crowd, sure I'd find him soon, sure I could do this without shrinking into myself and hunching over my phone.

I spotted someone from behind, talking animatedly, and it looked more or less like him, and anyway, how many men with thick wavy black hair could there be in this bar, and *anyway,* I looked hot, who wouldn't want to talk to me? I tapped him on the shoulder and he stopped talking and turned around and it was him. We smiled at each other and he stood up to give me a hug with a kiss on the cheek, then kept his arm strung across my shoulders as he introduced his friends, a pretty black woman with a sculpted 'fro and a surprisingly tall Asian guy with a good handshake, what a hip and casually diverse crowd. I forgot their names right away but it didn't matter because we were already hanging out anyway.

"You look like you need a drink," Josh said, and he was right, I did, and he guided me over to the bar and asked what I was having and I said, "Jameson on the rocks," knowing it was the cool thing to order, and he looked impressed and paid for it even though I must be the one who makes so much more money, although I don't know, people with knowledge of 3-D technology are probably more in demand than anachronistic print staffers. We made small talk by the bar as we waited for my drink, my wit on full display this time, and he smiled and toasted my glass with his beer when it arrived.

We stayed for three rounds at Jimmy Rhoda's, the crowd getting thicker and steamier around us, and then someone checked their watch and said we should probably go to Rocco's. Josh asked if that was cool and I nodded, smiling, and we all squashed into a cab, me for some reason in the middle but it was fine. Now the cab was cruising to Ridgewood, and Queen came on the radio and I pointed out we were listening to Queen on the way to Queens, and no one else knew the words but at least they all laughed and let the song play out, sing it Mr. Mercury.

Rocco's apartment was like a nice place with shitty furniture clustered here and there, a big black marble kitchen island piled high with beer and mixers, and we squished onto old couches drinking wet, cold cans of PBR while someone fiddled with the music on the wireless speakers that were scattered around so the music was coming from everywhere. Josh sat close and fetched me drinks whenever I wanted a new one and then I noticed a little white plastic bag, like the kind from a jewelry store, making its way around the circle and people were passing it with a teeny tiny spoon, dollhouse-size, and I squinted and focused even though I saw two spoons posing as one and realized it was cocaine, getting closer, and unlike Alex, unlike most of my friends in Calhoun, I'd never done it, so I probably shouldn't start now.

"I'm fine," I said, in what I hoped was a casual tone, waving my hand as it passed me by, and nobody said anything or seemed to mind, so it was fine.

There was a woman on my left with cool sleeve tattoos and I asked her about them and she was cool, too, an artist who'd designed some of them herself, and I asked her how old she was and she said thirty-one and that's only two years younger than me, so I felt better about that, too. We talked about a ton of things; I don't remember what, but we really liked each other.

Then someone announced it was time to go to the party and I was confused because I thought we were at the party already, but apparently this was just a pregame even though it was ungodly late, and Rocco's roommate was dancing burlesque at a warehouse party or something, and he could get us all in, so we were going to go. Who knew these things happened on Thursday nights? I think I said that aloud. We walked, laughing into the hot night, then Josh hung back a little so it was just us walking together, and I can't remember what we talked about, but he was smiling at me.

Oh, I think at one point the girl with the tattoos pulled me aside to tell me Josh is a really good guy and I smiled and beamed and was just, like, "I know."

Oh, and when we were almost at the venue I complained that I was starting to get sleepy and the girl said, "Here!" and got out the baggie and dipped her keys into the end and held it up to me, and I figured it was such a small amount that I went ahead and sucked it up into my nose, and I'm not sure it did anything, but it did sort of taste bad in there, like when you're congested and you sniff in some of that nose-clearing stuff. Afrin.

Then we were at the party and there was a big line outside, but Rocco knew to just walk to the front and say something and when we turned around he had entry passes like business cards for all of us, and we took them and showed them at the door and showed our IDs, too, and put everything back into our wallets and then the party inside was like a storm, flashbulbs and lasers and strobe lights and platforms with pretty people in lamé bathing suits dancing on them, and a mass of people dancing everywhere, like a whole shag carpet of dancing people. And Josh got me a beer and then we were dancing together, swooping around and letting the music pound through our skeletons, and I wondered why I never dance like this anymore, and then Josh grabbed my chin and kissed me, and it was kind of a gross, sloppy kiss, but we were both drunk so what do you expect, and then we were making out on the dance floor and I kind of giggled, remembering how Edie used to call dance-floor make-outs DFMOs, and then

Blackness.

Pain like lightning. I squeezed my eyes closed again for a moment, taking stock, then opened them into the light streaming through my windows. Normally I close the curtains before bed; normally I pull the blackout shade down behind them. I rolled over, something grinding along the inside of my skull.

I was in my own bed, fully clothed, my jeans torn at the knee. Josh was not beside me. I stared at the sheets while pieces of the night resurfaced like developing Polaroids: shots at Jimmy Rhoda's. An impassioned discussion with a girl at that kid's shitty apartment. My stomach churned: a house key hovering in front of my face, a tiny hill of white powder on the end. Music so loud it joggled my skull. How had I gotten home? Had I embarrassed myself? Fuck.

Everything hurt. Every inch of my entrails ached and roiled; my head buzzed with pain like it was a bell being struck, and my neck, back, and shoulders were one hard mass. Being awake hurt. Being *alive* hurt. And I felt a torrent of self-hatred, shame, and disgust singeing every nerve ending at the same time, over and over and over again.

Moving slowly, I sat up and crawled off the end of the bed, pausing there, the world flashing blue and white, to see if I'd pass out.

When I didn't, I lumbered toward the bathroom, hanging on to furniture as I passed. I sat on the toilet for a while, then swallowed four Advils, the bare minimum to have any effect. I drank two cupped handfuls of water, unsure I could make it to the kitchen for a glass. Then, almost crawling, I crossed to the dresser, took the antidepressant I'd missed the night before, and climbed back into bed.

I woke up to someone touching my shoulder. Tessa.

"How are you feeling?" she asked when I squinted at her.

I groaned.

"I brought you this." She handed me a huge Gatorade in my favorite flavor: orange. I struggled to uncap it for a moment before she snatched it back and opened it for me. It tasted like cold, flavored sweat.

"Here. For your head." She spread a damp washcloth over my eyes as I let out another groan.

"What are you doing here?" I said finally. So grateful she had her own set of keys, my hangover fairy godmother.

"You scared me last night," she said. "Once I got you into bed, I went home to shower and stuff, but I thought I'd come by before I went to work. Want me to email your boss and say you're taking a sick day?"

"That would be good. Thanks, Tessa. What happened last night?"

She sighed. "It's pretty serious, Linds. Maybe we should wait and talk about it when you feel better."

"No, no, no, I want to hear it now," I said, because who hears that and thinks, *Sure, let's delay?*

She chewed on her lip and stood up, crossing into the kitchen and returning with her phone. She sat on the bed next to me.

"So obviously you went out with . . . that guy," she said, "who I didn't know anything about. You ended up super drunk at a club and started sending me these really weird text messages that didn't make any sense, like you were talking about go-go dancers and . . . and trying coke and that you were angry with this Josh guy and didn't know how you'd get home." She swallowed. "So I made you send me a screenshot of where you were—thank god you could still do that—and I took a cab there, even though it was like four in the morning."

That uncomfortable hum all through my torso. "Thanks for that," I murmured.

"Well, so I pulled up and got out and realized you were in this little crowd on the side of the street and . . . and you were yelling at this guy, I guess the one you were there with? And you were incoherent but just yelling and kind of pushing and everyone was trying to calm you down, and there was a truck coming and suddenly you . . ." She paused. "Well, I can show you."

She held out her phone and it took a moment for me to make sense of what I was seeing. It was a shaky video of the dark scene, a group of us lit up by the sallow streetlights overhead; I made out the black woman and the tall Asian guy, plus Josh, his eyes wild. The one I barely recognized was me, definitely me, swaying and screaming and cracking both palms against Josh's chest, over and over.

Then suddenly I'd stepped forward and pushed with both arms, and Josh tipped off the back of the curb, toppling down to the blare of a big rig's horn as everyone in the circle screamed. The camera lens jerked around, then refocused on Josh lying flat on the ground, a pair of arms trying to help him up—Tessa's arms, her face popped into view, so she hadn't been the camerawoman, she hadn't recorded this—and the bang of a heavy truck door and the sound of a gruff man cursing, but the camera swung back to me, my eyes unfocused, staring, expressionless, at Josh's body at my feet.

The video ended and Tessa set the phone on her lap. "Is he okay?" I asked, tears streaming down my cheeks.

She nodded. "The truck stopped in time, thank god. He had the wind knocked out of him and he gashed his elbows, but he was otherwise okay. A woman—she was tall with tattoos? She was the one recording, and once she figured out I was your friend, she made me airdrop it onto my phone. She said . . ." She took a deep breath. "She said if you go anywhere near this guy Josh again, she's going to post it and tag it with your name."

I laid my head back and pulled the washcloth over my eyes. *This isn't happening.*

"What was I so mad about?"

"I don't know. No one told me."

I flipped the rag over to its cooler side.

"Lindsay, this is really bad."

Hot tears soaked into the washcloth.

"This is assault," she went on. "I'm deleting this, but . . . but I wish I hadn't seen it. That woman still has a copy. What is going on with you?"

"I don't know," I murmured.

"This is not you. You don't assault people."

"I don't know, Tessa. I don't know."

She stayed silent long enough that I slid the cloth up to peek at her.

"So this isn't the first time drinking made you violent," she said quietly.

I nodded.

"I think you should tell me," she said.

I pulled the fabric back over my eyes. Maybe like this, with the world blocked out and my forehead like an iron against the damp cloth, I could tell her about the Warsaw Incident.

"When I was twenty-three," I began, my voice small, "Edie and I went to this bar called Warsaw. It was in Greenpoint—this old Polish space with pierogies and Jell-O shots and weird beers and a dinky stage in the corner."

I swallowed.

"It was spring—the spring before everything went down, before Edie and Alex broke up, before Kevin left his trunk unlocked with the gun inside, before everything. There was an event at Warsaw, something Edie and I had RSVP'd to for the one-hour open bar, and I remember ordering two vodka Red Bulls, which came in plastic cups the size of Slurpees." I held my hands out, miming the double-fisting. "They were both for me, so I could keep drinking for free after the open bar ended. I have a flash of myself shortly after, holding a bag and freaking out; apparently I was so drunk, I'd taken my free swag bag, like a promotional tote bag, you know? And then I convinced myself I'd stolen it from someone else. Almost like dream-logic."

Tessa didn't say anything, so I went on.

"I started making eyes with this guy as soon as I walked in. Eventually we started chatting, and he kept circling back to me while still hanging out with his friends. I blacked out around that point in the night, but Edie saw the rest. Apparently he and I flirted for a while, then were apart for a bit, and then I saw him making out with another girl. And apparently I . . . I just lost my shit." Hot tears pressed into the washcloth; I wiped my nose.

"I was outside smoking when the girl came out by herself, and I . . . I *attacked* her, Tessa. I scratched her with my nails and just kept lunging at her, clawing and screaming." I let out a few rickety sobs. "I went for her face. I drew *blood*. I woke up the next day with what looked like rust under my fingernails and—and dried blood on my forearms." All I could remember from that night was a sense of rage, a deep conviction that someone was wrong, mingling with this weird elation, like bright barbs on top of a ball of fury.

I took a deep, wobbly breath. "Anyway, Edie succeeded in pulling me off her and shoving me into a cab, and the girl's friends came and grabbed her and Edie took me home. I'm so fucking lucky I didn't get charged with assault."

"You are," Tessa said, after a very long time.

"I know. The next morning I made Edie promise not to tell anyone, and she never mentioned it again." Of course, for years I'd believed that Edie could be trusted, that she'd never told anyone what had happened with my mom ten years earlier. But she had— she'd run to Sarah and shared that secret. Maybe she'd spread this one, as well. Maybe everyone knew about the Warsaw Incident, too embarrassed to bring it up but quietly disgusted by me.

"But now you know," I said. "So you can just stay away from me instead of finding out the hard way. Like Josh. Or Lloyd. Or Edie."

I lay stock-still for another long beat, until I began to wonder if Tessa was still there. Then I felt a kiss on my forehead, just above the towel.

"You get some rest, okay?" she said. "I have to go to work."

"Nooo, stay with me."

"I can't. But you'll feel better after you get some more sleep. Text me and let me know how you're doing, okay?" She gathered her things and left.

Three glasses of water and two pukes later, I managed to drag my laptop into bed with me and watch hours of a sitcom. Every blast of commercials, blaring and spastic, reignited my headache; every time, I rushed to mute it and then had nothing to do for ninety seconds but sit with my toxic, worthless, out-of-control self.

Eventually the trapezoid of sunlight sliding across my room disappeared into the ceiling. No one had called or texted me; outside there were birds singing, kids playing, people imbuing the world with bubbles of laughter and small, kindly acts. Not actively causing harm, not ripping others open at the seams so their blood would drip onto the ground. What was running through my head when I planted my palms on Josh's chest and shoved with all my might? Had dopamine spurted over my brain as his eyes bugged in fear, his arms flailing uselessly?

I made it to the bathroom in time to throw up again, words flooding my brain, the internal dialogue growing louder, louder, louder. I lay back down, paused the TV show, and opened up a new document. Email notifications flooded the side of the screen. I was about to X them all out when I froze: Tessa hadn't remembered to pose as me and email about being sick, had she?

"Shit," I barked aloud. It was almost five on a summer Friday, so my boss was already gone. I had pages I was supposed to ship today. Why hadn't anybody called me? I snatched up my purse, still crumpled in the hallway. Maybe her assistant was still in the office. Maybe I could make up something dramatic, something dramatic but not fact-checkable, so I couldn't have been in the ER, but maybe I'd witnessed someone getting in a crazy accident, and somehow my phone had died and my watch wasn't working and I'd spent all day off the grid in Urgent Care and then a police precinct—

My fingers, feeling for the smooth familiarity of my phone, stopped fumbling around in my purse and instead I dumped the contents onto the wood floor. Wallet, lipstick, gum, eye drops, pack of tissues. No phone in sight. I checked the zipper pockets, just to be sure. Let out another loud, low groan.

A few tears squeezed out of me, a single little sob over everything, my entire disgusting oeuvre.

I trudged back over to my computer. I wouldn't fiddle with the margins this time; I wouldn't open an old notebook and find space to glue in the entry. But the act of recording had always soothed me, the steady clack of my fingers against the keys.

> I've spent the entire day wishing I had some powerful depressants on hand so I could knock myself out for a while, but it wouldn't even matter because then I'd wake up tomorrow or in the wee hours of tonight and still be me. I'd still be this rabid, unpredictable stranger pushing against the inside of my skin. Sometimes I wonder who I'd be if things had gone differently. Maybe I'd be calmer and more competent, less prone to blanks in my memory and erratic behavior when handed a drink, if my brain hadn't been stewing since childhood in a constant bath of Prozac and Lexapro and Tofranil and Wellbutrin and Ritalin and Adderall and god only knows what else. If my parents hadn't been such fucking cowards. If they'd actually considered the long-term consequences of a fucking tsunami of chemicals crashing into a developing brain. I

can almost see the alternate timeline on Earth 2, the one
where little Lindsay just knew acceptance and love.

For now, though, I'm fucked. Fucked and fucked up, and
who knows how much is my own doing and how much
is my parents'. By now, it hardly matters. All I know is
my brain's so warped that a single bump of cocaine has
permanently screwed everything up. I'm scared—scared
of my brain, scared of myself. Today I told another person
about the Warsaw Incident. Now another human knows,
another living person with the knowledge that she should
stay far away from me.

I noticed that my arms and legs were freezing, my teeth chat-
tering as if I were out in the cold. I was sprinting toward a cliff
and couldn't stop until I'd leapt, until the ground below me gave
way to air. I let out a loud whimper and felt my fingers moving
furiously.

My parents were right to be afraid of me, to place a pill
next to my water glass every night at dinner and to not
let me eat until they'd seen it slip down my throat. I don't
know what's in me, why I'm like this. I didn't think that side
of me would ever show itself again. But it did, last night.
Now I know for sure.

A dizzying swoop, like I'd done something irreversible. I went
back to the top and added a salutation:

Dear Edie,

I read the whole thing over once as a bird screeched outside my
window. I moved the cursor to the trash icon. Then I just closed
my laptop, the draft left buzzing like a wasp trapped inside the
window screen.

Chapter 14

I managed to leave the house late the next morning, blinking into the sun in slight surprise that it all still existed. I picked up groceries and a bag of expensive coffee beans and whirred them in my coffee grinder, enjoying the growl and the slight thrill of a spinning blade, one that could take off my fingertips if it tried. Last night's freak-out already felt filmy and faraway; I remembered the jagged panic but couldn't actually pull it up again.

The text came an hour later, right as I wasn't thinking about him.

"Hey," it began, and I read it in Michael's voice: "How's your week?"

I leaned a few inches back, as if to distance myself from it. *Michael*. I thought of all the energy I'd spent on Lloyd when I was too young to know better—when I was indomitable and upbeat, convinced things would work out okay just because I'd seen a glimmer of a beginning. I thought of Josh, smiling at me over a pizza slice as the East River rushed by behind him. Again and again, I'd been so quick to disregard the million other ways things could turn out, the possibilities funneling out of Point A like latticework.

I texted back: "Can I call you?"

I saw him beginning to answer, but it didn't come through for thirty maddening seconds: "Sure."

It was an awkward conversation, as these kinds of chats always are—the first time we'd talked voice to voice in almost four weeks. Four weeks when I hadn't, for the first time, asked him to see me, testing the theory that if I stopped, he might evaporate like dew. He listened as I rattled off something about needing to feel respected even when I'm just casually dating, something about feeling like I was at the end of his priority list. I said, "This isn't working," like an actor with a script. He was so quiet. I pictured him fading away as he listened, becoming more and more transparent until he whiffed away like smoke.

"I'm sorry," he said, when I reached the end of my soliloquy. His voice was as diaphanous as I'd expected, molecules and air. "Guess I fucked up."

It hung there, and for a single second something split open in front of me, an alternate ending where he promised to do better and made a grand gesture and everything changed, so solid and real. It flashed in front of me and then blinked out just as quickly. The silence buzzed.

"Well, good luck with everything," I said, to pierce it.

"You, too," he said, and that was that. After we'd hung up, I found Alex's number in my contacts list and I stared at it for a moment before blocking it.

On Sunday, I woke up to an email from Mrs. Iredale. The subject line read "YOUR VIDEO," and my blood frosted over when I saw it. *She knows about the Flip cam video.*

Dear Lindsay,

I thought I had your email and I'm glad to see I have it here. You said you were putting together a video in memory of Edie and if you do, I would like to see a copy very much. I looked around to see if I have more videos to share with you but I don't since we never did have a video camera. I am of course thinking of her with the anniversary coming up this week and the video could be nice, and if you are free on Wednesday morning I always visit Summit Rock in Central Park on the anniversary, which was Edie's favorite place to play in the park when she was little. It is near West 83rd St. You are probably working but I thought I would ask. Should you wish to come along please call me before then. My number is in my email signature below.

Best,
Susan

Well, shit. The made-up commemorative video. Had she really been overcome with sentimentality, or was she calling my bluff?

At least she'd given me a reason to call her. Instinctively, I fumbled around for my phone, then groaned. I opened Skype on my laptop and turned off the video function—no need for Mrs. Iredale to see me in my pajamas. Then I copied and pasted in her number and listened to Skype's echoey ringing tone.

"Susan Iredale," she intoned. Why hadn't she changed her name when she remarried?

"This is Lindsay Bach. I just got your email."

"Oh, good."

I swallowed. "Finding footage for the video has actually been a little trickier than I thought," I said. "I spoke with some of our other friends, but it's actually hard to access video files from that long ago."

"I don't doubt it. That's why I was surprised you were making it."

I sighed. "I really appreciated your reaching out. I can send over a few clips I found, just of the Calhoun crew kinda hanging out." A couple of the Flip cam videos had to be PG, right?

"I'd like that. This time of year is always difficult."

"I'm sure. I also really appreciated your invitation to the park. I'll have to be at work, unfortunately, but it's nice that you . . . have a special spot for her."

"Yes, she always liked it up there, once she learned that it's the highest elevation in the park. You could see better from Belvedere Castle, but she preferred to just know she was on top."

I stared down at the keyboard. "It's cool that she grew up going to Central Park. I don't get out there often enough." I pictured Mrs. Iredale, wrinkled and jumpy and slight, and suddenly some strange, childlike part of me wanted her approval: a hug, forgiveness. "It's supposed to be beautiful this afternoon. Would you have any interest in going for a little walk around there with me?"

A silence, long enough that I was about to check if the call had been dropped.

"That would be nice," she said, her voice ragged. "How's two o'clock?"

I climbed out of the subway at the Museum of Natural History, pausing to ogle its dizzying facade, how something so large could sit right here in the middle of this teeming Lego city. The air felt crisp and dry, unusual for August. Exactly like the first morning Edie missed.

I pushed in between the trees and spotted Mrs. Iredale hunched on a bench, big sunglasses obscuring her face, her chin turned up to the dappled sunlight. We said hello awkwardly, and when she stood and began walking, I slowed my gait to let her lead.

"You know, you're the only one who reached out to me about her this year," she said, staring straight ahead.

"Oh my god," I blurted out. Not even her family members?

"I don't talk about her anymore," she said, "and no one wants to bring her up, as if I've forgotten all about her and they'll be reminding me of something terrible. As if I don't think about her every day." She whipped her head over to look at some Italian tourists as they passed; how oddly she moved.

"Oh, wow. Well, I bet a lot of people are thinking about her and just aren't sure what to say," I offered. "She . . . she touched a lot of lives."

"She did, didn't she?" We both froze to let a puppy barrel past, two kids in hot pursuit. "I always think about what she'd be like if she were still with us. She'd be thirty-three now, you know."

This was a chess game; if I was careful, I could win. "Do you think she'd still be in fashion? A stylist, like she talked about?"

"Maybe," she said. "She was so good at that kind of thing. But she was struggling to stay focused back then."

The near flunk-out Alex had mentioned. The one Mrs. Iredale had found so personally mortifying. I let the words out like someone leading a high-strung horse: *easy, easy*. "You know, I used to really struggle with ADHD myself, and Edie had a lot going on. It was a tough year for everyone, like you said the other week."

The path sloped upward and Mrs. Iredale's breath quickened. "It was odd," she said. "Fashion was her dream for so long. But then she just started to let everything slip. It was when she was dating that architect, that older man, and I think she was trying to seem adult with him and like a twenty-three-year-old with all of you." So the problem had begun earlier than Alex had thought. The mention of Greg evoked Josh; I felt a queasy pulse, tried to focus.

"From what I can tell," Mrs. Iredale continued, "she stopped going to night classes, and then fell behind on the course work, and then got so stressed out that she started to give up on the whole thing."

"Wow, that's tough," I murmured.

"And she didn't know this at the time, but her father's boss was loaning us the money for her tuition. If anyone had found out—if her father had known she wasn't even going to class . . ."

What? He'd do what? Down her with a bullet in her shitty loft apartment?

"So I talked to her about it. I told her the truth about how we were covering her tuition and she turned it around. Talked to her professors, got her grades back up. I was so proud of her." We'd reached the base of Summit Rock, and she sat on a bench, sliding her sunglasses up like a headband. The eye tic again.

Who else knows about this? Mrs. Iredale had snapped at Alex. It looked different in this new light. "Edie seemed so driven," I mused. "I'm surprised she'd slack on school stuff like that."

"Well, people reason differently at that age." She was using her psychiatrist voice again. "Their prefrontal cortices aren't fully developed yet; just think of yourself, the decisions you made at that age. How you thought things through."

Heat whooshed up through my throat and cheeks. "Good point."

It wasn't out of character, I realized suddenly. Avoidance was exactly how Edie had dealt with friendships once they became complicated. *She was always shucking people off,* Kevin had said. *She was the center of everything, and then she'd be gone again, leaving a bombed-out group in her wake.*

"That made it all the more distressing when Pat's boss told us he couldn't keep loaning us tuition money," she went on. "We were already on the verge of losing our apartment, but we'd shielded that from Edie, too. She'd just buckled down and brought up her grades, and then we pulled the rug out on her."

Right—the bad news Mrs. Iredale had come bearing the night of August 21. "But couldn't she just get financial aid?" I asked.

"She'd missed the deadline. Classes were about to start, in fact. I was going to see if I could pull some strings with the bursar."

"Then why rush to Calhoun to tell her?" It popped out of me like a hiccup. She squeezed her eyes shut, and I added, "The night she . . . the night."

"Oh, Lindsay." She jerked the sunglasses back into place. All at once, she seemed so frail and sad, the old witch in the woods. "I just needed to see her."

"But why?"

Mrs. Iredale looked up at the treetops. There was that crackly pause again, the same fissure I'd felt from Kevin, from Alex, even from Lloyd: The truth was finally going to rupture through. Why? Because I'd asked.

"You can tell me," I said, for what felt like the millionth time.

"I just had a horrible feeling," she said, "about Edie. I knew something was wrong. I fell asleep on the couch after dinner, and I dreamed it first: Edie and . . . and someone she trusted, and I couldn't remember what happened, exactly, but I woke up certain something was wrong, that something had happened to her. I'd never . . . I'm not a woo-woo kind of person, Lindsay, I'm a doctor, and nothing like this had ever happened to me before. But I just couldn't shake this . . . this *conviction*. So I got in a cab and started calling."

She dug in her bag, then dabbed her eyes with a tissue.

"She came out to see me, but she was looking at me like I'd lost my mind; she couldn't understand what that's like for a mother, to have these invisible cords tying you to your child. Are you a mother?"

"I'm not."

"So you don't know. You don't know." She blew her nose, composed herself. "I didn't go all the way to Bushwick to talk about our finances. But Edie asked about tuition. She asked about the apartment and figured out that we were going into foreclosure, which I hadn't planned to tell her. She figured this must all be about something else, that I was just panicking."

A line from Lloyd floated into my head: *She was, like, wild-eyed. Edie said her mom was freaking her out.*

"And then I left. I couldn't force her to come back with me."

"Wow. I'm so sorry." I pressed my palm onto her forearm. "I do believe you. About the premonition? I think that stuff is very real. Maybe scientists will figure it out someday, something with energy and . . . maybe quantum physics."

She laughed, embarrassed. "Thanks. I know it's silly. I'm glad Edie had a friend like you."

A balloon of discomfort in my belly. She turned to me. "Can you do me a favor? Can you tell me about those last days? With Edie? She and I hadn't spoken in a while, and it just . . . it'd be nice to hear about."

"I'm sorry, Ms. Iredale," I replied. "I wish I had more to tell you, but she and I were sort of . . . in a bit of a rough period at that point."

"A rough period?"

Why hadn't I lied, plucked a happy memory from earlier in 2009? "You know how friendships are at that age. We just needed a little space."

"Well, I hope you got it," she said, then turned away. "Sorry. It's just . . . I know she and Sarah were fighting, too. She was going through so much, with the miscarriage and everything, and it's difficult to know that none of the people she normally counted on were there for her."

Shame and outrage swelled, nausea with claws. *Your daughter was a bitch, Mrs. Iredale. Your daughter peeled us off one by one like strips of dead, sunburned skin, and—*

"Anyway, what do I know? It just shakes me to think about that dream. Here I thought someone else was trying to hurt her, but the person who hurt her was her."

Edie and someone she trusted. Someone who threatened to push her off the building, who'd wandered into the room at just the right time, who knew how to pick up a handgun, throttle high on the grip, click off the safety, nestle the trigger inside the crease of the pointer finger's knuckle. My heart pounded in my ears.

"Anyway, I'm sorry to be unloading on you." She stood and her purse slipped from her shoulder. She caught it awkwardly. "I should probably get going."

"You don't want to climb up Summit Rock?" I asked.

"I can't anymore," she replied, and left.

I stood looking up at it; I pictured tiny Edie scrabbling up its face, sunlight rippling off her Ariel waves. I began to climb it myself, thrusting my weight forward against its pitch. At the top, I looked around: dense trees in every direction, no real indication that this was the park's highest point.

Sometimes you can't prove something. There's no empirical evidence, no definite input from your senses. But you just know. You just know.

I looked down at my feet—black sandals, red toenails, the dirty hipster spelunking crammed so far into my past—and pictured how blood would flow over the rock's surface here, rolling outward and then channeling into its crevices. As I watched, the stone turned to glitter and something pitched up my spine. *I'm going to pass out,* I realized, and my head and knees dropped instinctively.

"Hey, lady, you okay?" someone called. I blinked through the glitter, which beat hard inside my skull and hands. *You're okay, just breathe, you're fine.*

"That lady looks like she's about to boot. *Lady,* you okay?" The rock was coming back into focus and I turned my head to see the teenager, wide-eyed and alarmed, clutching at her friends.

I opened my mouth to tell her I was fine, but what came out instead was a cough, an intense, body-racking hack that began somewhere deep and grew and grew and grew until my lungs squeezed shut and out came a stream of vomit, acidic and foul. The three girls gasped and made grossed-out noises. I spat and sat back on my haunches, crying.

"I'm sorry, I'm okay," I croaked, standing carefully. We stared at one another, and then I turned and walked away, a blotch of my fetid insides drying on the rock behind me.

I almost skipped work on Monday, thinking vaguely that I was in trouble for Friday anyway, remembering that I needed to get a new phone but what was even the point, and then at the last minute I pulled on a dress and hailed a yellow cab in front of my building.

On the bridge, Manhattan blared into view outside the window, the morning sun a spotlight on the whole jagged skyline. I leaned over and stared like a kid, noticing how all the stubbier buildings grazed the true skyscrapers' knees. How huge they must have seemed when they were first constructed; how solid and invincible. Now they were just background noise, anonymous and serving only to give the massive towers contrast.

A subway roared past us on the bridge and I jumped at the noise. In the rearview mirror, the driver's eyes fell on me.

"You okay?" he asked.

"Yep," I lied, although of course I couldn't be.

Bewilderingly, no one mentioned my absence on Friday. Truly no one would miss me if I were gone. I answered emails and passed story proofs in a fog, closing the door to my office as often as possible so that no one would try to speak with me. At night, I cleaned up my desk before I left, deleting some personal things from my hard drive and wiping the crumbs off the space around my keyboard. I walked all the way to the subway entrance and watched it for a moment, the frantic influx and outflow like ants at the top of an anthill. The breeze picked up, and I walked over to the ferry instead, feeling the floating docks bow under my feet. It was a half-hour walk from DUMBO to my apartment, one I desperately needed.

There was an air of ceremony to it, a farewell cruise, as I stood at the ship's stern, wind whipping in and out of my lungs so fast I couldn't control it. I stepped onto Brooklyn's soil and headed east along the cobblestone streets. I thought of Josh as I passed the old pizza place, praying I wouldn't actually see him.

A few blocks inland, I waited at a light with strangers, watching the stream of cars and waiting for my chance to jaywalk, to charge out into oncoming traffic and prove I wasn't afraid. My eyes fell on the man next to me, tall and blondish with a messenger bag strapped across a burgeoning gut.

"Greg?"

It popped out of me before I could think. I didn't feel surprised; I knew it was New York showing off again. So tiny and tightly folded, an M.C. Escher city.

He blinked at me. "Excuse me?"

"You're Greg Bentley, right?"

"Yeah . . . do I know you?"

We were missing the WALK sign; people streamed around us.

"This is weird! I was trying to find you a few weeks ago, and here you are."

"Trying to find me?" He shook his head. "I'm sorry, how do we know each other?"

"I'm a friend of Edie Iredale's. We met a few times when you guys were dating."

"Edie!" He smiled and his shoulders relaxed. "I haven't heard that name in so long. Sorry, what's your name?"

"Lindsay," I said, offering him my hand. He shook it eagerly. Despite Josh's insistence that his boss was an upstanding citizen, I hadn't expected Greg to be this warm. The whole situation felt peculiar, dreamlike.

"I was just thinking how it's been ten years," he said. "Were you working on a memorial or something?"

I blinked at him, processing. Finally I swallowed. "Yeah, for the anniversary. I was just tracking down some people who were important to her back then. And that was definitely you."

His green eyes twinkled. "She was really a great girl. Are you doing a digital scrapbook or something? Or a memorial site?"

I nodded again, slowly. What had I told Mrs. Iredale? "I wanted to see if there was enough material to make a memorial video. Or just compile some photos."

"Oh, well, I might be able to help, because I'm a photographer! An amateur one, but I'm sure I have some photos of her on my old laptop." He looked around happily. "Man, so funny bumping into someone from my former life. I just stopped into the office to pick up a couple things—I'm on paternity leave right now, actually."

"Congratulations," I said, and he thanked me.

Suddenly he unzipped his bag and dug around. "I have a better idea. I had a Flickr account back then, which all my photos went into. I'll write it down for you." He drew out a notepad, leather-bound and filled with graph paper. I peered at the pages as he flipped forward, noticing that he didn't have architect handwriting at all: It was impressively girly, a beautiful sweeping cursive, like the nineteenth-century letters you find in archives. I thought of Tessa's cool, pointy script, which would've looked more at home here. He jotted down a URL and a password and handed the ripped sheet to me.

I folded it up and slid it into my purse. "Thanks so much, Greg," I said, still stunned. "Really funny running into you."

"You, too! You'll have to send me the video or site or whatever you end up putting together." He produced a business card for me. "Have you talked to other people for it?"

I nodded. "Her . . . her mom, and her old roommate Sarah, just some old friends." Bringing up Alex, whom she'd dumped Greg for, seemed unwise.

He hooked his thumbs around the strap of his bag. "If you haven't yet, you should talk to her best friend. Jenny . . . Jenna, I think."

"Jenna," I repeated. "Do you remember her last name?"

"God, not anymore. But you remember her—Edie's roommate in Calhoun. The one she was really close with." He shrugged. "Although, come to think of it, they weren't talking much by the time we broke up. But you know what Edie was like. Anyway, great running into you!" He gave me another cheerful handshake and jogged across the intersection, never looking back.

I stood there for a while, the wind rustling my hair and dress. *Jenna*. Sarah and Kevin had gossiped about her as they played Jenga in one of my Flip cam videos, but I couldn't remember much else. I called Tessa from my watch during my long walk home. "I need your help with one more Edie-related thing," I said. "I promise I'm not being obsessive. I just need you to look someone up for me. I feel like she's probably in the case files somewhere, but I missed her. I'll check on Facebook when I'm home, but her name is Jenna something."

A BMW gunned through the red light just as I stepped off the curb; I jumped back, heart pounding.

"You said it's Jenna?"

"Yeah, Jenna. She was one of Edie's old roommates. I didn't know her at all and Edie literally never mentioned her, but Greg said they were close."

Tessa was quiet for a second, presumably taking notes. "Wait, you talked to Greg?"

"Yeah, I just happened to run into him on the street. Craziest thing. He was—"

I stopped talking as a new theory crashed through me: In the video, Sarah said that Jenna had been busted for selling drugs. Could that explain the Molly in Edie's system that night?

Was Jenna still living in Calhoun when Edie died?

"Lindsay, you there?"

"Sorry, I'm here." I motored around an old woman. "Can I call you again later? It's kinda hard to hear."

"Sure. I'm on it. I'm actually still at work, want me to come over?"

A curl of happiness that someone wanted to see me. Yet I hated the idea of making small talk while I should be at my computer, picking this final lock. "I think I'm just gonna order in. Kinda need a quiet night."

"A White Lotus Thai kind of evening?"

"Pad See Ew know me too well," I cracked, and she giggled appreciatively. We hung up and I headed home, hope billowing in me for the first time in weeks.

First I tried Greg's Flickr; the account existed, but the password didn't work. I emailed, texted, and called him from my watch, figuring a full-court press was my best bet here. Then I set to work finding Jenna.

An hour later, she was yet another digital ghost. I'd found her full name in an old email, but it was laughably generic—Jenna Smith—and I had no other identifying details to go on. Still, I sent it to Tessa and kept searching. The name returned thousands of hits, which I waded through with mounting annoyance: LinkedIn profiles and Instagram feeds and Twitter handles all devoid of real info and fitting neatly into my vague notions about this mystery woman—brunette, unremarkable, born sometime in the eighties. I couldn't picture her clearly, and no one with the name seemed to fit into my Calhoun network, no common Facebook friends or

LinkedIn connections. I shot off a few emails and messages to Jennas who sort of seemed to fit the profile, politely asking if they'd lived in Calhoun around 2009, but half the messages bounced right back.

I rewatched the video of Kevin and Sarah at the Levee. I wanted to smack myself for overlooking this: Here Sarah had offered up that Jenna had been busted for selling, but the drugs were Anthony's, and the two of them were probably sleeping together—meaning Jenna might have been the mystery caller who had brought Anthony to the scene. I filled out a FOIL request for the drug arrest records from that month—the Jenga video had a date, June 6—but I knew my lack of specificity about the actual day and charges would likely result in a rejection, or at best, a slower-than-usual retrieval. I hit submit and groaned in frustration, grabbing a fistful of hair and tugging it against my scalp.

Was this her? Was she just on the other side of all of this, somehow aware that I'd been investigating and feeling endangered enough that she'd cracked open Edie's email and sent me a vaguely threatening email? I answered my door to a dazed-looking man, holding out my bag of Thai food and looking winded from the climb. I thanked him and watched him slowly turn around, as if he'd been counting on more repartee.

Tessa finally called around nine, splintering my hope that she'd have more luck than I. "I can't find a damn thing," she reported. "There are a lot of Jenna Smiths, obviously, but I can't find anything tying one to Calhoun or even Bushwick. We could try to track down the lease—Will says they aren't confidential unless there's a confidentiality clause, which I doubt—but we'd need the landlord to hand it over."

"Well, he's dead."

"Shit, that's right." Tessa clicked her tongue.

"Ugh. And here I got so hopeful when I saw you were calling." I was eating the last of my noodles. Tonight they tasted kind of lame. "Thanks for trying, though."

There was a beat. "Well, I have other news," she said. "My co-worker helped me trace the IP address on that email."

"The one from Edie?"

"Right, the one from her address. I'm not—Lindsay, I'm not sure how to say this."

"What is it? Just tell me."

"Well, that's the thing, it's not—"

"Who sent it?"

"Okay, I don't . . . I'm not sure what this means, but the email . . . it came from you."

Static fizzed in my ears, the volume high. My insides all jolted in closer to my spine.

"What?"

"The IP address is yours. It shows that the email—"

"Like from my building? Someone was nearby?"

"Not nearby—from you. The same . . . An IP address is like your fingerprint. It's your coordinates on the internet. It identifies you by your specific computer, your laptop alone."

The room twisted; I grabbed onto the table for support.

"So what are you saying?"

"Lindsay, I don't know what else to tell you."

"You're saying I sent it?"

"You *did* send it."

"You're lying." She wasn't lying. I was the liar. I was the fucking crazy lunatic liar.

Her voice warning, rich with annoyance: "*Linds.*"

"You're insane! I ask you to be on my fucking side for once, and instead you're trying to manipulate me." I was falling apart; I was a shack tearing to pieces in the wind. I was spinning so fast I didn't have time to stop and ask if any of this made sense. "Admit it, Tessa."

There was a silence, so long and sharp and quivering that the world zoomed in on itself until it was the size of the speaker on the underside of my watch.

"You know what, Lindsay, I'm done," she said, and hung up.

PART IV

Chapter 15

ALEX

The apartment kind of sucked.

The Craigslist ad made it sound like there'd be high ceilings and tons of artists and a steady stream of music and partying and pussy. But this was, like, pretty fucking gross. The bedroom was smaller than my college dorm room. The kitchen was shitty and looked like it hadn't been cleaned in years. One of my new roommates had taken a kitten in off the street that was cute but kinda nasty, with matted hair and little bits of god-knows-what that caught in your fingers when you tried to pet it. She named it Animal. This was nothing like the house Lance and I had sublet over the summer in Philly.

But the part about people partying a lot, that was pretty true. My roommates seemed to have drugs tucked all over the place, so the good news was that they were constantly offering me something and the bad news was that they were all high pretty much all the time, lying around on the gross crusty sofa and staring at all my boxes with these freakity doll eyes. Kevin, the only roommate of the three who seemed to actually care about making music, would sometimes sit at his drum kit and jam with me, and the other kids would get up and dance like jerky strung-out puppets on the rug in front of them.

But it'd only been five days, maybe things would change. It was in the hottest part of the summer and we'd all just dragged ourselves here from various boring corners of America—Syracuse, Santa Fe, Cincinnati, Atlanta—so maybe we were just exhausted and trying to get our hometowns out of our systems before we started doing what we were all here to do, which was obviously to make decent art in our respective fields. Show our parents up for rolling their eyes at our BFAs and nagging us all the damn time to get the minor in computer science, just as a backup, "you were always so good on the computer back home." Well, Calhoun had once been home to the lead guitarist in The Sinks. So fuck you, Mom and Dad.

Except that Mom was coming to visit the next day and that was pretty sick. She'd look horrified and make a lot of disgusted noises, but then she'd know how to fit all my gear in my room, away from my weirdo roommates, and she'd probably drive me to IKEA to get a desk way less shitty than the one the dude before me left here, with its stash of expired condoms leaking and gross in the back of the second drawer. Sorry you couldn't get laid, brother.

It was almost late afternoon and Kevin and I were just hanging around the apartment, trying to get his turntable to work and switching on more and more fans as we sweated our balls off. We hadn't talked about it, but I could kinda tell Kevin hated the other two people in our apartment, too. They were shut up in their tiny rooms doing god knows what.

"So how do we find out what's going on tonight?" I asked at one point. First Friday in the new home. Seemed critical.

"Shit just goes down," he said, pulling a beer out of the fridge. Pretty sure it wasn't his. "People just keep their doors open."

Like the dorms. Okay. I'd liked the dorms enough. Hot girls wandering in and out of our room in search of vodka or pot or whatever. Just had to make sure the evidence was buried by the time Mom arrived at noon tomorrow.

Around eleven Kevin and I heard a booming dubstep bassline coming into our apartment from the left, so we ducked out in search of the source. It was three doors down with a bouncer out front collecting cover, but some girls in jorts arrived right when we did and grinned and giggled and did whatever it is girls do to gain free entry, and we kept our heads down and got waved in with the group, a Brojan Horse, if you will. Inside there was one of those stupid green light machines shooting beams like a sprinkler over a bunch of sweaty dancing people, and whiskey all over the kitchen with a short creepy guy watching over it and collecting five bucks a pour. Kevin spotted a ripped dude in nothing but sequined shorts and wandered off, and I leaned against the wall, waiting.

I saw a chick from the hallway pointing me out to her friend and I turned away, pretending to look for someone. They both moseyed over.

"Hey, did you sneak in with us without paying?" one shouted over the music. Her hotter, freckled friend stood behind her, smirking.

"Maybe," I shouted back. "Are you going to tell on me?"

"Not unless you piss me off," she yelled jokingly. Then, "What's your name?"

"Alex. What's yours?" I watched as her friend turned and left. The retreating girl had long, mermaidy red hair that swung as she walked, and I pictured myself running my fingers through it. This girl gave me her name, but I promptly forgot it.

"Wanna dance?" She put her hands on my wrists.

"Let's get a drink," I yelled back.

We took shots of off-brand whiskey, her grimacing and looking around for a chaser. She already seemed pretty drunk, like falsely confident; you know those people who pack all their ballsiness behind the safety of booze? When the creepy bar-guard wasn't looking, I took another pull straight from the bottle. The girl giggled delightedly. She was wearing a crop top and neon-green shorts. She didn't totally have the stomach for it, but she had a pretty nice ass and legs. Kind of a big nose and brown bangs scratching at her eyes, but cute. She asked if I wanted Molly, which was a form of X I'd heard of four hundred times that week and not at all in the twenty-two years before; she said it was clean, but I said no. I didn't feel like bothering. The electronic music was already getting less annoying, anyway. She told me she knew where to get it if I changed my mind. We danced for a bit, her pulling me over by her friends. The redhead was gone.

The whiskey started to wear off and it was still early, so I said I had to piss and left the apartment in search of something new. A floor up, I found a bunch of people in a circle toking up. Someone had bongos, fucking stupid. I ignored their stares and moved on. The hallway hit a fork and I spotted people standing around outside a door with the *shraaaaaw* of electric guitars coming out of it, so I headed that way.

I stopped in front of two girls and glanced around like I was lost, then smiled at the one who'd noticed me.

"You looking for someone?" she asked me, cutting off her friend.

"Oh, just my roommate. I live here."

"Here?" She gestured inside with her beer.

"No, just in the building."

"Us, too!" She introduced herself. I said hello and tried to remember her name. It was something dumb like Dallas. Not Dallas but something like that. I suck at names.

"I'm Alex," I told her. "Where'd those come from?" I grasped at the can, letting my fingers fall over hers.

"In here. There's a band that kinda sucks, but no one's watching the kitchen." I followed them inside and took in the three guitarists on the makeshift stage, one bassist and two dudes both convinced they were the lead. One wasn't bad, but they kept vying for solos. Embarrassing.

Dallas leaned against the counter with her back arched and asked me when I'd moved in and how I liked it and where I was from until her friend felt sufficiently left out of the conversation and made some pissy announcement that she was going home.

I was buzzed. Dallas had helped herself to another beer but seemed fine. I asked if she wanted to dance—there was another party down the hall with ridiculous house music. She grabbed my hand as I led her down a floor. I pulled my hand out and put it on her back, then just as we got to the door I slid it down for a quick squeeze of her ass. She looked surprised, then grinned.

I tried to convince the door guy that we'd already been inside, but he wouldn't hear it and I hadn't brought any money, so Dallas paid ten bucks for us to enter, which I felt pretty bad about. But she said she didn't care and yanked me out to the dance floor and pretty soon pulled my face in to make out. I was having a great drunken time until I opened my eyes and saw the Molly girl from earlier giving me the stink eye from like ten feet away, so I put my mouth up to Dallas's ear and asked if she wanted to get out of there.

"WHAT?" she shouted back.

I tried again, louder this time. She pulled my face in with her hand, closed my ear with her thumb, and purred into it, "Try it this way." I heard perfectly through the vibrations and also instantly got hard. I slid my palm around her jaw, pressed my thumb against the little piece of cartilage over her ear, and asked one more time. Hot.

We were both sort of sloppy by the time we staggered into my place. We kissed inside the doorframe and she enthusiastically pushed her tits into my hands. When she looked around and I blinked a few times to figure out which identical bedroom door was mine, I could tell she was a little grossed out. Animal looked at her and actually let out a long yowl. I pulled her toward my room and kinda yanked us both inside, closing the door behind me.

Standing there, she pulled off my shirt, belt, and jeans, like, really fucking fast. In the same few minutes I only got as far as unbuttoning her top. I started climbing the stairs to my loft bed, thinking she would follow, when she froze and said, "I actually have a full-size bed, cool if we go there?" Which sounded kind of awesome, a bigger bed where we wouldn't bonk our heads on the ceiling or die of heat as the night wore on. I kind of hated my room anyway. So I said sure and started to look around for my keys.

Which were, of course, nowhere to be found. I hadn't grabbed them before because I was just wandering around the building, and anyway, when did my three roommates lock the door? Did anyone in this fucked-up building? Keys were for outside, I told myself drunkenly. And her door was only a few down from mine and everybody else was in bed. So fuck keys. And fuck clothes. If I waited too long, she might think better of the offer. I grabbed her waist and told her we should run, *run*, to her room.

We made it there without seeing anyone else and were both laughing, doubling over, by the time we got inside her apartment and closed the door behind us. She led me to her bedroom—floor level, big bed, natural light—and I congratulated myself for the good move of getting away from my own miserable space.

The next morning, half asleep, she wanted to cuddle and cuddle and cuddle, and thinking vaguely about morning sex, I made no move to leave. "I have to gooo," I told her at ten thirty, but of course I was too comfortable-yet-hungover to fight it.

Ten forty-five. Eleven. At eleven twenty-five I finally stood up and asked to borrow some pants.

"For the twenty-foot walk of shame?" she teased, tossing me some plaid pajama bottoms.

I approached my door and tried the knob. Locked. So I knocked loudly, waited. Knocked again. Rang the buzzer. Leaned on the buzzer. And started to panic. Because my mom was on her fucking way.

I didn't have my phone. Dallas had the super's number in hers, so I tried calling, but he didn't pick up and she warned me he didn't work weekends. Or really ever. Dallas demonstrated that their door could be kicked open when it's locked, so we tried it on mine. Of course it didn't work and I got worried about breaking the door.

Panic. My mother was zipping off the highway by now, barreling down Flushing Avenue in Dad's Subaru. I started coming up with crazy schemes. I could just hide out until a roommate came back, worry my mother sick. I could knock on neighbors' doors, borrow some stranger's clothes, tell my mom I got locked out trying to get the mail. Dallas's suggestion was to just act like I had absolutely no idea what had happened the night before. I looked down at my way-too-small girl-size pants. "Uh, it's pretty obvious what happened."

New idea: the back door off the kitchen, the one leading to the fire escape over the alleyway. Locked religiously every time I checked, all three locks on the inner door and the deadbolt on the outer door, but it had been a Friday night, maybe some people had gone out there to smoke or something? Could I borrow some sandals?

Dallas gave me some also-way-too-small green flip-flops. Plaid pajama pants, doll-size sandals, my mother minutes away, I charged through the back alley to our little fire escape. I scaled up a few levels and the outer door was open and—the inside one, too! Thank the baby Jesus. I stumbled inside, half registering that the apartment was an absolute wreck. Dallas had climbed up after me, and I thanked her and shoved her out the door, telling her I'd bring back her clothes soon.

I pulled on jeans and a shirt, no time to do anything about my awful breath or gummy contacts. Then I grabbed Dallas's clothes and ran to her door, carefully *not* locking myself out this time. Her front door was ajar, so I gave it a token knock and wandered in, bleating "Hello?" Finally I came upon her standing in a bra and shorts in the kitchen, holding (I swear) a potato, and she gave me the strangest look and asked, "Did you kick in the door?"

I gave her an equally bewildered face. "No . . . it was . . . open."

Madison. I think that was her name. Or Addison? Something like that.

Then it was back to cleanup, throwing dishes in the sink, dragging beer cans to the trash. Mom burst in at noon on the dot. I was just playing it off like I'd overslept and hadn't gotten a chance to clean yet when Kevin sauntered in, all sex-mussed, and before he could open his mouth, I was, like, "HI KEVIN MY MOM JUST GOT HERE WHAT'S UP MAN?" He kind of chuckled and went into his room, locking the door behind him.

Mom was about as horrified as I expected. She could tell I was hungover, but at least she had no way of detecting that I'd almost answered the door in a pair of women's pants. Animal purred and rubbed her ankles and she made a face and raised her palms like she was convinced she'd pick up some serious disease in our apartment, avian flu or SARS or whatever. She asked me to lead her back out into the street and I took her to where Dad's sedan was parked, past the cigarette butts, empty beer cans, and not one but two sleeping bodies in the hallway and staircase.

"I don't want you living like this," she told me seriously as we weaved toward the expressway.

"It's what I can afford," I replied. "And besides, there's tons of talented people in the building. Who could really help me one day. The guitarist from The Sinks lived here."

"The who?"

"The Sinks. They're, like, millionaires now. You're the one always telling me to network or whatever."

She tapped her fingers on the steering wheel. "It just doesn't look safe. I mean, who were those people asleep in the hallway?"

"I told you to come later in the day."

"Noon on a Saturday is not exactly bright and early."

I was too hungover to come up with a reply. Ugh. Why are moms always awesome until they're actually there in person?

She turned to look at me and ran a hand over my shoulder. "I know you'll make it work like you always do. What's it like living with girls? Any cute ones?"

I wondered what she'd seen that'd tipped her off—maybe something in the bathroom. "Just one, and she has a boyfriend," I lied. "And I'm not really thinking about that. I want to focus on my music."

"Good for you," she said. A new song came on the radio and she turned it up using buttons on the steering wheel. I didn't notice her doing it right away and it was like the song magically swelled to swallow up the awkwardness.

At IKEA she went into Nazi shopping mode, whipping the cart one way or another when she had a new idea or saw something neither of us realized I needed. She tried to talk me into decorative pillowcases—shams, I think they were called?—even as I insisted I'd never be making my bed when it was lofted above my head.

"Oh come on, you don't want girls to be totally turned off by your room, do you?"

"Oh my god, Mom. That's so weird." It was so weird. It was so weird that it became the only thought I had for the next fifteen minutes. *Mom. You. Are. So. Weird.*

Afterward, she took me and Kevin out to dinner at this brick-oven pizza place, the only restaurant I knew about, and dropped us off on her way back to the hotel. Kevin got out a joint before we'd even gone into the building, when my mom hadn't even turned the corner. Inside, he told me that he'd heard that some hair metal band was having their debut or final or reunion or *something* show—can't remember—and he'd heard there'd be a ton of free booze and drugs.

We took a few shots and then followed the migration up two floors and a hallway over. There were dudes wearing Lycra and singing in big swoopy harmonies. There were girls in neon wigs. One chick was wearing a full fairy costume, a totally cheesy thing with wings that someone probably made for Halloween some year. I took a lollipop out of her basket and the girl next to me did the same.

She waved her lollipop at me and smiled. She had a big thick sheet of black hair. "Yellow ones are the worst," she said when the song had ended. "You hope it's going to be pineapple or something, but it's lemon."

I offered her my orange one. She smiled wide.

Fuck the real world, I thought right then. Fuck clean apartments and boring roommates and perfectly groomed cats.

Calhoun Lofts was my best decision yet, I decided. And I was right.

Chapter 16

LINDSAY

I stared at my watch, where Tessa's voice had been a moment ago. The news was having the strangest effect on me. I was stone sober, but I felt the long, downward brushstrokes I associated with the beginning of a pot high. Limbs loosening, spine turning to lead.

So I'd sent it, then. I'd sent it in my sleep or scheduled it inside a gap in my memory, my brain and mind operating on two different timelines. And my last stand, the cross on which I'd hung the belief that it could be somebody else, someone crazier than me, this whole paranoid delusion that a menacing other was threatening me for blowing on the embers of Edie's decade-old departure—it evaporated all at once. I'd sent the email, just as I'd tried to hurt Josh, just as I'd succeeded with Edie. This silly final scamper toward someone named Jenna felt embarrassing, gauche. It was just me, alone in my apartment with a steady pulsing sensation wafting downward from my skull.

It was just me, alone in SAKE with a dead body at my feet. The pistol shaking as my entire arm trembled. And then the only person who knew the real Lindsay, the monster, was gone for good.

I thought of the violence with my mother, with Lloyd, with Josh. At Warsaw. The anger, the graphic fantasies.

I needed to see the email from Edie again. I opened my computer and what popped up first was a document, the cursor blinking at the top.

Dear Edie,

I've spent the entire day wishing I had some powerful
depressants on hand so I could knock myself out for a
while, but it wouldn't even matter because then I'd wake up
tomorrow or in the wee hours of tonight and still be me.

Depressants. I didn't really need depressants. I had antidepressants, dozens of them, maybe hundreds, expiring in the top
drawer of my vanity. One kind, I remembered, had the narrowest
therapeutic range, prescribed at a level just south of toxic. Tofranil. I opened a new window and searched for it: lethal at 6.7 milligrams per kilogram of body weight. With 25 milligrams in a pill,
that would mean . . . seventeen pills. Maybe twenty just to be safe.
There was something satisfying and circular about it, the clear A
to B of my parents plying me with the long line of pharmaceuticals
that would eventually end me, too. I padded into the bedroom,
pulled the orange bottle out of my dresser, and sat on the bed,
clutching it in my hands like a chalice.

My eyes fell on my old diary, on the floor near a pile of shoes,
and I picked it up, dreamlike, and pressed it open, the gluey pages
crackling under the entries I'd pasted in.

> *I hate my parents and my teacher and my classmates and
> everyone here, so I'm going to become a writer and get rich and
> move away from them all. And I'm starting right here, right
> now.*

I closed my eyes and lay back on the bed, the notebook spread
open across my abdomen. What a miserable time that had been,
so miserable I'd spent two decades smashing it into the smallest
lockbox in the deepest corner of my mind. It occurred to me for
the first time that my disasters, the bloody calamities of my own
making, came like clockwork: at thirteen, twenty-three, and now,
pathetically, thirty-three. Jesus's final age.

Tears slipped down my temples, the right and then the left. I thought back to the night that had started it all. I was about to start eighth grade, but tall, suddenly and freakishly bigger and stronger than both my parents. But no, that's not the real origin; my parents had been suspicious of me for years by then, ever since I'd turned seven and begun to grow my own personality. I was a sullen child, moody and obsessive. And prone to tantrums, anger building up like steam under my skin and leading to something akin to a panic attack, though nobody called it that. "I can't get my breath down to *here*," I remember telling my mom, pointing at the bottom of my sternum and tearing up in alarm. And instead of acting, she watched me in fright until I was screaming and stomping and then called my dad down to spank me for my bad behavior. I never hurt anyone, but teachers labeled me a problem child and sent me home with pink slips and demerits for my parents to sign. Each one felt more confusing than the last, and after the panic was labeled anger enough times, I began to see it that way, too, the charged feeling blasting out of me on a shorter and shorter fuse.

I intuited that they wished I were chipper and sweet, like the other kids. When I wasn't acting out, I daydreamed through class and got too entranced by chapter books to answer when adults called for me; at the principal's urging, Mom took me to a hearing specialist, convinced I must be partially deaf, but I passed the aural tests with flying colors. According to the audiologist, I was just ignoring them. I remember Dad's frustration that night and the bright, flapping knowledge that I'd done something wrong, though I wasn't quite sure what.

The week after the hearing test, the first pill appeared next to my morning bowl of cereal. Ritalin, to help me focus. I began getting headaches, and at night sleep became elusive; as my Mickey Mouse clock ticked, I crafted pillow forts for stuffed animals and imagined the four legs of my bed came alive and whisked us off to foreign lands. Later, I switched to Adderall, which dried out my mouth and knotted my stomach. My spirits sank, but my grades improved. Dad kept taking me to the gun range, muttering about how I needed to master discipline. It was the one place where I knew he wouldn't yell at me.

And then I was thirteen, sullied by hormones and bad skin and inexplicable feelings, fury and fear and lust and self-hatred in a constant spinning wheel. One night, my parents and I were arguing about whether or not I had to keep taking piano lessons—a stupid, banal fight, but it became bigger, much bigger. Then Dad, irrational Dad with his sudden manic anger and his conditional love, leaned right into my face and hissed, "I don't know how we made you." As I stared back at him, a switch flipped, and when Mom—pathetic, submissive Mom who pretended to be laid-back but actually just put up with all his shit—grabbed my shoulder, I whirled around and hit her with all my strength.

It felt . . . amazing. As if my emotions, normally ricocheting around my interior, had finally found an out. I marveled at how clear and lucid I felt, the way the spinning wheel had stopped.

We were at the top of the stairs, and Mom took a step back as she grabbed at her face. Her feet shuffled, her eyes like two moons, and then she was falling, her hands clawing at air, the wooden steps making awful knocking noises as they connected with her back, her side, her shoulder, and, finally, her head.

I heard a noise in the kitchen; my computer, announcing that I'd received a new email. I picked up the bottle of pills and padded back down the hallway, listening to the maraca shake of every step.

A cheerful email from Greg with a new password to try. It was somehow cute and sad, now that I knew I'd killed her: affable Greg unwittingly helping me track down this imaginary killer, someone Not Me who'd forced their way into Edie's apartment to pick up a gun and push it against her temple. I imagined the rest of the Flip cam video playing out: It was probably Edie and this Jenna in there, in Edie's own fucking apartment, having a drink or a smoke or a bump or whatever, and I'd hung out for a minute, biding my time, until Edie and I were alone and my anger could break out, torpedoing around the room as the music from two floors up made the ceiling shake. I imagined the moment the red drops hit my white shoes, how my drunk, panicking mind had made the most basic of scrambles: pushing the gun against her fingers, typing something simple into her big black laptop. A lash-out not that different from the hard shove I gave Josh, a sweet kid who'd had the bad fortune of meandering into my path. I wondered what switch he'd flipped, what innocent remark had awakened the orange-red rage in me. I closed my eyes, mentally replaying the video Tessa had shown me of that night. The church-organ-like blast of the semi's horn, the chorus of screams. "I'm deleting this," she'd said, "but . . . but I wish I hadn't seen it."

My father had put it only a little differently. "We're going to say she slipped," he said, gripping my arm so that it bruised brown and green, "but we aren't going to forget this. You almost killed your mother."

I didn't accompany them to the hospital, instead locking myself in my room and watching out the window as the EMTs hoisted Mom into the ambulance, the side of her head soaked in blood. Dad paused to look up at me with pure hatred before clambering in after them. She had a severely sprained wrist and needed two stitches in her head, on a blob of scalp they had to first shave bare.

That Monday, I'd met Dr. Mahoney, a wiry-haired pediatric psychiatrist with a particular interest in aggression and disobedience. Every night for a week, we sat across from each other in uncomfortable armchairs, and through my braces I answered her questions in a small voice. Afterward I pressed my ear against her office door as she discussed with my mother everything wrong with me; "oppositional defiant disorder" seemed to be the problem, and the solution was both physical—weekly therapy, constant surveillance from the time I got home from school until bedtime, my door never closed, my computer time never unmonitored—as well as chemical. Three new pills appeared next to my dinner plate, and my parents eagerly watched me swallow them after we said grace.

The pills made me feel foggy and faraway, and for the first time in years, I could sleep at night. But that sleep had become a conduit for awful dreams: one where I found a long knife under my pillow and crept into the basement with it, then came upon Dad sitting on the weight bench in the dark. Another where we were at Uncle Bob's farm with targets tacked to trees, my ungainly hands curled around a rifle, and Mom didn't realize she wasn't supposed to walk out in front of us. Still another where I opened a kitchen cabinet and found it filled with handguns, ones I'd never touched in real life. Around that time, violent images began seeping into my daytime as well, quick bloody visions that still invade my mind decades later. I told no one. I was stuck with a head that'd never do anyone any good, not even after they'd brined it in a cocktail of drugs, not even after they'd pointedly moved all of Dad's guns into a gun safe, not even after my pickled brain realized its own constant narration could be inked down into writing and a path emerged: To Be A Writer Someday. That one hadn't panned out, either. Instead I was thirty-three years old and alone, a single pathetic generation, and I'd generated nothing but misery in my wake.

I snapped open the bottle, child-protection my ass, and shook twenty orange and white tablets onto the table. I shoved aside my empty Thai food containers and organized the pills into four even lines. Filled a glass of water at the sink and swallowed the first row, one by one.

As I waited to see what would happen, I tried the new password Greg had just emailed and opened all the photos at once. Fifty-six Edies appeared, each one like a finger pressed on a bruise. I let my sniffle turn into a sob as I clicked through them.

"I'm sorry, Edie," I whispered. "It should've been me."

I felt woozy, drunk. Edie on a carousel; Edie in a hammock; Edie in a kitchen; Edie picking apples. Edie unaware that she was already on a speeding train, that her trajectory was set and in under a year she'd live in the past alone, in old photos and videos, just echoes.

Near the end, something made me stop and scroll back a few images. I squinted at it and blew it up to full size: Edie at a party, people scattered around the hardwood floor, her holding up a large homemade card that read "When you're 22 . . ." across the front.

I leaned in closer, my heart speeding. The lettering on the card. Triangular and hip, handwriting I'd recognize absolutely anywhere.

And off to the right, a girl I'd otherwise barely notice, with light brown bangs covering her eyes and a nose that didn't look quite right, but those thin lips, lips and a crack of teeth that for the first time looked familiar.

Memories like flashbulbs:

That conversation right here in the living room, when I'd first shown Tessa the video. How she'd confidently recited all their names, Alex, Sarah, Edie; how after one viewing, she'd looked up and asked, "Where's Kevin?" even though I hadn't told her that the dark-haired guy was Alex.

Jenna, I thought wildly. *Mysterious, dissipated-into-the-dust Jenna.*

No. Absolutely not. But now the memories were strobing of their own accord:

The gun was in Edie's right hand, but she was a lefty like you.

Damien's little frown when he told me he'd cleaned up the audio so easily.

The deftness with which she'd hacked into my old email; the grave proclamation that the IP address was mine.

Six years back, the night I first met her, tipsy in a bookstore: *You look so familiar to me!*

With shaking hands, I typed four words into Google: *Jenna Smith,* plus *Teresa Hoppert.* The first result was a wedding announcement on the alumni page of an all-boys high school in Ohio: William Eric Hoppert ('02) to Jenna Teresa Smith.

She'd barely even bothered to conceal her former name.

I heard a clang behind me and turned around in time to see the deadbolt flop to the left. I thought about running across the room, moving at supersonic speed to throw my weight against the door, but before I could stand, the doorframe filled with the hallway's light.

Chapter 17

I wake up to the day I am going to die.

It narrates itself in my head like an audio file, *Today is the day you are going to die*, in a bit of a sing-song, "Mrs. Dalloway said she would buy the flowers herself."

I blink a few times before the brown line in front of me organizes itself into a floor. Then I detect pressure on my back and legs and realize I'm on it—I'm on the floor. The vibrations running directly into my left ear are footfalls. They must be hers. Man, my head hurts. If I could just roll my head back a little more, then I could . . .

Wait, what was I just thinking about?

Rolling over to see better.

No, before that.

It's gone, a weird little fish hook in my brain. Some black sideways lines sort themselves into table legs. A thought blinks on: empty Thai food containers way up on the top of this table. And something else on the table. I think like I'm pushing against my skull, like I'm trying to birth this memory. Finally it appears, a release: my laptop, open to something important.

Footsteps getting louder, coming closer. Instinctively, I squeeze my eyes shut. *Play dead.* Tessa squats in front of me, inspecting.

"You're fine," she says, then stands up. "Quit being so dramatic."

I discover both arms move if I tell them to, and I push myself up to a sitting position. I'm scared of her, though I can't remember why.

I try my vocal cords next. "What happened?"

"You killed your best friend, that's what happened," she calls from the kitchen.

My brain in a wormhole, warp speed: Edie bleeding, the video, my clumsy hand pushing open the door to 4G. Alex. Mrs. Iredale. Kooky, cryptic Lloyd, who was only maybe real. Greg. Greg's photo. Jenna.

"*You* did," I call back, like a petulant toddler. She doesn't respond and I try to stand up, my legs making a slow, delayed scuffle to get under me.

"Oh, don't bother," she says, walking back toward me. "You won't be able to stand."

"How did you . . . ?" I stop, puzzled. Another epic gap in my memory. Have I been drinking?

"White Lotus!" She perches on the couch a few feet away from me. "I know you always order the same thing."

"You . . . you drugged me?" The thought rises, spins like a dreidel, topples over.

She sighs, then stands and crosses to the table. "I thought I had to. Picked up your order and then paid a guy on the street twenty bucks to run it upstairs. But, sweetie, it looks like you also went ahead and drugged yourself. And here I thought I was going to have to draft up a suicide note. If I'd just left well enough alone, you'd have taken care of everything." She's quiet, her eyes sliding across the screen, rereading it.

With all my effort, I push my thoughts into a funnel. "Tessa, I don't know what you're talking about, but you don't have to hurt me."

She clicks the mouse a few times, then leans over the table and smiles down at me. "Isn't this like a goddamn slapstick comedy? Here I come over to stage a suicide and totally interrupt you doing it for real." She shakes the nearby bottle of Tofranil. "Seventeen pills, huh? Seems low."

She knows it's seventeen. She can read my mind. No, she just saw the search on my screen. *My screen*. Help, I need to call for help. My laptop is in front of her. My watch is somewhere in my room. My phone is . . . fuck.

"Oh, it feels good to be able to open up to you," she says, plopping onto the kitchen stool. "All this time I couldn't discuss it with anyone, but now I can talk to you!" She presses her hands together. "With your memory not recording anymore. *Again*."

I feel the tears before I even realize I'm crying.

Her face falls. "Linds, I didn't mean for it to end like this," she says. "I thought you'd just put two and two together and figure out that the evidence points to you having killed her, and then you'd come to terms with that and move on. Like I did." Her chin drops. "But now I don't really have a choice."

She's insane. For some reason this doesn't feel any more surprising than any of the other random facts I've uncovered over the last few weeks.

"I knew it was a mistake to become friends with you," she muses. "It was always sort of nuts. The one person in the world who could be a witness for the prosecution, if you ever realized what you'd seen."

I flail around for something to say, as if the possible responses are butterflies circling my head.

"So why did you befriend me?" I manage.

She shrugs. "I was keeping tabs on you, watching your Instagram and Twitter and stuff and kind of obsessing. At first it was just to keep an eye on you in case you ever talked about it . . . in case anything started to come back."

"And then?"

She smiles again. "Then I started to feel like I was getting to know you, Linds. Through the articles you were writing, and following your career as you worked at different magazines. And . . . and then one time you mentioned you were going to a reading and I decided to go, just to see you in person all those years later. Once I looked different enough, thanks to the hair and the nose job . . . and when I was sure you didn't remember anything."

A nose job! This feels wrong, a dirty trick.

"And maybe you could tell how much I wanted you to talk to me or something, because you came right up to me! You remember, you were there." She chuckles. "I was so fascinated by everything you had to say."

"I remember that," I offer. "It was fun! And then we got lunch."

"Fraunces Tavern on a weekday. It *was* fun." She rests her chin on her palm. "There was also this weird feeling that as long as I was there with you, I had a better shot at staying hidden. I could keep closer tabs on what you knew, right?"

Has the friendship really been that one-sided, me blathering away, her taking it in like a drain? "So the way we became friends is kind of crazy," I say, "but I still wouldn't trade it for anything. You're my best friend, Tessa."

She stares at me, then breaks into a little smile, and then starts to giggle. "I never liked having to go by my middle name, you know," she says. "You don't even know my name, Lindsay."

I don't know what to say, so what comes out is, "Well you don't know my real name, either," which isn't true and doesn't make any sense, but it does shut her up.

"Sorry this is taking so long," she says, like she's a hostess at a restaurant, like the table should be ready by now. "I just don't really wanna . . . I can't think this through until you're out. For good, not for two minutes like before."

I focus all my attention, *thinkthinkthinkthinkthink*, then remember a question.

I signal toward the computer with my chin. "You look pretty happy in that photo with Edie," I say, because I'm wily, Wile E. Coyote, *oh shit* that's why that's his name. "You were roommates, right?"

She gazes at it. Finally, a nod. "I knew her before that, through Sarah," she says. "Sarah and I were roommates first, with these two other girls. Then one moved out and Edie moved in." She whips her head toward me. "I was pretty happy with Sarah being several states away. I was not thrilled to hear that she'd moved back."

I work on it like a knot until it comes loose: that old apartment in Calhoun, the one pre-SAKE, with Sarah and Edie and two other women in it. One of them here in front of me.

"And you guys were friends?"

"I thought she was so cool, with her pretty hair and that gap in her teeth." I meant Sarah, so it takes me a minute to realize she's referring to Edie. "Out of everyone in the apartment, she and I were closest," Tessa is saying. "We'd stay up late at night after everyone else had gone to bed, drinking and talking. It was like a sleepover all the time."

"So what happened?" I prompt.

"We . . . I fucked up." Tessa's hand floats up to touch her collar, her eyebrows, her words finally slithering out from between her fingers. "She started dating that loser, Greg. Did you know she met him on Craigslist?" She waits for me to respond and I shake my head, shooting my eyebrows up like I'm astonished. "He was, like, ten years older than her and basically this sugar daddy, buying her nice stuff and taking her out for nice meals and never wanting to hang out with us—never wanting *her* to hang out with us. She just acted so different around him, so on edge. She was so busy trying to impress him that she stopped going to school, which is about the dumbest thing I'd ever heard. And he never made any effort to get to know us. Like Calhoun was this disgusting cesspool and we were these stupid little pieces of shit living inside it, weighing Edie down."

"And you hated her for picking him?" I offer.

"I didn't hate her," she says, like I'm an idiot. "I hated how he treated her."

"So you tried to break them up?"

"In the sense that I tried to help Edie realize how lame he was, sure. But you know how she was." She nods knowingly, conspiratorially, like we're war buddies gossiping about our commanding officer. I imagine distant gunfire, the two of us mud-smeared in a trench. "Super charming when she wanted to be—good at working people."

Another thought skates off like a water bug: my best friend

Tessa, apparently jealous, apparently wanting her best friend, Edie, all to herself. My being single all the time I've known her, unable to get a romantic anything off the ground. I'm close to connecting this when all the pieces fall apart in my hands.

Wait, what were we talking about?

"The really funny thing is that I never thought to just introduce her to someone new. And then we met that idiot Alex at a stupid Calhoun party and she couldn't stop gushing about him. She'd barely even talked to him; I went up to him, let him know I could get him Molly if he was interested, and I had no idea that that asshat would be the thing that finally broke up her and Greg, months after she'd stopped talking to me."

Why am I on the ground again? Am I dreaming?

"She'd suspected I didn't like Greg, so she put on a whole I'm-not-sure-if-he's-right-for-me dog and pony show, all leading up to her getting me alone and asking me point-blank: What do you think of Greg? And I told her in the kindest way possible, I—I thought she wanted to hear this and was thinking it herself, like, if someone just put it into words for her, it'd be crystal clear what she had to do next."

Her sentences are bouncing around like balls in a bingo cage.

"I told her, 'Honestly, I think you're too good for him. It seems like Greg puts a damper on all of your best qualities.' And her eyes went red. I'd never seen her look that way; the scary, quiet kind of furious, you know?"

She's speaking slowly, like this is the billionth time she's gone over it in her mind.

"And of course I immediately backpedaled, I didn't mean it, what do I know about their relationship, and I'm sure I'm reading everything so wrong, but she's not hearing it. She got up—god, I can picture it so clearly—she stood up from the couch, picked up both of our mugs of tea, walked into the kitchen and dumped them both into the sink, then walked into her room and closed the door, not slamming it, just, done. And that was it. She was done with me." She pauses to blow her nose as the tears drip on. "After that, it was like I didn't exist. We'd literally be sitting around in a group and I'd count how many times she acknowledged me, and it was always zero. I'd say something and it was like I hadn't opened my mouth; when she talked she'd bounce her eyes around between the other people there . . . and it caught on, she was so, like, alpha that everyone picked up the habit and would just cut me out of conversations. She unfriended me on Facebook and detagged every photo of us together. And all her little minions did the same. I felt like a ghost."

Her voice grows wavery and my gut contracts like a fist; I know how this feels, the full-body burn of trying to pierce yourself into a conversation and failing, nearby but separate, as if you're behind a sheet of glass.

"This went on for months. She even broke up with Greg and started sleeping with that loser Alex and it didn't even matter, I was still dead to her. I remember that winter, I got sick—like really sick," she says. "I was throwing up and couldn't get any food down for an entire week. Edie was barely even around—she was staying at Alex's apartment most nights, I overheard her saying something to Kylie or Sarah about me making the place a cesspool of germs. I was so weak that I fell once trying to climb back into my loft and just, like, lay on the floor, half in my room and half out, until Kylie found me and took me to the hospital."

I wish suddenly that Edie were here to defend herself, to tell her side of the story, one where Tessa was less of a beatific victim and more of an instigator.

"Then what?" I say.

Tessa wipes her tears angrily. "So she moved out," she continues, "she moved out and she had you as a best friend and she never looked back. It was awful." I realize I'm pushing my back against the bottom of the couch to disappear, to see if it'll swallow me whole. It scoots back six inches, all at once, making a weird monkey sound.

Tessa doesn't notice. "And I moved in with some other people in the building and tried . . . tried to move on. And I actually bumped into Edie at Hope Lounge shortly after she'd moved in with Alex. We literally ran into each other, so she couldn't ignore me. So I acted friendly, and then as we were talking, she grabbed this lanky guy who was walking by and asked if she knew him from somewhere. At first I was annoyed—she was obviously just trying to get away from me again—but he said he knew Alex, and the way she was nodding and smiling at him, it was too easy. 'Oh my god, Edie, did you see the way he was looking at you?'" she mocks in a falsetto. "'He is so into you. Yes, really. You should go over and talk to him some more, he's basically starry-eyed.'" She looks at me, puffed-up. "Moth to the flame."

I realize she means Lloyd, that she was the friend Lloyd had been describing when I spoke to him, that she'd manipulated Edie into pursuing him, and it's like a pinhole in the darkness, a little slit in a sheet of black construction paper. What's going on?

"I was glad to not be living with her," she continues. "That's also when I started selling."

My hands are batting around in the dust-bunny-infested earth I've uncovered by pushing the couch and they hit something, something I immediately recognize without even looking because of the thousands of times I've dug around in my purse for it, seeing with my fingertips. It's not in an alley behind a club in Ridgewood. It made it home.

"You started selling?" I say without comprehending it, because I need to keep her talking, because the easiest way is to be Pete the Repeat Parrot.

She nods, wipes her tears. "I always knew who to get stuff from, I had my guy in Calhoun, and I was always sending people his way. I'm not much of a drinker, as you know, but pot . . . relaxed me, I guess? Made me feel a little less anxious about living with strangers and having to still occasionally see all these people who'd betrayed me. Edie and Sarah and all their new friends. Like you."

I've lost what I'm supposed to say next; I'm onstage and there's a new line, but it's gone from me, flew out of my brain like a bird. A parrot.

"But then you started selling?" I repeat, and almost melt with relief when she nods like it's a good question. I've got my fingers around the case now and I'm inching it toward my lap, easy, easy.

"Yeah. My guy left New York and I figured out that stuff was coming from Anthony. I guess he figured either he could deal to his building or someone else would. So he needed a new middleman. That was also when we started hooking up." She pauses to glare at me. "And yes, I'm aware of the irony of hating Greg but being fine with fucking Anthony."

I don't follow. I feel two names rising out of the water like icon paintings, but I can't make them come into focus at the same time.

"Anyway, I started taking Molly regularly, which I liked a lot. It really . . . This sounds weird, but it really helped with the loneliness element. Like when I took it, that emotion just disappeared. Anthony asked if I'd be interested in selling for him, since he had to keep a low profile and only deal with a few people, you know, directly. It was pretty stupid. We all do stupid things when we're younger, I suppose. We feel so invincible."

An idea like a lightning bolt. "Edie used Molly that night."

She stops crying long enough to laugh. "Did she?"

I nod. The phone is close to my butt now and the thought comes into focus that she should not be staring at me, not good at all, nope. I speak before I lose it: "So you started selling for him?"

She doesn't seem to notice that I've said the same thing three times like a goddamn wind-up doll. Maybe she's on drugs now. Why am I on drugs again?

"I did. Free drugs for me. God, he was such a loser. I wasn't sad to see him go."

I don't understand. "I don't understand," I say.

"Oh, never mind," she says, "not important."

But I think that means it is important. I look back over my thoughts, like they're behind me.

"Tessa," I say. "You're my closest friend. I care about you." Have I ever said those words aloud? To anybody? I see another tactic: "I *love* you."

"Oh, for Christ's sake." She sniffs and shakes her head like she's done crying, then stands and looks toward the kitchen. "This is taking so fucking long. Do you have anything to drink?"

I almost protest and then realize she's moving away and this is my chance. I slide the phone out from under my butt, to the far side so it should be hidden from her, I think, and I hold down the button, but nothing happens, and I try to think what to do because it's dead, it's dead like Edie, it's dead like I'm supposed to be. It's dead like Anthony.

Holy shit. Anthony the landlord. Killed in a fire. Is *that* what she meant?

"What've you got there?" Tessa's amused, patronizing, and she crosses over to me with an ease I can only dream of and pushes me to the side so that I collapse into the fetal position. The phone is hers, it's in her hands, dead dead dead.

"Where did you even find this?" She's half laughing. "Lindsay, you said you lost your phone. Was it actually in your apartment the entire time? Don't you know how to geolocate it? God, Lindsay, how have you even made it this far in life?"

I'm crying now, stupid useless passive Lindsay with her conviction that everything was her fault and now it's Tessa's but mine, too.

"Oh, enough," Tessa says. "Here, you can sit on the couch. Help me." She grabs me under my armpits and waits until I shuffle my feet under me and then she plops me on the couch with a "Hup!" and then I'm sitting with terrible posture, sitting can kill you it's the new smoking, and she sits beside me, and it's just like a normal night when she comes to hang out with me except she's going to kill me.

"Linds, shhh, maybe this isn't so bad," she coos. "Hey, you were always so unhappy. Right? Glorifying your twenties, saying you don't feel like an adult, that nobody ever wants to be with you. Maybe this'll be better. I'll be right here with you."

I'm not listening though because I see something on the side table behind her, and I can't stare because then she'll notice and turn and see it, too, but it's there, and I can almost feel its smoothness in my fingers, and it's standing upright like it means business, like someone set it there carefully, and I don't know when, or how, or who, but probably Edie, dead Edie, Deedie, because there it is, directly behind Tessa. And I know she might be about to kill me, and I know that she might get away with it, but I also know that she hurt Edie, that's a fact, someone should tell Sarah and Kevin they were right all along. And so I pull together all of my strength, I gather it like coffee beans that just spilled all over the floor, and I lunge at her, I jump like a fish and turn halfway in the air, and it's balletic, I'm just like an Alvin Ailey dancer, the small one who looks like Edie.

I land with my head in her lap and look up at her and say as sweetly as I can, "I trust you, Tessa. I love you and I trust you and I know you know better than me."

And my gamble is right and she doesn't like this at all; she makes a face and wriggles out from me and I can't see where she goes, but this is my chance, so I whip one arm behind me like I'm doing the backstroke, and my fingers find it, and it's in my lap, and she's still talking, and her voice gets a little quieter, which means she's moving away.

And because it's from an era when we didn't want options options options, things were what they were and we didn't fault them for not being four hundred other things, too, and I know I can easily make it work, so I feel around with my fingers and then push it deep down into the couch cushions.

Remember this, I scream at myself. *Remember this remember this remember this.*

"Tessa," I call. "What happened after you started selling? What happened with Edie?"

She wanders back in. I hear her sit at the table, and I loll my head her way.

"Lindsay, there isn't much of a point. In an hour I'll once again be the only person who knows."

"Then you have nothing to lose," I announce, like I'm in a movie and it's go time.

"Fine," she says. I hear the crisp hiss of a La Croix opening, *tsst*. "It's been bottled up for fucking forever, so it's time you hear it. Since you have no idea despite being there." She glugs, exhales. "August 21, 2009.

"I was in my apartment alone. On a Friday night, as usual. I'd just toked up and taken some Molly, so I was in a weird sort of swirly mood. And someone banged on the door. So I open it and Edie is standing there with tears on her cheeks. I would see her around every now and then, but we'd been avoiding each other, obviously. I'm so surprised to see her and I think maybe she's going to hug me or apologize or something, but instead she looks at me and goes, 'Jenna, you have drugs, right?'"

She swallows hard, then takes another sip of seltzer. "And I . . . I was like, 'Sure, I have whatever you want,' and she was like—I remember this word for word—she said: 'I wanna forget. I wanna climb out of my life and feel good for a few hours.'" A heavy metallic sound; she's rolling the bottom edge of the can on the table. "So I suggested Molly, since it makes people feel happy and not over-think-y like pot." Her voice gets even smaller. "And also maybe because I know it makes you feel . . . connected to the people around you. I actually thought . . . I thought maybe we'd go back to being friends.

"So I gave her one and took another myself. And guess what, it worked like a fucking charm. Once it kicked in, she was super happy and peppy and excited to be hanging out with me. And she announced that she wanted to go out, she wanted to dress up and go find a party and dance and prove to everyone that she didn't give a fuck, so she was stripping, flinging clothes off around my apartment.

"And she . . . she sort of suddenly looked around and yelled, 'Fuck, I don't have any clothes here!' And we both just laughed and laughed and laughed. Just falling on the ground laughing. So she wanted to run into her apartment and change, and I was try-ing to get her to put some clothes on, but she was like, 'It's fine, it's fine, no one will see us, come on!' And she grabbed my hand and her clothes and took off running. It was so silly, like we were in a spy movie—she'd stop at every corner and look around it very carefully, she opened the door to the stairwell all, you know, mock covert—we were laughing so hard the entire way."

"Then what?" I say. Making my vocal cords vibrate is begin-ning to feel like a chore, like when you're too high and those mus-cles want to go to sleep.

She drums her fingers on the can. "So we went to her apart-ment. It was empty; apparently you guys were all getting wasted on the roof. She got out her laptop to show me something and then got distracted and went into the kitchen and announced that she was going to make us a snack. She was acting really weird, and I was especially confused because, like, I'd taken some stuff, too. But then before she could even pull any food out, she went back into the living room and was like, 'You have to see this,' and held out a gun she'd pulled out of god-knows-where."

The last line croaks up into a sob. She pushes back her stool and stands to rummage in her purse. She sets something on the table, but I can't turn my head to look. I don't want to hear the rest. I want to pause the story, maybe switch to a nice Pixar movie instead.

"She picked up the gun and kinda stared at it, and then she said, 'Kevin showed us how to use this, isn't it gorgeous?' And she clicked the safety off and then on again, kind of playing with it, and goes, 'Don't you love that sound?' And I . . . I was like, 'Hey, be careful, you should put that down.' But I was still trying to be nice because . . . well, I guess 'cause I didn't want to, like, yell at her when she'd just started acknowledging me again."

Tessa is pathetic. Suddenly I know this with certainty, like some-one's just read it to me from a book.

"And then the door opens and you fucking stumble in."

My heart clenches.

"Drunk off your ass, barely able to walk, you stagger right in and ask if we know where your other friends are and blink at us stupidly, and Edie puts the gun down and walks right over to you and gives you a big hug and goes, 'Ohh, Lindsay, I'm so sorry we've been fighting!'" She's using a nasal voice that doesn't sound like Edie's at all. "And she gives you some little speech about how she loves you and knows you're a good person and shit. And you try to tell us to come to the concert with you, but I point out that Edie is undressed, and off you go, stumbling back into the night like a wasted mess."

I know there's a stepping-stone in logic here, a leap from that to whatever came next, but I can't make it. This was nice. Why did this make Tessa so mad?

"So like a moron, I turn to Edie and expect her to make amends with me, too, but instead she turns to me and goes, 'Thanks for the Molly, but I don't think you're a good person.'"

Right, because you're a lunatic, I think, but I don't say it out loud.

"Such a fucking cunt." Her voice is small now, small and shaky like a Chihuahua. "And I felt this flash of rage and I grabbed the gun and lifted it, just to scare her, just to show her she's not the queen of everything, and then, right when I was about to drop it down . . ."

She scrapes back the stool and sits down again. She cries loudly for a few minutes, the kind of cry you have in private, hoping the neighbors can't hear you.

"You know, in eighth grade I took this geography class," she says weakly, "and the teacher passed around this, like, little ancient carving she'd gotten in Djibouti or some shit. And when it got to me I just—I couldn't help it, I pressed it just the littlest bit, and it snapped in two. And she was so crestfallen. It was like that. I just . . . squeezed."

"I don't believe it," I say, with effort. "You've rewritten it."

She snarls. "Oh fuck, what does it even matter. I can make the whole thing skewed in my favor if you want. She was threatening me, she said she hated me, she forced me to kill her in self-defense.

Is that what you want to hear? It doesn't matter, you won't be around to weigh in tomorrow."

I moan. She's quiet for a moment.

"And I squeezed it right as the band at the party hit this really loud note and . . . and the whole room shook, and for a second I thought it was just the music, but then Edie fell . . . she fell in slow motion and I saw the blood start to collect behind her and the song ended and it got so much quieter and I couldn't move, I was just standing there with the gun still in my hand as the blood got closer and closer to my feet."

She's quiet and I realize tears are rolling down my jaw and neck.

"So then I texted Anthony."

She pauses like it's my turn to say a line, but I'm silent. What's my line? Hello, prompter? Can we take it from the top? The whole audience leans forward, annoyed, the play can't go on until I remember my—

"Anthony had—he had a rule that if I ever got into a jam while I was dealing for him, I could call his burner phone. So I put the chain on the door and texted him to come up. God, I was feeling so fucked up by that point. Like I was in this insane nightmare and just had to wake up. Lindsay?"

Should I play dead? No, then she might kill me. I can't work out the logic of this, but I groan back anyway. "Mm-hmm?"

"Just checking. So I let Anthony in and he just keeps saying, 'Jesus fuck. Jesus fuck.' He told me to lock the door behind him, but not with my bare hands. So I used a tissue. And then he's staring at the body and goes, 'Pick up the gun.' I was shaking and I said, 'I can't.' He started yelling: 'Pick up the fucking gun!' and I was just saying over and over, 'I can't!' Then he points to the laptop open on the couch and goes, 'Is that her fucking computer?' and I said yes and he says, 'Get the fuck over there, open up a Word document, and type what I tell you. And wipe your fingerprints off everything.'"

A clang and a quick shuffle; she must have knocked her can over. Why is she doing this? Is it because it's her one and only chance to tell someone what the hell happened? I wish I'd never had anything to do with this. I notice with interest this cool black pool I could sink right into if I wanted.

"I remember I told him I wanted to call 911," she continues, "but he kept saying no. I think because of the drugs, because he was afraid I would tell, or they would figure it out, and he'd lose the building, everything. He just kept saying, 'Not yet, not yet.'"

She's shaking so hard, her shoulders and arms, that I can see it from here.

"My brain was going a million miles an hour, I didn't know if you'd told anyone what you'd seen, and I thought that everyone knew that Edie had cut me out the year before, everyone saw how upset I was, and there weren't any witnesses to show that it'd been an accident. So Anthony told me what to type and I put tissue over two fingers . . ."

"You opened up a new file?" I say this without knowing why.

She hesitates. "Oh, fuck it. Her diary was already up as a Word document and I saved it on a thumb drive on my keychain and then did control-all to delete all the copy. Then I typed what Anthony told me to."

This jiggles something in my brain, but I can't figure out what.

"I'm not sure why I took it," she says as if I've just asked her, as if she's on late-night TV and a charming host is interviewing her, all laid-back and chatty. Cameras appear all around us, stage lights beaming down on her at my kitchen table. "I guess I was thinking that if she'd written anything about how much she hated me, that might . . . that might not be good for me." She drags something heavy across the table, taps it. "And also . . . I don't know. I wanted it. This was my one shot at figuring out what she was thinking, this, like, enigmatic person I'd been close with once . . . and since she was already dead, it wouldn't do her any harm. Like me, now, telling you."

There's a thought that's a bubble at the bottom of a jar of molasses. It begins its long, slow rise to the surface. "You," I say, "made me . . . do it." That isn't right and I try it again from another angle, like opening up a tricky folding chair. "Made me . . . think I did it."

"You know, the only thing I really had to do was send an email from Edie's account. It's crazy, I had no idea you're legitimately violent. You almost killed that poor kid the other night. You really are out of control when you drink too much. You could have done it. Killed Edie. Why not?"

I can't remember what I did and didn't do. She's right: Why not?

She stands again and pushes out her breath like she's steeling herself. "Are you still not out? You're like a goddamn horse."

"Mmmph," I answer, then focus on pulling my lips into a shape; it's the middle of winter and they're frozen. Icicles crystallizing on my eyelashes, my breath white fog. "I'm here."

"Good, because I brought you something. Open your eyes." I do and something new surges through me, cold and sharp, because she's wearing white gloves and holding a gun out over my head.

"Why?" I manage.

"I don't know, *you* bought it," she says, casually, like a teenager.

"Okay," I murmur.

"Oh Christ, Lindsay, you didn't buy it. But it'll look like you did. I got it on the darknet. Mostly untraceable, but I ran it through your IP address first, so if anyone really looks, you bought it. Easy." *IP address.* That tickles something. None of my circuits are connecting and it's not fair, I want to be smart again.

"You know, this is momentous, I hadn't touched a gun in ten years before this one. Since I picked up Kevin's. Well, Edie picked it up, technically. Picked it up, showed me how to use it, because for once in her fucking life she decided to be nice to me again. Ugh."

I know I should be working out a plan, but the synapses in my brain have all sputtered out like a city grid gone dark, like a blackout . . . oh my god, I'm blacked out again, blacked out in a room with Tessa and a gun.

"Sweetie, I'm sorry," she says. "I really am. But you got your one pass already, and I just can't risk it. I mean, I spent years walking around in fear that someone would realize what I'd done, and it's like God or the universe or whatever gave me a second chance at life. And I used it, you know? I met Will, and he's wonderful, and we built this beautiful life and have a little boy or girl coming, and I just . . . I can't risk it. I'm sorry. I can't let you take it all away."

I'm quiet for a few seconds. "My pass?"

She sighs sadly. "This isn't the first time you've figured it out, Linds. Your thirtieth birthday. You were so drunk and so sad and alone, and you kept talking about Edie and looking at photos of her, and then suddenly you looked up at me, really stared, and then said, 'I know you.' And I kind of laughed and said, 'Of course you do,' and you said, 'No, from before.'" She laughs through her tears. "And I looked at you and I just . . . my heart broke in two. It was over. The jig was up. How do you come back from that? So I poured us more shots: 'Let's toast to old times! Tell me about Edie.' And you drank and drank and drank. I just kept putting shots in front of you. I was so scared that night, after I put you to bed and went home. I remember lying there next to Will and wondering if I should pack up and leave town. But then you texted me the next day. God, my heart was in my throat. And you asked if I could bring you Gatorade. Because you were so hungover. You had no idea. I literally fell to the floor with relief."

I blink a few times. "You didn't answer."

"I needed time to think. And I had to make sure that it wouldn't come back to you and that it wouldn't happen again. I thought about just cutting off all contact, but . . ."

I squint hard, remembering. "You yelled at me. Said I was mean."

"I didn't yell. I was terse. I told you you had to get your life under control, that you couldn't still be blacking out all the time. Which was true."

I poke at this but can't grasp it. My thirtieth birthday, when I was so awful to Tessa. Or was I?

I feel a new thought coming and I wait for it; I speak at just the right time, like it's a clay pigeon curving at its peak. "Did you kill Anthony?"

Her face contorts with pain. "Seriously? Of course not! Who do you think I am?"

I don't answer because it's a tricky question. Who is she again? Then a thought worms its way through, and I'm not sure I'll be able to say it because the grid's down, but I have to try.

"You," I say, "are a good. Person."

Silence, and I'm not sure I actually said it, and then she lets out a little cackle. "How can you even say that right now?"

She listens for an answer from me, but the city's gone dark; I forgot what I was thinking and my eyes won't open anyway, my mouth is done moving, my tongue is like a fat pink dead slug inside my mouth, and so I stay silent, and then that's an option, too, I'm out.

It's quiet. Tessa lets out a surprised laugh and mumbles, "Well, of course." I hear her move closer and I feel afraid, but it's a little faint stream of one single battery trying to light up the whole grid, it's faraway and ineffectual, just like me, I'm ineffectual and faraway. Music boils the air around us, it's my playlist, it's Edie's, it's so loud it's rattling my skeleton, the skeletons in my skeleton, where did I hear that?

Tessa shakes my shoulder and it moves all of me like I'm a huge dead sleeping-bag pink slug.

There's pain on the soft flesh of my upper inner arm, sharp and neon, she's pinching me there it hurts if she doesn't stop I'll have to—

And then it stops. I'm so glad it stopped, thank you, Tessa, bye now.

She lets out air like a balloon deflating, *pssshhhooo.*

I hear the sound of her cocking the gun and suddenly I realize this is it and I'm Edie, I can't remember if I'm Edie anymore and maybe it's 2009 now and I've become her and this is the end and there's pressure in my right hand and she's folding it, molding my fingers carefully like it's Claymation, like I'm in her stop-action film and right now she wants me to be—

The music hits a new hysterical triple-fortissimo as she slides my pointer finger into place and I don't think because I don't have time to. With every little atom of stardust left in me, I squeeze. Someone screams, Tessa or me or the music or Edie or inside my head, and there's pain and hot sticky on my arm, and then—

Chapter 18

S omeone's saying something, but I'm so tired that before I can listen I need to close my eyes and let myself back into the cool deep pool, the deep end, just for a minute, maybe Lloyd will be there and he'll do pull-ups on the diving board, if I can just

There's something over my mouth, maybe I'm scuba diving in the deep black sea, but when I look around it's not dark, it's so bright it hurts, and there's a man in white holding the mask over my mouth and I'm on my back on a table and my spine hurts and we're moving and

I'm erupting. I'm on my left side and it's bright and there are tubes shoved down my nose and someone's turned a torch on in my stomach. I retch and try to scream and I rip away at whatever's coming out of my face, but someone grabs my hand and starts saying something and it floats by, meaningless, a few times before I catch it: "You're okay, just relax, you're okay, keep your head down, that's it, you're safe, keep your head just like that, you're fine."

I keep erupting, my insides rushing out, a violent gush inward and then a big suck out, ocean waves swelling up my belly. Tears are pouring freely from my eyes. I try to ask what's happening, but there's something in my throat, something they need to remove, something keeping me from talking.

Someone reaches for my hand and I squeeze it. I breathe, my lungs struggling like I've just had the wind knocked out of me, and the voice keeps talking as I fight the mushrooming panic: "You're okay, you're fine, it's gonna be okay."

Finally the ocean stops and whatever's stuck inside of me starts to move, pain in my nose and throat and entrails as it slithers upward, I retch and retch and try to yell out but I can't, what's in there, what's in me? The hand around mine clasps tighter and someone touches my cheek tenderly, and then it's not to be nice, it's to grab the end of whatever's coming out, the bottom scratching me as it curves out my nostril.

"It's over, it's over, you're okay," the voice finishes, and the panic doesn't stop but it at least holds still as I gag and cough and roll farther onto my stomach. I look around and for the first time the shapes around me take on meaning: I'm in a hospital room, spotlit under bluish lights, with people in scrubs around me, busily doing things.

"What happened?" I ask, but it comes out like a croak. *They've taken away my voice,* I think wildly.

"You just had your stomach pumped. It's gonna be hard to talk." It's the same voice, a woman's, and I turn my head to look at her, pain grabbing my neck and torso. Someone's helping me to sit up and then the bed is moving under me, hinging up into a chair.

"Here. We need you to drink this." Someone else hands me a cup of something thick and black. It looks like the insides of a monster, whatever spits out when you cut its head off. I don't move.

"It's that or we put another tube down your throat," the man says, waggling it, and I take it. "It's activated charcoal. It's going to help your body get rid of the last of the imipramine."

Two fat tears roll down my cheeks. I nod and pull the cup up to my lips. The first sip tastes like cement, and I gag again. The rest I knock back in one long slug, *chug chug chug.* It works quickly and after a minute I grab around for a hand and am helped into the bathroom, my stomach creaking like an old wooden floor. Afterward I lie on the hospital bed, staring up at an ugly drop ceiling, realizing with sad resignation that, once again, I have no idea what happened the night before.

I must've fallen asleep because when I wake, Tessa's sitting next to the bed, smiling, and she leans forward and coos, "Hey, look who's up!" Softly, the tone you reserve for an infant.

"What happened?" My voice is still hoarse, like I've spent the night screaming.

She rests her hand on my arm. "You're okay, that's the important part."

I squint. "Why is your arm like that?" It's in a splint, midnight blue.

"I'm fine. More important, how are *you* feeling?"

I turn away and take in the ceiling again, the long rows of fluorescent lights. "I guess I mostly feel weak," I tell her. "I don't know what happened." A thought blooms: "They said they pumped my stomach?"

She smiles again and rubs my arm. "You're safe now, that's what's important," she says again.

I blink at her. "What were they pumping? What happened?"

"You don't remember anything?"

"No, I remember waking up here and they were fucking pumping my stomach." Distress is roiling again, a pot of water on the stove.

"It's okay, don't get upset. Here, I'll get the nurse." She stands and finds a button, ignoring my protests. It's an intercom; a crackly voice says someone will arrive shortly. She plops back into her seat.

"What's the last thing you remember?" she prompts.

"Not much," I say. "I'm really confused. I remember being at home and feeling upset and sitting on my bed. Then not much else." I have the feeling something bad happened, something very bad. I don't recall pulling out the secret bottle of whiskey. Did I start drinking?

"So you don't remember the antidepressants?" she asks, her eyes wide and blue.

I frown again. "I can't remember if I took my Wellbutrin last night," I say finally. This is hurting my throat, all this talking. "Why, what happened?"

"I mean, you'd just figured out—"

A doctor waltzes into the room, presumably a doctor with his white coat and cool, incurious eyes.

"I'm glad to see you're awake," he says, giving us both clammy handshakes. "How are you feeling?"

"Okay, I guess. My throat hurts. And my stomach." And strangely, something deep under my hip joints, little triangles of tender pain.

He nods, still towering over me. "Your stats all look good."

"She doesn't remember anything," Tessa calls out. "From last night."

He nods again. "Miss Bach, you'll be scheduled for a psychiatric evaluation. I can get you a wheelchair if you're unable to walk."

I shake my head. "I really just want to go home. Can't Tessa take me home?"

"We can't discharge you until you've had a psychiatric evaluation."

"Because I can't remember anything?" I gasp. "Do they think I have a brain tumor or something? And it's pushing on my . . . my hippocampus?" The memory center. I'm pleased with myself for remembering its name. Seems to bode well for my neurological health.

He glances at Tessa, then back at me. "No, we don't have any reason to believe you have a brain tumor. Do you have any interest in eating or drinking? You're well hydrated, but . . ."

I glance at the IV snaking into my arm. "I'm not really hungry, no."

"When your appetite returns, just stick with bland stuff. Toast, crackers, tea. Okay?" I nod, but it's Tessa who says okay.

"You're in from the OR, right?" he finally says, like he's been trying to work something out, and Tessa responds, as if they're speaking their own language: "Yeah, but I was already discharged, I'm fine."

"Would you like to speak to the psychiatrist as well?"

"I probably should, yeah." Her cheeks turn pink. "Are they gonna tell her . . . what happened?"

"Most likely." He grabs at his hip, like his phone has just buzzed. "Someone will be in shortly." And with that, he's gone.

We let the silence swell for a few seconds.

"Tessa, what's happening?"

"I don't want you to freak out. Okay? Everything's fine, I need you to know that."

"I'm calm. I'm, like, half dead, I don't even have the energy to get worked up. But I need you to tell me what the fuck is going on."

She chews on her lower lip, then drags her chair right up next to me.

"I came by your place last night," she says, "just to check on you. After I called you about the IP address from that email from . . . from Edie's account, and we fought on the phone. Do you remember that?"

I think about it. "I remember that phone call, yeah. But I don't remember your coming over."

She swallows. "I rang the buzzer and you didn't answer, and someone else was coming out, so I went up to your floor. And I could hear really loud music, like late-naughts music I wouldn't normally expect from you, and I tried calling but then remembered you lost your phone, so I tried banging on the door." She lifts her hand to her hair; her fingers are shaking a bit. "And I just got . . . a terrible feeling. I mean, the kind of stuff you've been telling me lately, all the stuff with Edie . . . I just got really scared. I was, like, wailing on that door. And finally I remembered I had your keys on me, so I let myself in, and you were on the couch, not coherent at all."

Her eyes glisten with tears, jewel-like. "And I ran over to you and you were saying all this stuff about how you were sure you'd . . . you'd killed Edie, and you just wanted to die, and I saw this empty bottle of pills out on the table and your laptop had a search up for how much it would take to kill yourself, and you were just totally,

totally out of it." She takes a sharp breath in. "I've never been so scared in my life, Lindsay. It was just . . . your *eyes*." She shakes a hand in front of her own brow. "Wild-eyed. And I was like, 'Hang on, hang on, help is coming,' and you—"

She swings her chin away, tears dripping. A few breaths, steeling herself. "You pulled out a gun. It was just sitting there next to you. And you held it up to your head and told me you would shoot yourself if I called 911."

A few loud sniffles; I'm frozen, riveted, unable to process what she's saying. It's the same tumbling sensation I felt when friends haltingly told me about Josh in the alley, about Lloyd's bruised eye, about the Warsaw Incident. How did I get a gun?

"And I didn't know what to do, I was so scared. So I waited until you relaxed your arm and then tried to grab it from you, and you somehow—" She peeks back up at my face, then looks down again. "It somehow went off. I'm *fine,* and the baby's fine, it just went into my shoulder and they said it was the best possible way it could've hit me. You and I are both okay. That's what's important. We're together, and we're fine."

She stares at me, then lunges in and wraps me in a one-armed hug, her tears forming a wet moon on my hospital gown. I hug her back, hard, scared of myself but also sinking into the warm bath of Tessa's attention, how she loves me and cares for me despite my being a sad and savage mess.

"I'm sorry I'm such a fuckup," I whisper, and she kind of coos.

It doesn't strike me until several hours later, still waiting for my psych evaluation and watching daytime TV, the irony: *I shot my best friend.* And not for the first time.

The psychiatrist looks like a bird and speaks with a thick Staten Island accent. She hands me pamphlets and demands that I find a therapist. She asks me twenty times if I'm having suicidal thoughts, not even varying the language much, and I keep repeating myself: Nope, nope, nope. She asks if I have someone to take me home and I reply that my friend Tessa is waiting for me. She frowns and glances down at her notes, then tells me I can leave.

Tessa sets me up in her guest room, no questions asked, with a well-thought-out suitcase she's put together from the mess of my apartment. She hands me my laptop the next day, wordlessly, and I notice there's no activity on it from that night, no emails sent or received, no record of files opened or websites visited. It's just as well—whatever I came across, whatever final nail I pounded into my own coffin, I probably don't need to see again. The night is gone, snipped out of my timeline, scribbled out of my personal history. Lost.

And Tessa, who found me, cooks delicious dinners and watches old movies with me, dutifully looking up critics' ratings and cueing trailers while I lie back and make the final call. She seems to get a vague thrill out of playing caretaker, watching over me like an old-timey nurse, Lindsay Flew Over the Cuckoo's Nest. At night, new pills keep me from dreaming, pills that Tessa carries around so I can't shake out too many at once, and I welcome sleep, a dip into the formless universe where nothing ever happened. It's only when I'm up that I remember what I've done. Twice, Tessa wakes to the sound of me vomiting and wordlessly pulls back my hair, holding it in a gentle fist like we're inebriated coeds.

Will is pleasant to me but seems quietly alarmed, like I'm an injured animal Tessa brought in from the sidewalk—an inconvenience likely to lead to more distress for her. He's working late in advance of a trial, so I see little of him, but he smiles tightly when we pass in the morning. Once I overhear them arguing through the wall and suspect he wants me out, and again, fuckup Lindsay is fucking up other people's lives. After a week, I move home while Tessa is at work. My apartment is neater than I left it.

I email my boss about a medical emergency, keeping things vague; I get an impatient note from her and decide to go in, indignant but also relieved to sink back into the drumbeat of working and calling sources and conferring with editors and jumping whenever someone knocks on my office door. Damien still has lunch with me most days, but I can tell he's uncomfortable; I don't know how much Tessa told him and I don't ask. He's never been great at dealing with real shit.

Tessa comes over most nights, and she's a rock, as ever, kind-faced and concerned and wordless when I try to thank her, to express some small piece of how she's keeping me sane. Sometimes I remember, in a rush, what must've happened, how I had to be the one left alone with Edie in her final moments. Primed for a friend fright, possibly newly aware that she was having sex with Lloyd. And I just don't know how the scene ended. On good days, I believe I left without ever touching Kevin's gun, my only weapon an especially poorly timed chew-out. But on most days, my brain weaves up an image that makes me cry or puke or worse: blood and brains and a body collapsing with a thud as music pounds through the ceiling.

Tessa and I fight once, a bizarre flare-up right after I've taken my sleeping pills, my logic just beginning to blink out. Tessa's doing something in the kitchen when my phone chirps, my shiny new phone with its sleek case and crisp sounds. It's a text from a number I don't recognize—not unusual, since my contacts didn't transfer over—and so almost without reading it, I write back: "Just got a new phone, who is this?"

"What?" I yelp aloud, rereading.

"What is it?" Tessa calls.

I go over it one more time. "It's from Greg, this guy who used to date Edie," I say. "Remember how I ran into him in the street? I'd asked him to send me some photos of Edie, but the password he gave me didn't work. He says he—" I look up, gasping. "He just remembered he had a Dropbox account from back then, apparently! He sent me another link to try. Not that I—"

Tessa crashes out of the kitchen and stands before me, her eyes dark. "You didn't write back, did you?"

I frown. "*Uh*, I wrote back to find out who it was."

"Lindsay, no." She shakes her head warningly, like I'm a dog. "*No*. That guy is the reason you met that little jackass who gave you coke and made you lose your phone and—and got set off on a really dark spiral."

I roll my eyes dramatically, about to tell her I don't want to look at the stupid photos anyway, and she raises her voice to a shout. "I'm serious! I will not have you talking to anyone in that circle while you're in this fragile state, here in—"

"What, in *your* house?" I start to stand. "What are you even screaming about? I wasn't even planning to write back to him, I just—"

I stop short, because Tessa has brought her fingers up to her collar and jabbed them to the side, the gauze-covered wound on her shoulder staring right at me. I sputter, my larynx shorting out, then hang my head. I've heard it as clearly as if she's said it: *This is where that led.*

"After all I've done," she says quietly, letting go of her shirt. "After everything."

She turns and walks back into the kitchen. I slump back onto the couch and block the number.

One night I demand a horror movie for no reason in particular; maybe I want something to jolt my system, to flick me out of this murky river of ugly, marbled feelings. I choose poorly and then panic when the bad guy pulls out a gun, creeping around the farmhouse while its inhabitants quiver with fear. I sniffle during a quiet moment and Tessa launches into action, turning off the movie, rushing to the bathroom, and returning with a box of tissues. She pats one against my eyes and cheekbones, a tender gesture that makes me cry harder.

"Too close to home?" she says after a few seconds.

I nod.

"Do you want to talk about it?" she asks.

I shrug. "Can't decide, which means I probably should."

She squares her listening face at me.

I suck in a breath. "I just can't believe I . . . I can't believe I hurt you," I manage.

She rubs my shoulder.

"It's really scary to feel like you're not in control of yourself, you know?" I say, and she nods, even though she doesn't know. "One minute you're feeling sorry for yourself and the next minute you're in a hospital having hurt your best friend. *Again*."

"You don't remember anything else?"

I shake my head. "It's just out of reach, like when you try to remember a dream later in the day."

"Well, listen." She pulls back her arm and mashes her hands together. "I was there, and Lindsay, you were not trying to hurt me. You'd just told me you loved me. Seriously, you were on your last leg and you said, 'You're a good person.' And it really . . . hearing that changed something in me. I looked you in the eyes and I decided you just had to make it, dammit, because where would I be without you? Who would I even be?" A pretty tear snakes over her cheek. "You know I'm here for you, right? I'm not going to let anyone hurt you, least of all yourself." She squeezes my arm. "I won't ever tell anyone anything you told me about Edie. Ever, ever, ever. And I'll make sure Damien doesn't, either. We're past that. Okay?" I keep my eyes on the couch cushion and nod. "Remember that," she continues. "Remember that. Remember that."

This jingles something in my memory, something unsavory, and I'm still for a moment, trying to catch it. Then I look up and Tessa is smiling at me, bright-eyed, and she lunges in for a hug.

A few nights later, I'm dicking around on my computer when I stand and knock a bottle of water onto the keyboard. An entire bottle, just squarely on it like the G key is a bull's-eye. I screech and lunge and promptly flip the entire thing upside down, and water pours out from between the buttons, a waterfall. I whimper and turn it off and jerry-rig a way to bury the keys in a beach of dry rice. Then I pop two of my sleeping pills—Tessa's left a dosage in my cabinet, in a tiny baggie—and go to sleep.

The next morning, I hit the power button, expecting little, and find that while the keyboard's unresponsive, the screen—and possibly the hard drive—seems mostly fine. At the repair shop, a woman with a half-shaved head tells me they can open up the keyboard and check for water damage underneath. I'm annoyed with myself but unsurprised; this is far from the worst thing I've ever done, left to my own devices.

I get a call a few hours later, from the same bored-sounding woman, it seems.

"So this is weird," she begins. "Did you install a keystroke tracker on your computer?"

"No. Did you?"

"What? No, I'm saying there's a keystroke tracker on your laptop. Which I came across as soon as I popped off the keyboard. Like a hardware one."

It takes another few seconds for it to clunk into place. "A keystroke logger." I know why I know what this is. Tessa installed one, years ago, to monitor her potentially cheating husband.

"Right, installed on your laptop. I mean, damaged by the water, obviously. But it's going to cost more if you want us to replace that, too."

Suddenly everything's fuzzy, TV static sprinkled over my brain.

"Are you able to tell who it's . . . whom it's transmitting to?" I ask evenly.

"I mean, it's totally fried from the water. You mean you . . ." She gasps. "Do you have, like, a stalker or something?"

"Can you tell when it was installed?"

"It's a newer one, we sell this. I think it only came out in the last month or two. Hang on, I can check if the serial number . . ." She's quiet for five seconds, ten. "No, we didn't sell this one. But it's only been out about six weeks. It's new."

I shake my head, order the static to melt away like snow.

"Okay. You can take it out. But just . . . keep it, I'll pick it up, too. And fix the keyboard. Is that all that needs fixing?"

"No, it's the hard drive, too. So it actually won't be ready until tomorrow."

I thank her and hang up.

Tessa is already there when I get home that night, chopping up root vegetables for roasting. She smiles and asks about my day as the butcher knife rolls against the cutting board, *thwack thwack thwack.* I've spent the whole subway ride home trying to come up with an alternate explanation, sifting back through my timeline for another moment my laptop was out of my sight or an innocent reason someone would need a log of every keystroke. Nothing.

I do my best to act normal, to control my smile and keep my body language open, shoulders and chest and tender pink neck exposed. I offer to help and clatter around cheerfully, checking in the cabinets for something missing that she'd deem necessary. I remark that I'm out of parchment paper, but she lines the baking sheets with tin foil instead. I knock my glass measuring cup to the floor, where it explodes into a glorious orbit of shards, but Tessa just sweeps it up, saying she doesn't need it for anything she's making tonight.

After dinner I order us cookies from a late-night bakery with notoriously lazy deliverymen, used to dealing with college students and potheads and other such poor tippers. When one leans on the buzzer, I pretend to begin getting up, but she murmurs, "I got it," and heads for the front door. This is my chance.

I find her laptop in her work bag, in standby, and quickly search for my name; the first file to pop up is a Word document with an inscrutable file name, created in 2009. I hear the front door slam and realize she's on her way back up; arms shaking, every nerve on fire, I airdrop the files onto my fancy new phone, watching as the

taskbar agonizingly slides to the right. I can hear her in the hallway now, slowing from fatigue on the last few steps. Heart pounding, I watch as the little icon switches to "processing," then turns
into a green check mark. As the front door creaks open, I slam
Tessa's laptop closed, heave it back into her bag, and busy myself
at the kitchen counter.

Tessa stays over for another two hours, and I keep smiling,
keep slowing my heart rate with deep breaths and praying she
can't see my blood vessels banging away in my throat and chest.
Feigning normalcy, something I'm practiced at, I've been doing
it for years. I tell her I'm sleepy—can't wait to hit the hay, but of
course I'll see you tomorrow, we can get brunch, get home safe,
text me when you arrive. She gives me a long hug and I try not to
slam the deadbolt too eagerly.

I watch through the window until her bike pulls out in traffic and then I open the document. At first I can't figure out what
I'm reading—it's first-person, but it doesn't sound at all like Tessa.
Entries are dated, and there are mentions of Sarah and Calhoun
Lofts, and nausea is blossoming in my belly and my heart is pounding inside my ribs and my brain is going *what the fuck, what the fuck,
what the fuck.*

July 1, 2008, just a month before Sarah and Edie came into
my life: complaints about an annoying dustup with a roommate
named Jenna; excitement and trepidation over a boyfriend named
Tyler. I scroll forward a few pages, to the Fourth of July: more sadness spinning toward this Jenna, and loneliness, isolation. "I had
the dream again," it reads, "lying on the floor with blood pouring
out of me, trying to cry out but I can't make a sound." A full year
before the bloody miscarriage and then her bloody end. This is
obviously Edie's diary. What the fuck is Tessa doing with it?

Darkness clouds the windows and I don't bother turning on
any lights. Edie kept writing, writing, writing, right up until August 21, 2009. The realization mushrooms: Jenna, the woman I'd
been thinking about just before . . . the night before I . . .

Then rapid-fire: how Tessa convinced me the IP address was

mine; how easily she cracked open my old email. How she couldn't clean up the Flip cam video's audio when Damien took care of it in one night. How much she seemed to know about all those Calhounies when I'd only shown her a single video, shaky and dark.

Tessa is Jenna; Tessa has been lying to me. Lying and then monitoring, installing a watchman to crouch inside my laptop and record my every move.

What do I do? I think about calling the cops, but I'm not sure what to tell them; this proves nothing, after all, and Tessa was the one who didn't press charges when I shot her, somehow. How had I shot her? Where the fuck had that gun come from? Suddenly it's funny that I haven't examined this harder. How skilled I've become at wiping my brain clean.

And how easy it would be to incriminate me if I did try to tell someone. "That's why Lindsay was suicidal, Officer, she showed me this old Flip cam video and requested the case files and really, killing Edie was all she was talking about for weeks. And she's dangerous, unfortunately. Here, I have footage of her pushing this kid into traffic a few weeks ago, outside a club in Ridgewood . . ." My stomach pitches, briefly threatening to expel everything, but I keep it down.

Whom can I talk to? Not my parents, not Damien; I call Sarah, my heart hammering as the phone rings, three times, four, then goes to voice mail. It's late; she's likely in bed, snuggled in a California King in her new Park Slope apartment. "PLEASE CALL ME ASAP," I text her, and then I delete the conversation, paranoid. I glance around the apartment, suddenly afraid of everything. The gun. The red wound on Tessa's shoulder. Whatever happened to the gun? Where is it now?

Finally, unsure what else to do and walloped with that post-adrenaline exhaustion, I get ready for bed and collapse into it, my bedroom door locked as a backup to the front door. I curse my landlord for not installing a chain; I briefly consider setting up a trap, *Home Alone* style, for anyone who dares to visit me.

For the first time in a month, I skip the sleeping pills. I'm out almost instantly, and my dreams are vivid and rich: Tessa wearing white gloves and waving the gun around. Anthony, tragic Anthony, burning up inside a beautiful building. Fear flooding my body, adrenaline and cortisol fighting off the effects of too many Tofranils, of too many Tofranils and something else altogether.

Remember this, I'd thought. *Remember this, remember this, remember this.*

I wake up blinking into the early-morning light, a bird singing too loudly outside my window: *oowee, oowee, oowee.* I grab my phone to check the time and my eyes fall on the voice memo app. The last time I used it, I murmured into the microphone about a dream, a dream where Edie was trapped inside my Flip cam and looking out at me from behind the—

I stumble into the living room and plunge my fingers into the dark spaces between the couch cushions. There are crumbs, and hair ties, and coins, but I need to physically flip the cushions to the floor before I spot it, dead against the black fabric: the Flip cam. The one I turned on in a brief moment of lucidity as the drugs took over my brain.

I stare at it for another moment, glossy in my palm, then lunge into the hallway and fling open the closet door. I yank things off the shelves, snapping open bags and boxes and piling them on the floor. I try the cabinets surrounding the TV, pulling out old magazines and dusty board games and outdated electronics, shit I scowl at as I shove it back into place. I move on to my bedroom, scattered with old notebooks, and I yank out plastic storage bins and fling through old purses and scarves and toiletries and expired medicine. I lumber back into the living room and run my hand along the dust behind my books.

It's on the third shelf, as I know it should be: the adapter. Everything in my insides surges toward the sky and I grab it, a small black coil, and rip at its ends to untangle the knots.

I sit down on my bed, locking the door behind me, and begin to cry again: Without my computer, I don't know where to plug this in. But the resolute part of me fights back, waving its little arms and stomping its little feet until I look again and see that the cord's end is unusual but not totally weird; I sift through more jumbled cords until I find a plug that fits, an old digital camera charger from the same era. I push it into the wall and an outdated graphic appears on the camcorder's screen: FLIP VIDEO.

I sit hunched on my bed for the full twenty-four minutes. I can't make out the words, but the affect seeps through—strained and quavering at times, then the staccato of sobbing. I play it a second time with my phone held up to its speaker, recording. I find the email Damien forwarded me from the online sound-cleanup app he used to snap my warble into focus: *Have you guys seen Alex?* I tap through to the program and upload the file. My finger lingers over the Filter! button, with an exclamation point like it's only meant for perky things, and then I press it.

It's ready in less than a minute and I listen again, comprehending this time, pausing when my own sobs get so loud that I can't hear Tessa's voice. It cuts off at the beginning of her 911 call, which sounds eerily like Sarah's—screeches, shock.

More hunches come to me like things I read in a book or maybe fact-checked in an article long ago—that Tessa sought me out, befriended me after changing her name and look. The button nose, the one I've always admired, now seems obviously fake. Greg helped me, he pointed me in the right direction, I think. And the White Lotus Thai . . . everything was off about it, even the delivery, though I can't remember how. But I'm certain Tessa was behind that, too.

I hear the deadbolt clink and look up at my locked bedroom door; behind it, I know, Tessa is navigating her way in. When I crack it open, she's dropping her keys and balancing a bag of groceries on her hip. For a moment, I see it: the Flip cam a flimsy weapon, beat into her temple over and over and over again until the skin bruises and splits open like a ripe stone fruit. Swelling pushing up through those wide eyes and that perfect nose, the one she didn't deserve, the one she got to trick me. Blood trickling out like juice as she fights back, waving both arms wildly, the groceries spreading out on the floor, eggs cracked on the hardwood.

I step out into the hallway.

"I thought I could make French toast," she says, smiling, then busies herself with the groceries. "Do you want to make us some coffee?"

I follow her into the kitchen, pressing the front door closed as I pass.

"What's up, you okay?" She's already whipped out a cutting board.

I clear my throat. "Sorry, I'm fine. I forgot to take my sleeping pills last night, so I'm kind of out of it."

"I gave them to you, right? Where'd you leave them?" She's taken off her sling, and with a fat chef's knife, she begins calmly destroying a pineapple, dismantling its spiny skin.

"Just in the bathroom. I'll take them tonight." *Fuck. Fuck. Fuck.*

"Sounds like we both need coffee then."

I stare at her, then shake my head. "Sorry. Right." I pull the beans and grinder out of the cabinet. What do I do?

She fries up our French toast and I suggest we eat in the living room, far from all my sharp objects. She agrees, still cheerfully so-liloquizing about her in-laws' concerns over how barky little Marlon will treat the baby.

"I thought it would be a whole power-struggle, territorial thing," she says, taking a sip of coffee, "but Will's dad was insisting dogs just get jealous and insecure. We finally looked it up at the table, and wouldn't you know it, he was right."

"Tessa," I break in.

"What?"

"I found the keystroke logger." How much would she admit to?

"Huh?"

"On my laptop. Like you used on Will. And I know I didn't put it there, so."

She pops a chunk of pineapple in her mouth and chews thoughtfully. "What are you saying?"

I take a deep breath. "Is it yours?"

A beat, a long one, and then Tessa's expression softens. "Linds, you don't know what it's like to have to stop your best friend from killing herself. It made me realize you're really fucking good at not letting on when you've hit rock bottom." She sets her fork down on the plate. "I just didn't want that to happen again. I'm sorry if that feels like an invasion of privacy, but I didn't know what else to do. I can't always be here to keep an eye on you, and . . ." She spreads her palm over her belly. "I mean, soon it's gonna be kind of hard to see each other at all."

I blink at her, then nod. We eat in silence for a few more seconds.

"There's something else," I say.

"Okay."

"I know you're Jenna."

She swallows, blinks. "Who's Jenna?"

"I remember you now."

Another silence, both of us frozen, and then, from inside my room, the sound of my phone ringing. We both turn to look at it as the hollow buzz starts again.

Then we're both moving, a race, and the dishes explode on the floor as I dash into my bedroom, yanking my phone off the nightstand just in time to see that it's a missed call from Damien. I'd thought Tessa was running for the same thing, but I look up and she's in the doorway with a knife from the sink, sticky with fruit juice.

"Give me the phone," she says, a hand outstretched.

"Tessa . . ."

"Give me the fucking phone. Don't test me."

I stare at her, then look down and begin frantically swiping. Home button, emergency call, 9—

She snatches it out of my hands and glares at me as it begins ringing again. She holds down a button to turn it off, then slips it into her back pocket.

"Okay, let's calm down," I say, lifting my palms. "Think this through. You don't want to hurt me."

"None of this was supposed to happen," she says as her eyes fill with tears. "I thought you'd just make peace with what you'd done."

"Tessa, put that down." I back farther into the bedroom and she follows, the knife tip shaking.

"I'm sorry, I can't, you can't know."

"Think this through. This isn't gonna save you. It'll only make everything worse."

She shakes her head. "I have to do it," she says. "I'm sorry."

The moment slows and I have time to take it all in: the knife quivering in her left hand, the tear that tumbles down her cheek, the sudden step forward with her left foot, and then—graceful, slow-motion—the right hand swooping out and closing around my wrist.

I jerk back and yank at her fingers with my other hand, and the knife darts forward, slices my knuckles. I scream and keep twisting, then shift my weight and land a kick to her gut. She shrieks and releases my arm, doubling over.

"I'm pregnant!" she screams, as if I'm the reckless one. "How could you!"

I scramble onto the bed and tumble off it behind her, shooting through the hallway and toward the front door. I hear her pounding up after me, and I'm a few feet from the door when she lands a tackle. My temple hits the hardwood floor and I see stars, millions of them, a dazzling image of the night sky.

She drops the knife with a clang and clasps both of my arms behind my back. A crash near my head as she pulls my lamp off the side table and then she's wrapping the cord around my wrists, again and again and again. A pile of slick photos topples from the end table, too, fluttering through a few feet of air together, and one lands upside down, tipped up against the table leg: Edie and me, pale in the camera's flash, on any one of a million anonymous nights.

This is it, then. I wonder what Tessa's planning next: a bottle of force-fed whiskey, perhaps, followed by a few handfuls of anti-depressants crammed down my throat. No, of course: a gunshot to the head, my fingerprints on the trigger, and a suicide note on my phone. *I love you, I'm sorry, goodbye.* Lucky for her, I never did delete any of the files that point to my obsessive research, my potential guilt—the case files, the Flip cam videos. The email from Edie. Her old diary, now trapped inside my phone.

Tessa climbs off me, and I take the opportunity to roll onto my back and sit up. She comes back with a gun in her hand—a decent one, I observe blandly, a Ruger 9mm. I look up at her and she meets my eye, staring as if across all ten years.

A bang at the door.

"Please help me!" I scream, before I can think. "She has a gun!"

Later I'll realize that my instincts were ahead of me, that I'd noticed she hadn't clicked off the safety yet. But I don't know it yet, so she just looks at the door in alarm, and I tuck one foot under me and stand and heave into her with all my might, the lamp dragging across the floor behind me, and the banging continues and I scream, "Kick it in!" and we both fall into a jumble, Tessa and me, and I can't use my arms to catch myself, and so her body breaks my fall.

The following hours and days I can barely remember, my brain hazing out like it'd just exhausted itself. 2009 all over again: sterile interrogation rooms, dazed calls and texts from other people in my life.

It's explained to me over and over again until it sticks: When I followed the link from Damien's email to the web-based audio app, I'd inadvertently uploaded the file into his account, where he'd found it that same morning. He called both Tessa and me, and then 911; he was on his way, but the cops beat him to my door.

Jenna Teresa Hoppert was arrested on the spot and charged with all sorts of things, most notably Edie's murder. I remember her stepping all over the fallen photos as two police officers led her out my front door.

I get three days off work, which feels simultaneously absurd and reasonable; I imagine my higher-ups deliberating over this, frowning and arguing over what feels right. The news vultures barely pick up the story, and I'm surprised, given that Edie was so young and beautiful and Tessa's and my jobs are both at least in the top quartile of interesting. There's a bombing in Dublin and no one cares about us washed-up hipsters, histrionic and grown. I'm relieved, I notice, taking stock of my emotions: grateful no one expects me to pant out the story like someone on a reality show. I feel a weird satisfaction in keeping it private, tucking it into the past where someday maybe it'll grow soft and smoky and eventually dissipate.

Damien keeps me company whenever I ask him to, and we take turns comforting each other when a wave of horror comes crashing through. For the first time, I see him cry, and after a few times he stops trying to conceal his tears from me. The lead detective checks on me regularly, like a sweet old neighbor, and he's reminded me a few times that I'll need to testify at the trial. It won't be for a few years, he says, which makes me feel sleepy and old, that this ordeal will stretch all stringy until I'm in my late thirties. Like I'm so adult now that three years is nothing. Do juveniles awaiting sentencing get the speedy public trials we've all been promised? Do they hurry things along for teenagers, for whom each month is a brave eternity?

Tessa never contacts me, but I know she's growing bigger, rounder, through some incredible yet banal alchemy, and though I can't explain why, I catch myself counting down the months until her due date. I don't speak to Will, either, but I feel a balloon of sadness every time I think of him; I know what he saw in sweet, funny Tessa, and he didn't deserve any of this. Damien talks to him sometimes, over email, I think, but I stop him the first time he tries to tell me how Tessa's doing, where she's being held, the legal calisthenics Will is performing on behalf of her and their unborn child. I have a feeling it'll be a girl, and I can't help thinking I'll meet her someday, know her as my shape-shifting friend's final iteration, giraffe-eyed and innocent and so sure of her goodness.

Word spreads quickly to Alex, Sarah, and Kevin, and one by one they reach out to say something kind, something supportive and nonjudgmental, never mind that I've been best friends with Edie's killer for years now. Kevin suggests a reunion sometime in the fall, and he somehow makes it sound jubilant and not at all macabre, and for some reason I agree and am surprised to find myself looking forward to it.

A few weeks before the gathering, Alex asks me to meet him, insisting there's something he needs to say; Damien persuades me to go and suggests I meet Alex at the restaurant across from his apartment in Chelsea, so he can keep an eye on things from his front window. I'm jittery on the walk from the subway, unsure I can look Alex in the eye without thinking about our faces sinking toward each other like magnets.

We hug hello and get seats at the bar, and I feel it on him, too, something high-strung and uncomfortable. For a few minutes, we make small talk. He tells me he and his wife just made a down payment on a house in Sleepy Hollow; I feign elation.

Then he leans in and asks it, and I have to admire the bluntness: how am I doing vis-à-vis my best friend turning out to be a psychopath, in so many words. It's a question that feels complex and corrugated every time I dip inside for an answer.

"It feels like a breakup," I tell him, "the kind where you trusted the person and they did something really bad, cheated on you or whatever. And then you look back and realize you were making a lot of excuses." I rub my fingers along the condensation on my glass. "And if I were younger, ten years ago or whatever, I would be freaking out about it, I'd be so embarrassed and ashamed that I let this person into my life."

He begins to protest, to come to my defense, but I cover him up: "I know, no, I'm saying that now that I'm older and wiser, I know not to be embarrassed, that that's a stupid reaction. I mean, part of me can't help feeling like there's a whole scales-falling-from-my-eyes, should-have-known-better element at play." I shrug. "But then most of me is like 'Fuck that. You are 100 percent not at fault.' It's funny, it's almost like all the dumb friend breakups and shitty guys from the last decade have prepared me for this. I've bounced back enough times to be like, 'Yep, somehow gonna recover from this one, too.'"

"Totally. With your bullshit meter intact. Good for you. At the end of the day, thank god you're safe."

"Exactly."

We're quiet for a minute, then he looks up.

"So I actually asked you to meet with me because I wanted to apologize."

It's one of those peculiar movie moments; I'm a few inches above my body, watching him speak.

"Lindsay, it was not okay for me to be flirty or whatever, and it definitely wasn't cool for me to kiss you. Jaclyn and I have been—it's been a rough year, we were struggling with some fertility stuff, but that doesn't excuse it at all. I took advantage of you when you were vulnerable and I'm ashamed and I really, really apologize."

Christ. It strikes me how strange it feels, hearing a man deliver an unequivocal apology. He looks away and sucks on his straw, like he wants to say more but knows he should quit.

"Hey, thanks," I say. "I really appreciate that. Obviously I'm not completely innocent there, but I appreciate it and totally . . . I forgive you, of course." I feel like a bad actor stumbling through lines, but I press on. "Also, I'm really looking forward to the reunion and everything, but after that, I think it's best if we're not in touch anymore." I swallow. "I'm just trying to focus my energy on, like, finding a healthy relationship, and you—it's not your fault, but this sort of takes up emotional space for me."

"Yeah, I get that. I'm really sorry."

"I know." I gaze out the front window; two sparrows alight on a tree that blocks my view of Damien's apartment. Then I look back at Alex, and we exchange a brave smile. "It'll all be okay."

"It will." He plays with his napkin. "And I've got some other news."

"Oh yeah?"

"Jaclyn's pregnant."

I squeal. "Congratulations! You're gonna be a dad!" A little peal of sadness: Yes, I just told Alex it was over, but this makes it real.

He chuckles, beaming. "I can't believe it. I know this is an over-share, but between you and me . . . I was really worried. Fertility-wise, I mean. Because the last time I was trying, it was with Edie, and nothing came of it. Thank god, in retrospect, but yeah."

I start laughing, which is probably the wrong reaction, but everything about this is suddenly hilarious. What a thing to tell me, seconds after discussing our near affair. "You and Edie were thinking about having a baby? In *Calhoun*?"

"I mean, trying-not-trying. God, we were stupid. It was this half-baked, unspoken idea we'd had, probably because things were not going super well in the relationship even though we loved each other so damn much." He jangles the ice in his drink, takes a final sip. "It was, like, the ultimate idiotic hipster choice. Thank god that didn't materialize."

Edie's unborn child—I can't believe it. I thought I'd die without knowing what had happened. I consider telling him, then lean on the bar instead, waving for the server. "This man's going to be a father!" I call, pointing.

The bartender offers us a round on the house. I order another Diet Coke and Alex gets a look on his face and then orders a pickle-back, beaming through the server's eyebrow flash. I smile, too, as we watch him pour pickle juice into a glass and whiskey into a shot glass, then smack everything on the table with an eye roll.

Picklebacks. A 2009 classic, and Edie's favorite.

We raise our drinks high, each waiting for the other to propose a toast.

"To Calhoun," I say, and we clink.

"Didn't you used to write?" he asks as he slams his glass onto the counter.

It's not at all what I expected him to say. "Me?"

"Yeah. Poetry or something."

"Essays. I did. That was a big era for navel-gazing. So yeah, I spent a lot of time being really, really in my own head. Or up my own ass, maybe."

"Hey, don't minimize it. They were good. I remember that piece you had in *n+1*."

"Oh my god, I haven't thought about that in years." I lean back, remembering. That pretentious lit mag . . . I'd been so excited when they'd published my reported essay on the social politics of a kickball league. And a bit shy about it, so that I'd posted about it on Facebook but hadn't mentioned it to the gang. But Edie had bought a bunch of copies and spread them out on their coffee table like a bouquet. That was actually really sweet of her.

"All I'm saying is, I got my guitar out of the basement last week," Alex says. We grin at each other and then hide our faces behind our water glasses.

When I get home, I open up my photo archives from that summer, choosing one at random. It's an outtake. We're at Coney Island, having just tumbled out of a smelly sedan Alex borrowed from a bandmate. Sarah had set her camera with a timer on a barricade and then sprinted over to where we were standing, but she was still running when the shutter clicked, and Kevin was beginning to tip over from his one-legged Captain Morgan pose, and Alex's mouth was open yelling at Sarah to hurry up, and Edie had further ruined the photo by tickling my ribs with the hand she'd wrapped around me, so that the rest of us were mid-drama and

Edie alone gazed at the camera, smiling beatifically. Only it wasn't ruined, I see now. I check the date: May 23, 2009. It was perfect.

A few nights later, at home in my pajamas, I sit down at the kitchen table and write an essay; it's about finding in my best friend's sudden and scary incarceration a support network I'd heretofore failed to notice, a whole hammock of loved ones I'd always been too closed off to really see. I give it a headline, Losing a Friend But Finding the Love, and read it over, making changes as I go; I like it, crisp and honest, so I look up Modern Love's submission guidelines and hit send with a little spritz in my chest. I get the automatic reply saying I'll hear back within twelve weeks, and so I do the math, projecting myself into twelve weeks from now when I'll have a yes or, more likely, a no, and I smile at the fact that all those weeks feel solid, that I can trust the months to unspool for another fifty years like a ball of yarn.

Another week passes in the familiar rhythm of sunrises and sundowns, the days growing shorter, impervious to the drama that rumbled in and then out of my bones. One Tuesday, the mail guy drops off a stack just as I'm leaving my office for the day, and I find among the time wasters a card with my name and work address handwritten on the front. The address label is a couple's initials, and it takes me a moment to recognize one as Sarah's.

I slip the envelope into my purse and rip it open on the subway. It's a cool letterpress card with a sheet of printer paper folded inside, and I smooth out the creases to read it:

> Dear Lindsay,
>
> I hope you're well, and I hope you don't mind my sending this to your work address—I don't have your home one. I wanted you to have our new address, and I figure, who doesn't like receiving mail? ☺ I'm super excited to see the

whole gang in October. Kevin is going to stay in our guest
room, which will be fun.

Anyway, lately I've been fixating on some things I said
during our meet-up at Skylight Diner, and I just wanted
to reach out directly. You know, no more keeping things
bottled up, like in 2009.

I stop reading and blink around the packed subway. There's
a little boy asleep against his mother's shoulder; a college-age
woman reading a book with a slick cover design and an obviously
ironic title: *Self-Esteem for Dummies*. I think back to the last few
months, the self-suspicion and disgust camped in my chest, the
paranoia shining back out onto other people. It felt familiar yet
wrong in my body, like software meant for a much-older operating
system. I take a long sip of air and continue reading.

I said some sort of nutty things that day. About Edie,
especially. She was a really amazing person and I feel
bad that I was talking about her being manipulative or
narcissistic or whatever and how she had made so many
enemies. She was also charming and free-spirited and
loving. Remember that time she threw a fancy cocktail
party in our crummy apartment with a tablecloth over a
card table she borrowed and bodega flowers in a vase on
top? That was just as much Edie as the cold or shrewd
person I was trying to make her out to be. I guess what I'm
saying is, we all have a choice, and I choose to see her as
a beautiful person in that stage of my life. And similarly, I
count you as someone super important to me. Now that
I'm back in the city, I'd love for us to get together more.
And, you know, talk about the present and the future, not
just the past. Call me anytime!

XO,
Sarah

I read it twice, then lean back in my subway seat and close my eyes. There's another dichotomy I've been playing with: There's the Tessa who felt overcome with anger, sick with exclusion and hurt. The Tessa who felt backed into a corner and frenzied from the lack of options. But that's only her from a certain angle, through a certain lens. And, of course, there's the Lindsay wallowing in her childhood, pawing through the old anger and jagged violence, and the one here on this subway, finding a way forward, seeing her own pitfalls and learning how to avoid them. We all get to choose.

The train is climbing now, steadily escalating like a plane after takeoff. It breaches the surface and we're on the Manhattan Bridge, the train gasping as if for air. The two skylines are there again, behind us Manhattan's sawtooth horizon, and out front Brooklyn's outline light-studded and bone white. I picture Edie, a million Edies an arm's reach away from one another in that old chamber of mirrors, carefully sketching out the day's events, documenting a twenty-four-hour period that mattered because it happened. I see infinite universes spanning out around her and in all of them but this one she's alive and beautiful and going on thirty-four, her skinny freckled arms wrapped around her friends, tickling their sides and laughing into the molecules around her.

Acknowledgments

First of all, unspeakably huge thanks to you, the reader. You chose to buy or borrow this novel, and that blows my mind. I am eternally grateful.

This book never would have happened without my incredibly supportive New York family, including Julia Bartz, Leah Konen, Abbi Libers, Erin Pastrana, Megan Brown, Jennifer Keishin Armstrong, Paul Schrodt, Kate Lord, Emily Mahaney, Michele Hirsch, Alanna Greco, and many others—I'm so grateful for your encouragement and love (and, often, hilarity) throughout this five-year process. Thanks for talking me down, pumping me up, cheering me on, setting me straight, and making it clear you always have my back. I'm especially indebted to the brilliant friends who read and commented on early drafts. Love and gratitude to my non–New York friends as well, including Lianna Bishop, Katie Scott, Blaire Briody, Kate Dietrick, and Jen Weber. I am so very blessed to have you in my life.

Thank you to my incredible, unstoppable agent, Alexandra Machinist—I'm still pinching myself that I get to work with you. Huge thanks, too, to Hillary Jacobson for finding me in the slush pile and forever changing my life.

I'm very grateful to my astute, insightful editor, Hilary Rubin Teeman; I couldn't have asked for a better collaborator and guide. And big, big thanks to the bright and brilliant Jillian Buckley and the entire outstanding team at Crown. I'm awestruck.

Thank you to all the wonderful editors, bosses, and colleagues who've helped me hone my craft over the years. I feel lucky to have worked with so many talented, amazing women.

To those who shared their technical expertise—Loren Bartz, Thomas Sander, and others—thanks so much for your time and help. (All departures from the realm of possibility are, of course, my own.)

Shout-out to the party friends, hipster dudes, and memorable Brooklyn characters who made 2009 a hell of a year. Special thanks to Booters Liebmann-Smith for getting me past McKibbin's front doors.

Finally, thanks to my parents for turning us into avid readers and encouraging us to pursue our passions (even if you guys find the whole writing thing a little bewildering). I'm also grateful for the enthusiasm of my extended family, especially Tom Denes and Nagypapa and Nagymama. I love you.